Taking The Long Way Around The Barn

by

Eli Mayhew

Panther Creek Press

Spring, Texas

Published by Panther Creek Press
SAN 253-8520
116 Tree Crest
P.O. Box 130233
Panther Creek Station
Spring, TX 77393

Cover photograph by Chris Bumgardner
Cover Design by Nancy Heard

Manufactured in the United States of America
Printed and bound by Data Duplicators, Inc.
Houston, Texas

1 2 3 4 5 6 7 8 9 10

Library of Congress Cataloguing in Publication Data

Mayhew, Eli
    Taking the long way around the barn

I. Title   II. Fiction   III. Western

ISBN 0-9718361-2-4

For Kris and Colleen, our two horse persons, and for Lloyd and Rusty, their persevering husbands. And especially for Chester. This is, after all, his story. He was every bit as bad as this book portrays him. He was never this good, except in our hearts, where he is and shall forever remain. In typical Chester fashion he up and galloped off to that great pasture in the sky before we could get this book published. But that's okay, he couldn't read anyway. As far as we know.

A veritable multitude of classmates and critique group mates, far too many to mention by name, suffered ad nauseam through various iterations of this book. A special thank you to each of them as much for their stamina as their comments and suggestions. At the risk of offending those not mentioned, I would like to pay special homage to the original "Writers in the Hat", Kristl Franklin, Jack Crumpler, Joyce Harlow, John Garrett, Errol Howery, Pepper Ross Hume and Ledia Runnels. One could literally bring yesterday's newspaper to this group then sit back and take notes. By the end of the session you would have plenty of material. John Garrett provided the line, "I don't care if you're the Pope, go ask God." And Jack Crumpler gets credit for the chortling chicken.

Likewise, my eternal gratitude goes to the "Friday Night Group," Linda Helman, Betty Joffrion, Bobbi Sissel, Charles Lowrie, Colleen Thompson, Bill Laufer and Jack Crumpler (again). They may not want to take credit for this nonsense but their help and encouragement were invaluable.

Also, a special note of thanks to my son, Rusty, and to Ann Anderson, who figured out how to get this "masterpiece" from a glorified typewriter to a genuine, readable disc.

Finally, I must express my deepest and heartfelt appreciation to Dr. Guida Jackson, teacher, mentor and, most importantly, friend to this and many other struggling writers. After one of my readings, Guida suggested to the class that I was probably anal retentive. That's just like Guida, always there with constructive criticism.

*Any serious social issue that cannot be avoided
or otherwise ignored shall be addressed with understated absurdity.*

The Code of the West

One

Rux Tuttle sat in the cab of his pickup in the pre-dawn darkness, staring into his old black hat. The solution to his current dilemma sprang from the hat and startled everyone present except Rux, who was the only one present and accustomed to such acute insight. Cowboys are like cats, he concluded. They stay up and howl all night and they can see in the dark

Ten minutes earlier Rux had emerged from his bathroom to be greeted by the hairy backside of Harry Beauchamp, *ungloriously* wrapped in the golden silk legs of Harry's latest girl friend. Both Harry and the possessor of the legs were either unaware of or unconcerned with the presence of their host. Always sensitive to the courtesies required of the host, Rux retrieved his hat and boots and exited room 711 of the Evergreen Hotel, not unmindful of the significance of the room number.

Harry did not need that particular room to get lucky. Luck followed him around like a herd of mares in season. Harry needed Rux's room as a neutral breeding ground away from his wife and the husband of the girl with the golden silk legs.

I should have said no, Rux thought, but Harry's the boss. Why look for trouble? It finds you often enough. When it does, sometimes you have to put on your Texas Ranger act and fight for truth and justice, or some such nonsense. But if you know trouble is coming around the bend, get off the trail and let it pass.

Harry was just enjoying the fringe benefits of being one of the world's top trainers of Arabian horses. Gatherings like this, the 1986 Scottsdale Arabian Horse Show in Paradise Park, Arizona, provided opportunity for spouse-swapping and other assorted escapades for those among the elect.

Harry's wife, obviously not among the elect, would be at the show arena looking for him. Rux liked her and did not like covering for her husband. The clever solution emerging from Rux's hat suggested he have coffee at the coffee shop across from the arena. This would give Harry time to show up and explain his whereabouts to his wife, and give Rux a chance to visit with the pretty, dark-haired waitress at the diner.

Rux parked in front of the abbreviated restaurant and stepped into the frigid air of a desert winter morning. "Brilliant," he said to himself. In his custom of conserving speech he used the word in simultaneous reference to the solution for his dilemma and the scene inside the coffee shop.

Even in her pink uniform with the white apron the waitress cut a striking figure as she stretched to pour water into a tall coffee urn.

The spell cast by the girl shimmering in the glow from the bright lights above the counter captivated Rux as he hurried into the restaurant, certain that her skirt would be hiked well up her neatly formed thighs. As usual, he arrived at the counter just as she finished pouring and set the pot beneath the spigot. For all he could tell, her shins might have gone all the way up to her hips.

"Good morning, Rux," the waitress said, with a smile that would mesmerize swarming sharks. "Aren't you the early bird. What'll it be? The usual?"

"Hi, Sam. Yeah, usual sounds good. Got a horse in the first class today."

Rux mounted a stool at the end of the counter, right across from the waitress' assembly line of knives, forks, spoons and napkins being packaged for the breakfast rush. The waitress relayed his order to the cook and the distinct aroma of stale grease mingled with the smell of freshly brewing coffee.

She resumed her utensil packaging, acknowledging Rux by cutting her dark, seductive eyes to meet his. Rux knew what would follow. In two minutes, she would fill her Pyrex coffee pot from the large urn, then transfer a suitable portion to his cup. While pouring, her eyes would again meet his with the same fleeting glance that bewitched him into momentary oblivion. After four days, Rux thought, this routine had probably gained ritual status.

On Thursday, the first day of the local show preceding the big Scottsdale show, he had stumbled into the diner, foggy-headed and bleary-eyed after only two hours' sleep. All that day an opaque vision of a gorgeous, dark-haired girl with a brilliant smile wandered around the edges of his awareness. Rux made no attempt to identify the source of his subliminal gaiety, assuming her to be his fantasizing about one of the pretty young riders participating in the show.

Friday morning he had again arrived at the diner just as they opened. The fantasy merged with the waitress tending the coffee urn behind the counter, and the napkin stuffing, coffee pouring routine from the day before repeated itself.

The waitress introduced herself as Sammi Stone, from Houston. Being somewhat more clear headed than the previous morning, Rux promptly invoked the ageless right of cowboys to flirt with pretty young waitresses.

During the course of their conversations over the next two days, punctuated frequently by her rushing off to wait on other customers, he learned that she had a nine-year-old daughter. Sammi also made a point of letting him know she was a country and western singer looking. As best he could gather from her disconnected story, she had left Houston in a hurry to get away from some unsavory relative involved in drug dealing.

Waiting tables at this little eatery on the outskirts of Phoenix provided temporary employment until she could save enough to go on to Los Angeles and pursue her singing career.

"Coffee will be ready in a minute," Sammi said, easing Rux out of his trance. "How did you do in the horse show yesterday?"

"Aw, just fair I suppose. Qualified a couple of horses for the championship classes today. A few others that should have qualified didn't."

"That's too bad."

"Them's the breaks. They're still eligible for the Regionals coming up in April. Whole idea is to win a championship or reserve championship at a regionals show to be eligible for the Canadian and U. S. Nationals."

Sammi drew coffee from the urn into her Pyrex pot and had barely filled Rux's cup when Harry's wife plopped onto the stool next to him.

"Morning, Rux," Dottie Beauchamp said. "Have you seen Harry?"

"Mornin', Dot. Naw, I ain't seen his ugly mug yet, but it's early. He'll be along soon, I reckon. He's showing Chester in the Halter class."

Sammi produced another cup and asked, "Coffee, Ma'am?"

"No, thanks," Dottie said. "I'm sort of in a hurry."

Dottie scurried out the door as Sammi took the coffee pot and a cup to the far end of the counter to wait on a trucker.

Rux took off his hat and ran his fingers through his thick, reddish brown hair, feathered neatly above each ear to accommodate the hat. A groom with hands steady enough to body clip a horse could usually be depended on to trim your hair at just the right angle so as to conform to the hat's band.

He replaced the hat as Sammi returned, the protocol being that a cowboy always removed his hat in the presence of a lady except when seated on a horse, in a bar or in a restaurant. Inside a truck was optional, depending on whether you were short enough to keep the hat on without scraping it on the top of the cab. Rux, at six-foot-three, wasn't.

"Who's Harry?" Sammi asked.

"Her husband. He's back at the hotel bang—uh, entertaining a friend."

"That's not what you told that poor girl. You said you hadn't seen him."

"Well, I wasn't exactly lying. I said I hadn't seen his face yet, although the part I did see bore strong resemblance."

Sammi's dark eyes danced with laughter. "That's preposterous," she said, then retreated to the other end of the counter to take the trucker's order.

"Listen, Sam," Rux said as she returned to the napkins, "does your little girl like horses?"

"Sure, we both do."

"Most of the classes today are the finals. I think you and your daughter will really enjoy them. Why don't you bring her over when you get off?"

"Why thank you, Rux. That's very thoughtful of you. I get off at eleven. We'll be out early this afternoon." She hesitated. "I need to tell you something about Missy, Melissa, my daughter."

Sammi left to wait on two cowboys at a booth by the window. She returned with Rux's scrambled eggs, French fries and a large bottle of Tabasco sauce, and attempted to continue her story. "Anyway...." Sammi again rushed off to take care of another order. By the time she returned, Rux had finished.

"Listen, Sam. I need to get to the show. If you want to get back into singing, I've got a friend up in Pine Knot who owns a bar. Name's Deke Ball. They have live entertainment on weekends, and there's a Mexican couple living at his ranch that I'm sure would look after your little girl while you're working. It ain't Hollywood, but it's better than pushing potatoes in Paradise Park."

"Gosh, that would be great." Sammi wrapped her tiny, soft hands around Rux's large, callused left paw. "I don't, I mean, well, there's other things you need to know."

"I'll see you at the show this afternoon. You can catch me up then. Here's Deke's number. I'll call and tell him about you." He threw down a last swallow of coffee and headed for the door.

Rux drove across the highway to the show grounds. He had this vague sensation of riding over the hill not knowing if Indians were on the other side. It wasn't that he minded helping Sammi if he could, even though he barely knew her.

Cowboys naturally doted on attractive young waitresses. But her shadowy references to an elusory past made him wonder if she might be running from something, or someone. He didn't need any loose Indians in his life.

Rux allowed the old pickup to settle among the giant horse trailers and hauling rigs dominating the exhibitors' parking lot at the show grounds. He shuffled through the sawdust avenues separating the endless rows of concrete stalls and ducked inside the elaborate yellow-on-brown tapestries draping the Le Fleur Arabians horse condominium.

Behind the false front, The pungent odor of liniment, oily leather and manure combined to make his eyes water. Young grooms busied themselves feeding, watering and grooming horses, the mascot terriers and anything else that moved. Dottie, obviously wishing to avoid the grooming process, sat motionless in a deck chair by the changing stall.

Chester, fresh from a bath he would just as soon have skipped, stood cross-tied in a grooming stall. A girl combed through his long mane with the tender care of a mother coddling her child.

"Hey, Rux," the girl said. "How do we look this morning?"

"We look great," Rux said. "Good enough to win if you ask me."

The male groom painting the horse's hooves was not given to coddling. "Chester ain't no Halter horse," he said. "If anybody but Harry was showing him he wouldn't even be here."

"Aw, give Chester a break," Rux said.

In truth, though, he had to agree with the boy. Harry Beauchamp's reign as one of the top five or six Arabian horse trainers in the country gave any horse he showed an edge with the judges. Chester needed an edge in Halter. The four-year-old, dappled gray, purebred Arabian gelding had good conformation and a dazzling ring presence that could win him ribbons in Mare and Gelding Halter classes at local shows, maybe even a Regional championship. But Rux and Harry knew his national potential rested in performance, probably the Cutting Horse and Working Cow Horse competition.

Rux watched Harry arrive, this time with a decently clad backside. The trainer engaged in a brief but animated conversation with his wife, then ducked into the changing stall. He reappeared in short order, dapper in his white fedora and black riding suit with the white silk lining. Even his little toothbrush moustache had been tinted with Grecian Formula to match his outfit. Harry exhibited the swagger of his lofty position.

Rux handed him the whip and Chester's lead line, and hustled to the show ring entry gate to gauge the disposition of the competition. He did not envy the judges. The horses in a championship Halter class would be difficult to choose between, based solely on their conformation. All else being equal, the judges would be impressed by a horse snorting and prancing with his tail high in the air. Most of the trainers had their horses agitated into a controlled fury when they reached the gate, hoping to get the judges' attention with a dynamic entry.

Chester normally ambled up, half asleep. But when the gate opened he would roar in with the passion of a Mongolian horde. This time he found his Mongolian passion before he arrived.

Rux could not believe it was the same horse. Chester had been his usual docile self when he left him with Harry only a few minutes before. He had not seen him this active since they first started breaking him.

When the gate opened, Chester balked at first, then lunged into the ring in response to Harry's whip. He pranced and snorted like a wild stallion accepting the challenge of a young suitor to his mares. Harry had some difficulty running the horse along the rail. Chester alternated between trying to circle away from his trainer and racing past him. Once the ten horses were lined up for the judging, Chester constantly circled and shied until his turn came. Harry managed to get him to stand in place and stretch for the judges, but Chester shook and lathered with the violence of a sizable earth tremor.

"Something's wrong," Rux said to the groom who had joined him at the gate.

Rux reached to take the lead line from Harry as they came out of the arena. Harry handed it to the groom, who rushed Chester back toward the stalls.

"What the hell's wrong with Chester?" Rux asked.

"Nothing," Harry said. "He's just hyper. That's what you want for Halter. We took the blue ribbon, didn't we? If he'll show off like that, maybe we should show him at Halter in the Regionals."

Ash Chalmers, Chester's owner, walked up and exchanged congratulations with Harry. Rux left the two men talking and headed back to the stalls, still puzzled. "Pepper," he said to himself. "Damn you, Harry. The only way Chester would act like that is if you peppered him."

Rux wondered if Ash knew what had happened. Ash had his own ranch but generally sent his national caliber horses to Le Fleur's for training by Rux and showing by Harry. He didn't seem like the sort that would be cruel to his horses, but national champions meant big dollars.

Chester stood in the wash rack, calm but still shaking as the groom rinsed him. Rux examined the horse for evidence of ginger in his nostrils and rectum, or liniment on his front hooves, but found nothing. If anything had been applied the groom had already removed it. Rux grabbed the groom by the arms. "Did you pepper him?"

"Come on, Rux. I'm just the poor miserable groom. Take it up with Harry."

Rux groused but let go. The groom was the poor miserable groom and he was the poor miserable barn trainer, green breaking the horses for Harry to finish and show. Any groom or barn trainer who crossed a top trainer like Harry ran the risk of being blackballed out of the Arabian horse industry.

Rux took Chester to the far end of the show grounds and let him cool in the high desert air. The warm February sun soothed the horse but not Rux. "Chester," he said to the horse, "this ain't gonna happen again, not if I can help it. Me and Harry are going to have ourselves a little discussion. I'll get Mr. Le Fleur involved if I have to."

Rux liked Sonny Le Fleur. Le Fleur Arabians in Scottsdale had been his home and place of employment for the past five years. Their lavish facilities rivaled any of the magnificent Arabian horse ranches across the country. Except for being cooped up in a stall the better part of their adult lives, the horses fared better than most people.

Most people didn't have to accept a bit in their mouths, although Rux chewed on one at the moment. He led Chester back through the rows of stalls to the banner proclaiming "Le Fleur Arabians." All the show barns proudly displayed their trophies and ribbons across the front of their elaborately curtained stall areas. The more ribbons and trophies you could display, the more customers you were likely to attract. But no trophy, ribbon or potential customer warranted peppering a horse, Rux thought.

He placed Chester in his stall, filled his water bucket and tossed him a flake of hay. Rux checked the changing stall. No one was present, although Harry's black coat with the white lining hung neatly on the portable clothes rack. He prowled the stall areas. Other grooms and trainers were busy applying Vaseline, hoof polish and show sheen to horses who knew from experience that such pampering meant work. No one had seen Harry.

Rux kicked at the shavings and loose dirt as he made his way through the old wooden barn and around the rodeo arena, then out to the main show ring. Harry must suspect something, he thought. He sure is making himself scarce. Naw, that cocky little rooster had no fear of his barn trainer, even if Rux dwarfed him. Since his next class wasn't until after the lunch break, Harry had probably gone back to the hotel for another quickie with the girl with the golden silk legs.

Rux watched the big, high trotting horses whipping around the ring in pursuit of the amateur-owner-to-ride English Pleasure championship, then stomped past the porta-potties and across the makeshift dirt street to the show office.

"Hi, Rux," the pretty hostess said as he stuck his head in the door. "Want a donut?"

"No, thanks. Looking for Harry Beauchamp. Seen him?"

"Not this morning. I heard his horse won the Halter championship class though. Nice going."

Rux felt someone nudge him. "Come on, Rux," a voice said from behind him. "Get in or out. You're holding up progress."

Rux stepped inside to let the man enter. He recognized him as one of the directors of Region Seven, although he couldn't recall his name. "Sorry," Rux said. "Aren't you one of the directors?"

"Sure am," the man said. "Can I help you?"

"Maybe. Come on outside if you have a minute, I'd like to talk to you." Rux led the man to the center of the dirt way, out of hearing of the office and the porta-potties.

"Listen," Rux said, "did you see the mare and gelding halter class this morning?"

"Sure did. Your horse won, didn't he?"

"Right, but the point is, that horse is normally not that hostile. I think

Harry peppered him."

"We've heard rumors of that going on. Considering the value added to a horse by a national championship I'm not surprised some trainers'll resort to drastic measures to win. Can you prove that?"

"Unfortunately, no. By the time I got back to the stall, the groom already had the horse cleaned up. But I broke that horse, trained him since he was a yearling. I'd swear to it."

"I appreciate that. But you know as well as I do, Harry will deny it. And I suspect the groom would also. We're doing our best to put a stop to this. It's just that we can't accuse someone without hard evidence. I'm sure you understand."

The director promised to investigate. Rux's charges would be kept in confidence until they could be supported. Rux didn't care about confidence. He thanked the man, retrieved his truck from the parking lot and drove back to the motel.

Neither Harry nor the girl was in his room. Rux packed his clothes, checked out and walked across the lobby to the restaurant. The hostess seated him in a booth near the back so he could watch the entrance for Harry.

"Good afternoon," a cheery voice said. "May I get you something to drink while you look over the menu?"

Rux pushed his hat back and looked up at a tall, leggy blonde. She obviously recognized him, although he could not place her at all.

"Oh, hi," she said. "Haven't seen you since this morning."

"This morning?"

The girl laughed. "With Harry," she whispered.

Rux embarrassed himself by looking at her legs. "With Harry. Right," he said. "I'm looking for him. Do you know where he is?"

"No, and I don't want to know. I've about had enough of that twit. I'd like to fry his little butt."

"Me too. Why don't you bring me an iced tea and maybe we can think of something."

An hour later, Rux found Harry at the Le Fleur stalls, all duded up and ready for his next class. Harry, lounging in one of the deck chairs, stood when he saw Rux approaching. Something has alerted him, Rux thought. He wasn't sure if word of his accusations had gotten back to him or if Harry could sense the danger in Rux's purposeful strides.

Harry greeted him in a tense voice. "Where have you been? We have a horse going in the second class this afternoon."

Rux kept a polite distance between his face and Harry's, thanks primarily to the brims of their hats. "Never mind where I've been, Harry. Did you pepper Chester this morning?"

Harry stepped back, stumbling over the deck chair. "That's none of your business," he said. "You get paid to have my horses ready, and I get paid to win. Don't you ever question me."

Rux thought seriously about making a question mark out of Harry's nose.

Harry's normal voice returned, his confidence apparently bolstered by the presence of the grooms poking their heads out of the stalls. "Have you made these accusations to anyone else?" Harry asked.

"Yeah. I told one of the directors. I expect they're gonna be watching your horses pretty close from now on."

Harry turned as red as the Sedona desert. "Get your gear and get out!" The words were accompanied by spit. "You're fired!"

Rux was surprised at his own lack of reaction. Normally, he would have pounded Harry into the dirt. Instead, his fists relaxed and he took a step back. "Fine," he said. "I got no desire to work for a man who would do that to a horse. I'll pick up my stuff at the ranch and be gone."

One of the grooms said, "Wait a minute. What about the horses that aren't staying for next week's show? I drove Rux's truck over but I can't drive the big rig. Rux has to do that."

"Okay," Harry said. "Rux, you can't leave these horses stranded here. Wait until after the show and drive them back to the ranch. Then you're fired."

"That's just like you. Fire a man and then try to put conditions on him. You don't own people like you do horses."

"I may not own you, but I know you. You're not going to leave those horses here."

Rux knew he was right. "Fine. I'll get the horses home, Harry, but you stay outta my way. You better hope I never lay eyes on you again."

"Don't make things worse than they already are," Harry said. The squeak returned to his voice. "I can see to it that you never work in the Arabian horse business again."

"Maybe you'd better, 'cause if I ever hear of you peppering another horse I'll use your wimpy moustache to clean it off."

"Are you threatening me?"

"No, I was complimenting your moustache." Rux shoved his hands in his pockets and stomped off towards the exhibitors' parking lot. I should have jerked Harry wrong side out, he thought. But I had to make sure he gets back to his girl friend in one piece.

* * *

Rux spent the afternoon at Le Fleur's ranch gathering up his belongings.

He felt no great remorse. White stucco barns with tiled roofs and floors never had the feel of a working ranch as far as he was concerned. Pole barns with corrugated tin on top didn't have to be hosed down every night. But horse owners willing to house the Le Fleur staff in expensive hotel rooms near the show grounds when the ranch was only thirty minutes away would not be too impressed with a pole barn.

"Speaking of pole barns," he said to the whippet lounging in the glass-enclosed trophy room, "I might just go home to Texas, check on Daddy."

Rux headed for the phone in the office, calculating the time since his mother died. Five years? he thought. Man, it doesn't seem that long.

He left the day after the funeral. Harry Beauchamp had just hired him and only agreed to two days off. Rux was prepared to tell Harry to shove a worming tube up his nose and blow the job out his ears. But his father had insisted he would be fine, and that Rux go on back to Scottsdale.

Over the years Rux would call his dad, always intending to go home and check on things. But each time Daddy assured him everything was okay, the cow still gave milk and the chickens still laid eggs whether Rux was there or not. No need to hurry home unless he could bring rain.

Jeremiah Tuttle's familiar West Texas twang interrupted the phone's ringing. "Hal-ow."

"Hey, Dad, it's me."

"Me who?"

"Rux, your son."

"Rux? I don't know any...Oh! Rux! My favorite child. How are you, boy?"

"What do you mean, favorite child? You only got one. I'm doing good. How about you?"

"Aw, fair to middlin', I suppose. You still in Scottsdale?"

"Yeah, but I'm thinkin' about heading that way for a while."

"Seems like I remember you was comin' about a year ago. You must be takin' the long way around the barn."

"I know. Seems like something always comes up. But my job's played out up here. Reckon I'll be along soon."

"Well, in your case 'soon' is relative. Guess I'll look for you when I see you comin'."

"Sounds good."

Around ten o'clock, Rux returned to Paradise Park. The cool of the desert evening reminded him that summer was still several months away. He exchanged his pickup for the large tractor-trailer rig and pulled up in front of the stalls.

"Hey, Rux," Ash Chalmers called as he climbed down out of the cab.

"Can I talk to you for a minute?"

"Sure, Ash. What's up?"

Ash grabbed hold of the side loading ramp and helped Rux lower it to the ground. "Heard you had a run-in with Harry this afternoon."

"Yeah. Harry peppered Chester today. I've known that horse since his mama weaned him and so have you. He's never been spazzed out like that before."

"I know," Ash said. "And I won't tolerate cruelty to my horses. I told Harry I was taking Chester back as soon as the show ended tonight. Hate to lose a top trainer like him, but looks like the horse market is imploding anyway. You needing a job?"

"Appears that way. Harry fired me, then re-hired me to haul the horses back to the ranch. I'll be gone as soon as that's done. You know of anything?"

Ash followed Rux to the back of the trailer and the two of them lowered the rear ramp. "Would you mind dropping Chester off at my place on the way?" he asked. "I might could use you. I've got several other horses and a couple of kids that need training, but I've also got a lot of money tied up in horses that may not be worth much anymore. If you wanna stay around until after the auctions next week we'll see how things look. Your welcome to bunk at our place."

"Best offer I've had all day. I'd be grateful." Rux stopped the groom carrying water buckets into the trailer. "Don't worry about watering them. It's only a thirty minute ride. Just give them some hay to occupy their attention until we get there. And put Chester on last. I'm gonna drop him off at Chalmers."

Rux stepped out of the way to let the grooms load the horses. "Ash, even if things don't work out it's mighty kind of you to offer to take me on."

"You may not be so appreciative if the market collapses. I'd like you to stay with me as long as you can. If you need to be looking elsewhere I'll understand."

A glimmer of a thought that he might not get home right away stole into Rux's well-guarded repository for sensitive feelings, then flickered away. "Sure," he said. "I've been bumming around the horse business for almost twenty years now. It ain't like someone's got a light in the window waiting for me to come home."

Ash laughed. "Well, we do. Evening, Dottie."

Rux turned to find Dottie Beauchamp wandering out of the shadows behind him. "Oh, hi Dot," he said. "Need a ride back to the ranch? Understand Harry's staying over."

"Thanks, Rux. Yeah, Harry's feeling pretty low after Ash took Chester away from him. He'll get no pity from me, but he has his girl friend for that. Let her pump him back up."

"His girl friend's got no use for him anymore, either," Rux said. "But she agreed to put up with old Harry for one more night. He'll be plenty high when she gets through with him."

"She's that good, huh?"

"I wouldn't know. But we fixed him up an ecstasy suppository. Pop that sucker in and he'll be high for a month."

"How did you come up with that idea?"

"Only way we could figure out how to get pepper up his butt."

Dottie and Ash almost collapsed with laughter. Rux helped Dottie into the cab, shook hands with Ash, then climbed in and fired up the diesel. He eased the rig onto the highway, mindful of his cargo of expensive horses. At least one entertained himself by trying to kick the door off the trailer.

"What's making all that racket?" Dottie asked.

"Oh, probably Chester trying to assert his manhood, which he no longer has."

"Maybe we should do the same for Harry. Then he could spend his time kicking the door off the trailer rather than some poor girl's bedroom. Who invented a creature like him anyway?"

"Chester's not so bad."

"I meant Harry."

"Oh. Well, they've probably been with us since the beginning. As I recall the story of creation, God stood on the shore with a broom sweeping little critters back into the sea until the one deigned to evolve in Their image finally washed up. While this was going on one of the unwanted burrowed itself in the mud and escaped the wrath of the broom."

"Aren't you mixing metaphors?"

"Is that what they're called? Anyway, this unwanted little metaphor eventually evolved into a prurient species. They show up from time to time at places like Sodom and Gomorrah, the Left Bank in Paris, and the New Orleans French Quarter."

"And among an elite group of Arabian horse trainers."

Harry's wife withdrew into her thoughts. This allowed Rux to revive the image of Sammi reaching for the top of the coffee urn. He still-framed the scene and adjusted it slightly to place her on stage, sporting a frilly cowgirl dress.

His mental revelry interrupted itself and reminded him he had not seen her at the show. Of course, when he invited her, he hadn't planned on getting fired and spending the afternoon at the farm. He had remembered to call Deke about her. With any luck she would soon be performing in Pine Knot.

The thought that he might not see her again distressed him, but she was younger and way out of his league. Besides that, her disjointed references to Houston and drugs raised a caution flag. Sammi had said the culprits were someone called Peter Ossip—or was it Peter Rabbit?— and Hector, probably the turtle. Her friend, Tyrone, helped her load a U-Haul and disappear in a hurry.

Or was Tyrone the bad guy and Peter Rabbit and Hector Turtle her friends? It didn't matter. No way he would wade into that cesspool. Houston is another world. He thought.

Two

The fading of Sammi Stone's fears had been so gradual as to escape conscious perception. The surprisingly warm sun of late February embracing her in the cold mountain air brought an easy feeling, nudging Sammi into the notion that she had found a safe harbor.

She shed her denim jacket, unbuttoned the top two buttons of her white cowgirl shirt and leaned her head back. The sun chased away all but a hint of chill. She doubted if anyone else would consider Moose Ball's Bar and Grill as safe from anything except a snow storm. But Deke Ball had welcomed her like a lost child, and Pine Knot seemed far off the beaten path. No one would look for her here. The dulling of her anxiety brought a determination for vengeance.

Sammi propped her elbows on the top step of the stoop leading into the restaurant's kitchen. She stretched her legs in front of her, shoved her jeans further down on her hips and chuckled for the hundredth time over Deke's explanation for the name of his bar.

"'Moose' is my nickname," Deke had said without explanation or apology.

Sammi remembered thinking the nickname certainly fit his bulk. But the name had been adopted for more commercial reasons.

"This old bar's been here since the forties," Deke said. "I always dreamed of owning it some day. Bought it when I retired from the Army."

Deke would always cock the foot of his artificial leg and emphasize the word "retired" when he spoke about the ending of his military career. His "retirement" had been prematurely brought about by the loss of the lower portion of his left leg in Vietnam.

"Town's church folk objected to me calling it 'Moose Ball's'," Deke said. "They argued with some merit that every mountain hamlet from Arizona to Idaho had an Elk Horn bar. That should be good enough for Pine Knot, they said, even if there are no elk in the area. After all, there are no moose either. But they wouldn't deny a man the right to use his own name. So I named myself 'Moose' and that settled the issue."

Recalling Deke's easy resolution of his name problem caused Sammi's thoughts to wander back to Houston, and her own unsettling dilemma. The distance in both time and miles allowed her to reconstruct, without terror but not without sorrow, the events that caused her sudden departure two months earlier.

The return of Adrianne Godfrey had clearly been the catalyst that stood Sammi's world on edge and sent it spinning out of control. She tried to picture Adrianne's angelic features, her photogenic face that would have made a Los Angeles plastic surgeon envious. But the image was invariably overshadowed by the Adrianne that returned to Houston after her singing career failed.

Her formerly porcelain-like skin appeared sallow, as though she wore corn meal for makeup. And she was no longer flat chested.

"Couldn't make it as a singer," Adrianne had said, volunteering answers to questions Sammi had been too polite to ask. "I did get a job with a chorus line in Vegas, but that requires more than singing and a pretty face. They insisted on a boob job."

Sammi's eyes moistened as she recalled Adrianne smoothing her hands over her blouse. "I was happy with what I had," Adrianne said. "Figured they'd be good enough to nurse my babies some day. Hell, now I could nurse a school bus."

Sammi wasn't sure if she meant the bus itself or the kids riding it, but Adrianne looked like someone smuggling softballs. They had been friends for eight years. Peter Del Ossio, Sammi's husband, recently her ex-husband, was the agent for both of them.

Under his tutelage they took voice lessons and attended modeling school together. Sammi tried to assure Adrianne that Peter would get her singing career back on track.

"Show business is a tough life, babe, trust me," Adrianne said. "I'm working as a dancer at the Gentlemen's Preference Club. "Adrianne's watery eyes had darted between the ground and some unseen object behind Sammi as she added in a husky whisper, "And I work for Hector Romero."

Those words still stung. Sammi knew Hector had a string of prostitutes. Several of them, like Adrianne, were former clients of Peter's who did not make it in the music world but needed to support a drug habit acquired in the process of trying. Sammi pleaded with Adrianne to let her help. They agreed she must get free from Hector, but neither knew how. Pimps did not let their girls just walk away.

Sammi hugged her and both of them cried, ignoring the midday heat of the mall parking lot and the curious stares of the passers by.

"I'll call you," Adrianne said.

Those were the last words Sammi ever heard from her friend. Two days later, Adrianne died of a drug overdose.

Sammi scootched over to make room for the fry cook trudging down the steps with a garbage can. She looked at her watch and realized the band was awfully late. Inside, Deke yelled into the phone demanding their whereabouts. A stiff back and the smell of fresh garbage prompted Sammi to resume her cogitation at the board fence separating Moose Ball's from a cow lot, somehow overlooked by Pine Knot's urbanization.

Houston, never having left her thoughts, reasserted itself. She knew

Peter supplied his clients with whatever drugs they needed, and she also knew Hector sold crack on the streets. But she never suspected Peter and Hector were partners. Her confrontation with Peter over drugs in general and Adrianne's death in particular turned violent.

Peter did not brook insubordination. She moved out and filed for divorce. Melissa, Peter's daughter by his previous marriage, came with her, a twist of events that delighted Peter. He never wanted the child, but her mother had abandoned them when Melissa was a baby. Sammi was the only mother the girl ever knew.

A week after the divorce was final, the Houston police banged on her door in the middle of the night, brandished a search warrant and turned the apartment upside down. They did not find the drugs they were looking for.

She knew Peter had set her up. He accepted the divorce but not the fact that he was no longer her agent. She and Missy left the next day. They did not leave a forwarding address.

Deke called from the back door. "Bad news, Sam. The band ain't gonna show. You'll have to go it alone until we can get another one."

"I'll try," she said. Sammi turned back to the cow lot, hoping Deke could not see her sniffling and wiping tears. No point in involving him, she thought. I've already unloaded on that poor cowboy in Paradise Park more than I should have. But, chances are he wouldn't know anyone in Houston.

The old horse in the cow lot deposited an ample supply of road apples, confirming the solitude of Pine Knot, Arizona. "No one will find us up here," Sammi said to the horse. "Tyrone will know what to do."

Tyrone Dedman had befriended her in junior high school even though the caste system forbade him from associating with whites. Everyone assumed Tyrone's father to have been black since his birth mother was white. Tyrone himself made chimney soot pale.

She blotted her eyes on her shirt sleeve and quickly made her way back to the stoop. "Nice outfit," Sammi said to Deke as she slipped past him through the kitchen door. "I need to make a phone call."

"Thanks. Use the phone in my office. Close the door if you want to."

In the week she had known him, Sammi had never seen Deke dressed in anything other than a white apron over a red plaid shirt and khaki pants. She concluded it must be some type of uniform.

"It's okay, you can do this," Sammi whispered to her shaky fingers trying to slip into the proper holes of the rotary dial. On her third try she conquered, in proper sequence, the phone number for Tyrone Dedman's adopted grandmother.

"Sammi, how are you, dear? It's so good to hear your voice. Tyrone's not here. He's either working or at Mama Henry's, shooting pool. Shall I have him call you?"

"No, that's okay," Sammi said. "I'll try to reach him at Mama Henry's."

Sammi thanked her and dialed Mama Henry's. She waited as the voice that answered the phone yelled "telephone for the Dead Man."

"Hey, Sam, what's up?" Tyrone said when he came on the line.

"I need your help, as usual." Sammi related the story of the aborted drug bust, emphasizing her strong suspicion of Peter's involvement. "That's why I left in such a hurry. I'm sure he and Hector are into dealing. Who knows what else. He may be just mean enough to claim I kidnapped Missy. I'm really scared."

"Lemme conversate with a few folks," Tyrone said. "See maybe we can get a posse rounded up and headed in the right di-rection. I don't wanna know where you are, right?"

"No, I don't mind if...Oh, I see what you're saying. Plausible deniability in case the police want to talk to me."

"Plause is cool. Call me back in a week or so."

Sammi's hands trembled so badly she missed the cradle twice as she tried to hang up the phone. I had no right to involve Tyrone, she thought. I'm secure in my little mountain hideaway but he's on the streets down in Houston. Peter and Hector will know how to find him if they think he's helping me. I should call him back and tell him to forget it. I'll call the police myself.

Sammi reached for the phone but couldn't force her hand to pick up the receiver. "I'll call back later," she said to the phone. "After practice."

Another safe haven existed inside her music. Strumming the guitar quieted her hands and the words to her songs soothed her mind. But the solitude proved fleeting. Ten minutes after she started, Sammi had exhausted her repertoire of medleys she could do solo.

"Deke," she said, "I'm inventing chords out here. I only know three songs I can accompany myself on. My guitar playing is just not that good."

She twanged a discordant chord, then slapped the strings to silence the instrument. Deke roused himself from behind the bar and lumbered toward the stage. Uh oh, Sammi thought. I'm in trouble. Deke's heavy red beard and bushy eyebrows made it difficult to read his expression, but his walk seemed more determined than normal. She quickly began picking the lively melody to "Good Hearted Woman."

Deke stood at the edge of the stage with his tremendous arms folded. The arms rested neatly on top of a barreled chest that had yielded a few inches to the pull of gravity.

"Not bad," he said as Sammi finished. "Look, Sam, don't worry about

21

it. All we get in here on week nights is the locals and they're all so in love with you they won't notice if you miss every other note. I'll get another band here by the weekend."

"Can you at least get a piano player? There's a keyboard back in the dressing room. Who plays that?"

"Oh, that belongs to Rux."

"Rux?"

"Yeah. You remember Rux, the guy who sent you up here."

Sammi tried to find a hint of teasing in the furry face. "Sure, I remember him. I just didn't picture him as a piano player."

Deke laughed. "And just what did you picture him as?"

"I guess I...." Sammi searched for her boots hiding beneath the guitar. "He's nice. I just didn't think he looked like a musician." She glanced up to find Deke's eyes prodding her. "I'm not getting out of this, am I?"

The normally stern blue eyes beneath the bird's nests brows twinkled with obvious delight. "No," Deke said. "Why wouldn't you picture Rux as a musician?"

Sammi looked to the bartender for help. He merely stood at the end of the bar with a mischievous grin. "Well," she said, "he's so big. And his hands. He looks like a cow puncher who literally punches out his cows."

The roar from the two men rattled the beer mugs drying on the counter behind the bar.

"Please, guys, I don't know. You're getting me in a lot of trouble here."

Deke finally controlled himself enough to motion Sammi toward the dressing room. "You're probably right," he said. "Them old hands been mangled by punching ornery cows, balky horses and trailer hitches that won't hitch. Not to mention a few bar fights. But he still manages to beat a tune out of this contraption. Look here."

Deke opened the closet door in the dressing room and stepped back for Sammi to look inside. Several speakers, a drum machine and a Kaypro computer stared back at her.

"What is all this?" Sammi asked.

"The Rux Philharmonic Orchestra, minus the conductor, of course."

Sammi turned to look at Deke. The blue eyes still twinkled.

"What? How? What are you talking about?" she asked.

Deke sidestepped over to the keyboard. "This," he said. "Don't ask me how, but Rux wires the computer and drum machine to the keyboard then back through the speakers. Some new interface technology lets him play the keyboard and produce the sounds of a whole band."

"I've heard of that. But it's highly technical. It seems so...unRuxlike."

"More to that boy than meets the eye," Deke said. His eyes were laughing but the tone of his voice now seemed more serious. "I can usually get a band out of Phoenix or Flagstaff. But if they get a gig in a bigger city, like as not they just don't show. Half the time they don't even bother to call. Rux comes up occasionally and fills in for me when I get in a bind."

Sammi fingered the keys, playing a silent tune and trying to imagine a ham-fisted cowboy producing the sound of an entire band. "Could he possibly come up this weekend?"

"I was hoping. Called as soon as I found out about the band, but the ranch where he was at said he didn't work there no more. Feller said he heard Rux was headed back to Texas."

"That's too bad," Sammi said. Genuine sadness tugged at her, an emotion for which she could not readily account. After all, she had hardly known him. "So," she said, sweeping her arm over the keyboard and toward the closet, "this is the real world of Rux."

"I dunno, Sam. Somewhere, underneath the rawhide and behind all the corny jokes, I suspect there just might be the soul of an artist. But I ain't never seen it."

"And, if he's gone back to Texas, I guess we never will."

"Could be."

Sammi tried to picture the square-jawed, square-shouldered cowboy hulking over a keyboard, playing a piano concerto. Instead, her aesthetic logic produced Rux's handsome, bronzed face, green eyes betraying his attempt to hide a devilish grin behind his coffee cup. "Well, so much for the piano player. Let me go back and work on a few more songs."

Sammi returned to her stool on the stage and searched her mind for any song with simple chords. As she sang, images of Tyrone and Rux, two men at opposite ends of her universe, kept flitting in and out. All the songs were sad ones.

Three

Rux lolled on a precipice of the Mogollon rim above an endless valley. He surveyed all his earthly possessions and pondered on whether he might be the wealthiest man alive. At the moment his earthly possessions consisted of a faded red, fifteen-year-old Ford pickup, a once white but now mostly rusted two-horse trailer, and the newest and most prized of all his treasures, Chester.

Scottsdale, the Mecca of the Arabian horse world, disappeared from his rearview mirror before dawn. Rux wanted to be in Albuquerque by dark. And he had only one hundred dollars for gas money to reach Texas. Nonetheless, he was detouring through the mountains to say good bye to his old army buddy, Deke, and to show off his good fortune.

Chester lounged in the trailer, nibbling at his hay bag more for the purpose of strewing than consumption, while simultaneously relieving his bladder. Rux had stopped at the roadside turnout for similar relief, lacking both the luxury of a trailer bedded with wood shavings and the convenience of an owner with a shovel to assure a reasonably clean abode for traveling.

Rux did not consider himself particularly religious, due more to his bachelor ranch hand life than to indifference. Nonetheless, he could not help but think someone upstairs had taken a liking to him. A year earlier, Chester would have sold for forty thousand dollars. Last night, Ash Chalmers had given him to Rux for nothing more than a promise to give him a good home.

Over the last twenty years, Rux had watched as the small, family-oriented Arabian horse business burgeoned into an over-hyped marketing scheme. Prices for top stallions and brood mares had inflated to over a million dollars. Breedings to a champion stallion could cost up to ten thousand dollars, live foal guaranteed of course. The stallion would gladly service your mare as many times as needed, but the market sustained itself solely on the greater fool theory.

The sales at the Scottsdale show confirmed Ash's fears. The Arabian horse market had collapsed under its own weight. The last of the greater fools sat in auctions and watched their one hundred thousand dollar horses sell for two thousand. There were rumors of horses meeting with fatal accidents, particularly if they were insured.

Rux carefully straddled the remnants of the trailer's running board and admired his horse. He knew Chester could achieve national stardom, and every trainer and show judge who watched the horse work agreed.

Rux reached in and scratched Chester's withers. "Yessir, big fella," he said. "Fame and fortune are just around the bend."

Chester farted. He would be equally unimpressed with Pine Knot.

The aroma of the horse's flatulence blended nicely with the exhaust from a geriatric truck doddering into the turnout. Rux was immediately distraught. The advanced age of his pickup defined a cowboy. The gasping relic predated his Ford by at least ten years. Its equally distraught driver hardly gave the appearance of a cowboy.

The man either belonged to the clergy or had his shirt on backwards. Rux decided to address him by a church title until he knew for sure. "Need any help, Padre?"

"Guess I do. Hi, I'm Tom Richter, Rector of St. Mary's Parish. You know anything about trucks?"

"Rux Tuttle. 'Bout all I know is they ain't broke in good until they'll start when you throw your hat at 'em. Looks like this one's about there."

"She starts okay. It's the running part that seems to be the problem."

Rector Richter looked like a steer wrestler, but Rux had never heard of a rodeo Rector. Since St. Mary's sounded Catholic, he assumed Rector Richter had something to do with the priesthood.

"I drive her over to the Apache Reservation at Whiteriver twice a week," Rector Richter said. "Every time we make it back, we consider it another miracle of the Red Sea crossing."

Rux laughed with Rector Richter although he did not understand the pun until the Padre nodded towards the door of the old truck. Apparently it once belonged to the Caldwell Cattle Company, but all that remained of their logo was a faint red "C" on the door panel.

Rux said, "Best thing would be to jack up the radiator cap and drive another truck under it. Short of that, let's see if we can find enough baling wire and chewing gum to keep you one step ahead of the Egyptians. You ever do any bulldogging?"

Rector Richter chuckled. "No, although I did play football in high school. Chicago. Might have played college ball or even pro, but I committed to the priesthood at an early age."

Rux engrossed himself in the old truck's carburetor. "Commitment's important," he said, although he could not recall ever having committed to anything beyond staying out of the bush in Vietnam. "You have a church over at Whiteriver?"

"A small mission. Trying to protect our turf, I suppose. Some of the Apaches are into the Native American movement seeking their heritage. I think that's good from an academic standpoint. But several of our parishioners are confusing their ancient spiritual beliefs with their practice of Christianity."

Rux wondered if Rector Richter felt the same way about Baptists.

"I've been working with a young couple who are sort of the unofficial leaders of their old religion," the Padre said. "Modern day shamans, I suppose."

"Sounds like Joe Hawkins."

"That's right. You know Joe and Auren then."

"Joe hangs out at Moose Ball's. Once he's sufficiently fire-watered he's into his sun dance and seeing visions of the white buffalo."

"Maybe we should consider a nonalcoholic communion wine."

"Who's Auren?"

"Auren's his wife. Pretty Indian girl from Oklahoma. Cherokee and Comanche I understand."

"Wife, huh. Good. Maybe she can domesticate the great Apache warrior a little. Then again, maybe not."

Rux applied all the modern medicine he could to Rector Richter's truck. Any further miracles required a fair amount of faith healing. He waved the Padre behind the wheel and told him not to stop until he got to town.

Rux followed the Red "C" into Pine Knot. The town typified the rural mountain communities of eastern Arizona recently discovered by valley residents. Once quiet villages currently provided convenient ski resorts in winter and a respite from the punishing desert heat of summer.

Pine Knot's original town square now served as the town's historical district. Its old barbershop, hardware store, Moon Palace Cafe and other staple establishments had been replaced with antique stores, gift shops and bistros. Condominiums and other real estate developments, fueled by Pine Knot's three-hour proximity to Phoenix, overshadowed the old town itself.

The bistros and the two new wood and glass restaurants, each with a large round fireplace centered in the bar, competed for the overflow from Moose Ball's Bar and Grill.

Rux strode into Moose Ball's, tilting slightly forward in the manner of men who wore boots and balanced in the saddle. Even at midmorning the place was dark, the only source of light seemingly coming from the beer signs.

"Rux, you old war horse," Deke bellowed, bounding from behind the bar to bear hug his friend and former adversary. Deke's mass engulfed him even though Rux's size might near matched that of Rector Richter.

Throughout his army career Deke himself had been trim and muscular. He could haul ass with the best of his troops. Now, he had to make two trips. Eighteen years of the good life at Moose Ball's had taken its toll.

"How you getting along, big'un?" Rux asked.

"I ain't gittin' any longer, that's for sure. How 'bout a beer?"

"Grab us a couple and come on outside. I want to show you my new pride and joy."

"Outside? She too damned ugly to bring into a dark bar?"

"Not she, he."

"He? Coming out of the closet after all these years, are we? Wait a minute. There's someone else here looking for you."

Rux turned and found himself staring into the fascinating eyes of Sammi Stone. He hoped his startled surprise didn't register on his face.

"Sam. By golly it's good to see you again."

"Hello, stranger," Sammi said. She extended her soft hand to him. Rux politely wiped his own hand on his shirt before accepting hers. As he did, she lightly touched his cheek with her fingers.

"Oops, sorry," Rux said. "I left early this morning. Didn't plan on meeting up with any pretty ladies today or I would've shaved."

"That's okay," Sammi said. "We're glad you're here. Deke tried to call you earlier. We thought you had gone to Texas."

Rux knew they were ignoring Deke but he could not pull himself away from her eyes. "That's where I'm headed," he said. "But I couldn't leave without saying goodbye to Deke. I didn't know for sure if you came up here. Glad you did, though."

Deke said, "Me too. She's been great. Listen, Rux, we lost our band. You in a hurry or do you think you could stay on a few days and help us out?"

"All depends," Rux said. He finally thought to let go of Sammi's hand.

"On what?" Deke asked.

"Whether or not you can accommodate my new family."

"Sure we can," Deke said. "What family?"

Rux stifled a laugh. He took Deke and Sammi by the arms and guided them toward the door. "The one you thought was too ugly to bring inside. Come on, I'll introduce you."

Rux led them out the door and to the parking lot at the side of the building. Sammi still looked puzzled, but Deke obviously figured out what was going on as soon as he saw the trailer.

"Good lord," Deke said. "What have you gone and gotten yourself into now?"

"Wait here," Rux said. He left his wards a safe distance from the trailer while he backed the horse out. "Deke and Sammi, meet Chester."

The horse, sensing his cue, snorted and pranced like the stallion he once was.

"Dang, he's nice," Deke said. "Where'd an old stall mucker like you come by a nice piece of horse flesh like this?"

"Chalmers gave him to me. Had more horses than he could feed."

"I hear that. When my daddy sold his stock and deeded the ranch to me, he told me never to own anything that ate while I was asleep."

Sammi walked up and patted Chester's neck. The horse responded by nuzzling her hair as if he was about to eat it. "Nice horse," she said.

"Thanks," Rux said. "Do you ride?"

"Used to, when I was younger. Deke's got a couple of mares out at the ranch we've ridden a few times."

"Ah," Rux said, turning to Deke. "So you do own something that eats while you sleep."

"Couple of Daddy's old cow horses he couldn't bring himself to get rid of. I can't vouch for their eating habits. Look, if you're a mind to stay, you can turn Chester out with the mares. Sammi and her little girl are staying in the house, but you can bunk in the foaling room in the barn. How about it?"

"Couldn't turn down an offer like that," Rux said, smiling at Sammi. "But Miz Stone here may be a little above performing with a funky old piano player like Henry."

"Who's Henry?" Sammi asked.

Deke laughed. "Part of his nonsense. You'll get used to it. Y'all come on in and see if you can work up a few numbers for this weekend. I'll tie Chester to the fence out back and let him graze."

Deke took Chester's lead rope and led him off behind the building while Rux and Sammi made their way back inside.

Rux hauled the synthesizer keyboard and other equipment to the stage. Sammi pitched in where she could, stringing wire and retrieving pliers and other assorted tools for him.

Once everything was in place and properly tuned, Rux asked, "Okay, Madam. What type of instruments would you like in your band? We can do just about anything up to a one hundred string orchestra. I'll provide the piano from the keyboard."

"This is incredible," Sammi said. "Where did you learn all of this?"

"Not from my daddy, that's for sure. He saw to it that I acquired all the skills necessary to survive on the West Texas plains. Ranching, roping, riding, building, fixing anything mechanical, and football. But he did indulge my mother one fantasy. When I was about five or six, still young enough to be under her womanly influence, she gave me piano lessons."

Deke and the bartender guffawed from the bar.

Sammi frowned at them and asked Rux, "And you continued your piano all these years?"

"Not exactly. By the ripe old age of seven my manhood would no longer permit such feminine pursuits. But a seed had been planted, I guess.

Now, how about a steel guitar, a base, and a fiddle? Maybe some harmonica or a little banjo?"

Rux could see Sammi playing songs in her head, trying to pick out the various instruments that accompanied her. "No big deal to program them in," he said. "We don't have to use them."

"Okay," Sammi said. "But how did you master all this if you haven't played the piano since you were seven?"

Rux slipped the software into the Kaypro and began selecting the voices for the synthesizer. "Like I said, a seed had been planted. When I got to be a teenager, I sat down at the piano and taught myself to play. Got my computer training in the army. When the synthesizers and midi interface software came out, well I guess one thing just naturally led to another. I'm ready when you are."

Sammi picked up her guitar and tuned it with the keyboard. "Let's try an easy one first," she said.

"How about 'Clyde Played Electric Base'?"

"That's simple enough, but I don't think it has a part for me."

"Sorry." Rux flipped through the menu on the computer. "Can you do 'Texas When I Die'?"

"Sure. Give me the beat. Slow at first."

Rux could sense an immediate rapport develop. The blending of her guitar with his melee of sounds required more time, but by late afternoon they had put together enough numbers for an evening's performance.

"You guys are a natural," Deke said. "Why don't you try a practice run tonight with the locals? Rux, take Chester on out to the ranch and get settled in. You got a clean shirt?"

"This one's reversible, just like my shorts."

"Good. How long can you stay?" Deke asked.

"I can stay a bit, I suppose."

Rux was more than glad to help but he doubted he would last long up here in the cold and snow. He had wandered from ranch to ranch since his Army days, but always managed to land in a warm climate. Even the winds that occasionally chilled Scottsdale on a cloudy winter day irritated him. But a week or so in the mountains with Sammi could prove tempting.

Rux headed for his truck, welcoming the break. Sammi's love ballads had filled the musty saloon like the perfume of gardenias on a warm summer evening. Her closeness rapidly reduced him to jelly. His truck would provide sanctuary for him to regroup.

The cause of his ungrouping climbed into the pickup beside him with a smile that would melt jelly into flavored water. "Can I ride with you?" Sammi asked.

"Sure." Rux picked up his hat to study the secret message inside.

Cowboys' hats, like their trucks, were required to be of a certain vintage. 1976 was a good year for hats. The secret message inside still read "Acme Hats."

Chester struggled to maintain his balance in the trailer as Rux eased the pickup along the narrow, rocky path leading from the highway to Deke's ranch.

"I need to tell you about Missy, Melissa, my daughter," Sammi said. "She's nine, pretty as a picture and loves horses. But she's, well, not really my daughter."

Rux noticed a hesitancy in her voice. "How's that?" he asked.

"She's the daughter of my ex-husband, by a prior marriage."

"Oh." Rux assumed there was more to the story but Sammi did not continue. And it was not his nature to pry. Unable to muster up an understanding look or think of something appropriate to say, he simply squinted unnecessarily at the winding road and checked the side mirror to be sure the trailer still followed. It did.

"Her mother decided she wasn't cut out for motherhood and left when Missy was a baby. Her father all but ignored her."

"Well I swan. I can't imagine a grown man doing that to his own child. Never had any kids of my own, far as I know. I did have a wife once."

"Once? What happened?"

Rux's lack of fondness for talking about his ill-fated marriage approached his lack of fondness for his ex-wife. But he sensed Sammi wanted to shift conversation away from Missy. "Long story, short marriage. In No Water, the small ranching town in West Texas where I grew up, we tended to pair up in high school and marry shortly after graduation. Unless pregnancy required an earlier wedding. Betty Jo Follmer and me followed this ancient custom but skipped the pregnancy part."

"I'm touched. I thought chastity went out with the fifties."

"We never knew it came in. The one thing a Baptist mother fears more than premarital sex is unwed motherhood. They rely on the pastor's assurances of eternal damnation to keep their daughters pure through about age fourteen. Beyond that, they equip them with a working knowledge of the art of the diaphragm to protect their family's reputation from the ravages of the teenage male population."

"Are you making this up?"

"Mostly, but not the part about me and Betty Jo and our failure to procreate. She assured me I was the greatest thing produced by No Water since the Dairy Queen. The depth of her passion for me almost matched her contempt for small town life. She needed a ticket to the big city."

"And did you?"

"Did I what?"

"Take her to the big city."

"Not exactly. Betty Jo figured any guy who could play football, build a barn, work on cars and fix her television set could do just about anything. But she didn't figure on the draft. I drew a high lottery number and Uncle Sam shipped me off to Vietnam shortly after our wedding."

"She didn't wait for you, right?"

"Oh, she promised to wait faithfully. And she did. Until my bus topped the hill and disappeared from sight. Then she piled into a pickup with Cecil Parmalee and headed for the bright lights of Fort Worth. Her 'Dear John' letter beat me to Saigon. I expect she used a form letter from a do-it-yourself divorce kit."

"Sort of impersonal, huh?"

"You might say that. She used all the right words, like forgiveness and understanding and so forth. But the salutation read 'To Whom It May Concern'."

Rux would just as soon have quit the story at that point. He still enjoyed reliving the conclusion to this iniquitous saga. But the telling of it without offending the tender ears of a young lady he hardly knew required less colorful language than that to which he was accustomed. He continued only after Sammi's persistence.

"Well, complete devastation sounds trite. I swore I would never forget her. Sack cloth and ashes came to mind, but the Army prefers drinking. It's more in keeping with the rites of manhood plus it gives you an excuse when you throw up on someone else's bunk."

"You didn't."

"Didn't what?"

"Throw up on each other's bunks."

"It's a time-honored military tradition. Anyway, I indulged a weekend binge during which I proposed to at least two prostitutes. I forgot Betty Jo's name, although I did remember her as having the physique of a bulldog and a face that would stop an eight-day clock."

"Nice choice of words. Your English teacher would be proud of you."

"I doubt that. Our English teacher was Cecil Parmalee."

The truck topped a ridge and began the long descent over rocky tire tracks. The path wound through sparse native grasses to an old, two-story house with a wide porch across the front and a small stoop on the back. The green-painted siding of the house appeared badly weathered, although the cinder-block barn looked freshly whitewashed.

Deke's ranch arrived just in time. Rux had used up his prose. Chester definitely had not. As they drove toward the ranch house, the horse loudly announced his presence to the mares in the pasture.

Rux dropped Sammi at the house and continued fifty yards further down the makeshift road to the barn. He parked at the pasture gate and opened the trailer doors, then took the horse's lead rope and clucked, letting him know it was okay to back out. The big, gray gelding stepped cautiously to the ground and shook vigorously.

Because he suffered the ignominious fate of his gelding at the relatively late age of three, Chester retained some of the mannerisms of his former life. Rux knew he would not back away from a fight with a stallion, and kick chains were necessary to preserve the automatic watering trough in his stall at Le Fleur Arabians.

Conventional wisdom held that a gelding could safely be hauled next to a mare. Rux gave Chester credit for wisdom but not conventionalism, recalling how the horse relieved the boredom of his first trip by chewing sizable gaps in the long, silky mane of the mare beside him. Sonny Le Fleur and Harry Beauchamp were not amused.

Rux opened the pasture gate, ushered Chester inside and removed his halter. The two mares at the far end of the pasture answered Chester's clarion call and he set out to gather his new herd. The mares were amenable until they discerned their would-be leader's altered state. They returned to their grazing and proceeded to ignore him. Chester returned the compliment, obviously realizing the stallion's duty is to assemble and protect his herd. Dining with them is not required.

Rux replaced the chain on the gate and collected his saddles and tack from the truck. As he shuffled though the barn toward the tack room, a slight figure emerged through the back entrance.

"Emilio, you old wetback," Rux said. "Why ain't you been deported yet?" Rux laughed as he shook hands with the small Mexican man. "Where's your better half?"

"Welcome back, Rux. You know I'm legal. Juanita's up at the house. She stays with the little girl until her mamma gets home."

"She lost any weight yet?"

"Naw, but she's going on a diet tomorrow. You know how that goes. Deke called, said you'd be staying in the foaling room. Here, let me help you."

Emilio took the saddles and followed him to the tack room. Rux had no idea whether Emilio and Juanita were legal, and did not care. They occupied the double wide behind the barn and generally kept the place from falling apart. That should be good enough to satisfy the I.N.S.

A large, yellow cat with a stiff back leg hopped off an old trunk and rubbed his jaw against Emilio's boot. "Who's this?" Rux asked.

"Howard. He's a stray we picked up in town. Stays out here and keeps the rat population in check."

"Don't look like he could move quick enough to catch rats, with that jake leg he's got."

"He does, though. You'll hear him at night scurrying around in the rafters. I can't figure out how he even gets up there."

"What happened to him?"

"We ran into him in the parking lot at Howard's Supermarket. Juanita wouldn't let me put him out of his misery. That's the best the vet could do with his leg."

As they returned to the open area of the barn, Juanita waddled in with Sammi and a young girl close behind.

Juanita said, "Rux, come here boy. You owe me a hug."

Juanita stood less than five feet in height and was about as round as she was tall. Emilio towered over his doughy spouse by at least an inch but was muscularly thin, giving him the appearance of a large ant.

Rux grinned and bent to allow Juanita's embrace. "When are you and me gonna run away together?" Rux asked her.

"Soon I hope," Juanita said.

"Me too," Emilio said. "I need to find another cook who fries everything with lots of grease and gravy."

"You still feeding him rabbit food with all those herb and vitamin drinks?" Rux asked.

"Sure," Juanita said. "See how healthy he is." Her playful pat intended for Emilio's rear found only the baggy seat of pants designed for a more ample posterior.

Sammi interrupted the frivolity before it descended to an R-rating. "Rux, this is Missy."

Missy was definitely as pretty as a picture, Rux thought. In fact, she could have been a portrait of Sammi at an earlier age, with the same dark hair, olive skin and dark eyes. No one would ever suspect they weren't mother and daughter.

The tiny princes in blue jeans was tall yet slight, and she still maintained the innocent elegance of preteen youth. Missy carefully studied the pattern drawn by her boot in the dirt of the barn floor, then briefly met Rux's gaze with a shy smile.

"Hello, Mr. Rux."

Rux grinned like a new daddy.

* * *

When Rux and Sammi returned to Moose Ball's that evening he still wore his grin along with a clean shirt and dusted off hat and boots. His boots would stay clean for a while. Sammi and Missy had him walking about three feet off the ground.

Except for the name and entertainment, Moose Ball's resembled every other Elk Horn Bar from Arizona to Idaho. Large, rounded pine logs formed both the exterior and interior walls, exposed rafters and cross beams. Massive support beams, strategically located, obstructed the view of the stage from every table. Mounted heads of moose, elk and bighorn sheep, logos of defunct railroads, and the obligatory neon beer signs liberally decorated the walls.

The crowd clamored for Sammi as Rux eased behind his keyboard for his warm up act. Friendly hoots and cat calls greeted him. They knew his opening farce better than Rux.

"Hello, I'm Henry Eweolfard," Rux said, playing the melody to his first number. "That's spelled E-W-E-O-L-F-A-R-D-T. The 'T' is silent."

He continued playing until someone from the audience yelled, right on cue, "Sing the song Henry, you old fart."

Rux boomed out several songs in his gravelly voice that ranged somewhere between Hoyt Axton and Johnny Cash, then introduced Sammi. She stepped across the stage and into the spotlight. Soft pink roses appliqued on her white shirt matched the color of her jeans. The cheering violated the town's noise ordinance by several decibels.

Rux gave her time for numerous bows, then cued up their first number. Immediately, her graceful presence and full, rich voice captivated the audience and left the maestro of the Rux Philharmonic spellbound. An afternoon of practicing with her had not prepared him for this. The energy of a live audience lifted Sammi to another level.

Rux could not understand how someone so beautiful and talented had escaped the attention of Nashville. But for the moment she belonged to Pine Knot. He levitated even further.

By three o'clock the next morning the bar had long since closed and the two performers neared exhaustion. The patrons refused to leave even though most of them were due at work in a few hours. Their effusiveness flowed out of Moose Ball's and shook water from toilets in the surrounding buildings. The afternoon practice had permitted time to program and rehearse only ten numbers. All of them had been recycled several times. Rux and Sammi were winging it with any song they both knew when Deke mercifully pronounced Moose Ball's closed for the evening.

Even then, the crowd exited slowly. Most of the men milled around the stage, waiting their turn to greet Sammi. Tears streaked her stage makeup as she hugged them and placed kisses on several bald pates.

Deke finally shooed the last patron out the door. He stumped back to the table where the bartender had set up cups and a pot of hot tea with lemon and honey. "Man," he said, slumping into a chair, "you two must be exhausted. I was wondering if they were ever gonna let you quit. Can't say as I blame 'em, though. That show was absolute dynamite."

Rux pushed his hat back and downed a cup of tea to soothe his raw throat. "Hey, thanks, Deke. You didn't tell me Miz Stone here would blow the room away when we went live."

Even in the dim tavern lights Rux could see Sammi blush as she pondered her empty cup. "Thank you," she said. "But I think the Rux Philharmonic had something to do with it."

Sammi's dark eyes met Rux's. Her smile surpassed the sum total of all the gorgeous sunsets he had ever seen. While he waited for her last comment to fully register, Deke interrupted the slow motion process.

"You guys better head for the ranch," he said. "Big night tomorrow, or tonight, I guess. A lot of the weekend skiers will be here."

"Right," Rux said. He unraveled his lanky frame from the chair and offered Sammi a hand. "We'll need more than ten numbers. Think you'll feel up to practicing again tomorrow afternoon?"

Sammi took his hand and pulled herself up. "Sure," she said. "I've got to get Missy off to school in about four hours, but I'll get some sleep after that. We'll try for right after lunch."

They bade Deke and the bartender good night and headed for the truck. The crisp air of the winter night greeted them as they stepped out of the old bar. Sammi shivered and hugged herself. Rux placed his jacket around her shoulders as he opened the truck door. Sammi's same tired smile offered a silent "thank you."

The light chatter of their earlier ride to the ranch yielded to an exhausted but not unpleasant quiet. Rux could feel an easy harmony with his new partner, something beyond just their music. He wondered if she felt it as well. Probably not, he decided. Just another of his teenage infatuations. He knew he should have grown out of this stage by now but, what the heck, it was pleasurable enough.

Rux noticed Sammi take something from her purse and pop it into her mouth. "Downers," she said. "I need them to relax after a performance, particularly tonight. Want some?"

"No thanks. I prefer something more natural." He knew that didn't sound right. "Like exercise I mean." Worse, he thought. "Maybe Juanita has some herb concoction we could use."

Sammi laughed. "You're digging yourself a nice hole."

"I know. I have a habit of that."

He pulled up to the back porch of the ranch house and turned off the motor. "Good night, Miz Stone," he said. "Thank you for a lovely evening. Tell Juanita I'll give her a ride down to the trailer."

"Thanks, I'm sure she'll appreciate that. Good night, Mr. Rux."

Within a few minutes a groggy Juanita stumbled out the back door and climbed into the pickup. "Mighty kind of you, sir," she said.

Rux cranked the engine and eased along the make-shift gravel road toward the barn. "Least I can do for the elderly," he said.

"Elderly, schmelderly. Watch your tongue. How was the show?"

"Great, you need to come see it." Rux grimaced at the noisy squeaking of his brakes as he stopped in front of the house trailer.

Juanita opened her door and slid to the ground. "I'd love to see the show, but I'm the baby sitter, remember? You want a wake up call?"

"No, thanks. See you tomorrow. Buenos snowshoes."

"It's Buenos...oh, never mind. I'm half asleep. I think your lug nuts are loose, anyway."

* * *

On winter evenings the concrete walls of the foaling room abandoned any pretense of capturing the sun's warmth, leaving the small cubicle chilled with cold mountain air. The sparsely furnished room contained a bed, an old rocking chair and an electric heater. The "kitchen" consisted of a miniature refrigerator and a hot plate occupying most of a badly scarred wooden table.

A small window faced the house and a large picture window permitted oversight of the adjacent stall, used for mares thought ready to foal. A helping hand could be available if needed, although Rux knew mares to drop their young in pastures without human intervention. The horses probably preferred the pasture approach.

Foaling stalls with adjacent viewing rooms were undoubtedly conceived by someone with millions invested in mares and breeding fees. In better times, Le Fleur's staff included a full-time veterinarian.

Rux noticed a can of coffee and a pot on the table. He checked inside the refrigerator and found a quart of orange juice and a pan of biscuits. "Bless you, Juanita," he said. "I'd better get some groceries tomorrow."

He shucked to his underwear, dismissed the idea of exercise and flopped on the bed. An hour later he found himself contemplating the vapor light that illuminated the yard between the house and the barn. Maybe I should get up and exercise, he thought. Performing, plus looking into the most fascinating dark eyes for the better part of his last twenty-four hours made sleep impossible. Winter in the mountains with Sammi Stone would be tempting.

Naw. Some agent will discover her long before then, and she'll be gone. Deke can most likely get another band by next weekend. I'd best quit dreaming and get on down to Texas.

Four

Some time after his shower and during his shave, Rux became conscious of the fact that he was actually up. He walked to the window, located the sun and calculated the time to be before noon. But what day? He returned to the mirror, tried to wipe off the fog and realized it was in his head.

"Good grief," he said to his bloodshot eyes. "I shaved off my moustache." Then he remembered he had shaved it off years ago, under similar circumstances. Only half of it at first.

One hour, one pot of coffee and one pan of biscuits later, Rux climbed into his truck and drove up to the house. Sammi, all decked out in white jeans and a pink and green plaid shirt, greeted him from the back porch.

"Howdy, Ma'am," he said. "Could you use a ride into town?"

"Be right there. Let me grab my purse."

Probably needs her "uppers," Rux thought as he waited. She ought to try getting up on a half-broke horse. That'll get you going. Guess I should have worked Chester this morning, or maybe I did and just don't remember it.

"And how are you this morning?" Sammi said, climbing in the truck. "Did you sleep well?"

Rux goosed the gas pedal and headed for the highway. "One thing training horses and singing in bars have in common is lack of sleep," he said. "Drunks stay up late and horses get up early. Actually, it gets so hot down in Scottsdale during the summer we'd work the horses at night. You rested up enough for another long performance tonight?"

"Absolutely. Let's see if we can get down about ten more songs today. But last night was fun, even when we were making up stuff. What did you think?"

"Who had time to think? You're right though, it was fun."

Sammi pulled her long hair into a pony tail and captured it with an elastic band. "I thought we worked real well together, right from the start," she said. "Are you sure you have to leave after this weekend? You and I could be the Rux Philharmonic's choir."

Rux rounded a curve too fast and swerved back into his lane. Driving and watching a well-endowed lady with her arms behind her head at the same time could prove hazardous. Heck of a time to ask me about staying, he thought. "We'll see," he said. "I imagine Deke already has another band lined up for next weekend."

Sammi, still fiddling with her hair, cut her dark eyes at him and smiled. "Maybe not."

This isn't fair, Rux thought. He would have just as soon kept the scenario going, but the parking lot at Moose Ball's arrived.

Inside, Deke was on stage, fooling with the keyboard. "Hey, guys," he called. "Everybody all right this afternoon? Rux, how do you get noise out of this thing?"

Rux helped Sammi up on the stage, then slapped hands with Deke. "Try turning it on," he said. "You gonna take my place when I leave?"

"I can if all I have to do is turn it on," Deke said. "When you planning on leaving?"

Rux leaned over Deke and flipped the keyboard's power switch. "Soon as you get another band, I suppose. You got one lined up yet?"

Deke banged several notes. "Naw, not yet. After the way you and Miz Stone here performed last night, I kinda hoped y'all mighta talked about teaming up. Putting an act together, just the two of you."

Rux looked at Sammi, busily picking at her guitar, then back at Deke. "Did kind of come up in the conversation this afternoon," he said. Rux suspected a conspiracy. If Sammi would have started fiddling with her pony tail again, he would have known for sure. She didn't, but she sure gave her guitar a funny grin.

* * *

Around four o'clock the next morning, Rux stumbled into his bed again, wide awake. He recalled another thing training horses and singing in bars have in common. Things are seldom routine. Every day, or night, is a new adventure. The last two days of his life were the exception. Friday had been a repeat of Thursday.

After their afternoon rehearsal, he and Sammi had a total of twenty-three songs. Plenty for one evening's performance. By midnight, they had gone through all of them twice and were winging it again. The mixed crowd of locals and weekenders all but rocked the old building off its foundation.

The bluish glow of the vapor light extended from the barn to the house. Sammi appeared on the back porch, wearing a light colored robe. Obviously, her downers had not worked any better than Rux's exercises. Would she really want to team up with him? he wondered. Temporarily, maybe. But she has way too much talent. Sammi belonged in Los Angeles or Nashville.

He belonged right where he was, on a too-short double mattress in a glorified tack room. Going back to West Texas and sleeping in his old boyhood bed would be like a vacation at the "Walled-Off Astoria." He would stay as long as Deke needed him. But it would be kind of like buying new boots a size too small. They look nice, but you never quite get accustomed to them.

* * *

On Saturday morning, Rux stood before the shaving mirror and decided a routine had indeed developed. Saturday morning repeated Friday morning, even to the point of fearing he had shaved off his moustache. He ignored the light tapping he could hear, assuming Howard to be rummaging around in the attic after mice.

"Rux, are you up?" Sammi called from the other side of the foaling room door opening into the barn.

He stumbled to the door and almost opened it before he realized he wore only underwear and his hat. "Just a minute." Pants were located and utilized, and the door tardily answered.

"Good morning," he said, trying to adjust his vocal chords to hide the croak. "I was just having coffee, would you like a cup?"

Sammi laughed. "Do you always have coffee with shaving cream all over your face?"

Rux stepped back to let Sammi in. "Yes, it flavors the coffee better than milk. Are you always this chipper so early in the morning?"

"Actually, no. It's almost eleven." Sammi switched on the hot plate and dumped several spoons of grounds in the percolator basket of the coffee pot. "It's Saturday, no school. I get to sleep in. Would you like to go trail riding with Missy and me?"

"Sounds great. Young Chester's been in the pasture a couple of days. Don't want to spoil him."

"Or his trainer. We'll bring him up and get him brushed for you. Come on out when you drink all the cream off your face."

Sammi giggled her way out the door as Rux returned to the shaving mirror. He poised the razor over his cheek, raked off the excess foam with his finger, then tasted it. "Yuck, think I'll stick to black coffee."

"Morning, Mr. Rux," Missy said as he walked up to the wash rack where she had Chester cross-tied. She met Rux's eyes briefly, then returned her attention to combing the horse's tail.

"Hi, Missy." Rux sat his western saddle and head stall on an old trunk. "You got him looking real nice. Did he give you any trouble?"

Missy released the tail and turned to face him. "Not really. He didn't want to come up, but Emilio helped me with him. He's really beautiful."

Just like you, Rux wanted to say but didn't. She smiled just like Sammi. "Thanks. Yeah, he gets a lot of attention in halter classes, but he's really more of a performance horse."

Missy stepped out of the wash rack to let Rux get Chester tacked up.

"Could I ride him sometime?" she asked.

Rux grunted as he tossed the saddle on, not from effort but to gain time to think of an answer. Sammi walked up with one of the mares and rescued him.

"Okay, boys and girls," she said, "are we ready to ride?"

"Just about," Rux said. He took the head stall from Missy and slipped the D-ring snaffle bit in the horse's mouth. "Chester can be a handful, Missy. He hasn't been under saddle that long, and Arabians are naturally feisty. Let's see how you handle your mare. Course, we better talk to Mom about this."

"About what?" Sammi asked.

"Mom, I'm going to ride Chester," Missy said. "Eventually." She rubbed Chester's muzzle and took the mare's reins.

Sammi retrieved the other mare from her stall. They led the horses outside and rode across the pasture to the back gate. Missy cantered ahead of them, leaned down and flipped the gate chain loose. She straightened in the saddle and eased the horse through, pushing the gate ahead of them.

"I'm impressed," Rux said to Sammi. "How long has she been riding?"

"We spent a couple of summers at my grandparents' farm before they passed away. I taught her what little I know. Until we got here, though, she hadn't ridden for about three years."

Rux followed Sammi through the gate and waited as Missy repeated her maneuver and re-latched the chain. "Nice job," he said as Missy cantered her horse past them. "She rides well," he said to Sammi. "You must be pretty experienced at this."

Sammi pulled ahead of Rux as they entered the narrow trail winding up the ridge. She kept her mare at a steady walk while she twisted in the saddle, rested her hand on the horse's rump and continued her conversation with Rux. "Some," she said. "I rode a lot when I was growing up. I spent my summers and quite a few weekends at my grandparents'."

Rux's mind eased considerably as he watched Missy make her way up to the top of the ridge. He had not known what to expect when Sammi first told him about the girl. He could not remember being nine years old himself. Maybe he skipped that year.

Missy proved a pleasant surprise. She paused at the top of the ridge to wait for them, then galloped off once they came into sight. Rux held Chester back as Sammi's mare struggled up the last few yards of the steep incline. The horse got her rear end under her and scattered gravel as she lunged over the rocky lip of the ridge.

Chester hopped up to the top with his usual flare of arrogance. Sammi rode beside him along the wider ridge trail.

"By the way," Rux said, "I noticed she calls you Mom."

"Yes. I'm the only mother she's ever known. Only real parent for that matter, and I'm not much of one. I've been so focused on my career. But I couldn't leave her with her father."

"She's the spittin' image of you. Does she know about her birth mother?"

"Yes, we've talked about it. I don't have any family either. Guess we sort of cling together out of necessity."

Rux asked, "What do you think about her riding Chester?"

Sammi watched her daughter for a moment before answering. "I think she can do it. She has good riding instincts. Her problem is in dealing with something she has to memorize. She reads slow, and math is an absolute nightmare for her."

"I know the feeling. Ain't never been much on math myself."

"She seems to be improving, though. I think the smaller school up here will help. And Juanita gives her a lot of vitamins and stuff."

"Could be the riding is helping her also. I know they teach riding to retarded kids, the ones we used to call Mongoloids. Improves their motor skills, which is mostly mental. May even improve Missy's math grades."

Sammi looked at him with raised eyebrows. "I didn't quite follow the math connection."

This girl's even got beautiful eyebrows, Rux thought. And they look natural. If she paints them on she does a good job. "Getting a horse to do something is just a matter of figuring out what he'll respond to. Then you use that to nudge him into doing what you want."

"Okay, but how does that relate to math?"

"Simple. If you have a problem requiring a mathematical solution, figure out what Einstein would do, then nudge yourself in that direction."

"Rux?"

"Just a theory. It's all relative." Rux reined Chester to a stop and motioned Sammi to do the same. "Listen."

A faint howl echoed from the mountains to the east.

Missy galloped her mare back down the trail to meet them. "What is that?" she asked.

Rux said, "Sounded like a wolf. Didn't think there were any still around here. Ranchers cleaned them out years ago. They won't bother us, but Howard better stay close to the barn."

Sammi said, "We need to head back anyway. By the time we get the horses and ourselves cleaned up it will be time to leave for Moose Ball's."

As they turned the horses to retrace the trail back to the ranch, Missy let her mother lead. "Rux," she asked, "wolves aren't dangerous to people, are they?"

Rux noticed she had dropped the "Mister" part of his title. Not out of any disrespect, he assured himself. She's just getting used to me. That's good. "No," he said. "They hunt in packs, but they wouldn't attack three people on horseback."

Missy rode in silence a while as they eased the horses down over the crest of the ridge and made their way along the narrow trail winding through the scrub oaks. Once the trail widened she stopped her mare and let Rux and Chester come up beside them. "Will horses fight wolves?" she asked. "Is that why the wolves wouldn't attack us?"

Sammi turned in her saddle and smiled back at them, obviously anticipating his answer.

Rux said, "Not generally. A horse's first instinct is to run from danger. That's why they're so skittish. They have excellent hearing and their eyes can see in several directions at the same time."

Sammi asked, "What about mares with a foal? They are very protective of them."

"That's true," Rux said. "In the wild, several mares will stand in a circle around a foal, with their rear ends facing out. Any wolf trying to get to the foal would get kicked to death." It occurred to Rux that a nine-year-old child on foot would be about the size of a new foal. No need to worry, he thought, Sammi wouldn't let her stray too far.

"Wolves are pretty crafty," he said. "They'll split up and a couple of them will try to lure the mares away from the foal. But the mares don't fall for it."

Missy galloped ahead and again opened the pasture gate, then started her horse in a lope toward the barn.

"Make her walk," Rux yelled. "Don't let her think she can run back to the barn."

By the time Rux and Sammi arrived, Missy already had her mare untacked and was rinsing her off. "I'll clean the horses up and put them back out in the pasture," she said. "You can go on in and get ready for your show tonight."

Rux took the reins from Sammi and whispered to her to go ahead. He would stay and help Missy, if needed. He untacked the mare and Chester, slipped on their halters and tied them next to the wash rack to await their turns.

Rux returned the saddles and bridles to the tack room and busied himself wiping everything down. He was close enough to the wash rack to hear if any problems arose. Ten minutes later he walked back. Chester and the two mares had been washed, groomed and pampered more than most kids. Like most kids, Chester preferred to be dirty.

"Got 'em all washed?" Rux asked.

"All but Chester," Missy said. "I washed him once and tied him in the wash rack to dry while I turned the mares out. When I came back he was filthy. Did you or Emilio let him loose?"

Rux laughed. "Rinse him off again and come back here where he can't see you."

Missy dutifully washed him again then hid with Rux. They watched Chester chew on the rope until he worked it loose. He walked outside and rolled in the dirt, then resumed his position in the wash rack as if no one would notice.

* * *

A misty rain collected on the windshield as Rux and Sammi wound their way into town. Rux had dutifully put on clean jeans and a fresh white shirt, and dusted off his hat and boots. Sammi's powder blue jeans bore little resemblance to his faded ones beyond similarity in color. She, too, wore a white shirt, but hers had little blue cowboy boots across the front.

"Looks like we coordinated our outfits," Rux said. He wanted to comment on the little boots, but considered their location and decided against it.

Sammi commenced her pony tail machinations again, making it difficult not to steal an occasional glance at the little blue boots.

"Have you decided if you want to stay over and perform again next weekend?" she asked.

The smile and another inviting, come-hither look from her dark eyes accompanied the question.

"I'm thinking hard on that," Rux said. He almost sideswiped a pickup parked on the shoulder of the highway.

"Dang," Rux said, braking the truck. "I think that's the Padre. Looks like he's having problems with the Red 'C' again." He pulled onto the shoulder and backed to the stranded vehicle.

Rector Richter climbed out of the cab. "Hello, Rux," he said as Rux and Sammi walked back to his truck. "Nice to see you again, especially right now. You're handier than Triple A."

"Hello, Rector Richter," Rux said. "You having more trouble?" He turned to Sammi. "Do you know Sammi Stone? We're working together at Moose Ball's."

"I don't think I've had the pleasure," Rector Richter said, taking Sammi's offered hand. "How are you?"

"Fine," Sammi said. "Nice to meet you. Can we help?"

The Padre laughed. "I'm afraid I've had to call on Rux's good services before. Can't seem to keep this old truck running. Rux, do you mind looking at it again?"

"Glad to," Rux said. He lifted the hood and asked Rector Richter to try cranking the engine. "Same old problem, let me adjust the fuel mixture and see what she does. Sammi, why don't you wait in the truck with Rector Richter so you don't get all wet? We won't be long."

The Red "C" soon choked and stammered well enough to send the Padre on his way.

"I'm staying out at Deke Ball's ranch," Rux said to the Padre. "I know you're busy tomorrow but why don't you bring the truck out one day next week? I'll get some parts and we'll rebuild the carburetor."

"Thank you," Rector Richter said. "Seems like every time I'm stranded you come along. God surely works in mysterious ways."

"So do carburetors," Rux said. He and Sammi waved as the Red "C" sputtered onto the highway. They hurried into Rux's truck to avoid the mist.

Sammi said, "Looks like you're committed to be here next week."

Rux smiled as he checked his mirror, then pulled onto the highway. "I guess," he said. "Your daughter has adopted my horse, anyway."

Five

Rux's time warp continued. Saturday night's performance duplicated Friday's. Sunday morning, the same bloodshot eyes stared back at him from the shaving mirror. "Ah ha," he said. "There's no pattern of consistency here. This time I remembered about the moustache."

No one would be tapping on his door any time soon, either. The whole ranch clan, Sammi, Missy, Emilio and Juanita, attended services at the Baptist church on Sunday mornings. Only the heathen cowboy and other soulless animals were left to sleep in.

Two cups of coffee and a pan of biscuits later, Rux stumbled into the barn and retrieved a halter, lead rope and lunge whip from the tack room. Outside, a gray mist camouflaged the mountain rim. Chester, grazing at the far end of the pasture, attempted to blend into the fog but two sorrel mares gave him away.

The horses looked up as Rux opened the gate to let himself into the pasture. They eyed him for a moment, then returned to their grazing, obviously pretending not to have noticed the halter, lead rope and whip.

Okay, Rux thought, we'll just see whose curiosity gets the best of them. He walked over to the pipe gates forming the round pen, stepped inside and clanged the entry gate to be sure he had the horses' attention. Rux picked up a rake and began working the soft sand from the center of the ring to the deep rut around the perimeter made by pounding hooves.

The horses watched but made no move to come over. Rux took off his jacket, hung it over the gate, and continued his raking. "Wish they'd hurry up," he mumbled. "It's cold out here."

The horses obliged. In a few minutes all three of them were sniffing at the coat. Chester grabbed it, tossed his head in the air and turned to run. The mares stampeded, but Rux already had Chester by one ear.

"Wanna trade?" With his free hand he extracted his jacket and slipped the halter on.

Chester ambled into the round pen as if that was what he came over for in the first place.

Twenty minutes later, Missy scampered up to the round pen, still in her Sunday dress and shoes. Rux had Chester bridled up and working himself into a serious lather. "Hi, Rux. Think I can ride him today?"

"I dunno, Missy. I've seen him dump some pretty good riders when they got too heavy on the reins."

Sammi, Emilio and Juanita joined Missy at the fence. "Let her try him in the round pen," Sammi said. "I think she can handle him."

While Rux thought on his response, Missy scampered off to change into her jeans and boots.

Rux soon knew he had lost a horse. Girls and horses naturally bonded. He'd seen it before. The girl who groomed Chester at Le Fleur's cried bitterly when he left, although Chester did not belong to her and never would. At the horse's first show she bought him a blue silk cooler with his name stitched in broad white letters. She bought herself a matching jacket with Chester's name on the back above an embroidered Arabian horse. The cooler and the jacket cost her a week's pay.

Rux stood in the middle of the round pen and circled to watch Missy and Chester. The horse was a little too much for her, but she learned quickly.

Chester, the master of bolting at the first hint of trouble, transformed himself into a paragon of patience. Each time Missy got out of balance, he would shift himself to accommodate her. If that didn't work he would slow his pace until Missy could get back in control.

Rux had her trying to balance with her legs. The reins were tied to the saddle and Missy rode with her arms spread-eagled. "Stretch your heels down and squeeze with your knees," he said as they went in a slow canter. Missy giggled when she lost her balance and had to grab the saddle. Chester stopped, waited for her to get her seat again, then walked off slowly as Rux clucked to him.

I don't believe this, Rux thought. I'd best get my horse and get on to Texas. Otherwise, we're gonna break another girl's heart when we do leave. Deke can get another band. I'll fix the Padre's truck Monday and be gone.

* * *

By the end of April, Rux gave up on his time warp notion and took to rationalizing his presence in the Arizona mountains in the dead of winter. For a while, he couldn't risk leaving for fear of getting caught in a snow storm while trying to negotiate Route 666. At this altitude snow storms might occur as late as June, maybe even August.

For some time now Rux had puzzled over a strange sensation. As he walked into Moose Ball's with Sammi for their Friday evening performance, it finally hit him. He was comfortable. And more than just plain old cowboy contentment. Cowboys can rest easy in most any circumstance, except maybe when they pitch their bed roll over a cactus.

The old bar, not unlike a thousand others he had been in, felt comfortable. In just two short months he had gotten comfortable with a lot of things — the foaling room, Rector Richter and the Red "C," Missy riding Chester. Most of all, he had an easy feeling with his new singing partner.

Joe Hawkins yelled, "Give 'em hell, Henry," as they made their way to the dressing room. Rux laughed and waved back.

Sammi walked ahead of him, wearing her pink jeans and white shirt with pink roses. Her pony tail flipped about as she greeted first one customer, then another. This isn't real, Rux thought. I need to find a good cactus.

He didn't find one in their performance. Two months of practicing and performing had allowed them to really get in sync. For four hours, Sammi simply overpowered everyone in the room. Her accompanist was no exception.

They closed with Linda Ronstadt's and James Ingram's "Somewhere Out There." Rux even managed to hit his high notes, although not particularly strong. Sammi staring into his eyes as they sang did not help his voice modulation.

Deke finally had to close up again to cut off the calls for encores. Even then the crowd milled around the stage, not missing the chance to josh Rux and hold hands with Sammi. Rux swapped lies with several cowboys, only half aware that Sammi's conversation with three strangers suddenly assumed a more ominous tone.

From the corner of his eye he saw her whirl into hurried retreat. One of the strangers appeared intent on vaulting to the stage in pursuit, but his less than graceful attempt became even more ungainly as Rux's stool caught him square in the face.

With Chief Broken Nose's rapid descent to the floor Rux re-cocked the stool and spun in a wild-eyed rage, stalking the other two with malice aforethought.

Though not a fighter by nature, when riled he became unmanageable. Almost. Sheriff Mo Mohlmann's .357 Magnum staring him in the face had a rather sudden calming effect.

"Easy Rux," the sheriff said. "Everything's under control."

The sheriff had one of the strangers by his pony tail, so tightly the man's eyes formed little slits. The last of the trio stood frozen in his tracks. Chief Broken Nose probably did not agree that everything was under control. Blood covered most of his silk shirt.

Sheriff Mo instructed Deke to get the man some ice. "You gentlemen drive up from Phoenix?" he asked the trio.

Chief Broken Nose blubbered something unintelligible.

"Yeah," Slit Eyes said through his stretched lips.

"Where you staying?"

"Don't have a place yet," Slit Eyes said, again without moving his mouth.

"Everything's full here. You best drive on back."

The sheriff spoke in a nondescript monotone but obviously conveyed a clear message. He holstered his gun and released Slit Eyes. Chief Broken Nose's two compadres gathered him from the floor and led him outside. The sheriff followed them out.

"Nice shot, Rux," Joe Hawkins said as he took the stool from him. "Hope I'm never in the way when you decide to give more etiquette lessons on the proper use of a piano stool."

"I hope you're not either," Rux said. "Sorry. Where's Sammi?"

"Right there," Joe said, nodding his head toward the back of the stage.

Rux turned and found Sammi huddled among Deke and two other men. None of them seemed anxious to leave. "You okay?" Rux asked.

"I think so," Sammi said.

Sheriff Mohlmann came back in the bar and, just to make sure everyone knew it, stomped heavily to the stage. "What was that all about?" he asked Rux.

"I don't rightly think I know," Rux said. "First thing I knew...."

Sammi came to his rescue. "Those three men told me they were here to take me back to Houston."

Sheriff Mohlmann lifted his hat and scratched his balding head. "Back to Houston," he said. "That where you're from?"

"Yes, sir."

"I take it you don't want to go back," the sheriff said. "Least not with them."

"No, sir."

Sammi, obviously still unnerved, attempted to sit down on the edge of the stage. Sheriff Mohlmann took her elbow and assisted her to a more graceful descent.

"Fine with me," he said. "Deke, why don't you get the little lady a drink?"

The sheriff picked up Rux's stool and examined it, then looked at Rux. "Humpf," he said. "Hate to be that fella. Have to go home and tell my friends a piano player broke my nose with his stool."

Rux laughed. "Considering the way I play, that may be the highest and best use for the stool."

Sheriff Mohlmann "Humpfed" again and returned his attention to Sammi, who sat choking on a brandy. "You know those guys?"

"The one Rux hit with the stool is my ex-husband, Peter Del Ossio. The man with the pony tail is Hector Romero. He's a small time pimp and drug dealer. The other one I didn't recognize. One of their henchmen, I suppose."

"Sound like nice folks," the sheriff said. "Young lady, you can stay here in Pine Knot as long as you like. Any more strangers try to bother you, you let me know." He threw a playful head lock on Rux. "That includes this guy."

Sheriff Mohlmann released his hold, picked up Rux's hat and handed it to him. "Don't think those three will be back," he said. "All the same, be careful."

The sheriff walked to the door, looked over the parking lot, then turned back to the small group knotted in front of the stage. "Rux, you might want to think about getting a license for that stool. Good night, now."

The group re-focused their attention on Sammi. Deke asked, "You feel like you can make it out to the ranch?"

Sammi handed him the glass of brandy. "I'm fine, now."

Deke said, "Rux, it's a little chilly out. Why don't you go warm the truck up for her?"

Rux headed outside, thankful for the chance to be alone for a minute. The sheriff's gun had calmed the heat of his anger, but only a few degrees. He still needed to hit someone else. He fired up the engine and waited, hoping Sammi would take her time.

She did, but not enough. His rage still had him shaking worse than a kindergartner on the first day of school. Sammi climbed in, slid across the seat and hugged him. She was shaking with equal vigor. The old truck shook naturally. Sammi released her hug but clung tightly to his arm.

"Are those the guys you told me about back in Paradise Park?" Rux asked. His voice quivered in sync with the truck and its two occupants.

"Yes. I suspected Peter and Hector were working together. Now I'm sure of it. I can't figure out how they knew where to find me."

"Lot of folks up here from Phoenix, and you're making quite an impression. My guess is, word's getting around the music world." Rux shifted into drive and eased the truck into the street. "I expect there'll be some agents along pretty quick."

"Peter's my agent, or was. He spent a lot of time and money trying to help me get a start in show business."

"What happened to change your mind?"

"A good friend of mine, another one of his clients, died of a drug overdose several months ago. Her singing career went bust and she ended up working as one of Hector's prostitutes. I'm fairly certain Peter supplies the crack and Hector peddles it. That's why I got out."

Rux freed his arm from her grasp and put it around her shoulders. "Did Peter say why he wanted you back in Houston?"

"We may be divorced but he still considers me his property. That was always a problem. To him, I'm not a wife or a client, I'm a possession. If I couldn't make him millions as a singer he'd have no qualms about turning me over to Hector."

They drove in silence for a while. Rux's shaking stopped. His anger seemed to be building toward a firm resolve, although he had no idea what he was resolving to do.

Rux said, "In Paradise Park you also mentioned a Tyrone. How does he fit into all this mess?"

"Tyrone's a good friend. I've known him since we were kids. He, Hector and I went to school together. Hector's always been pig puke. Is the heater warm yet?"

"Sorry." Rux flipped the heater on for the comfort of his passenger. His own temperature had risen steadily ever since she slid in the truck next to him.

"When we were about twelve years old, Hector accosted me in the hall at junior high school. I have no idea why, probably acting out something he saw in a TV sitcom."

"I can understand that. At that age, boys are little more than gonads with feet."

Sammi's laughter, the conversation and her closeness all combined to aggravate Rux's need for a cold shower. Against his better judgment, which he exercised only in hindsight anyway, he asked, "So, what happened?"

"Nothing and everything. Hector had me pinned against the lockers. Tyrone grabbed his long hair and slung him against the lockers on the opposite wall. Then all the black and Mexican boys jumped in."

"You started a gang fight?"

"Not me, Hector. All the black girls and Mexican girls cheered for their side to annihilate the other guys."

"Where were the teachers?"

"They fled with the few white kids to the relative safety of the classrooms and cheered for them to annihilate each other."

Much to Rux's regret, the truck dropped over the ridge and into the little valley housing Deke's ranch. He stopped by the back porch to let Sammi out and pick up Juanita.

Sammi kissed him lightly on the cheek. "Thank you. I feel a whole lot safer up here with you than I ever would in Houston."

"My pleasure." Man, Rux thought, if she only knew how many ways I meant that. "Tell Juanita not to rush."

Rux watched her ease out of the truck, smile back at him, then hop up the steps and into the house. He killed the engine and slumped down to

50

where the back of the seat caught his neck. Gradually, his mind erased the image of Peter and his bloody nose and replaced it with a vision of a pretty, dark-eyed girl. Even old cowboys can dream, he assured himself.

"You old fool," jerked him out of his reverie. At first, Rux thought he was talking to himself. Then he realized Juanita was climbing in the truck.

"Oh, hi," he said, pulling himself upright.

"Heard you had a little trouble tonight."

Rux chuckled as he cranked the truck and started for the trailer. "You know how boys get when you turn them loose in a bar. Before the night's over we're gonna be playing king of the mountain, trying to impress the ladies."

"Well, you certainly impressed one of them, present company excluded. You're going to get yourself killed."

Rux pulled to a stop in front of the trailer. "Nah, just a little harmless fun. I knew the sheriff was right behind me in case things got out of hand."

Juanita reached over and patted his arm, then stepped out of the truck. "You be careful, my friend. Good night."

"Buenos nachos."

"Oh, good grief."

Rux figured it must be forty degrees inside his room. He opened the window. A cold shower, push ups, sit ups, stretching and a hot shower all did nothing to calm his anxiety. He replayed the fight in his mind enough times to get it mostly out of his system. But he could not quiet the music, or the mirage of a titillating dark-eyed girl singing to him.

He flopped on the bed for the tenth time and, like the nine previous flops, sat up and looked out at the vapor light. The mirage appeared on the back porch, wearing that same light colored robe. Obviously, Sammi needed better downers. Rux indulged himself in a brief fantasy, then dismissed it.

What would a captivating young starlet want with an old coot like him? He was at least ten years her senior but looked older, thanks to the desert sun that gave him the appearance of a weathered saddle. He convinced himself there were no Indians over thirty. They just looked old. He lay back and studied the underside of his pillow.

Rux jumped when the door creaked open.

A soft voice whispered, "Rux it's me, Sammi."

"Thank goodness," he said, pulling the blanket over him. "I was afraid it was Emilio."

Sammi giggled as she stepped across the small space and sat on the edge of his bed. "You idiot. Why do you have it so cold in here?"

"Oh, sorry." He sat up and closed the window, then lay back down and propped himself on his elbows so he could face her. He thought, if she fixes that pony tail now, I'm not responsible for what happens. They can

51

hang me in the morning. She didn't.

"I couldn't sleep," Sammi said.

"So I gathered. Me neither. Too much excitement, I guess. You gonna call the sheriff?"

"Why?"

"Remember what he said about strange men bothering you?"

"You're not—well, yes you are. But you're not going to bother me, are you?"

Sammi placed a soft hand on each of his temples and gently massaged them. Rux appreciated the darkness. He knew any second now the pounding in his chest would blow the wax out of his ears. He forced himself onto his left elbow, freeing his right hand to reach for her.

Somehow, their lips met, gently at first. Then harder. Rux, always in control and possessing the ability to make tough decisions under pressure, decided right then and there another month or so in the mountains was not such a bad idea. Chester was born and raised in the desert, but horses could adapt to any climate.

Sammi gently extracted herself from his grasp and stood. They faced each other in the darkness for a long, silent moment. The shadows hid her eyes. Good, Rux thought. Pretty eyes had always been his downfall, although he could not recall whether Betty Jo Follmer had eyes. If he spent any time at all transfixed with the eyes of a beautiful woman, Rux was in trouble. His trips to the dentist were infrequent but he always fell in love with the dental assistant.

Almost imperceptibly, the front of her robe fell open, then slid to the floor. Rux's involuntary nervous system scootched him over to make room for her as she lifted the blanket and slipped under it. He reminded himself not to fall in love again. But deep in the recesses of his mind a voice he never heard said, "It's too late, stupid."

Rux managed to mumble through the T-shirt being pulled over his head, "Were you ever a dental assistant?"

Six

Sammi slipped into Deke's office and closed the door. The night before had ping pong balls of conflicting emotions bouncing off the inside of her skull. The past three months had been like a dream. She knew it would end, wanted it to end. Even in this out of the way hamlet an agent would find her.

But that was the problem. Peter had found her.

Sammi shuddered. The image of Peter and Hector emerging from the crowd still haunted her. How could she have ever loved Peter? Or did she? Perhaps he had been just a means to an end, as she had been to him.

She sat in Deke's mammoth, overstuffed chair and hugged herself. Do I really want to leave here? she thought. I'd miss these rough-and-tumble, salt of the earth guys. Deke, and the sheriff, and Rux. Sweet Rux, that big galoot. He was there when I needed him, in ways he doesn't even realize.

In ways I didn't realize until last night. How many men tough enough to knock down a mule could be so tender in bed. But Rux may not always be there to protect me, and if he's not I'd better be sure Peter isn't either.

Sammi shook her head and dialed Mama Henry's.

"May I please speak to Tyrone?"

"Dead Man, phone."

"Sam, how you be, woman?"

Sammi assured him of her well-being, then inquired about him, his grandmother and Mama Henry. "Peter and Hector were here," she said.

"No way. I don't even know where you at. How'd they find you?"

"I'm in a little town called Pine Knot, in the mountains of eastern Arizona. We've been performing before a lot of people who come up from Phoenix. Rux thinks word's gotten around in the music community."

"Who's Rex?"

"Rux. He's my singing partner, and my band."

"Cool. What happened far as Peter and Hector?"

Sammi explained her confrontation and the fight."The sheriff ran them out of town, so I doubt they'll be back here. But I can't stay in Pine Knot forever."

"Listen, I tipped my sources at the po-leece 'bout our boys bein' into crack dealin'. I'll see maybe somethin's goin' down."

Sammi felt her throat tighten. "No Tyrone. You've done enough already. Don't get involved any further. It's too dangerous."

"Hey, Sam, don't worry over me. Down in the streets punks snitch on other punks all the time. Peter, he smart enough to figure it out but he don't know about me. Hector? That home boy so dumb he need Peter to tell him when to pee."

Sammi laughed. "You remember what our eighth grade math teacher used to say about Hector?"

"Yeah. Put his brain in a woodpecker's butt and he'd fly backwards. Waste of a good woodpecker, you ask me."

"Seriously, Tyrone, let it go. What will you do if they come after you?"

"I just shut down by bidness enterprises and be headin' for Pine Nuts."

"Pine Knot. We'd love to have you. What business?"

"Nursery."

"Nursery? You're taking care of babies?"

"No, plants. Filadandruff, stuff like that."

Sammi couldn't stop giggling long enough to correct him. Finally, she said, "Philodendrons. Where do you get your plants?"

"Borrow 'em off the back of a nursery up the street. I take back what I don't sell."

"Nice profit margin."

Sammi hung up and hurried back to the stage. Rux had the Rux philharmonic cued up and ready to go.

Deke called from behind the bar, "Sammi, everything okay?"

Sammi turned to face Deke and started to answer with a "no", then hesitated. She looked at Rux. He grinned and tipped his hat. Peter, Hector and Tyrone slipped into a far away corner of her mind.

"Yes," she said to Deke. "Everything's fine. Beautiful, in fact."

Seven

Two things not required for cowboying are television and air conditioning. The stuffy air of Moose Ball's generated by a warm July afternoon competed with the incessant noise of the television for "most annoying" as Rux tuned his keyboard. Sammi, off running errands and overdue for practice, added to his annoyance.

I shouldn't worry about her, he thought. I'm just the interim piano player—and lover — until she heads off for the big time. When that happens I'll mosey on down to Texas. But in the meantime, I'll worry over her. And enjoy every minute of it.

Rux hit the off switch, stood and kicked his stool back. Danged if I ain't getting comfortable in my old age, he thought, not to mention a little bit stupid. I gotta be moving on.

"Getting warm in here," Rux said to Deke. "Think I'll wait outside."

Deke wiped sweat from his forehead with his apron. "Wait a minute, I'm coming, too." He grabbed two beers from the cooler and followed Rux out to the back stoop.

Overcast skies greeted them, but no rain. The June rainy season was reluctantly passing in favor of the warm, sunny afternoons and cool nights of mountain summers. Deke settled himself on the stoop, handed Rux a beer and directed him to sit on the overturned watering trough.

"You ever think about air conditioning this place?" Rux asked.

"Naw, don't really need it. Only a couple of months in the summer when it gets a little stuffy, but just during the heat of the day. It's usually cooled off by the time the crowds get here in the evening. Way you and Sammi been packing them in, though, I'm thinking I need to enlarge the place. Put in more tables, and a bigger kitchen."

"Sammi's packing 'em in, not me." Rux lifted his beer to take a swig and found himself nose to nose with a honey bee. The rest of Deke's comments finally sank in. "You know," he said to the bee although his remarks were directed at Deke, "you're not going to keep Sammi. She's way too good for Pine Knot. Some agent is going to come along and whisk her off to L.A. or Nashville or some place. Then you're gonna be back to the beer hall bands."

Deke downed the rest of his beer and reached his hand out for Rux to pull him up. "Yeah, I know," he said, using Rux's grip to leverage his bulk up from the stoop. "Just wishful thinking, I suppose."

Rux watched Deke pirouette on his plastic foot and stomp into the kitchen. Not bad for a three-hundred-pound, one-legged man, Rux thought.

The sight still pained him. He had known the two-legged Deke, in a different bar, a different time and a different place.

He watched the moisture dripping from his bottle form tiny craters in the dust between his boots as he recollected a burly, redheaded master sergeant bursting through the door of Rux's favorite watering hole in Cam Ranh, South Vietnam.

Sergeant Derrick Ball made sure everyone present understood three things: he was a lifer; he made it his personal mission to kill every Charlie he could find; and rear echelon wharf rats serving their tour of duty as clerks in the supply depots of Cam Ranh Bay were barely one rung up the social ladder from Charlie.

Rux and his fellow wharf rats tried to ignore the intrusion, but Deke got louder and louder as the afternoon of drinking extended into evening. Finally, Rux had enough. He raised the stakes by impugning Deke's parentage. Deke returned the compliment by challenging the sufficiency of a certain part of Rux's lower anatomy. More sober heads kept them apart, but Deke's challenge could not be ignored.

The next day, Rux volunteered for duty on a re-supply chopper making a run to Deke's Company's command post. He had no idea what he would do when he got there, other than to be sure Deke knew he did not fear the bush.

Deke's platoon began shuffling in just at dusk. Rux spotted his quarry from the bunker and started out to meet him. The events of the next few minutes froze in his mind without sequence.

"Incoming!" someone yelled.

The mortar shells whined and exploded, flares lit the sky with an eerie green glow, the grunts outside the wire dove for cover, and a provident arm jerked Rux back into the bunker by his shirt collar. All simultaneously.

The howitzers answered, mercifully avoiding the grunts on the perimeter who were busy shredding the jungle foliage with small arms fire. Rux watched the two hounds that had snarled and snapped at each other all day finally hurl themselves into mortal combat with all the fury of centuries of inbred hate. They fought in syncopated rhythm with the dark, cacophonous symphony produced by the beating wings of the angel of death.

The thunder reverberated in Rux's stomach, uncorking seltzered adrenaline. Through the haze of his own sweat he could see the field lights. The crowds on both sides of the field screamed as the bands blared opposing fight songs at each other. Dim scoreboard lights showed time running out with the game in the balance. Rux wanted the ball.

The bunker provided no field of fire without risk of hitting the perimeter grunts. Rux focused on where he last saw Deke Ball and was one step out of the bunker when an explosion rocked the same spot. A large body went airborne and plopped on the wire with the virtuosity of a Raggedy Ann doll.

In less than thirty seconds Rux made his way through the barbed wire maze that had required ten minutes to navigate in broad daylight. He hoisted the Sergeant over his shoulder and again groped through the wire. The run back to the bunker took most of a minute.

Deke was not a man to suffer in silence. The entire battle front quieted as combatants on both sides strained to identify the source of the bellowing heard even above the cannonade.

Morphine finally eased Deke into his present surroundings. "Tuttle? What the hell you doing here?"

Rux grinned. "Special recon, Sarge. You invited me, remember?"

"Gawddamn wharf rat. Git yourself killed out here."

The Captain interrupted. "You oughta be glad he's here. We're taking serious grief. Tuttle pulled you in off the wire."

"Damn," Deke said. "First I git my ass shot off then get it hauled in by a gawddamn wharf rat."

The medic bandaged Deke's mangled leg as best he could before loading him on the medevac chopper. Deke and Rux flew out of the bush together. Neither ever returned.

Sammi brought Rux back to 1986, CONUS, Pine Knot, Arizona, Moose Ball's and the watering trough. "I'm here," she called from the back door. "Ready whenever you are."

"Be right there." Rux finished his beer and searched for a garbage can that was not already overflowing. Ready for what? he thought. It was Friday. Every Friday since the fight with Peter and Hector, Sammi had come to the foaling room after their performance. He never asked or assumed, preferring to enjoy the mystique of a "chance" encounter.

And the affair was never mentioned outside the foaling room. This, he knew, was to protect Missy, as it should be. Cowboys are like that, he thought. Take your comfort where you can find it, but always be considerate of women, children and horses. It occurred to him that he wasn't going anywhere as long as Sammi and Missy were here.

* * *

Friday evening produced another rousing performance, both at Moose Ball's and in the foaling room. Rux felt Sammi's familial instincts finally wrestle her from under the blanket.

"Rux, I'm borrowing your boots. I'll bring them back before you get up. My feet almost froze running across the yard."

"How well I know. Nights are still cold up here, even in the summer. I think I'll invest in an electric blanket."

Rux retrieved his boots from the back porch around noon. He could see Missy lunging Chester in the round pen. The horse obviously felt compelled to uphold the reputation of frisky colts on a cool morning. Chester had almost jumped out of his "pajamas," Missy's term for the horse's cooler.

The pajamas began to slip, causing Rux to hurry from the porch. If the cooler worked its way down to his feet, Chester would be doing the ballistic ballet off the fence. Rux slid to a halt in the soft dirt outside the round pen.

"Hi Rux," Missy said.

Rux stuffed his hands in his pants pockets and casually propped one foot on the fence. He felt like a gunfighter trying to save face after backing down from a shoot-out. "Hi Miss. Need any help?"

"No, we're fine."

Chester patiently lifted each foot, allowing Missy to remove the cooler tangled around his legs. Horses can't grin, Rux thought. But he knew Chester would if he could. Chester was registered with the National Arabian Horse Registry under some unpronounceable Arabic name. Since it began with the letters "c" and "h", "Chester" prevailed over "Knot Head" although the latter was frequently used, particularly in his early training. At the moment Rux had second thoughts about which name fit the horse best.

"Let's work in the barn," he said. "You'll have a little more room."

"Sure, here." Missy tossed him the cooler.

Rux opened the gate, then followed her and Chester into the barn. He watched as she expertly checked the head stall.

"Give me a leg up?" Missy asked.

Rux cradled her knee and eased her onto the saddle-less horse. He had her riding bareback to develop the habit of controlling her horse with her legs. He helped her up and she started Chester in the walk, then cued him into a slow canter.

"Good," Rux said. "Nice and collected. Guide him with your legs."

"Can I trot him?"

"Okay, but keep a tight rein. Don't let him get too fast."

Rux watched her bubbling as she gained confidence. Missy continually surprised him. It may take her a little longer to learn some things but once she grasped it she could perform as well as anyone. She certainly knew her way around horses, and Sammi encouraged her.

He worried Sammi might be pushing the child beyond her capabilities. He still didn't know how much he could trust Missy's judgment. And Chester was, well, Chester.

Chester, being Chester, took care of the problem. The horse seemed to have a sense for children.

Rux watched as Missy increased the horse's pace, then apparently realized she was slipping. Rather than jerk hard on the reins she gradually let go and slid to the ground. Rux ran to her, yelling at Emilio to head off Chester at the barn door. Emilio need not have bothered.

Chester stopped as soon as he sensed he was riderless and returned to Missy. He sniffed her as though he couldn't figure out why she was lying in the dirt, then wiped his wet muzzle on her shirt. Missy was laughing too hard to get up.

Guess I oughta quit worrying about them, Rux thought. But I'm still not sure a kid this age has a firm grasp on the concepts of time and distance. He vividly remembered their "short" ride to a natural bridge Emilio had shown her.

"How far is it?" he had asked. "It's only an hour until dark."

"It's just over the ridge a little ways."

Two hours later they made their way home in the dark.

* * *

Several weeks later, Rux himself seemed a little uncertain of the elements of time and distance. The summer had collapsed into a pleasant blur, one he would just as soon continue. In the back of his mind he knew winter would come in due time, and he still knew the driving distance to Texas. Like the five years since he left, the urgency of returning always seemed to get side tracked.

I'll be headed home soon, he convinced himself. Just taking the long way around the barn, as per usual.

Rux, Sammi and Missy sat on the second row of the wooden bleachers lining the vast arena of the Pine Knot Fair Grounds. A giant, single-span metal roof shaded the east stands from the afternoon sun while the open sides allowed the breeze to mingle barn smells with the hot dog mustard.

Bales of hay and a two-foot high white picket fence created an island in the center of the show ring for the Pine Knot Arabian Horse Club Summer Classic. The organist, announcer and show judge, when she was not judging, sat smugly within the little enclave although it would hardly deter a horse. Rux explained the nuances of the various classes to Missy, who sat in rapture.

"Can Chester do that?" Missy asked, watching girls work their horses through the various gaits and patterns of the Equitation class.

"Sure he can," Rux said before he realized where Missy was headed. "But its not natural for him. See how they have their necks arched and their rear ends tucked under. That makes them elevate in front and trot with that high, rounded motion. Chester has the neck and the rear end propulsion, but he'd rather drop down and chase cows. Most horses would, I guess."

"I bet he could win this class."

"This class judges the rider, not the horse. These girls compete with all the civility of hockey players, and their parents are worse. They'll pay thirty thousand dollars for a good equitation horse and at least that much for training and riding lessons."

"Couldn't you train us?"

"I suppose, but these horses have been in training for years. They've had so much schooling they're called 'push button' horses."

Rux looked to Sammi but she was no help. It was not his place to protect Missy, he thought. But she would have to compete against these girls, at least in the Equitation medal class where there was no age category. They were all older, and normally paid Missy scant attention. Rux shuddered to think how they would react to showing against someone this young and inexperienced.

He suspected Sammi might be trying to live her own childhood dreams through Missy. She should have understood what her child could not, the imminent shattering of a fairy tale existence.

I don't want any part of that, he thought.

Eight

In Scottsdale, it had been hard to know exactly when fall arrived. Most species of cacti were evergreen, as far as Rux knew. But Pine Knot knew no such limitation. By early October the air had cooled considerably and the hillsides displayed orange splotches among the green.

Rux stood at the rear door of the barn, absorbing the scenery. He mentally complimented Mother Nature on her handiwork, then turned and admired his own. Missy and Chester circled the interior of the barn in flawless fashion.

With some effort and a lot of patience from her coach and her horse, Missy had mastered the techniques of the double bridle and the cues to invoke the desired gait. Endless practice produced a horse and rider that literally moved as one entity, exactly what the equitation judge looked for. They would be ready to compete in the fall show this coming weekend.

Rux had three worries. One he expressed to Missy after she reined the horse to a halt in front of him. "Missy, you're not going to hurt Chester or his feelings. It's unnatural for a horse to arch his neck and move forward from his rear end at the same time. But he will if you help him. Keep just enough pressure on the curb bit to make him bring his nose down but not enough to where he fights it. You want his head steady as a rock. Then sit back and squeeze with your legs to get his rear under him."

"I'll try," she said, and trotted off again.

She was still too gentle, but Chester's inclination to show off in the ring should offset that, Rux thought. Her bigger problem was her inability to memorize patterns quickly.

All Equitation classes required the rider to demonstrate their skill by taking their horse through a series of circles, figure eights, stopping, backing and sometimes cueing for the wrong lead. The pattern would normally be posted several classes ahead of the Equitation class, allowing time for the horse and rider to get it down pat. They would deal with that when the time came.

Sammi, Juanita and Emilio joined him. Sammi asked, "Well, how do they look? Are they ready for the show ring?"

"Gittin' there," Rux said. "One problem, though. Proper ring attire is required. We need to get her an equitation suit."

"Oh, I remember that," Sammi said. "Seems like the riders were all wearing clothing similar to a man's pin stripe business suit. Ties and everything."

"Right," Rux said. "With jodhpurs boots and a derby hat. The pants need suede in the inner seam for better gripping."

"How much does all that cost?" Sammi asked.

"With a dress shirt and matching ties, the entire outfit could run seven hundred dollars. A small price to pay if you had already invested fifty thousand dollars in a horse and riding lessons, like her competitors' parents have."

Sammi shoved her hands in her jeans pockets and tried to punch a hole in the dirt with the heel of her boot. "I don't have that kind of money," she said.

"Not a problem," Juanita said. She placed her arm through Emilio's who stood imitating Sammi's pose. "Emilio here will contribute his dark blue pin stripe suit. He only wears it to funerals, anyway. I can tailor it to fit Missy and install the suede."

Emilio grunted his agreement.

Sammi said, "Oh, that's so sweet of you. But I can't ask you to do that."

Juanita unleashed Emilio and hugged Sammi. "You didn't ask," she said. "We volunteered. If we have to attend a funeral between now and the show, Emilio won't mind a little suede in his crotch. We'll let you and Rux pitch in for the hat and boots and the other accessories."

"Be happy to," Rux said. "And Chester can contribute his once thirty-thousand-dollar self."

Missy and Chester roared by in a fifty-thousand-dollar trot. Their audience applauded. "Looks like we're all set," Rux said.

Sammi, Juanita and Emilio left to find the funeral suit and Rux headed for the wash rack to help Missy. What are we doing? Rux thought. Pushing this poor kid out in a show ring. What happens when she's out there all by herself, in front of a crowd, and forgets the pattern? Fancy clothes and a classy horse won't solve that.

He stopped as he approached the wash rack and watched Missy, busily untacking her horse. Her green Izod shirt and brown pony tail were covered in a thin layer of barn dust. He wanted to hug her, to tell her everything would be okay. But she didn't belong to him. Maybe the girls she rides against will sort of take her under their wing, he thought.

* * *

On Thursday afternoon, Rux had the trailer hitched and the truck loaded by the time the school bus arrived. Missy waved and hurried into the house. She returned shortly with her new equitation suit, neatly pressed and hanging in a clothes bag.

"Got your boots and hat?" Rux asked.

"Right here," Sammi said, handing him a duffel bag.

"Okay," Rux said. "Everybody pile in...Oops, forgot the horse."

The forgotten horse was soon loaded, and Rux climbed in the cab with Sammi and Missy. He cranked the truck and eased up the gravel drive leading from the barn to the road. As they passed the house, Emilio and Juanita were on the back porch, he with his hands in his pockets and Juanita with hers on her hips.

"First class is at six," Rux yelled.

"We'll be there," Emilio called back.

Juanita wagged her head and grinned.

"I know what you're thinking," Rux yelled to Juanita. "How could a cowboy forget his horse?"

Thirty minutes later they drove into the field that served as the parking lot for the Pine Knot Fair Grounds. Twenty or thirty pickups with trailers and a couple of big rigs were already there. Rux pulled up to the stalls to unload. In front of his pickup a smallish, gray-haired man was backing a beautiful chestnut stallion out of his bright red ten-horse trailer. He appeared to have several more horses still in the trailer.

"That's what we need," Missy said.

"Sure," Rux said. "Then Chester could invite some friends along to play poker while we're hauling."

"Horses can't play poker," Missy said.

"Sure they can," Rux said. "How do you think Chester lost his...uh, never mind."

"Lost what?" Missy asked.

"Your mother will explain it to you. I gotta go check on our stalls. Be right back."

Rux hustled through the stall area and found the show office. He made a point of getting stalls next to one of the large farms where several of the other girls rode. He hoped they would warm up to Missy.

As he walked back, Rux passed two girls riding a couple of very nice horses toward the practice arena. The girls appeared to be several years older than Missy. He tipped his hat to them and said, "Afternoon, ladies. Nice horses. What classes are you girls showing in?"

Both girls smiled. The tall, skinny girl with short brown hair said, "Thanks. We're in thirteen-and-under Equitation and English Pleasure." She reminded him of a stork. The smaller girl had tiny wire-rimmed glasses perched on her pinched nose, giving her the appearance of a mouse.

"Good luck," Rux said.

He returned with their stall assignments, unloaded Chester and the equipment, and sent Missy with her horse to let him walk off the kinks. He lined Chester's stall with shavings and set a cot and the equipment in the extra stall.

"Are you sleeping out here?" Sammi asked.

"Yeah. Can't leave old Chester out here by himself. That's the joy of being the trainer and the groom. How's Missy doing with the other girls?"

"Oh, they kind of took to her at first. Mainly out of curiosity I think. Once they realized she was showing they pretty much shunned her."

"I was afraid of that. This is dog eat dog."

"She'll be okay. The others don't associate with her at school anyway. They're on the same campus but junior high has its own building."

Missy returned with Chester, cross-tied him in the aisle, and soon had his coat shining like a circus seal. Rux volunteered to blacken his hooves with hoof paint while Sammi helped Missy get into her funeral-slash-equitation outfit.

Rux stuck himself twice trying to pin Missy's number on the back of her coat. She was as cool as the mountain air. He had entered them in a thirteen-and-under English Pleasure class. They wouldn't do much so far as ribbons were concerned, but it would allow Missy and Chester to get a feel for the ring before the Equitation class. Missy needed it, but Chester had never met a show ring he didn't like.

"All set," Rux said. "Come on, I'll give you a leg up."

He tossed her up, then wiped off her boots. "How do we look, Mom?" he said to Sammi.

"We look great, if I do say so myself," Sammi said. She had Missy's pony tail twisted into a ball and held in place with pins and a hair net. The new, navy blue riding hat sat snugly above the bun.

They followed Missy and Chester to the practice arena. Rux watched them carefully as they walked, trotted and cantered among the other horses warming up. The other riders and their trainers were watching them also. Rux leaned over to Sammi and whispered, "She'll get some attention."

The loud speaker announced that the class ahead of them was in the line up. Missy and the other riders made their way down the large runway to the main arena, with parents and trainers frantically trying to keep pace. The other horses nervously turned, circled and pranced as they waited for the gate to open. Chester, with his usual "who cares" expression, stood with his head drooped and mouthed his bit.

Once the gate opened, the fifteen-year-old push button horses providing the competition mattered little. Chester was full of himself. Rux and Sammi watched him snort, bridle up and prance through the first half of the class. Rux occasionally glanced at the judge. Missy and Chester clearly had her attention.

They placed third. From Missy's reaction you would have thought she won the championship. From the reaction of the competitors and their parents, you would have thought she had just lanced her rivals in a jousting match. Only cold, silent stares met Missy and Chester as they left the ring. None of the pretentious congratulations normally offered to the winners were heard. Missy did not seem to notice.

Rux noticed. He had received the accolades of parents whose child won on a horse he trained, and also felt the wrath of those whose child lost with one of his horses.

"Congratulations!" He and Sammi called simultaneously as Missy and Chester rode out past the group of parents and trainers clustered by the exit gate. Missy beamed. The stork and the mouse trudged out of the arena, apparently ribbonless.

Emilio and Juanita came out of the stands and joined Missy's entourage on the trek back to the stalls. Missy hopped off, hugged her mom and then hugged Rux.

"How did we look?" she asked.

"You were beautiful," Sammi said.

"Just great," Rux said. "Obviously the judge thought so. You were in against some pretty good horses." He replaced Chester's double bridle with his halter and crossed-tied him again.

Juanita said, "Let's get Chester cooled off and bedded down, then we'll go to the cafe back down the road and celebrate."

Missy smiled her shy, "aw, shucks, it really wasn't anything" smile, carefully hung her ribbon on the wire mesh of Chester's stall, and retrieved her jeans and shirt from Rux's temporary bedroom. "I'll run change in the restroom," she said. "Be right back."

They just had time to treat Missy to lemon pie and a chocolate malt before Sammi reminded them she and Rux were due at Moose Ball's and their little rider had school tomorrow.

"Tough break, kid," Rux said. "Emilio, why don't you and Juanita take Missy with you? I'll get Sammi to drop me back at the fair grounds after we get done at Moose's."

Outside, Emilio held the door of his truck open for Missy and waited while she hugged her mom and her trainer again.

"Take care of Chester for me," she said to Rux. "We'll be out right after school tomorrow."

"You bet," Rux said. He and Sammi waved as Emilio pulled onto the highway, then Rux opened the door of the Ruxmobile for Sammi. "I told you," he said.

"Told me what?"

"Your daughter has adopted my horse."

During the fifteen-minute drive into Pine Knot the two of them were as giddy as teenagers on their first date.

"Missy has really warmed up to you," Sammi said. "Now I have to share her hugs. I'm jealous."

Rux gave her a "horse bite" on the knee. Sammi squealed and tried to pull his hand off. "Stop, stop. That tickles."

Rux relaxed his "horse bite" grip but left his hand on her knee.

"Please, no more," Sammi said. "I'm serious, but I'm not actually jealous. You've done wonders for her. She's really come out of her shell."

Rux reluctantly accommodated Sammi's seriousness and returned his hand to the steering wheel. "She has come a long way," he said. "Just in the last six weeks her riding skills have improved tremendously."

Sammi took his hand and returned it to her knee. "You don't have to be that serious, just no more horse bites. You're right, though. Her teachers tell me even her school work is getting better. I think you, Chester and Juanita must be miracle workers."

"Juanita, maybe."

"Aw, I'm so disappointed. I always thought you could walk on water."

"Depends on how many alligators are chasing me. But then I'd be running, not walking. What is Juanita giving her?"

"It's a combination of vitamins, minerals and herbs. I don't know exactly what. She forces it down me every time she gets a chance."

"Uh huh. Probably the same stuff she chokes down me and Emilio."

A dense fog floated among the rafters of Moose Ball's, an aromatic blending of smoke from cigarettes and the grill. The place was packed, mostly with their Thursday night locals talking loudly over the noise of the juke box. It took Rux and Sammi several minutes to work their way through the crowd and to the small dressing room behind the stage. All of the women had to hug Sammi, all of the men wanted to hold hands with her, and both sexes had to josh Rux about something.

"Ten minutes," Rux yelled to Deke as they finally squeezed past the bar.

Deke slung ice off a beer bottle and gave him a thumbs up.

Rux waited in the hall while Sammi changed into one of her stage dresses. When she gave him the okay, he slipped into the toilet-sized dressing room to put on a clean shirt and wipe off his boots.

Sammi twisted on her stool to face him. "I shouldn't have said what I did about being jealous of you and Missy. Actually, I'm glad she feels comfortable enough to hug you. The only time I ever saw her try to do that to her father he backhanded her."

She turned back to the mirror, leaving Rux to mull over whether to make further inquiry about what happened between Missy and her father. He figured he knew Sammi well enough, but wasn't sure it was any of his business. Sammi obviously read his mind, an enigmatic if not down right dangerous venture.

"I'm sure Peter didn't mean to harm her," she said. "He just went into an uncontrollable rage, something inside him he didn't even know existed."

"A common problem among the male population."

Sammi checked herself one last time in the mirror, stood and again turned to face him. "Will you try to be serious for one minute?"

"One one thousand, two one thousand...sorry."

"I suppose Peter's still rebelling against his mother." Sammi returned to the mirror and began fussing with her hair. "She raised him in the Pentecostal church. He tried everything to please her, even learned to babble so it would sound like he was speaking in tongues."

"Seen that myself," Rux said, busily brushing the dust off his hat and boots. "Tent revival came to No Water when I was four, maybe five. Young enough to still be in short pants because I remember my legs kept sticking to the wooden folding chairs."

"I'd like to see that."

"What, me in short pants? No you wouldn't."

Sammi shellacked her hair with spray. "Why not?"

"You know why cowboys can't wear short pants, don't you?"

"Never mind."

"I thought so. Anyway, my buddy sitting next to me had to go to the bathroom, but his momma wouldn't let him. Some poor Mexican was in the pulpit carrying on about how he had died, and after three days God brought him back to life. Everybody got real quiet, waiting for his description of heaven."

Sammi apparently gave up on her hair and plopped her white cowgirl hat on her head. "I think the same guy visited our church one time," she said. "He dies a lot."

"Makes sense. We had already been through two spontaneous tongue speakings. I guess my buddy figured he had nothing to lose. He jumped up and started babbling like an irritated A-rab. Next thing we knew the whole crowd was on their feet, waving their arms and babbling like crazy. My bud's momma fainted."

"And?"

"And what?"

"What happened to your friend?"

"He peed in his pants."

Sammi screeched with laughter. Rux tried to shush her as someone rapped on the door.

"Everybody all right in there?" Deke asked.

"One of us is," Rux said. "Be out in a minute."

Sammi said, "I thought you were going to be serious."

"I am serious. You were saying about Peter?"

"Yes, that's how we met."

Rux put on his hat, pulled it low on his brow and checked himself in the mirror. "You met at one of the Mexican's resurrections? I need a shave."

"You don't have time to shave. Yes, well, no. But that's close. I used to sing solos at our church. Someone told Peter about me. We're late. You better go out and do your opening."

"Right." Rux jerked the door open, imitated Jackie Gleason's "away we go" pose, then pecked her lightly on the cheek. "Look out, here comes Henry," he said, launching himself toward the stage.

* * *

Some time after two o'clock the next morning, Deke swept the last of his patrons out the door and ushered Rux and Sammi to Rux's truck. "Great show tonight, guys," he said. "Both of you were really wired."

"Thanks, Deke," Sammi said as she climbed in the truck beside Rux. "I don't know if Rux had a chance to tell you. Missy got third place in her very first class at her very first horse show. We were excited when we got here."

"Glad you explained that," Deke said. "With all that carrying on you two were doing in the dressing room I thought maybe I needed to get you a 'do not disturb' sign."

Rux slammed the truck door and threw his hat out the window at Deke. "For your information," he said, "I'm spending the night with my horse."

Deke roared, picked up the hat and handed it back to Rux. "Tell Missy I said good luck tomorrow, or I guess it's today by now. See you guys tonight."

The old truck shuddered in the cold night air, then gradually yielded to Rux's urging and made for the highway. Rux asked, "You don't mind dropping me at the fair grounds and driving home by yourself, do you? I could take you to the ranch and come back and pick you and Missy up after school."

"No, you don't need to do that. Nothing happens up here. I feel perfectly safe. I don't think I ever want to leave."

"Not a bad idea. You were going to finish telling me about Peter."

"Oh, right. Where did I leave you?" Sammi snuggled against him and reached a cold hand inside his shirt.

Rux flipped on the heater. "At the revival."

"The revival, yes. Peter came several nights in a row. Sat right down near the front." Sammi chuckled under her breath. "He dazzled all the girls in his sharkskin suit and brown wing tips. We all knew he was an eligible bachelor. I think every single girl in the audience responded to the preacher's invitation. They confessed to sins they hadn't even committed yet just to get a closer look at Peter."

"One of those girls being the young Sammi Stone?"

"No, I sang in the choir. I asked him to take me home after the service. Poor Peter. He was ten years older than me. I was still a senior in high school."

"What happened?"

Sammi shifted against him and remained silent for a long minute. Finally, as Rux pulled up to the stalls at the fair grounds, she said, "I seduced him."

Rux wanted to drive around the grass parking lot so she could continue. Sammi nudged him out of the truck and slid behind the wheel.

"That's all I'm going to tell you," she said. She reached out the window, cupped her hand behind his neck and pulled his face to her. "Take care of Missy's horse," she said, and kissed him hard on the lips.

Rux stepped back and watched her drive away. He pulled on his hat and walked to their stalls. Chester, lying on his feet, lifted his head as Rux came up. "Good night, Missy's horse," he said.

* * *

Rux spent Friday tending to Chester and helping the show officials keep everything moving. He was tempted to enter the working cow horse competition but opted to help with the calves instead. This was Missy's show. He would save Chester for her.

That afternoon, the judge posted the equitation pattern an hour before the class. Rux stood with Sammi in the middle of the practice ring and grilled Missy. They were ready.

"Sam," he said. "I originally just wanted Missy to compete and have fun. Now, I want to win. Not just her class. I want her to win the equitation medal."

"What is that?"

"That's a class where all the girls under eighteen compete for a medal. The winner is automatically qualified for the U.S. Nationals."

"Do you think Missy can win that?"

"No. It doesn't matter how good she is. These girls have waited for years to get their shot at a national equitation championship. Several of them are preordained to represent this area. The judges have watched them for years and know who they are. It would be political suicide to give the medal to a newcomer, particularly one so young."

"I don't know, Rux. That's a lot of pressure for her first show."

"So far pressure hasn't bothered her. Lets see how she does with the pattern in the Equitation class coming up. You can think about it and let me know."

The parents and trainers rejoined their jostling ritual as the riders made their way to the arena. Once the horses went in and the gate closed, the jostlers all rushed up to claim a spot along the fence.

Missy looks good, Rux thought. But the pattern will be a real test. Chester's got it memorized, if she doesn't confuse him with too many wrong cues. He agonized through ten minutes of ring exercises and then the additional twenty minutes it took six riders to complete their pattern.

Finally, the judge lined them up, did her obligatory walk in front and then in back of the horses, and turned in her score card. Another wait. The loud speaker clicked on. "First place goes to rider number Six One Two, Miss Melissa Stone."

Emilio and Juanita whooped and yelled from the stands. Rux and Sammi joined them from the gate, overwhelming the polite applause from the other spectators.

Missy trotted out with her blue ribbon, trying hard to contain her grin. The stares from the parents grew colder and longer. Again, Missy steered Chester down the walkway and toward the stalls, apparently not noticing. Rux hustled to keep up with her, but Sammi pulled him back.

"Rux," Sammi said, "let's enter her in the medal class, just for spite."

"My thinking exactly."

The medal class was the third class Saturday morning, but the judge posted the pattern Friday evening before they left. Missy had plenty of time to learn it, and they could brush up the next day before the class. She can't win, Rux thought, but her challengers and their parents would know she should have. So would the judge.

* * *

Chester and a hard cot roused Rux early Saturday morning. He wandered over to the restroom to wash up and brush his teeth, aimlessly glancing at the bulletin board as he passed the show office.

"Oh, no," he said, rushing to the pay phone. "Sammi, get Missy up and out here right away," Rux shouted. "They've canceled the first two classes and the judge posted a new pattern. We'll only have a few minutes to go over it before she has to go into the ring."

Missy got three tries to unlearn the old pattern and memorize the new one. Chester was ready, but he depended on her for his cues.

"She'll be all right," Rux said to Sammi as Missy and Chester roared into the ring. He knew better. Missy had not hit every part of the new pattern in any of her three rehearsals.

Missy went through the performance part in good fashion. The judge was watching. She would be the fifth to go in the pattern.

"That helps," Rux said. "She can see what the other girls are doing."

The stork and the mouse were no help. Each of them had a hard time convincing their highly trained horse to do what their trainer had grilled into them. Two of the other riders ahead of Missy performed beautifully.

Missy hit the first four requirements of the pattern without a hitch. "She looks good," Sammi whispered.

"She does," Rux said. "But in her practice runs she kept forgetting to cue him for the wrong lead after coming out of the figure eight. It's unnatural for both of them."

"Why?" Sammi asked.

"When horses canter in the show ring, they prefer to lead with their inside leg to help them balance in the turns. In equitation, judges will test the rider's skill by requiring them to canter down one rail on the outside, or wrong, lead."

Missy worked Chester through the figure eight in good fashion, stopped, then backed him five steps as required. She hesitated. Rux held his breath, and watched helplessly as Missy gave Chester the cue for the inside lead.

Chester ignored the cue and began to canter down the rail on an outside lead. Rux glanced quickly at the judge as soon as Chester took off. From that distance, he was sure the judge could not have seen Missy touch Chester with her outside heel, which meant the inside lead. The judge noted something on her card. Missy continued the pattern as though nothing had happened.

Rux accurately gauged the judging procedures for the Equitation medal class. The medal went to a seventeen-year-old who had been to the nationals twice. This was her last chance at the elusive national prize. The judge assumed there would be other chances for the dark-haired girl in the pin stripe suit, Rux thought.

After the class, Missy congratulated the winner. Back at the stall, she hugged her horse, hugged her mother and hugged her trainer. Rux picked her up and squeezed her. "You were great, Little Lady. You won that class hands down."

Missy beamed. "No I didn't. I missed the cue on the canter down the rail."

"Yeah, but that's all you did wrong. I don't think the judge could see your cue from where she was standing. And you didn't let it flusterate you. That's a lot of poise for someone showing for the first time. Plus you realized your mistake. You're a natural, kid."

Rux noticed the loathsome glances from the stork and the mouse, grooming their horses nearby. He didn't envy Missy having to go back to school with them. But they were in another building anyway. Tomorrow should be no different.

"Rux," Missy asked, "when we get back to the ranch will you draw up some patterns for me? Chester and I will practice every day after school. I promise, I'll never miss another cue."

"Sure, Miss. But don't worry about missing a cue. Everybody does it once in a while. This was your first show." He eased the bits out of Chester's mouth, handed the bridle to Missy and threaded the horse's muzzle into his halter.

As he fiddled with Chester's tack, Rux watched Missy and Sammi head off to the restroom so Missy could change her clothes. He knew the other girls and their moms would be there doing the same thing. Apprehension tugged at his euphoria.

He and Sammi had let their feelings overrule their judgment. Missy should not be showing against these girls, certainly not in something as competitive as the medal class. She would get crucified at school if she did come into contact with the older girls.

He would humor her with patterns to practice at the ranch. Showing again required some serious cogitation.

Nine

Sammi forced herself to think, a device used to keep her from falling asleep. It also gave her an excuse to stay a few more minutes with Rux, the current and frequent occupier of her thoughts. She tried to conjure up words to describe him, but it was like looking at someone through a prism. Each time she pictured him she saw the same rogue but in a different light.

Even though she could not physically see him in the darkness, her present image of him comforted her. His large, rough hand massaged her thigh with the gentleness of a kitten. A myriad of needs she could not completely fathom pulled her to their Friday nights—or early Saturday mornings—foaling room rendezvous, but it meant leaving Missy alone in the house. Sammi knew she had to get back in case Missy woke up and found her missing.

Rux's sleepy voice said, "You're seducing me again."

"I've never seduced you."

"Sure you have. Just like you did poor Peter." He lifted the blanket from her and whispered, "And I can see how you did it."

Sammi found his ear and nibbled it. "You can't see anything. It's too dark."

"Cowboys can see in the dark. So can horses."

"That's preposterous." Sammi jerked the blanket back down. "Your horse is not in here with us, is he?"

"Why, are you going to seduce him, too?"

"Stop that. I've never seduced anyone. Help me find my robe, I've got to go."

"It's on the foot of the bed. You told me you seduced Peter. If you don't believe I can see in the dark, tell me how you did it."

Sammi slowly eased her leg from under the blanket, hooked the robe with her foot, and pulled it under the cover. If anyone would understand her youthful escapades with Peter, it would be the hairy brute trying to take her robe away from her. "Rux, stop," she said. "I've go to get back to the house."

"Not yet, I'll get cold out here. You can have the robe if you tell me how you seduced Peter."

Sammi surrendered temporary custody of the robe and snuggled closer to him. "I invited him to come by after school to have tea with my mother and me. Purely by oversight, I neglected to tell him my mom wouldn't be home from work until an hour after he was to arrive. But it wasn't my idea for him to come early. I just happened to be wrapped in a towel when I answered the door."

"Poor baby," Rux said, releasing the robe to her.

Sammi sat up and smiled inwardly as she slipped into the robe. Maybe, she thought, it's Rux's easy way of putting everything in a humorous vein, but she had never before been able to relive her marriage without sadness. And she certainly had never shared her memories with anyone. Rux didn't ask further, but Sammi continued anyway.

"Peter waited on the porch while I got dressed. Was it my fault my only clean shirt happened to be missing the top two buttons?"

"Aha," Rux said. "The old cleavage trick."

Sammi self-consciously pulled the collar of her robe around her neck. "For a while, we sat on the couch. I remember playing connect-the-dots with the polka dots on his tie. Next thing I knew, the tie, shirt and everything else were flying all over the place. I got pregnant, we got married. End of story, I'm going."

Rux grunted as Sammi crawled over him. She swung her legs off the edge of the bed and swept her feet in search of her shoes.

"Pregnant?" Rux asked. "Did I miss something? I thought you said Missy was not your child."

"I did...didn't I." She gave up on her shoe search, pulled her knees up under her chin, and debated with herself. Telling him all this provided a kind of unburdening, comical relief. But how much further should she go? Could she trust Rux with her innermost secrets, with all the pain and sordid details?

"Please remember, I was only eighteen," she said. "Peter did not know I was pregnant at the time we married. When he found out he flew into a rage. He had plans for me, singing lessons, modeling classes, performances. Pregnancy and child bearing just did not fit in. Plus he already had Missy to worry with. No more children, period."

Rux obviously guessed the abortion. "I'm sorry," he said.

"Thank you." She could feel Rux squirming behind her. Another hurried attempt to find her shoes succeeded. Properly shod, she hopped off the bed, found the electric heater and flipped it on.

"You can't go now," Rux said.

"I'm not. Just a minute." Sammi pulled the heater and rocker closer to the bed so as not to have to talk above a loud whisper. She settled herself in the chair to continue her tale.

"There was no marriage after that. Peter demanded, and I performed. Whether in the bedroom or on the stage."

Rux sat up, wrapped the blanket around himself and propped his feet in front of the heater. Sammi leaned over the bed and pulled back the window curtain. The sky behind the vapor light still appeared dark. "How long have I been here?"

"Probably half an hour. You'd better get back."

"Okay, just a couple of more minutes. You remember me telling you about my friend who died of a drug overdose?"

"Yeah."

Sammi could feel the hurt building in her chest. She slipped back to the bed, seeking the shelter of Rux's powerful arms. Her voice trembled as she continued.

"Her name was Adrianne Godfrey. She and I planned to get her into a rehab center, away from Hector. At the time I didn't know about Peter's connection to Hector."

Sammi's tears flowed in earnest, but now they were born of anguish. Rux held her close against his chest and rocked quietly.

"It's okay," he said. "You need to get back in case Missy wakes up."

"Just one more thing, I'll hurry. I asked Peter to help us."

Sammi blew her nose on something Rux handed her, gave it back to him then realized what she had done. "Was that your T-shirt?"

"That's okay. It's reversible, too."

"Ugh."

Sammi trembled trying to hold her laughter in, then felt herself begin to shake violently. Rux wrapped the blanket around her and pulled the heater closer with his foot.

"Don't torture yourself," he said. "I never should have asked you about this."

Sammi felt like an old car trying to crank as she shook, sniffled, and then swallowed hard. "No, I wanted to tell you."

The orange glow of the heater flickered in Rux's eyes as he held Sammi at arm's length and queried her in silence. Finally, he asked, "You think they killed Adrianne?"

Sammi took Rux's hands from her shoulders and pulled herself back to his chest. "No," she whispered, "Peter's not that kind of person." Everything in her body told her to stop, to get back to the house. But she had come this far. There was one more thing Rux needed to know.

Sammi sat up, wiped her eyes and dried her fingers on the hair of Rux's chest. "I'm sorry," she said, trying to dry him with her forearm. "There's a lot of pressure, performing night after night. You don't feel it because everything you do is lighthearted and fun. But sometimes we needed something to get us up for a performance, then something else to come down off the high.

"Peter got us whatever we needed. I was never hooked, not like Adrianne. But I've been there."

"But not now?"

"No. You're my natural remedy. You keep me off the peaks and out of the valleys."

Rux stood and pulled her to her feet. "First time I ever been called natural anything. I wish you didn't have to go, but you'd better. I'll get dressed and walk you to the house."

"No, don't. Please, I'll be okay." Sammi tore herself away and rushed out the door before she could change her mind. The cold night air sobered her as she hurried to the house. What have I done? she thought. All Rux did was tease me about seducing Peter. He didn't ask to walk through my personal hell.

Sammi slipped quietly into the back door, tiptoed up the stairs and peeked in on Missy. Still asleep. She eased down the hall to her own room and collapsed on the bed. Maybe Rux is right, she thought. I am seducing him, wrapping him ever so slowly in my web.

For the first time since the abortion, Sammi wanted a man as a part of her life.

She got up, shucked her robe and climbed into her flannel pajamas. They were cold. Sammi jumped back into bed and under the covers, and tried to force her mind to go blank. It would not. Her exhaustion had apparently triggered another adrenaline rush.

How are you going to make Rux a part of your life? she taunted herself. We are so different. I want a music career, a recording contract, platinum records. Rux would be happy driving to the Grammy awards in his old truck, if he would go at all. He'd rather be right here, working the ranch and riding his horse.

She folded her hands behind her head and Rorschach tested the shadows made by the vapor light on her ceiling. A big, white stucco house emerged, with an orange, Spanish tile roof. A matching barn sat across a green field. Black fences enclosed the pastures. Rux and Missy would love it here. So would Chester.

Ten

Rux never knew Emilio to give long speeches. He assumed this stemmed from the fact that he thought in Spanish while attempting to speak in English. Each time Emilio paused to search for the correct words, Juanita finished his sentence for him. No one knew what language she thought in, if she thought at all.

"It's mucho caliente up here," Rux said as he tossed the hammer to Emilio and climbed down the ladder from the roof of the loafing shed. "Glad we waited until the weather cooled a bit before we tackled this job."

Emilio grunted his agreement and handed Rux a cup of lukewarm water. The crisp air of a fall morning had gradually yielded to the warming sun. By mid-afternoon the tin roof would grill mountain oysters.

"I think we're in trouble," Rux said. "Here comes Juanita and it's not three o'clock yet."

The two laborers squatted in the shade of the partially completed tin roof and watched Juanita approach. Her five minute waddle from the barn provided a welcome excuse for not continuing their roof repairs.

"Grassyass, Señorita," Rux said as she handed him a thermos of cool water.

"That's gracias, Señora," Juanita said. "You two look like you could use a break. Rector Richter called. He's going over to Whiteriver tonight for a church meeting. Wants to know if you two will go along and help Joe Hawkins round up his cows."

"They need cows for mass?" Rux asked.

"No," Juanita said. "Joe's fence is down and the cows are out. He wants to mend the fence and get the cows back in before dark. The Padre will be by for you in about half an hour."

* * *

Joe and Auren Hawkins' modest frame home posed neatly on a little knoll among tall pines. Below the knoll a small pasture of brown grass separated the pines surrounding the white house from the endless forest of the mountains.

"I appreciate you coming over to help," Joe said as he, Rux, Emilio and Rector Richter examined the barbed wire lying harmlessly on the ground. "Bought these heifers last spring and intended to sell 'em before winter, but the price dropped. They're out in the woods some place, I suppose."

"Glad to help," Rux said. "Just remember this when you guys decide to go on the war path again."

Joe grinned. "We'll be happy to round up your cows before we scalp you, paleface."

"I know you will," Rux said. "If you and Emilio want to get started on the fence, the Padre and I will see if we can find the heifers." Rux retrieved his rope from the Red "C" and headed off across the pasture with Rector Richter.

The cool evenings had nipped the hardwoods just enough to coax some of their leaves into the brilliant red and orange of fall, dotting the green of the woods with splashes of color highlighted by the retreating sun. "This is what the creation must have been all about," Rector Richter said.

"Rounding up cows?" Rux asked.

"No, the landscape, the coolness of evening after a warm day. Where's your poetic side, Rux? By the way, how are we going to get all those cows back to the lot?"

"I'll get a rope on the bell cow. If we lead her in the rest will follow."

"How do you know which one's the bell cow?"

"The one with the bell."

"I don't think Joe has a bell on any of them."

"Well, I guess we'll just pick out the orneriest one."

Rux got a rope on one that proved her orneriness. She did not relinquish her new found freedom easily. Rector Richter tugged on the rope while Rux twisted her tail. She rewarded his efforts with her best green cow patty.

All the cows were in the dusty feed lot and Rux had his boots cleaned by the time Rector Richter's ten renegade Apache catechumen arrived. Each of the men, including Joe Hawkins, had attached to his rosary a medicine bag made from a bull's scrotum.

The fledgling congregation met in the home of Joe and Auren. Rux had no difficulty seeing why the tribe acceded leadership to them. Joe's angular frame stood almost six and a half feet, at least a head taller than any of the other men. Although Apache, his deep set eyes and large, hawk-like nose gave him the classic handsomeness of the eastern Indians.

The boys at Moose Ball's generally described Auren as pretty. An obvious understatement, Rux thought. The slight suggestion of oriental features made her dark eyes even more fascinating. He tried not to stare, but Auren would not have noticed. She seemed mesmerized by the Padre.

Rector Richter bore good news. He produced a letter from the Bishop informing them that money had been appropriated for their first church building.

The women giggled. The men grunted. Rux took this as a sign of their approval. Joe took the letter and promptly dubbed it the "Red 'C' Scrawl."

Like all good and perfect churches, the little group began the process of immaculate deception — organizing. Over the protestations of their clergyman, they elected a chairman and secretary-treasurer. The entire parish membership sat as a committee of the whole to make magnanimous decisions, like where they would meet next week.

Rector Richter buried his face in his hands as they adopted bylaws, even though no one knew what they said. Joe assured them that they were copied from the bylaws of the Whiteriver Lions Club, and no one knew what theirs said either.

On the trip back to Pine Knot, the Padre seemed satisfied all had gone relatively well, in spite of their organizing efforts. Rux commented about the medicine bags.

Rector Richter said, "That's what I mean about them confusing Christianity with their old pagan practices. Many of them still think each man receives his own power from the spirits. They carry little trinkets in their medicine bags that represent their power. Somehow they relate that to the rosary."

"At least they carry them rather than wear them under their breechcloth like they used to," Rux said. He did not share with the Padre his mental image of a bunch of Indians sitting in church with their hands under their breechcloths fingering their rosary beads. The church's inreach program would take on a whole new meaning.

The Padre said, "Emilio, Rux, I'm extremely grateful for your help today, and for all the work you've done on my truck, Rux. May I treat you to dinner at the new bistro tomorrow? Bring Juanita, Sammi and Missy as well."

Rux said, "Sure, long as the bishop appropriated enough funds. You ever broke bread with Juanita before?"

"Can't say that I've had the pleasure."

"Boy are you in for a treat."

* * *

The bistro's pretty teenage hostess smiled at Rux as she ushered their party of six to a large round table next to the roaring fireplace. They were barely seated when the busboy arrived with a tray of six glasses of water.

Juanita caught the boy's arm before he placed the glasses on the table. "Hold on a minute, Buster," she said.

She extracted a brown bottle from her purse and proceeded to shake several drops of the bottle's contents into each glass. "Oxygen," Juanita said in reply to the busboy's quizzical expression. "Kills all the impurities in the water."

The busboy gingerly lifted each glass with his fingertips, distributed them around the table, and left hurriedly.

Rux saw Emilio's eyes glance heavenward just before the menu covered his face. Rector Richter appeared to be making the sign of the cross over his glass. Missy gulped her water as if its oxygenation was an every meal occurrence.

The waiter arrived for drink orders.

"Coffee for me," Juanita said. "Black."

The place buzzed with a mingling of varied conversations from the myriad of tables. Rux hoped the din masked the lecture each of their party got as they ordered.

"Catfish are bottom feeders," Juanita scolded Sammi. Rector Richter received a firm reminder that a sixteen-ounce New York strip steak was a lot of red meat. "Roast pork loin?" she said to Rux. "Do you have any idea how long it takes your system to digest pork? At least a week."

"And you, Ma'am?" the harried waiter asked Juanita.

"A dozen raw oysters, with Tabasco."

Emilio ordered the vegetable plate."

Juanita somehow managed to direct the conversation at her own table while at the same time eavesdropping on the couple seated next to them. Throughout the evening she kept the Padre and his guests abreast of the man's efforts to impress his date, obviously trying to lure her into his bed.

"The drunker he gets, the prettier she gets," Juanita said.

Rector Richter made the mistake of quoting Winston Churchill's famous retort to the lady who accused him of being drunk. "'Yes, madam, I am drunk'," the Padre reported Winston as saying. "'And you are ugly. But tomorrow I shall be sober'."

Juanita leaned over to the young man at the next table and said, "Your girl friend may be ugly, but at least she's sober."

Rector Richter rested his elbows on the table and hid his eyes behind his large hands. "Mister Churchill would be very proud," he said.

The Padre declined Rux's invitation to join them at Moose Ball's Friday night, even though Rux assured him Juanita would be at home with Missy.

* * *

The patrons packed into Moose Ball's were rocking the rafters in anticipation of the entertainers. Rux had left Sammi in the small dressing room behind the bar, allowing her to absorb the crowd's excitement. The energy of a live audience gave her all the stimulant she needed. Rux burst in and gave her another one anyway.

"You remember Lee Wiley Willcox, my lawyer friend from Scottsdale who's always threatening to retire and open a horse ranch with me? He just told me Evan Vaughn is here."

"I remember Lee Wiley. Who's Evan Vaughn?"

"He's a big-time agent from L.A. And he ain't here to audition the piano player, that's for sure."

Sammi jumped up and hugged him. The first "Oh, Rux," rang with excitement. The second one sounded more apprehensive. "Uh oh," Rux said. "That's not good news?"

"It is and it isn't. Remember what happened to my friend, Adrianne, after she was 'discovered.' It's a teenage dream I'm not sure I want anymore. Even if I did I couldn't do it without you."

"Go out there and knock 'em dead, Sam. Hang on to your dream. We'll handle whatever comes out of the chute." He squeezed her and planted a light kiss on her forehead, careful not to muss her makeup, then made his way to the stage.

The crowd greeted him with their usual mixture of rambunctious applause and razzing. Rux kept his opening short. He doubted if Evan Vaughn would be too impressed with Henry Eweolfardt, but he would be more than impressed with Sammi Stone.

Rux introduced her, then felt himself tingle all over as she swirled into the spotlight. Her eyes sparkled in competition with the rhinestones studding her powder blue cowgirl dress, casting a spell over her audience in a way she never had before. The intensity with which she sang one sad love ballad brought tears to her eyes, but her voice never broke.

The women in the crowd cried with her, as did Joe Hawkins. The great Apache warrior tended to become a maudlin souse when he drank.

The Rux Philharmonic performed brilliantly, along with Rux the accompanying singer in the duets. I've got to give her every chance, he thought. His own dream of stardom, long since dead, tried to force its way into his awareness, but he would not let it surface.

This night would be Sammi's alone. There could be no room for a broken down cowboy with minimal talent. He agonized between not wanting the performance to end and wanting to know Evan Vaughn's reaction.

After the show, Rux let Sammi talk with Vaughn while he helped Deke and Sheriff Mohlmann pour black coffee down Joe Hawkins. The Indian always refused a ride home and Mo always made sure he sobered enough to make the forty mile journey to Whiteriver without scalping himself on some farmer's fence.

"Think you can make it home now?" the sheriff asked Joe.

"Great Apache warriors always make it home," Joe slurred. "My trusty steed knows the way."

Rux and Sheriff Mohlmann helped Joe outside and sat him astride his ancient Harley. Joe cranked the kick starter with his massive boot, belched in unison with his motorcycle, then inched his way to the street.

"The other way," Sheriff Mo yelled as Joe turned the wrong direction out of the parking lot. The great Apache warrior made a flourishing U-turn, grinned at the sheriff and roared off toward the highway.

Rux noticed Evan Vaughn searching for his car and rushed inside to find Sammi. "What did he say?" he asked, his excitement betraying his feigned dispassion.

"Who?" Sammi teased.

"You know who. Vaughn."

"Oh, Evan Vaughn. Well, he flowered me with compliments but begged off until tomorrow. He appeared to have done his part to make Moose Ball's bar profitable for the next month. But he did say he had a business proposal for me and he wants to discuss it with a clear head. We're going to meet back here at noon."

On the drive to the ranch Sammi asked Rux six times how long it was until noon. Rux knew she would have asked a seventh time had she not fallen into an exhausted slumber.

Noon came too soon for Rux. He and Chester were in the process of winning their second straight national cutting horse championship when a soft hand shook him awake. "It's almost eleven," Sammi bubbled. "We need to be going."

"Five minutes," Rux mumbled. "I need one more go round to qualify for the finals."

"What finals? Don't you remember my appointment with Vaughn?"

"Never mind, I'm up. Give me twenty minutes to shower and shave."

"Ten? Please? I can't be late."

Fifteen minutes later, Rux heard his truck firing up. He gave up on shaving, washed the lather from his face and hustled out to the truck carrying his shirt and boots. Frigid air reminded him a norther had blown in overnight. Sammi helped him into his shirt while he drove, and the heater blessed his bare feet with warmth.

"Nothing like a warm truck on a cold morning," Rux said.

"Nothing? You can't think of anything else to warm you?" Sammi held tightly to his arm.

"Well, okay. A warm truck or a warm horse."

Sammi pushed herself across the seat in a mock pout. "Please don't tease me. I'm extremely nervous."

"I'm sorry. Come back over here and keep me warm."

The old truck quivered in the cold wind as Sammi alternated between twisting her hands in silence and incomprehensible babbling. Rux pulled up at the front door of Moose Ball's. Sammi slid out of the truck, then looked back at him with the apprehensive expression of a toddler spying the pool on her second day of swimming lessons.

"I'm nervous," she volunteered for the fifth time.

"I wouldn't know if you didn't keep telling me. Don't worry, you'll be fine."

Rux and Deke drank coffee and dawdled at the bar, a discreet distance from the booth where Vaughn sat with Sammi.

Deke said, "Looks like I'm prob'ly gonna be needing a new singer."

"I'd say you probled right, and a new band, too. I don't think your customers are going to put up with me without Sammi."

"I couldn't put up with you without Sammi. Truth is, though, I'm kinda getting used to having your mug around. Sure you don't want to stay and hook up with a band? You're welcome to move into the house if Sammi and Missy leave. Maybe we can talk Willcox into leasing the ranch and you two can start your horse training business."

"Tempting, although I've never been really sure how serious Lee Wiley is about that. I think it's mainly a distraction from the pressures of his law practice. Anyway, I need to get back to Texas and check on my dad."

A lifetime plus fifteen minutes later, Rux and Deke waved to Vaughn as he left, then fell over each other rushing to the booth.

Sammi leaned across the table and grabbed Rux's hands as soon as he slid into the booth. "I've got a contract," she said. "Vaughn wants me to come to L.A. right away. He's arranged a studio for a demo tape. Thinks there are several labels that will want me. I can't believe this!"

Her excitement threatened to change the magnetic poles. She failed to mention Vaughn's lack of interest in Rux, but she didn't have to. Rux knew musicians and their unions were very protective of their positions. They didn't look too kindly on someone who could replace an entire band with a keyboard and a computer.

Vaughn would put Sammi with a good band and backup singers for live performances and Nashville Network tapings. The music studio would mix the sound for her recordings. It took a place like Moose Ball's to utilize Rux's novelty, and then only in a pinch.

Experience had steeled Rux for the inevitability of this moment. Cowboys belonged with their horses and old trucks. Anything else, particularly Sammi, was a diversion. A pleasant diversion to be sure, but one born of illusion and predestined to early extinction.

Rux leaned back and pushed his hat up from his eyes. He grinned like a bear at a barn dance. "That's great, Sam. I knew you could make it. Just a matter of time."

Losing her would rip his guts out. Protocol required him to cover them with his hat, walk through the door with dignity and just ride away. He slumped over the table and stirred in his empty coffee cup. He cut his eyes toward the window and watched the blowing snow. How the hell could he ride off into the sunset in a snow storm?

Such is the fate of a cowboy, he thought. Don't plan. Just play the hand you're dealt.

"Rux, I need you to watch Missy for a few weeks until I can get settled and find a school for her. Maybe I can locate a place where you and Missy can work horses. I'll be back as soon as I can. We'll load up Chester and all ride out together. Will you do that for me?"

What is this? Rux thought. The illusion had taken a strange twist. His guts were not on the floor, and the door for dignified walking through disappeared. A frantic search of his hat failed to produce either of them.

"I dunno, Sam. There's nothing I wouldn't do for you and Missy. But my portfolio barely includes horse training and piano playing. Parenting ain't exactly my strong suit."

"The two of you will do fine. She trusts you. Juanita and Emilio can stay in the house with her. You don't have to cook or anything. Juanita can do that. Just look after her, like you do now."

Rux thought about Rector Richter and his commitment to the priesthood at an early age. It seemed a little late for him to be committing to anything now, particularly to looking out for a young girl who desperately clung to the only mother she had ever known.

He looked again at the whirling snow flurries, then resumed his hat studying. The wind of the West Texas plains blew with the force of a frustrated witch on Halloween, but it wasn't this cold. And No Water wasn't that far away.

Eleven

Real men tell time by the sun. No self-respecting cowboy dared to wear a watch, although some were known to carry one in their pocket if they had an appointment. Rux paid homage to this creed by glancing at the cloudy sky, then calculating the time based on events as he scurried from the barn to the back porch.

Around one, he thought. Sammi's plane left Phoenix at nine and the Baptist church was just letting out when he drove through town.

"I could do with some groceries," he said, while silently acknowledging that the hollow feeling inside him stemmed more from anxiety than hunger. The emptiness had blossomed as he watched Sammi's plane back away from the loading ramp.

He had no particular dislike for airplanes, but they did grind at his innards with a certain sense of foreboding. Every time he flew in one he sat next to a fat lady with a weak bladder and a strong body odor. In self defense he learned to ask for a window seat and purposely neglected to scrape the manure from the instep of his boots.

Driving his truck proved much more satisfactory. He could see the countryside, and if he had to ride shoulder to shoulder with a female he could normally find one with less weight than a heifer. In high school he drove his dad's old 1948 Studebaker pickup that had the stick shift on the floor, right where your girl friend sat. Shifting presented a lot of opportunities, although his ribs were always sore.

Even still, the cause of his uneasiness had not been the plane as much as the small hand that slipped into his just as the plane disappeared from sight. Missy had said nothing, but from the corner of his eye he saw her holding up her little chin and fighting back tears.

She didn't have much luck. Neither did Rux. He felt like an overloaded pack mule, but he had promised Sammi he would do it. And he would, just as soon as he figured out what "it" was. The ultimate "it" seemed clear enough — take care of Missy until Sammi got back from Los Angeles. The details were a little vague, but he had Juanita and Emilio for that.

"Rux, I'm sorry," Missy had finally said.

Rux knew her girl-child voice had been created before eternity for the sole purpose of melting the heart of every man blessed with the gift of hearing.

"I had no right to ask you to give Mom your hat. I know it's a magic hat that tells you what to do. I've seen you study it when you're puzzled over something."

Until that moment, Rux's awareness of his hat studying habit existed only in his subconscious. All cowboys did it as far as he knew. He probably learned it from his dad. And now he also knew why.

Old cowboy hats did indeed have magical powers, but the ignorance that comes with adulthood prevented him from realizing it. Only the innocent insight of a child could have discerned this.

"No, no. That's okay, Miss," he said. "Moms need hats too. I should have thought of it myself. I've got my new Sunday-go-to-meetin' hat I need to break in anyway. Your mom and the hat will be back soon enough. If not, we'll go fetch them."

On the drive back to Pine Knot, he and Missy had talked about riding up on the ridge and cookouts in the snow, and how different it would be in Los Angeles. Now, pondering the clouds from the back porch of Deke's old farmhouse, Rux wondered if "it" might involve more than riding and cookouts.

The warmth of the kitchen eased the chill momentarily as Juanita opened the door. "Sammi's on the phone," she said. "You want to talk to her when Missy gets done?"

"Sure." Rux shook the snow off his coat and stomped his boots on the mat before stepping inside. He, Emilio and Juanita stayed in the kitchen so as not to eavesdrop on Missy's conversation. Rux could see Missy in the living room putting on a brave face even though Sammi couldn't know it. The tinkling of spoons stirring in cups of coffee attempted to muffle the child's conversation.

Juanita had the table filled with little cups, perfume bottles and other paraphernalia she had brought over from the trailer to decorate with. One wall of the kitchen already displayed several copper Jell-O molds.

Rux said, "Juanita, you would have loved the house I grew up in. Outside of marrying my dad and birthing me, my mom's whole existence revolved around collecting pretty things. I mean she had plates, paintings, glasses, thimbles, buttons, artificial flowers, anything that could be hung on a wall or put on a shelf."

"Sounds like you lived in a museum," Juanita said.

"That's what my dad used to say. Antique glass display cases were everywhere. We couldn't turn around or close a door without jarring something off the wall and breaking it."

Juanita moved several of the items to the sink and tossed dish towels to Rux and Emilio. "You guys can dry after I wash them," she said. "Don't break anything. Rux, could we infer your dad did not appreciate your mom's decorating talents?"

Rux sipped his coffee and watched Emilio gingerly accept a slippery perfume bottle from Juanita. "Oh," Rux said, "I'm sure he appreciated the decorating, just not the rate at which it took over the house. We managed to stake out a couple of rocking chairs five feet in front of the television, but even that five feet suffered frequent encroachment. It was like trying to keep weeds out of a garden."

Rux accepted a tea cup for drying, since Emilio obviously intended to make a career out of toweling off the perfume bottle.

Emilio said, "These things multiply worse than weeds. And their incestuous breeding produces mutations more ghastly than their parents."

"You two are ridiculous," Juanita said, handing Emilio a small ceramic owl.

"No, I'm serious," Emilio said. "See that little gold plated eagle? He mated this owl one night and produced a whole flock of cloth and glass chickens, ducks, cardinals and wrens."

Rux laughed. "I never thought of that. But now that you mention it, we started out with just a hall tree and a Murphy bed. I bet those two got together and begat the brass lamps and soda fountain stools. Maybe even the imitation Persian rug."

"You guys are running that into the ground," Juanita said. "Here, dry these squirrels. I'm sure your dad could see the television just fine."

"Not really," Rux said. "He finally got a portable radio for his tractor. But it wasn't just the television. Mom spent every waking moment dusting and cleaning her collection. As soon as she finished the entire house it was time to start over."

Juanita rejoined them at the table with the last of her freshly washed knickknacks. "I'd love to see your mom's collection," she said.

"You may be looking at part of it," Rux said. "I suspect Dad hauled every last item to the resale shop after Mom died. He swore all he needed was the bed, rocker, TV and enough cookware to make coffee and heat up meatballs and spaghetti."

Rux checked the living room to be sure Missy was still on the phone. He leaned over the table, motioned a thumb in Missy's direction and whispered, "Juanita, I guess you've been through all this before."

"Been through what?" Juanita said.

"You know...this. Child raising, parenting, whatever it is we're supposed to be doing with Missy until Sammi gets back."

"Oh," Juanita said. "Well, no, I haven't. I never had any kids. Other than you and Emilio. How about you?"

"Closest I came to raising a kid was nursing a baby goat with a bottle after our neighbor mistook its mother for an antelope."

"Maybe we should call someone," Juanita said.

"Like who?" Rux asked.

"How about Rector Richter? Juanita said.

"He's a priest," Rux said. "How would he know anything about parenting?"

"He's the rector of a school," Juanita said. "Wouldn't he know something about child raising? At least he could give us moral support."

Emilio took an exaggerated slurp of his coffee to get their attention. "She'll be fine," he said. "What can happen in two weeks?"

"Plenty," Juanita said. "What if she decides to go lollygagging off with her new horseback riding friends?"

"She won't," Rux said. "Remember, the girls she competed against at the horse show pretty much ignored her. We need to keep our eyes open, though, just in case."

Emilio said, "You two are letting your imaginations get the best of you. We can't watch her every minute. What are you going to do when she's in school?"

Rux slapped himself on the forehead. "That's right, she'll be in school. Maybe one of us should go with her."

"Shhh, here she comes," Juanita said. "Act natural."

Rux scooted his chair back and attempted to lean against the wall. Emilio propped his feet on the table. "Not that natural, you idiots," Juanita said.

Rux misjudged his angle of repose and banged the chair into the wall with a severe jolt. He tried to look very casual under the shower of Jell-O molds falling on his head.

Juanita rolled her eyes and lifted Emilio's feet from the table.

Missy entered the kitchen and asked, "Rux, are you okay? Mom wants to talk to you."

"You bet, Miss." Rux righted his chair and stepped over the Jell-O molds. "Watch them little tin things, they're dangerous."

Rux hurried into the living room, leaving Juanita and Missy to redecorate the kitchen. He could still hear Emilio chuckling as he picked up the phone.

"What's all that racket?" Sammi asked.

"Nothing. We're just moving the chickens inside so they don't freeze. How's L.A.?"

"L.A.'s beautiful. What chickens?"

Rux lowered his voice. "Hey, you run off to the big city, I gotta do something to keep warm. Where are you?"

"I'm at the hotel. Rux, you won't believe this place. It's like a palace. I even had a chauffeur-driven limo pick me up at the airport, a polite little oriental named Richard."

"You sure it wasn't a Toyota? I never heard of a Japanese car called Richard."

"Not the car, the chauffeur. I think he's Filipino or something like that."

"Probably the wild man from Borneo."

"He's very nice. Vaughn and his staff are treating me like royalty."

"Get used to it, Sam. You deserve it."

"Maybe, but keep my place warm at Moose Ball's, just in case."

"The only kind of royal treatment you'll get up here is a condo share of the throne in the ladies' room. I assume your palace has an indoor toilet."

Sammi's boisterous laugh forced Rux to hold the phone away from his ear. "Yes," she said, "and a king-size bed with satin sheets. When you come, I'll buy you a pair of satin pajamas."

Rux glanced toward the kitchen, hoping this conversation remained very private. "That won't work," he said. "I'd just keep sliding off the bed."

"You can hold on to me."

"What'll you be wearing?"

"Nothing."

"I'll be right there. Send wild Richard back to Borneo."

Somehow even Sammi's giggling sounded sensuous. "I miss you," he said.

"Rux, it's just been four hours. But I miss you too. I'll find us a place and be back for you and Missy as soon as I can."

"I'm still thinking on that," Rux said to himself after he hung up. Teasing with Sammi was one thing. Actually going to California meant more than king-size beds and satin sheets.

He would take care of Missy and get her back with Sammi, but planning beyond that eluded him. The last thing he recalled planning was how to get a jalapeño suppository up Harry Beauchamp's rear. He still planned to go back to Texas. Some day.

* * *

Well before dawn the next morning, Rux busied himself about the foaling room and watched for lights in the kitchen. What's keeping them, he thought. The school bus will be here in an hour.

When the kitchen light finally flicked on, Rux grabbed his new hat and hustled across the frozen grass to the house. Juanita appeared at the window behind the sink, bundled in a heavy flannel robe and apparently still asleep. A freshly shaved and fully dressed Emilio opened the kitchen door before Rux knocked.

"Morning, Rux," Emilio said. "Come in. Heard you stomping your feet on the porch."

"Morning, Emilio, Juanita. Where's Missy?"

Juanita groused, "She's getting dressed. You two don't need to be quite so early." She shooed Rux and Emilio out of the kitchen until she could get Missy fed and off to school.

Rux made sure the girl had her warm jacket and her lunch. The three guardians hustled back to the kitchen after seeing their ward safely aboard the school bus.

"Parenting can be frenzied at times," Rux said.

"You should have spent more time with that goat," Juanita said. "Well, I got one child off to school, guess I better feed the other two."

Twenty minutes later, Rux found himself sharing Emilio's usual fare of fresh juiced carrots and celery with hot cracked barley cereal. And bacon.

"Bacon?" Rux asked.

"Sure," Juanita said. "It comes from the Mother Earth Organic Food Store."

Since Juanita took Emilio's natural foods diet seriously, Rux assumed the bacon to be soy bean. Or it could be meat from hogs raised on organic slop and allowed to wallow only in mud certified by the EPA to be free of toxic wastes.

Emilio got only the purest of foods, although Juanita herself was known to slip into town rather frequently for a breakfast of biscuits and sausage at McDonalds. Her diet always started tomorrow.

Rux stirred his cereal, spooned up a large bite, then quickly returned the contents to the bowl. The mush appeared to be saturated with little brown critters.

"Juanita," Rux said, "I don't mean to be impolite, but there's fleas in my cereal."

"Those aren't fleas, they're flax seed. They clean out your gall bladder. Now quit complaining and eat, drink and be Mary, or Jo Ann, or whoever you want to be."

Juanita handed each of them a mug of hot chocolate made from crushed macadamia nuts and tofu milk.

"Not bad for macadamia nuts," Rux said, wiping the liquid moustache from his upper lip. "But I understand the Macadamians ain't too fond of the harvesting process."

Emilio and Rux tried to beat each other to the back door, knowing the last one out would catch a pot holder in the back of his head. Hopefully without the pot.

"We'd best work outside for a while," Emilio said, heading for his trailer.

"Good idea. I got horses to tend to."

Rux made his way to the stalls where he had left three blanketed horses last night. He led them out, one at a time, and turned them loose in the back pasture. Chester sniffed at the fresh snow, pawed it, then roared off after the mares.

Heck, Rux thought, this cold doesn't bother him at all. If he can tolerate this after spending his whole life in the desert, I might could even get used to this parenting business. One thing's for sure. A few more nights in that cold foaling room and I'll welcome the chance to slide off them satin sheets, particularly with Sammi there to hold onto.

He shook his head to clear the image and headed back to the tack room. The first morning of parenting had gone okay. Between himself, Emilio and Juanita they should be able to muddle through. How much could go wrong in just a few weeks?

Twelve

Sammi slid from between the satin sheets and fumbled into the heavy terry cloth robe provided by the hotel. The digital number on the clock flipping from seven-fifty-nine to eight-zero-zero interrupted her half-conscious stare and reminded her she was awake. She sat back down on the bed and tried to shake her brain cells into their proper firing sequence.

Why am I so tired? she thought. I've been in bed almost ten hours. Her hand slid on the linen as she attempted to push her weary body up from the bed. "That's why," she said. "I spent all night chasing my pillows. I guess Rux was right, but how would he know about sleeping on satin?"

Move, she scolded herself. A phone call to room service produced a lame promise to deliver coffee before Richard arrived. She had an hour to shower, shave her legs, and do her hair and nails. "Don't be late," Evan had said. "This is a business appointment, not a cocktail party."

"I am not nervous," Sammi lectured to her toothbrush, making her third try to hit it with the toothpaste. "I'm just excited. Today, I get the news on my new band and recording sessions. Please hold still."

The toothbrush cooperated just long enough to receive a slight smattering of the paste.

* * *

"Good morning, Ms. Stone," the receptionist sang. Sammi and Richard entered the white carpeted offices of Evan Vaughn and Associates at exactly nine-fifteen. "I'll let Mr. Vaughn know you're here. May I get you anything? Coffee? Tea?"

Richard accepted the coffee but Sammi declined. She had remembered to brush her teeth again after drinking coffee at the hotel, but didn't remember if she had breath freshener in her purse.

Richard sat in the chair opposite her and smiled while stirring his coffee. "Sammi, relax," he said. "You're among friends. Everything's fine."

His calm voice and soft oriental features relieved her tension a little. She closed her eyes and leaned her head back, then realized her carefully styled hair would be crushed by the high, winged-back chair.

Oh, to heck with the hair, she thought, and this dress and these high heels. I wish Rux was here.

By nine-twenty-nine, Sammi felt perfectly at ease. At precisely nine-thirty, the receptionist ushered them into Evan's office.

"Sammi, how are you?" Evan said. He walked around his desk and accepted her hand.

Richard said, "If you will excuse me, I'll be in the conference room."

Sammi acknowledged Richard with a brief smile and turned back to Evan. In the dark, reflective window glass behind the desk she half noticed Richard open the door to the adjoining room, step inside and close it. She tried to focus on Evan's words, inviting her to sit down. But something from the conference room had jolted her attention.

When the door opened, the window had reflected for just an instant the image of a tall figure wearing a white slouch hat.

The name "Peter" floated in from a distant fog at the same instant Sammi recognized his all too familiar handsome face.

"Peter," she gasped. "What is he...." Sammi felt herself turn back to the conference room door. She wasn't sure if she would faint, wet herself, or had already done both. "What is he doing here?"

Evan retrieved her purse from the floor, took her arm and guided her into one of the plush chairs facing his desk. Sammi could hear her inner voice saying, "Don't lose it, don't...." Too late. She had already buried her face in her hands and the heavy sobbing came involuntarily.

Time and surroundings blended together without meaning, but at some point she realized the office contained only her and Evan. He sat silently behind his desk. Sammi found a lipstick smudged tissue in her purse and blotted her eyes.

"I need to go," she said.

"In a while. I guess I should explain some things."

"No, please, just let me go." Sammi smoothed her skirt over her knees in an effort to keep her legs from trembling. "This never happened. I'll go back to Arizona and you'll never hear from me again."

Evan stood, walked around to Sammi and sat on the edge of his desk, facing her. His blue shirt with white collar and yellow tie complemented his tan face. Sammi's dry mouth quelled her urge to spit on him.

"Leaving is not an option at this point," Evan said. "I have an arrangement with Peter. He's interested in your career, as am I. We both think you are good enough to go to the top of the charts. To do that, we need you here in Los Angeles.

"I have a band lined up for you to try out with, and I am arranging for a recording studio to cut a demo tape. All you have to do is perform, like we all know you can."

Sammi avoided Evan's hard blue eyes. She had been duped. Everything about him repulsed her, his smile, his manicured hands, the smell of his cologne. She edged her chair back and stood, shakily, holding on to the chair. A deep breath allowed her to walk to a large bronze of wild horses surging from the credenza.

She ran her fingers over a flowing mane of the bronze as she whispered, "Chester. Rux, I need you."

Behind her, she heard the conference room door open and close again.

Sammi turned to assure herself it was all a bad dream. Peter sat on the edge of Evan's desk watching her. Obviously, Evan had left the two of them alone.

"Hello, Sam," Peter said. "It's nice to see you again."

So calm, so sweet, so disarming, Sammi thought. I hate this.... At the same time her tortured psyche was mustering up bile and venom, something lifted a corner of her antipathy and peeked out. The eighteen-year-old Sammi Stone was still enamored with him.

Oh, god, no! Sammi yelled inside herself. That Peter doesn't exist anymore, never existed. Mentally, she grabbed the corner of her wrathful veil and closed it. Forever.

Somehow, her shoes had remained under the chair. "I have to get back to my daughter," she said.

"*Your* daughter? How is *my* daughter?"

"Why do you ask? You've never cared about her before."

"True." Peter took off the slouch hat, carefully placed it on the desk and shook his head, letting his wavy blond hair nestle over his ears. "I assume you left her in Arizona, along with your singing partner, Henry, or Rux, or whatever his name is."

Sammi studied her former husband. There was something different about him. Ah, his nose. She remembered his encounter with Rux and the piano stool.

"Melissa is being well taken care of, if you really are concerned about her."

"Well...." Peter pushed himself from the desk, folded his hands behind his back and began pacing, like a lecturing professor. "This is working out nicely. Missy is out of the way and you're here."

Sammi reached behind her and gripped the bronze with every intention of smashing it into Peter's face. The bronze didn't budge. "I need to throw up," she said.

"Try to compose yourself. Think for a minute. You have a great opportunity here. Don't blow it."

Sammi turned around to grip the bronze with both hands. It still wouldn't move. Damn thing must weigh a hundred pounds, she thought. Well, why not. She sensed Peter stop directly behind her. Soft, firm hands gently held her shoulders.

"My little Sam."

The words were almost a whisper, his tone smooth, almost sensuous. In spite of herself, Sammi drifted back—beyond the drug dealing, past

Adrianne, before the abortion. They had loved each other once.

She stepped out of his grasp and turned to face him. "Rux and I are more than singing partners," she said.

"I guessed as much. Look, I can accept that. Whatever existed between us is over. But not our shared dream of making you a top performer. I'm still a damn good agent, and so is Evan. We can make it happen."

His easy voice continued. "Stay with us, Sam. Give it a chance. Missy and Rux Henry will be fine for now. All they need to know is that you are busy recording and working with the band. Once we get the recording contract, bring them out if you like."

Sammi looked at the numerous photographs adorning the paneled walls. They all pictured neatly posed artists who had made it to successful careers. Each photo contained a handwritten note to Evan, thanking him for his help.

Ten minutes ago she had walked into this office with her dream in full focus. Slowly, reluctantly, it began to resurface. She faced Peter.

"Ours will be strictly a business arrangement. There's no reason Missy and Rux can't come out now."

"Rux doesn't fit in. He's kind of fun to watch but he's not Grand Old Opry material, not by a long shot. You're going to be very busy touring with the band. Missy and Rux would be a distraction."

Peter fingered his crooked nose. "Besides, I don't think Rux Henry and I get along too well."

"I'm sorry that happened. What about Hector? And your drug dealing?"

"Over and done with. Everything's cool."

Sammi again sought the comfort of the bronzed horses. She remained facing the credenza for several minutes of agonizing silence.

"How long" she asked, "before Missy and Rux can come?"

"That depends on you. Evan already has the wheels in motion. If you fit in with the band and the demo tapes go well, a few weeks. Worst case scenario, maybe a month or two."

Sammi took a deep breath, then let it out slowly. "Let's do it."

Behind her she heard the conference room door open, presumably ushering in Evan and wild Richard from Borneo.

"Richard will drive you back to the hotel," Evan said. "My secretary will call you this afternoon with the appointments. Let her or Richard know if you need anything in the meantime."

Sammi retrieved her purse and shoes and trudged out of the office with Richard. Her feet felt as heavy as the bronze. She thought, I really do need to throw up.

* * *

The posh hotel room with its king-size bed and satin sheets now felt like a prison cell. Sammi stripped off her clothes and showered again, desperately needing to remove the grime from Evan's office. The pounding of the hot water did little to soothe her headache as her mind raged with self-communion.

Every fiber of her being said go back to Pine Knot. But the brass ring hung right before her eyes. All she had to do was reach out and grab it. This might be the best chance she was ever going to get. It might well be her last.

If she could only talk to Rux. He would know what to do. But telling him about Peter's involvement would be inviting disaster.

Sammi had an eerie feeling Peter and Evan would be watching her every move. She turned the shower off and quickly wrapped herself in a towel. "Stop this," she chided herself. "No one is watching you." Still, she hustled into her jeans and shirt, and abandoned her poofy hair in favor of a pony tail.

Rux's old black hat residing on the closet shelf next to the hair dryer gave Sammi new resolve. "Rux will know how to handle this." She retreated to the bed, picked up the phone and dialed, then hung up before anyone could answer.

She pounded her fist into the pillow, trying to clear her head. Why am I so confused, she thought. I told Peter I'd do it. Everything's arranged. All I have to do is perform. Missy and Rux will come out in a few weeks, just like we planned.

In spite of her rationalizations, the nagging doubts continued to pluck at her feeble brain.

The solution emerged. Evan had given her a generous advance for expenses. She had at her fingertips the most effective catharsis ever devised by man. Or woman. A shopping mall adjoined the hotel.

Sammi grabbed her purse and jacket and hurried out the door.

Richard, lounging comfortably on a plush leather couch in the lobby, greeted her as she stepped off the elevator.

"Hi, Sammi." The friendly tone of his voice now had a chilling effect. "Can I drive you somewhere?"

"No," Sammi said. "I'm just going for a walk."

Yellow-gray clouds trapping cool air against the concrete of the city did little to relieve her chill. Sammi ducked into the shopping mall and stole a quick glance through the glass wall to see if Richard had followed. He did not appear on the sidewalk.

Don't be so paranoid, she chided herself. But it occurred to her to call

96

Tyrone. It would be foolhardy to take Peter's word that he was through with Hector and drugs.

"Excuse me," Sammi said to the security guard. "Is there a pay phone here?"

The man pointed to a bank of phones by the rest rooms. No booths with doors to close for privacy. Sammi thought, anyone standing near me could hear every word I say. "Thank you," she said to the guard, and boarded the escalator up to the next level of shops. The guard was probably hired by Peter and Evan to keep an eye on her.

Sammi joined the elderly mall walkers hustling up and down the corridors at a brisk pace. Her legs gave out before the gray panthers did. She stopped at the food court, ordered an Orange Julius and found a secluded table. The lunch crowd had not yet arrived. The aroma of the Orange Julius reminded her of Evan's cologne.

Sammi carefully eyed the lady with blue hair operating the Orange Julius stand. She had to be the mother of the receptionist in Evan's office.

Around eleven-thirty, the lunch crowd replaced the gray panthers. Sammi gathered her rejuvenated legs and rejoined the fray. Two hours later, her *unjuvenated* legs guided her back to the food court. A grumbling stomach insisted she eat, but she could only stare at her hot dog with sauerkraut. Something about it reminded her of Hector.

She cut off a piece of the wiener for his head, arranged strands of sauerkraut for his pony tail, then stabbed her makeshift voodoo doll violently with her fork. The prongs of her plastic weapon shattered. "Figures."

Even the clerks in the phone store did not know where she could find a singular phone booth. Sammi's languishing in the mall corridors would have survived perpetuity had her finite body not threatened to come unhinged.

Darkness had replaced the yellow-gray sky when the mall finally regurgitated her. Sammi debated whether this had to do with the lateness of the hour or her frame of mind.

"Probably both," she said as she merged into the sidewalk traffic. A lone telephone station grinned at her from the side of the building. It offered only a little metal dish for privacy, but at least no one else would be on the phone right next to her.

Sammi stood as close as she could to the dial as she punched in the number of Mama Henry's, then dropped in three quarters on instructions from an electronic operator. The line was busy. Sammi fully expected the pay phone to keep her seventy-five cents. It did.

She dialed again and deposited more coins.

"Mama Henry, it's me, Sammi," she said to the familiar voice that answered.

"Sammi, child, how are you? It's so good to hear from you."

"I'm great," Sammi lied. "Is Tyrone there?"

"Sure. Let me pry him away from the pool table."

"Tell him to hurry, I'm on a pay phone calling long distance."

Sammi surveyed the sidewalk as she waited. Everyone appeared to be moving. She startled when she heard Tyrone call, "Hey, Sam, what's up?" Then she remembered the phone.

"Hi, Tyrone. Just wanted to see how you were, and if you had heard anything from your police friends about Peter and Hector."

"We all be fine here. Last time I talk with my police contact he say they at a dead end. Nothing to...."

Tyrone ended abruptly as the telephonic slut demanded more money. Sammi obliged and said, "Tyrone, are you still there?"

"Yo, I'm here. Where'd I lose you?"

"You were saying the police were at a dead end."

"Right. If them home boys be dealin' they good at it."

"Okay, let's leave it at that for now. I'll get back to you as soon as I can. Thanks, buddy."

She could hear Tyrone chuckle at her use of their old school days term. "Hang loose, Sam," he said. "Lemme know if I can help."

"No one can help," Sammi said to herself after she hung up. She gathered her heart from around her knees and walked back in the hotel. Richard still sat on the couch, reading a magazine.

"Hello," he said. "Enjoy your afternoon of shopping?"

"Not particularly." How does he know I've been in the shopping mall all day? she wondered.

Richard stood, stretched and followed her into the elevator. "Mr. Vaughn's office called," he said. "I retrieved your messages from the operator."

How? Sammi wanted to ask, but did not.

"You have an appointment with Earle Steiner's band tomorrow at four o'clock. They're playing at the Elk Horn Saloon. Good band. I think you will fit in well with them."

The elevator stopped on the tenth floor. Richard followed her toward her room. "You also have an appointment with a recording studio on Thursday, eight o'clock."

"A.M. or P.M.?"

"P.M."

Sammi stopped at her door. She wondered if Evan's instructions included Richard spending the night in her room.

"Good night, Richard," she said as she inserted the card key in the slot on the door handle.

"Good night. I'll meet you in the lobby at three tomorrow."

Sammi closed the door and leaned against it. Three tomorrow, she thought. Good. I'll have all morning to shop.

Deep inside she knew the shopping was just a distraction to avoid making a decision. Maybe she would just shop for the next three weeks and see how things developed.

* * *

Richard's Dockers and Izod shirt were clearly out of place in the Elk Horn Saloon. Jeans and boots were the acceptable culture. Sammi blended right in. They stood by the door a few seconds to let their eyes adjust to the dim light inside.

Sammi thought, this place is Moose Ball's cubed. She glanced up. Steel girders and painted air conditioning ducts formed the indoor sky instead of the exposed log beams in Deke's bar.

Richard led her through a maze of red and white checkered table cloths. Miniature kerosene lanterns adorned hundreds of round tables.

Earl Steiner's Red Neck Band blasted the room with an old Merle Haggard tune. Richard guided Sammi over to the stage when they finished.

"Hey, Richard," the lead singer called out over the speaker system.

Richard stepped up on the stage and shook hands with the singer and each of the other four band members. "Guys, this is Sammi Stone."

The lead singer, who turned out to be Earle, took her guitar and helped her to the stage. Earle introduced her to each band member, then offered her his stool.

"Evan Vaughn has told me a lot about you, Sammi," Earle said. "He's very high on your singing. Want to give it a try?"

"Sure," Sammi said. "But I have to warn you, I feed off the energy of the crowd. What you hear now will sound twice as good when we have a live audience."

She took out her guitar and tuned it with the band as they discussed songs, tempos and keys.

After several trial runs on the first few bars of "Sweet Memories," Earle asked, "How about it, guys, everybody ready to jam?"

"Hey," the drummer said, "Richard looks live enough for an audience. Get on down, my man."

"I'm gone," a grinning Richard said. He began a slow clap more or less in time with the easy rhythm.

Sammi missed her entry by half a beat, but picked it up quickly. She focused on the blue glow of the Pabst Blue Ribbon Beer sign and let the music spin Richard, Peter and Evan into temporary oblivion. Only after the last twang of the steel guitar finished echoing from the metal rafters did she refocus on the room.

Richard, three janitors and the bartender all stared at her in stunned silence.

Sammi wondered if that meant they were that good or that bad. She nodded in meek acknowledgment of what she hoped was their noiseless applause, then turned to find the band in a similar muted pose.

"Man," Earle finally said. "If you're twice as good as that, I can't wait."

"Thanks," Sammi said. She felt warmth in her cheeks and found a sudden fascination with the toes of her boots. "I guess I like that song."

Two hours later, Sammi's plea for mercy fell on deaf ears. The band was in a groove and wanted to keep going. Richard and the bartender finally rescued her with hot lemonade to soothe her raspy throat.

"Enough," she said. "Don't you guys have a gig tonight?"

"You're right," Earle said. "We're just excited to have you. Can you practice again tomorrow? If we get a few more songs down I think we can go live this weekend."

"Does that mean I'm hired?"

"You were hired the moment you sang the first note. I'll work out the details with Evan."

Sammi felt her face blush again. "Thank you," she said. "You guys are really great."

"Gang hug," Earle yelled to the band.

Sammi suddenly found herself in the massive embrace of the five free spirited young men, bouncing up and down and chanting, "Gang hug, gang hug." Her playful cry for relief again went unheeded, which was okay.

Sammi's initiation into the Red Neck Band lured out long forgotten memories of laughing and singing with her friends at church youth revivals. The world seemed back on its proper axis.

The newest member of the Red Neck band finally freed herself from the gang hug. As she and Richard negotiated their way back through the tables to the door, the band cranked out their version of "Good Hearted Woman."

Sammi turned and waved. What a great bunch of guys, she thought. This is going to work, I can feel it.

Richard wheeled the Lincoln across the parking lot of the Elk Horn Saloon. A speed bump simultaneously jolted the car and Sammi's buoyancy. The Lincoln continued smoothly, but the world tilted again.

"Where to?" Richard asked.

"Back to the hotel."

The terseness of her reply was obviously not lost on Richard. He drove in silence while Sammi watched the endless parade of traffic and concrete freeway hillsides.

Richard parked in the hotel's garage and took Sammi's guitar from the back seat. Sammi dutifully accepted each courtesy as he opened doors and pushed the elevator buttons to see her safely, and securely, back to her room.

"Look, Sammi," Richard said after she unlocked her room and took her guitar from him. "I know you're angry with us, and you have every right to be. Evan should have told you about Peter from the beginning. But you were great today. You can lose yourself in your music and float high above all this on a magical cloud. Am I right?"

Sammi let her eyes trace the flowered pattern in the beige and maroon carpet. He was right, but she made no attempt to acknowledge or answer the question.

Richard was not much taller than Sammi, and she could sense him trying to make eye contact with her. After a moment, he half turned toward the elevator, then faced her again.

"I understand," he said. "I wouldn't want someone manipulating me like that, either. Just try not to think about it. We'll get you a good manager and a recording contract, and everything will come up roses."

Richard reached into his jacket pocket and produced a small cellophane bag with several blue pills. "Here, take these," he said. "They'll make you feel better."

"What are they?"

"Blue velvets. You need to mellow out a little. I can get crack if you prefer."

"I don't need anything."

As she opened the door to step into the room, Richard stuffed the package with the blue pills in her jacket pocket.

"Just in case you change your mind," he said. "Good night."

Sammi closed the door, deposited her guitar in the plush chair opposite the armoire with the mini-bar, and flopped on the bed. Her mind would not go numb in spite of her instructions that it do so. She sat up, kicked her boots off and threw them at the closet door. Practice again tomorrow, she thought, and the recording session for the demo tape on Thursday. I can stick this out until then. We'll see what happens.

Her jacket and shirt flew across the room after the boots while Sammi adjourned to the bathroom and washed makeup from her face. The towel blotting the warm water gradually moved from her forehead to her chin, revealing dark brown eyes staring back at her from the mirror. The soulful eyes reminded her of Missy.

"I miss you, little baby," Sammi said to her own reflection. "I miss you too, cowboy," she said, letting her eyes wander down the reflection of her body. "Everything was going so great in Pine Knot. Do I really want to get mixed up with Peter again?"

Sammi slipped off her jeans and donned the fresh robe left by the maids. She ordered a tuna melt from room service, then called the ranch.

"Hi, Mom," Missy said. "How's everything going?"

"Great. I signed on with a great band today, my recording session is Thursday, and...." Thirty minutes of exuberant small talk later, Sammi was satisfied Missy and Rux got the message.

All is well in Los Angeles. Blah.

* * *

At exactly 7:30 on Thursday evening, Sammi's Borneoan chauffeur wheeled the Lincoln to the curb in front of the hotel.

"All set?" Richard asked, holding the door open for Sammi to enter the back seat.

Evan Vaughn greeted her with a friendly smile. A business discussion regarding the band quickly dissipated into an uneasy silence as they made the thirty minute drive to Hollywood.

Richard parked the Lincoln in a lot with patches of asphalt more or less covering old red bricks. The bricks matched the exterior of the conglomeration of fifty-year old buildings separating the parking lot from Hollywood Boulevard.

Creepy, Sammi thought. Maybe I'm doing a demo tape for a horror movie. Whatever, let's just get it over with and get out of here.

"This is Hollywood Boulevard?" Sammi asked Evan.

He held the door of the Lincoln open for her to exit. "It looks worse in the daylight," Evan said. "She's old, but the lady is still famous. When we get around front you will see the stars in the sidewalk with names of famous actors and actresses."

A solitary light hanging from the corner of the building guided them to the side street leading back to the boulevard. The sidewalk stars were barely visible in the shadows cast by the awnings of the buildings.

Richard and Evan led Sammi past storefront shops to a doorway opening into dark wooden stairs. On the second floor, they were greeted by a large mahogany door with unpretentious gold letters announcing "Polaris Studios."

"Here we are," Richard said, opening the door and ushering Sammi and Evan into a modest-sized reception area.

"Hello Richard, Evan," the man sitting behind the desk said. The man rose and shook hands with Sammi's companions. "And this must be Sammi," he said with a friendly smile.

"Sammi," Evan said, "say hello to Alex. He's the manager and chief engineer here."

Alex, dressed in blue jeans and a blue button-down dress shirt with no tie, bowed slightly and accepted her hand. His gentle demeanor and the comfortable setting of the reception area eased Sammi's apprehension a bit. She noticed for the first time the tasteful Victorian furniture and the numerous gold records and publicity photos lining the walls.

"May I show you around?" Alex asked.

The small, bespectacled engineer took Sammi's arm and proudly gave her a quick review of several of the gold records Polaris had produced for a host of well known bands and artists.

"I hope I can add to your collection," Sammi said.

Alex smiled his disarming smile. "Of that, I have no doubt," he said. "But first things first. Let's get you a good demo tape cut and we'll take it from there."

He led them into a large room behind the reception area. A scuffed wooden floor connected four carpeted walls. A grand piano and a set of drums resided at the far end of the room.

"This is where our bands set up," Alex said. "And back here is our control room." He pointed to a glass panel in one of the carpeted walls.

Sammi followed Alex into the control room, where she was introduced to two sound engineers cramped among speakers, monitors and the largest mixer she had ever seen.

"You will record in here," Alex said, opening the door to a smaller cubicle, also separated from the control room by a glass panel. "We call it our 'cry room'."

The sterile room contained only a recording mike suspended from the ceiling, headphones and a stool.

One of the sound engineers said, "We have the songs you requested cued up on tape. The background music will be piped in through the headphones. We're ready whenever you are."

Sammi stepped into the cry room, tried on the headphones and adjusted the mike. "I guess I'm a little nervous," she said.

"Take your time," Alex said. "There's no hurry. Why don't you get your guitar and warm up a little, get a feel for the room and the equipment? Just let us know when you want to start."

"Thank you," Sammi said. Richard brought her guitar. She tried several songs, but each time her voice sounded thin.

That's what's wrong, she thought, catching her image in one of the glass walls. I'm all dressed up in my powder blue dress and white boots, ready for a show. But there's no audience. She turned to the control booth and said, "I've never performed under glass before."

"Relax, you'll get used to it," Alex said through the headphones. "We're going to cut a lot of records right here."

"I hope so. Do you have any hot lemonade?"

"Sure," Alex said. "We'll get it for you. We're going to pipe in the music for your songs. Close your eyes and get the feel of it. You're on stage at the Hollywood Bowl."

The Hollywood Bowl did not materialize. Rux and Moose Ball's did. The hot lemonade cut some of the thinness in her voice but did little to lift her out of her mental quicksand.

I've got to try, she chided herself. One good demo tape, one good recording contract, one good manager to deal with Vaughn and company. Just try.

Sammi picked up the words to the tune coming through her headphones. After a few bars, her full voice returned. "I'm ready," she said.

Three takes later, Sammi looked hopefully at Alex behind the glass panel.

"Not bad, Sammi," he said. "Not bad. Your timing and the quality of your voice are great, but we need a little more enthusiasm. Let's do one more take. Remember, you're on stage. Feel the audience, make them laugh, make them cry."

I want to cry, Sammi thought. This isn't working.

Half way through the next take, the background music stopped.

"That's enough, Sammi," Alex said. "We're all tired. Let's call it a night."

Sammi hung her headphones on the mike, picked up her guitar and dragged herself back through the studio to the reception area. Evan and Richard were waiting with Alex.

"Nice going, Sammi," Alex said. "Let us work with what we've got. If it isn't what we want, I'll set up another session."

Richard, Evan and Sammi drove back to Los Angeles in the same icy silence. I'm sure Alex told them, Sammi thought. There's no way he can get a decent demo tape from tonight's session. I was just out of it. I need a real audience, not some glass booth. On the other hand, if Rux can produce a whole orchestra with his little computer and synthesizer, who knows what Alex and his engineers can do with all that equipment?

Richard pulled into the garage underneath Evan's office building and stopped on the second level behind a lonely BMW. Evan opened his door, then reached back and patted Sammi's knee.

"We'll be fine," he said. "There will be other sessions."

Shut up, Sammi wanted to scream, but didn't. She simply nodded and mumbled something that passed for "good night."

Richard drove to the hotel, and again parked in the garage and walked her to her room.

"Sammi, he said, "you're still way too up tight. Just relax a little and you will be fine. Can I get you anything?"

Sammi reached into her jacket pocket for her room key and felt the cellophane bag with the blue velvets. "No," she said. "I have everything I need."

Thirteen

Missy placed her tray on the table and glanced around the school cafeteria. Somehow the place seemed strange but she couldn't tell why, exactly. Dark blue curtains still hid the stage, and bright sunshine bouncing off the concrete parking lot still created rainbows in the wall of windows. The familiar clatter of kids hummed around her just like any other lunch period.

She did not understand why they left Houston. It was difficult to make friends in a new place. She had several friends in her class at her old school. One girl in particular, Pam, had been her best friend since the first grade.

Pam's mother worked during the day. Missy's mom worked mostly at night and on weekends. After school, the two girls played together at Missy's until her friend's mother came for her.

The kids in her class at the new school were friendly enough, but it was not like having a best friend. The girls she had met at the horse shows were older, and were over at the junior high building. They weren't very friendly anyway. She would like to have at least one friend like Pam, the girl in Houston.

And now Mom was gone. The meeting in Los Angeles was very important, Mom had said. She wouldn't be gone long, and Rux, Juanita and Emilio would take care of her until she got back. Then she and her mom would move to Los Angeles. Rux and Chester were coming, too.

Missy thought she understood. Rux, Juanita and Emilio were nice, and a lot of fun. But they were grownups, not friends. Horses were her friends now, especially Chester.

She walked out to the playground, plopped into an empty swing seat and watched the boys playing kickball. Though the air was cool, the midday sun felt warm on her face. Maybe she would just sit here all day.

Swinging in the sun was much more pleasant that dealing with arithmetic. Everything about numbers confused her. She didn't understand them and couldn't recall the rules from one problem to the next.

Juanita had her on a strict regimen of herbs and vitamins to correct the problem, but as far as Missy could tell it had not helped. Juanita assured her it would. Just give it a little time.

Missy felt two girls standing beside her but dared not look up.

"Hi Melissa. We'd like to talk to you for a minute," one of the girls said.

Missy looked up, surprised. She recognized the two from the horse show. The tall one had brown hair, cut short so that she looked even taller.

The other girl, barely reaching the taller girl's shoulder, had a pinched nose and wore glasses.

Missy remembered Rux talking about two girls at the horse show. He called them the stork and the mouse. Each had ridden a big, high stepping horse. Both girls had worn brightly colored coats in the English Pleasure class before changing into the traditional dark suit for the Equitation. Neither of them won a ribbon as best Missy could recall.

"Sure," Missy said, forcing the word around a large lump in her throat. "Please, sit down."

The stork and the mouse exchanged nervous glances, then surveyed the playground swings.

The stork solved the dilemma. "Let's find a bench. We'll be more comfortable."

Missy joined them, but her comfort level sank.

"We saw you at the horse show," the mouse said. "You're a good rider."

"Thank you," Missy said. "Chester's a very good horse. Both of you did well also."

"We'd like you to join our riding club," The stork said. "Several of us ride together on weekends. Would you like to ride with us?"

Missy wished she had Rux's old hat. Often she had seen him peer into his hat when faced with a decision. And he was the smartest person in the world, except for Juanita. She knew everything.

Juanita didn't even own a hat, but Missy suspected she wrote messages in Rux's. "I'll have to ask my mom."

"Okay," the mouse said. "But first you have to go through our secret initiation. You can't tell your mom about it."

"What is that?"

"You have to make a trail ride at night, by yourself," the stork said. "Do you know where Kott's Lake is?"

Missy had never heard of it. "Not exactly," she said.

"We can show you," the stork said. "It's easy to find. It's about ten miles from Pine Knot if you take the highway, but not that far if you cut across the mountain. You can follow an old logging road that runs behind the Ball ranch. That's where you live, isn't it?"

"Yes, but I'm not permitted to ride trails by myself, even in the daytime."

"That's the whole point," the mouse said. "You have to sneak out. No one but us will know. Everyone in the club has done it. There's a full moon this Friday. It'll be easy to pick up the old logging road. Do you know where the natural bridge is?"

"Yes." Missy's comfort level rose with the excitement.

"All you have to do is take that trail on past the bridge and you will come to the logging road," the stork said. "Go east away from town and you'll come to the lake. You will be back before anyone knows you're gone."

* * *

Missy's apprehension grew steadily as the afternoon wore on. Maybe I should tell Rux, she thought. But he would tell her mom and that would be against the rules.

She hopped off the school bus and looked over the ranch. Rux was working on a fence beyond the barn. Missy ran to the kitchen.

Juanita greeted her as she came through the back door. "Hello, Missy. How was school today?"

"Okay, I guess." She accepted the handful of pills and glass of water Juanita handed her. "I have to go talk to Rux," she managed to say between swallowing vitamins."

"You have homework?"

"Yes, I'll be right back."

Missy raced out the door and across the carpet of brown winter grass separating the house and the barn.

Juanita called from the kitchen window, "Watch where you step. You got your good shoes on."

Rux saw her coming and hooked his claw hammer on the top fence rail. "Hey, little lady. You missed second base. Better run back and touch it or you'll be out."

Missy slowed and looked behind her. "Where?"

"Right there." Rux pointed to what looked to be a pile of dried horse droppings.

She ran back and kicked the "base", which turned out not to be dry underneath.

"Aw, Rux, these are my good school shoes."

He was bent over the fence again, but she could see his grin.

"Do you know where Kott's Lake is?" Missy asked.

"Sort of. I think it's east of here."

"How far? Could we ride up there?"

"I'm not sure. But it's up in the mountains a ways. I'm guessing that would be a pretty good ride. Why?"

"Oh, nothing. Just curious."

* * *

Chester greeted Missy with a low, guttural nicker, the soft sound a mare makes to her foal. Missy waited to see if Rux heard. No movement came from the foaling room. She circled away from the barn to the hay shed in the back pasture where she had left her tack.

They were soon under way. The trail was easy to find in the bright moonlight, even though she had gotten a late start. She couldn't leave until Rux got in from Moose Ball's and went to bed. The moon was high but still brilliant.

The frigid air numbed her, but Missy had a jacket, her gloves and a rain slicker with a hood. Occasionally she would lean forward and warm her nose against Chester's neck.

She passed the natural bridge and shortly picked up the faded tracks of the old logging road. Missy paused to recall the directions. Pine Knot would be to her left, Kott's lake to her right. It wouldn't take long.

Clouds occasionally obliterated the moon, leaving her in fearful darkness. She did not stop. The road always reappeared with the moonlight.

Near the top of a ridge the road divided, forcing her to pause. She did not remember her new friends saying anything about which fork to take. The left fork appeared to go down over the ridge while the right fork apparently continued upward. Rux had said the lake was up in the mountains. She took the right fork.

Missy began to question her choice as the road climbed over large, flat rocks, then disappeared altogether. She wished she had Rux's hat. Or at least the wisdom written in it by Juanita. A sudden gust of wind told Missy Mother Nature was about to provide her own brand of wisdom.

Dark clouds eliminated the moon totally. Blowing snow, driven by strong wind gusts, whipped at her sideways. Missy pulled on her rain slicker and turned Chester back toward the fork. But the road and the moonlight were gone. They wandered through large boulders and pines with no particular direction other than following the down slope of the terrain.

Missy trembled violently. From the cold, she convinced herself, although she wanted to cry. The shaking left her bone weary and exhausted. She could cry, she thought. No one would hear her. The realization of that released the tears.

Crying relieved some of her tension but Missy still needed to rest. The leeward side of a mass of boulders allayed the insistent wind.

Missy dismounted and climbed to a small crevice. She pulled her legs up, tucked the rain slicker under her and rested her head on her arms. "We can't be too far from home," she said to the horse. "But you look like you need a break. We'll rest just for a minute."

Deep sleep came easily.

Missy startled, and almost slid off the rock. The snow had stopped and the moonlight blinked off and on as clouds darted across the night sky. Oh, no, she thought, I forgot to tie Chester.

The horse stood at the base of the rock, knotted reins draped loosely over the saddle. His pose mimicked the motionless boulders as he cocked his ears forward and stared into the trees. One ear flicked backward as Missy called to him.

"Chester, what is it?" She lifted herself with her hands to edge back down the rock, then froze. The eerie sound of wolves howling echoed across the mountain.

"Oh, no," she whimpered. "Chester, please don't run. Come here, boy." she scooted down the rock to the ground. Though trembling and sobbing, she somehow managed to climb back in the saddle. Wolves won't attack a horse, she assured herself.

The flickering moonlight revealed no trace of the trail.

"Go home, Chester. Go home."

Fourteen

Without waking, Rux eased into twilight slumber between conscious and unconscious, The kind of sleep where you can hear yourself snore and manipulate your dreams. Rector Richter would be by soon for more help in keeping the Red "C" from extreme unction. Until then, Saturday mornings were a time for orchestrating dreams in anticipation of Sammi's return.

The subject of his dream faded as someone knocked on the door.

"Rux, are you awake?" Juanita called.

"Do I want to be?"

"Have you seen Missy this morning?".

Rux suddenly became very awake. He fumbled into his pants and jerked open the door. "What did you say?"

"I can't find Missy. She was asleep when we went to bed last night. Normally she sleeps late on Saturday and comes down for breakfast about nine. I checked on her at nine thirty. She's not in her room."

"Maybe she got up earlier and is out fooling with the horses. Did you ask Emilio?"

"He hasn't seen her. I've looked in the barn and around the pastures. Chester's gone also. Do you think she went trail riding by herself?"

"She shouldn't, but maybe she did. I'll saddle up one of the mares and go look for her. If Rector Richter shows up, tell him I'll be back shortly. She wouldn't go far."

The mare's disposition soured considerably when Rux opened the barn door enough to lead her outside. The landscape, whitened with several inches of fresh snow, did not suggest a day for casual trail riding. Bright sunshine offered little comfort from the stiff north wind.

The horse attempted to bow her back when Rux mounted, but firm hands and taut legs convinced her to head out across the pasture to the back gate. Rux picked up one of the three trails they normally used and spurred the mare. The snow yielded no sign of tracks, but could have covered them up as well. He wasn't exactly sure when the snow had stopped, although he recalled the storm blowing in around two o'clock. Surely, he thought, Missy would not have ridden out in the middle of the night.

Twenty minutes of riding turned up no sign of a lost girl or a lost horse. Rux reined the mare around and loped back to pick up another trail. As he neared the ranch he heard horns honking. Good, they've found her, he thought. He hurried the mare back to the gate.

His good news turned out to be Emilio and Rector Richter driving around the pastures honking, apparently hoping a lost Missy would find them.

Emilio hopped out of the truck and opened the gate for Rux. "Maybe you better go call the sheriff," Emilio said, "see if he can get us some help."

Rux nodded and squeezed the mare into a steady gallop. Inside the house he found Juanita in the living room with the phone cradled between her shoulder and her ear. Her hands waved in an awkward disunion, mocking a hand bell choir without the bells.

"Here, it's Sheriff Mohlmann," Juanita said, handing the phone to Rux. "I'm not making any sense."

"Rux, what's going on out there?" the sheriff said. "Best I could tell from Juanita she hasn't seen Missy since last night."

"We think she's out riding. One of the horses is missing also. I didn't think she would go far but we can't find her."

"There's a lot of wilderness out behind you. She may have gotten lost. Highway Patrol's got a chopper. Let me get them moving and I'll be right out."

Rux slapped himself up side the head. "Sheriff, you still there? How far is Kott's Lake from here?"

"Hold on. Lemme look at a map. I'd say thirty to thirty five miles from Pine Knot, maybe twenty from where you are. Why?"

"Missy asked me about it the other day. Never occurred to me she would try to go up there. How would she get there on horseback?"

"Looks like there's an old logging road a couple of miles north of the ranch."

"How would I get to the road in my truck?"

"There's a cutoff from the road leading to the ranch, but the logging road plays out several miles before it gets to the lake. It might be quicker to take a horse and pick up the road behind the ranch. I'll send a deputy with a radio so we can stay in touch."

The fifteen minute wait for the radio proved an eternity. The sun said noon as Rux and the mare again headed out the back gate toward the natural bridge. He loped the horse as best he could through the rocks and trees, reaching the logging road about half an hour past the natural bridge.

"Sheriff Mo, this is Rux. Come in."

"Go ahead, Rux. Over."

"Are you airborne yet? Over."

"Not yet. Should be here any time now. Over."

"Okay. I'm on the logging road, headed up the mountain. Call me when you're leaving with the chopper. Rux out."

The road provided better footing than the trail. Rux spurred the mare into a hand gallop, slowing her when she needed to catch her wind.

Apprehension and determination set his jaw. They would find Missy. He was sure of that. But how would he explain this to Sammi?

This parenting business sure has its drawbacks, he thought.

He walked the mare and leaned down to study the road bed. There was still no evidence of hoof prints. He dismissed the thought that he was just guessing Missy came up here. Right now, he needed assurance that he knew what he was doing.

I'll find her pretty quick, he thought. Chester could make it to Kott's Lake and back on three legs. My guess is they're headed straight to us right now. He spurred the mare again.

The radio crackled. "Rux, this is Sheriff Mo. Come in."

Rux reined the horse to a slow walk. "Rux here. Over."

"We are airborne. Should be over you in about ten minutes. Are you still on the logging road? Over."

"Yes. Over."

"Okay. If she's up there you'll find her. We'll crisscross the area between the ranch and the lake. Chopper out."

Rux continued at a slower pace, looking for side trails and listening for sounds from a horse or a lost child. Although, he thought, Chester's probably not lost. He'll find his way back to the barn if Missy will let him.

He topped a ridge and skidded to a halt. The helicopter clattered overhead. Rux looked up and waved as the chopper paused over him, then motioned them to continue on.

A few yards farther up the ridge the road forked, heading off in two different directions. The left trail led down off the ridge and the right one appeared to wind further up the mountain. Rux took off his hat and contemplated it. If Missy came up here, he had no way of knowing which way she went. He studied the two trails, trying to figure out what Einstein would do. He'd probably be in the chopper, Rux thought. Wisdom from the hat interrupted his version of calculus.

"She went up," Rux said to the mare.

The horse flicked one ear back in acknowledgment.

"I told her Kott's Lake was up, like up in the mountains. Let's go."

He wheeled the horse around to the right fork. Radio static summoned his attention. "Rux, this is the sheriff again. Come in."

"Rux here. Over."

"We've got her. She's coming down the mountain, right toward you. Maybe half a mile. She sees us, appears to be all right. Over."

"Got it. Is there more than one trail up there or will I meet her if I take the right fork? Over."

"Only one trail. We'll stay here until you catch up to her. Sheriff out."

Rux charged the mare up the trail, guiding her over rocks and around pine branches. Within two minutes an obviously tired horse with his equally exhausted little rider plodded out of a pine thicket toward him.

As soon as she saw him, Missy stopped Chester and slid to the ground. Rux rode to her, dismounted, and swept the child into his arms.

"I'm so sorry," Missy tried to say through her blubbering.

Rux was in no better shape to carry on a conversation, but did manage to shush her. "It's okay, Missy, I'm here."

Rux freed one hand and gathered up the reins of both horses as the chopper approached. The noise of the helicopter lowering over them drowned out Missy and spooked the horses.

The radio crackled again. Missy clung to his waist while he freed his other arm to pluck the radio from his belt.

"Rux, this is the sheriff. Can you hear me? Over."

"Barely. Over."

"Everybody okay down there? Over."

"I think so. Let me see if Missy can make it to the ranch on horseback. If not, maybe you can set down on the logging road and pick her up. Hold on. Over."

Rux hesitated, then pulled Missy from him and knelt down to face her. "Are you okay, Miss?" he asked.

Missy nodded.

"Can you ride on back or do you want the helicopter to pick you up?"

Missy looked at Rux, then up at the chopper. She had taken her hat off and the wind from the helicopter's blades whipped her hair in several directions. She shouted to make herself heard.

"I can ride."

"Okay, Sheriff," Rux said into the radio. "We can make it back to the ranch. Thanks for your help. Rux out."

Rux watched Sheriff Mo and the pilot wave as they banked hard right and headed down the mountain towards Pine Knot. A welcome silence settled around them, interrupted only by the wind swaying the trees and Missy's sniffling.

He pulled her to him, then slackened the reins to let the horses root in the snow for the sparse mountain grasses hiding among the rocks.

"I'm sorry," Missy managed to say before the tears came again.

"Hey, everything's okay now. You ready to head back?"

Missy nodded. Rux picked her up and sat her on his mare. He climbed up behind her and took Chester's reins.

"You all right?" Rux asked.

Missy smiled and wiped her tears. "I am now."

They plodded along in silence for several minutes, winding their way down to the logging road. Missy leaned against Rux and let her head slowly drift toward her chest, bracing herself periodically as the horse eased around the rocks.

"Rux," Missy whispered, "you were right about the wolves."

"Really?" Rux said. "Did you run into them?"

"We heard them. Chester...." She paused, obviously trying not to cry again.

"It's okay, Miss. You can tell me later."

The tears came in earnest.

Once they reached the smoother grade of the logging road, the mare's easy gait rocked Missy to sleep.

Sheriff Mohlmann, Rector Richter, Juanita and Emilio were waiting for them at the back gate. The crying and the "poor babys" started all over as Rux lowered Missy to Juanita. Emilio took Chester's reins and the Padre drove Missy and Juanita to the house in the Red "C."

"How's she doing?" the sheriff asked as they walked the horses to the barn.

"She'll be okay, I think," Rux said. "A little shook up, as you might imagine. They apparently ran into some wolves. But she actually nodded off to sleep on the way here."

"I'm sure she's exhausted," the sheriff said. "Did she say how long she'd been gone, or how far she went?"

"No. Hard for her to talk without crying."

Emilio asked, "Have any idea why she went off up there by herself?"

Rux took off his hat, wiped his forehead with his sleeve and shook his head. "Don't know. Guess after she's rested a bit she'll tell us what's going on. Sheriff, you need to fill out some sort of report?"

"Eventually," the sheriff said. "Got to explain what we were doing with the state's helicopter. No rush, though. Main thing now is to be sure the girl doesn't need any medical attention. I'll go on up to the house in case I'm needed. See you guys in a minute."

Twenty minutes later, Rux and Emilio joined the rest of the adults in the kitchen. Missy had been given a hot bath and put to bed. Juanita, still rumpled from her long day of worrying, was rummaging in the refrigerator looking for sandwich makings.

Rector Richter poured coffee as Juanita ferried bread, lunch meat, cheese and various fixings to the table.

Sheriff Mo dug a knife into the mayonnaise and slapped a healthy dose on his bread. "Juanita," he asked, "did Missy say anything about where she was going, or why?"

"Not really. She's worn out. I'll try to find out more when she wakes up."

"Or when you wake up," Sheriff Mo said. "Looks like you could use some sleep yourself, little lady."

"Oh, hi, Miss," Rux said.

All four heads swiveled to the door leading into the living room. A slump-shouldered little girl in red pajamas and Winnie-the-Pooh house shoes got as far as the door and leaned against it.

Juanita said, "Come over here and sit down, baby. Couldn't you sleep?"

Missy climbed into Juanita's lap, her long legs almost touching the floor. "I'm not sleepy," she said. Her droopy eyelids suggested otherwise. "I wanted to explain to Sheriff Mohlmann what happened."

Juanita shifted in her chair so Missy would be facing the sheriff, and brushed the girl's hair out of her eyes. Missy took a hand full of potato chips, apparently collecting her thoughts.

"Sheriff Mohlmann," Missy said, "I'm sorry. I really am. I knew better than to go up there by myself."

"Never you mind, Missy," the sheriff said. "All of us do things we shouldn't now and then. Where exactly is the 'up there' you went to?"

"I was headed to Kott's Lake, but I didn't make it. We got caught in a storm...." Missy looked at Rux, then back to Sheriff Mo. "Somewhere up on the mountain. So we turned around to come back. Only by then we...I was lost. Chester knew the way back. I just gave him his head and told him to go home."

Sheriff Mo threw coffee down after the half sandwich he had just eaten in one bite. "What's at Kott's Lake?"

Missy looked around the table, then lowered her head.

Rux sensed the need to break the tension. "Fish," he said.

The laughter relaxed everyone a little, including Missy.

Sheriff Mo picked up the tease. "You went fishing? Without a fishing pole?"

Missy displayed an embarrassed smile. "No, two girls at school asked me to join their riding club. They have a secret initiation. You have to ride by yourself up to Kott's Lake and back, at night. No one outside the club is supposed to know." She looked at the sheriff. "I guess I didn't make the club, did I?"

Sheriff Mo leaned back in his chair. "I don't know if there is such a club, but I don't think any of them have made a ride up to Kott's Lake and back. That would be a hard two days' ride through some pretty wild country. I'm not sure I could find my way up there even in the daylight."

Missy lowered her eyes again, then looked up at Sheriff Mo. "There are wolves up there," she said.

"I know, "the sheriff said. "Ranchers killed them all off years ago. But some self-righteous environmental group trapped a bunch down in Mexico and released them up in the mountains again. Rux said you ran into them."

"We heard them," Missy said. She began to tear up again.

Juanita pulled Missy tight against her breast. "Oh, no," she said. "What happened?"

Missy cried softly for a minute, then composed herself. "I got down to rest, and I didn't tie Chester 'cause I was going to get right back on him. But I must have dozed off. When I heard the wolves howling I got scared Chester would run off."

"Well, obviously he didn't," the sheriff said.

Missy nodded. "He stayed to protect me. And he got us home."

Juanita lowered her to the floor and stood up. "I think you should try to get some rest. Sheriff, do you need anything else?"

"Not right now."

Juanita wrapped her arms around Missy and guided her to the living room. Missy turned as she got to the door. She paused and caught her breath. "Chester didn't run," she repeated.

"Horses are like that," Rux said. "They'll protect someone they really love, even if it's against their natural instincts. One more thing, Miss. Who were the girls that put you up to this?"

"I don't know their names. They were at the horse show a couple of weeks ago."

Rux asked, "Was one of them tall like a stork, with short brown hair? And the other one short, mousy looking?"

"Yes, that's them."

Missy and Juanita continued their trek up stairs. Rux stepped to the counter, retrieved the coffee pot and filled everyone's cup. "Do you know who those girls are?" he asked the sheriff.

Sheriff Mo slurped down his coffee, stood and picked up his hat from the rack by the back door. "Think so. Guess I'd better have a little talk with their parents. This could have been a disaster."

Rux followed him through the living room to the front porch. "Listen, Sheriff, do you think it's a good idea to say anything to the parents? Missy has to go to school with those kids. They could really make it hard on her."

The sheriff walked down the steps and opened the door to his patrol car. "Can't afford to let this happen again. Next time, someone could get seriously hurt. I'll be sure the parents tell the kids not to bother Missy. Besides, half the town is wondering what that chopper was doing up here. Need to tell them something."

"You're right," Rux said. "Why don't you tell everyone Missy just rode over to Kott's Lake and back, by herself. Didn't need the chopper after all."

Sheriff Mo laughed as he climbed into his car. "Sounds good to me."

* * *

Late that evening, Sammi returned Rux's call. He was just as happy Missy spoke with her first, while Emilio retrieved him from the foaling room. Rux stopped in the kitchen, but stood close enough to the door to hear Missy explaining her venture to her mother. She was apparently making sure Sammi understood no one else was at fault. Finally, she said her "I love yous" and "good-byes," and handed the phone to Rux.

"Listen, Sam. I am so sorry. I had no idea...."

"Rux, it's okay. Please don't feel like you have to apologize. I'm as shocked as you are that Missy would do something like that. You got her back safely, that's the important thing."

"Well, me and Chester. Mainly Chester."

Sammi laughed. The conversation continued with their usual teasing, but their was something in her tone that bothered him. He dismissed it as the stress of learning about Missy's ordeal.

"Sam, are you coming back?"

"I, uh, well...."

Rux could hear her breathing during the long pause.

"Do you think I need to? Is Missy okay?"

That really stumped him. He had expected her to be rushing to the airport. "I suppose. She seems fine now. I guess I kinda thought, well, you know. She might need you."

Sammi hesitated again before responding. "Missy said everything was okay. I don't think she'll do anything like that again. I have another recording session for the demo tape next week, then I'll be back. Do you...is that all right with you?"

This time Rux hesitated. Something was wrong. "Is everything okay?"

"Sure, why?"

"Nothing. Yeah, another week is fine with us if you think Missy can handle this without you."

"Oh, Rux, don't...."

A long silence followed what sounded like Sammi choking back a sob. Rux pictured her holding a hand over the receiver, trying to compose herself. Guess it's just my day for consoling crying women, he thought.

"Sammi?"

"Yes, I'm here. Sorry. Look, I'll check back with you tomorrow night. If anything comes up in the meantime, call me here at the hotel. Give my love to Juanita and Emilio. I can't tell you how much I appreciate everything you guys are doing for me."

Rux walked back through the kitchen, conveyed Sammi's message to

Juanita and Emilio, and headed for the barn. Countless stars decorated the night sky but shed no light on his perplexity. Sammi seemed genuinely upset, as he expected her to be. So why would she wait another week to come back?

Oh, well, he thought. What can happen in a week?

It occurred to him that he had asked that exact same question last week.

Fifteen

A week later, Rux struggled out of a deep sleep, trying to determine if he was dreaming or if he had actually heard a distant scream. Lights were on in the house, suggesting he had better go check. A haggard Emilio opened the back door.

"What's up, amigo?" Rux asked.

"Come on in, Rux. I don't know. We heard Missy scream and rushed up to her room. Juanita seemed to understand as soon as she saw her. She asked me to stay down here."

Rux and Emilio paced the kitchen floor, exchanging nervous glances like expectant fathers as they waited for Juanita to come downstairs.

"Amigo," Rux said, "we need a caffeine fix."

Emilio shrugged, extracted the hot macadamia nut cocoa powder from the cabinet and set a pot of milk on the stove.

Juanita finally lumbered in, slumped into the straight-backed dining chair and adjusted her bulk to envelop the cane seat. Dawn would not appear for another hour.

"Nothing to worry about," she said. "Missy started her period."

"Period!" Rux said. "Are you sure? She's only nine."

"She's ten now," Juanita said. "A little young, but it happens."

"Good Lord," Rux said. "Juanita, I'm so glad you're here."

Juanita ladled several spoons of hot cocoa into a saucer and gently blew it. "Why?" she said. "Are you going to start yours too?"

"Juanita, I'm serious," Rux said in a rare moment of seriousness. "What would have happened if you hadn't been here? I wouldn't know how to deal with anything like this."

"I told you, you should have spent more time with that goat. No, forget that. You're right. Everything is fine for now. I explained to Missy what was going on, and she seemed to understand. But this is a very delicate time in that child's life. She needs her mother."

"Sammi'll call tonight," Rux said. "Maybe she'll have some news about when she's coming back."

"Let's hope so," Juanita said. "Meanwhile, Rux, you'll have to be the father figure for Missy. Heaven help her."

Rux leaned over to Emilio and whispered, "What's a father figure?"

Juanita rolled her eyes and reached for a pot holder. Rux and Emilio headed for the back door.

* * *

An hour later, Rux and Chester were on the trail. Chester hesitated to gather his footing, then lunged up the sudden incline in the trail leading to the rim above Deke's ranch. The horse did not seem to mind the cold.

Rux kept first one hand and then the other tucked between Chester and the saddle blanket to avoid frost bite. He thought seriously on how to stick his nose under the blanket and stay in the saddle at the same time.

Down below, the ranch meant walls to be painted, fences to be mended, horses to be tended and stalls to be cleaned. From the top of the rim the snow-dusted buildings gave the appearance of a Christmas card scene.

Rux had the feeling he had stepped outside the world and was viewing it as it really existed. He also felt as though he had stepped outside himself.

Since he left home his life had been free of entangling alliances, excepting of course his romance and marriage with Betty Jo Follmer. The big-time trainers in the Arabian horse industry were always wife-swapping or getting involved with their clients.

Rux never qualified for the big-time, being relegated to green-breaking horses along with the younger trainers aspiring to reach Lothario status.

For the first time in his life he had a responsibility, a delicate child he could not walk away from even if he wanted to. And he missed Sammi.

How did I get caught up in all of this? he wondered. The answer floated back to him as if she were right there, behind the counter pouring his coffee, smiling her shy smile and cutting her eyes to meet his.

Their love affair he could understand, at least from his perspective. Sammi seemed to rely on him for security, like an old blanket. But now she had apparently invited him to share her life, trusting him with Missy.

He couldn't even muddle through the child rearing part, at least not without Juanita. Throwing in with Sammi and her soon to be glamorous lifestyle of a country and western star would take some serious hat studying. Looking at yourself could be painful, he decided.

"Come on, Chester," he said, reining the horse around to retrace their trail back to the ranch. "We need to find the quickest way to get these two women back together. Meanwhile, one of us has to be a father figure, and I doubt it'll be you. Nothing personal, you understand."

Chester kept his ears forward, obviously more interested in the trail ahead than the babbling of his rider. "Tell you what, Chester. If Sammi's not back in a week, me and you and Missy will just pack up and go to California."

The snow had stopped and a hint of blue sky appeared in the west. As soon as the weather cleared, Rux and Joe Hawkins were due to help Ray Talliferro put up a new fence. Stringing wire would be a relief, he thought. How much trouble can I get into building a fence?

Sixteen

Great Apache warriors earned their lofty position in battle. Less ominous circumstances did not require the holder of the position to assert his dominance, particularly if a meaningful wage hung in the balance. Apaches had always been survivors.

A week of relatively mild weather had allowed Rux, Joe Hawkins and Ray Talliferro to string a new barbed wire fence around most of Ray's front pasture.

Joe leaned his large shoulders into the hammer, keeping the barbed wire stretched tight against the fence post while Rux nailed.

Clouds had been gathering for the last hour, and the wind had begun whistling through the pines.

"Better hurry," Joe said. "You gonna be trying to hit them nails in a snow storm."

"Let's finish this post and give it up," Ray said. "It's already colder'n a Klondike miner's tweet twat."

Joe hoisted the wire spool onto the open tailgate of Ray's pickup parked in the bar ditch as Ray fired up his old D-9 tractor.

"Want me to drive the truck up to the house for you?" Joe asked.

"Naw," Ray yelled over the clattering of the ancient engine. "Go on home before the snow gets any worse. I'll come back and get it after supper. It's parked far enough off the highway. Nobody will bother it till I get back."

Rux tossed his tools in the back of Ray's pickup and headed for his truck.

"Buy you a beer?" Joe yelled to Rux.

"You ought to get home before this storm cuts loose," Rux said. "But if you're headed into town I'll meet you at Moose's."

Joe pulled up the collar on his jacket and mounted his Harley. The old war horse fired on the first crank. Rux knew it could not do otherwise. A warrior trusted his steed to move quickly if the need arose. Snow swirling in a cold wind suggested need had arisen. The great Apache warrior headed for Pine Knot and Moose Ball's.

Rux followed dutifully in his truck. We ought to be headed for the house, he thought. But he could always spare a few minutes for a friend, particularly one buying the beer. If Joe Hawkins offered to buy the beer, it usually meant he needed to talk about something.

Rux had asked about Auren several times during the course of their fence building. Joe always answered with a terse reply, then changed the subject. Rux wondered if there might be trouble in the old teepee.

"There's gonna be trouble if he doesn't slow down," Rux said to himself as the motorcycle disappeared into the blinding snow.

Rux ducked into the door of the bar, glad for a momentary respite from the biting cold. Joe had a table and two beers waiting.

"Thanks," Rux said. "Joe, what are we doing in these mountains in the dead of winter?"

"I was born here, I'm used to this. Old West Texas boy like you ain't, though. Why didn't you head on down to Los Angeles with Sammi?"

I wish I had, Rux thought. But the issue is not me and the weather, it's getting Missy back with her mother. "Aw, she's with a real band now," he said. "Even doing some recordings. That ain't no place for a worn out old cow puncher with more broke knuckles than he's got fingers."

Joe slid his hunting knife off his belt and laid it on the table, tilted his chair back and downed half his beer. "Well, I'm no music 'connie sewer' but I gotta tell you, there's magic between you and Sammi. Everybody can see it when you perform. Not just your voices. Your bodies seem to blend without touching."

"You ain't finished your first beer yet and you're already getting poetic on me."

"That's why you're not supposed to give firewater to us redskins. In all seriousness, though, whether you perform with Sammi or not, you ought to be thinking on marrying her and raising that little daughter of hers."

Rux laughed and lifted his beer mug in a toast. "Why not?" he said. "Here's to wishful thinking and more drinking. How's that for cowboy poetry." At least I got the child raising part, Rux thought to himself. "Speaking of dreaming, how did you meet Auren?"

"Met her at a powwow in Chickasha, Oklahoma. We used to travel around the country with a group of native American activists protesting the desecration of our ancestral burial grounds."

"What'd you do? Lay down in front of the bulldozers?"

"If it got that far we'd let the ancestors take care of themselves. We weren't anxious to join them. Usually, though, a state agency was involved, either wanting to display the remains or issue permits to a developer wanting to destroy a burial site. We tried to shame or intimidate the people in the agencies."

Rux could readily understand how most bureaucrats would be intimidated by the mere presence of Joe Hawkins. The hawk-like stare of this massive figure with a long, black pony tail and arms hanging almost to his knees would test the resolve of any white man. Joe claimed to be the reincarnation of the great Apache chief, Mangus Colorado. No one disputed him.

Joe said, "One poor guy down in Texas even resigned. Somehow, he thought we were a threat to his family."

"What gave him that idea?"

Joe chuckled and took a drink. "Nothing. He kept making the point that the burials involved were Karankawa, and they were known to be cannibals. I just reminded him that he himself was Jewish and, at one point in their history, the Jews were trapped and starving, so they ate their own children.

"I also told him of an old Indian legend about a band of Karankawas that once killed a Jewish settler, and out of respect for his religion they ate his children."

"He resigned over that?"

"Well, I did add that, if he wasn't careful, we would bury him and eat his children. Not as a threat, mind you, just a little biblical allegory."

Rux choked on his beer.

"Occasionally," Joe continued, "we could get some politicians on our side. But Auren proved to be our best weapon. At every protest television cameras and still photographers would capture that haunting beauty of her dark eyes, looking off in the distance as though she could see the pain of our ancestors in the next life."

The storm drove in a couple of Joe's drinking buddies. They hollered their beer orders to Deke as they made their way to join Joe and Rux.

One of them greeted Joe with his usual, "Hold on to your scalps boys, the Indians are on the warpath again."

Joe slapped both men on the back and mockingly reached for his hunting knife.

"Ain't you supposed to check that thang with the sheriff when you come into town?" one buddy said.

The barmaid arrived with the beer before Joe's cronies settled in their chairs.

"Knife's harmless," Joe said. "Sheriff don't wanna be checking my real weapon."

Rux knew what their comeback would be and figured Joe was just getting his revenge in advance. Joe's drinking buddies always hoorahed him unmercifully for spending his evenings at Moose Ball's while his lovely wife waited at home. They all used their most sensuous prose in referring to Auren. Most of them did not even add the tag, "for an Indian," normally used by white men in describing a native American.

His cohorts assured Joe they were all there because of their wives, but they wouldn't be if they had someone like Auren at home. Joe did not disagree.

124

"Auren is a goddess," Joe said, "and I worship the very ground she walks on. But I am a great Apache warrior. Warriors come and go as they please. Our women understand this."

The buddies spewed beer across the table, unable to control their laughter long enough to swallow.

"Hey, Rux," Deke yelled from the bar. "Sammi's on the phone."

Rux ducked behind the bar and covered his free ear, trying to block out the noise of the juke box and the afternoon revelry. "Hi, Sam, where are you?"

"I'm in Bakersfield. We have a gig up here."

"Heck, I was hoping you were at the Phoenix airport, calling for me to come pick you up."

"That's sweet. I wish I were, but I can't come back just yet. We have several gigs lined up, and I still need to cut my demo tape."

Her last remark sounded ominous. The taping should have been done a week ago. "What happened on your earlier tape session?"

"I've had two, but my singing is flat. There's no emotion. I didn't realize there is so much difference in performing before a live audience and in a sterile studio. There's no crowd to feed your energy. I need something to get me pumped up, excited, like when we're playing at Moose's. You know, the place gets to rocking and you can't help but get high."

The word "high" struck another chord. Rux remembered their conversation about drugs to get high for performances. It would be just as easy to take uppers if you needed a high to record. He thought their mutual "exercise" after the shows had convinced her she didn't need the drugs.

"Does Vaughn have any suggestions?" he asked.

"Yes, he's got me listening to tapes of live performances and doing some pop psycho stuff before I go in. Maybe that will work eventually."

"Should I bring Missy on out?"

"Oh, I would love to have you and Missy here. But right now we're on the road, and I really haven't had time to find us a place to live or a school for her."

"She really misses you, Sam. She needs you."

"I know. I'm such a bad mother. But you guys are doing fine. It won't be much longer, I promise."

After the conversation, Rux sat behind the bar and studied his new hat. I guess another week or so won't make that much difference, he thought. But I've got to get my old hat back. This one's useless.

He toyed with the idea of calling Sammi back to inquire about the well being of his hat, then realized he didn't know where to reach her.

Rux hurried out to the ranch to be there when Missy's bus arrived.

Once satisfied that she was safely home, fed and sufficiently entertained for the evening, he returned to Moose Ball's for his Thursday evening performance. The crowd would be small, mainly a few locals willing to brave the weather and some of the skiers in town for the week. Plus he could not provide the charisma of Sammi Stone, but then, who could?

Joe sat alone as Rux reentered Moose's. Rux shook the snow from his hat and coat and tossed them in the dressing room. He went back to check on the Indian, although he was sure he would find him sober. No matter what time he began drinking, Joe always paced himself so that he would not be totally drunk until closing time.

"How's it going?" Rux asked.

"I'm cold and I'm sober," Joe said. "Why don't we move closer to the heater and have another drink?"

"I've got to get started on the show. Don't you think you should go on home? Auren's probably pretty worried with you out in this storm."

"I am a great Apache warrior," Joe started into his spiel.

"I know," Rux interrupted. "Great Apache warriors come and go as they please. I was here earlier, remember? I'm sure it would please your wife greatly if you were at home with her on a night like this."

"Deke won't appreciate you running off his customers. Here's to wishful thinking and more drinking." Joe hoisted his empty mug and signaled for another beer.

Rux leaned across the table and grasped Joe's arm. "Whatever the problem is," Rux said, "Drinking ain't gonna solve it. I thought warriors faced their enemy head on."

Black eyes glowering from beneath a heavy brow reminded Rux why the bureaucrats wilted underneath Joe's stare. But he thought he detected a twinge of pain just before heavy eyelids curtained the man's inner soul.

"Maybe...there ain't no enemy to face," Joe said, and exchanged his empty mug for the full one brought by the barmaid.

"Maybe," Rux said. He slapped Joe on the back and headed for the stage.

Rux's mellow voice had left with Sammi but his raspy singing fit well with the honky-tonk music. He normally ignored Sammi's love ballads still in the computer, but for some reason their closing number, "Somewhere Out There," kept rattling through his mind as he performed. Without knowing why, he cued up the song and gave his best rendition of Sammi's lead. The bar and the audience faded as he closed his eyes and sang to the soft, sweet face of Sammi Stone.

He finished with the keyboard flourish and opened his eyes. The entire bar had stopped chattering and sat staring at him. He sought out Joe through the glare of the spotlight and nodded to the great Apache warrior. "Here's to wishful thinking, and making those wishes come true."

Joe began a slow applause. Gradually, the audience joined him, building into a standing ovation that threatened to blow the doors off the old saloon. For a brief moment Rux sensed Sammi on stage with him. He gave the Rux Philharmonic a much needed break.

Several hours later, Joe concluded his festivities as he did every night by announcing he would henceforth be known only as "Hawk, the great Apache warrior." This clued Deke to eliminate the beer and serve several rounds of hot coffee.

"Snowing pretty good outside, Joe," Sheriff Mohlmann said. "Why don't you let me drive you home?"

"No need. The Hawk will follow the white buffalo."

Rux and the sheriff trailed behind Joe as he made his way outside and mounted his Harley with sufficient dexterity for the ride home. It would be a long, cold journey back to Whiteriver, but Joe assured them Apache warriors often endured the elements.

"The white buffalo leaves clear tracks in the snow for warriors to follow," he said.

Rux wondered if the stupid buffalo might leave tracks for Sammi to follow home from L.A.

* * *

Friday mornings were tough. Rux usually got to bed well after midnight but insisted on getting up to see Missy off to school.

He made his way to the house, noticing the snow had stopped and the skies seemed to be clearing. The smell of freshly brewed coffee greeted him as Juanita opened the door before he could knock.

"Rector Richter just called," she said. "Joe's been in an accident out on the Whiteriver highway, about ten miles beyond Pine Knot. He wants you to meet him there."

Rux stood speechless for several seconds. He spun and hopped off the porch, then turned again toward the kitchen door. "How's Joe?" he asked.

"He didn't say, but it doesn't sound good when they bring your priest to the accident scene. Call us when you know something."

"I will. "Rux ran to his truck and sped out of the yard. As was his nature, he imagined Joe would be okay.

The scene in front of Ray Talliferro's farm convinced him otherwise. Joe's motorcycle rested quietly behind Ray's pickup, apparently having been dragged from underneath the truck. The Padre knelt over Joe, or what was left of him, lying on a stretcher behind the ambulance.

Sheriff Mohlmann and a deputy busied themselves around the pickup while Ray and his wife stood several feet away, holding each other and crying. Rux walked over to the Talliferros and placed his arms around them. Their trembling would have registered on a seismograph.

"I forgot about that damned truck," Ray sobbed. "Sat down to watch television after dinner and plum forgot about it. Remembered it this morning. That's when I found Joe."

"It's okay," Rux said. "The truck is way off the road. No one should have hit it. Don't blame yourself."

Ray looked up at Rux and tried to respond, but his voice choked. Rux left them with their neighbor from across the highway and waited for either the sheriff or the Padre to finish their official business. The ambulance finally left with Joe, and Rector Richter came over to Rux. The priest was so badly shaken he could not immediately speak.

Sheriff Mohlmann joined them. "Looks like the white buffalo led the great Apache warrior right towards Ray's new fence," he said. "Appears Joe realized it at the last second and swerved, directly into the back of the pickup.

"Tailgate was down, but I'm not sure it would have made any difference at the speed he was going. The motorcycle and Joe's lower torso slammed up underneath the truck, and the top half of him slid into the pickup bed. Almost cut him in half."

"How could you tell how fast he was going?" Rux asked.

"By the distance his eyeballs traveled beyond their sockets. Padre, will you go over and tell Auren?"

"Sure," Rector Richter stammered, his voice barely audible. "Rux, can you come with me, in case we have to tend to the cows or anything?"

"Glad to," Rux said. His skills at consoling new widows graded even below his parenting, but he sensed the Padre needed him for moral support.

A half awake Auren greeted them at the door in her bath robe. She carried a hair brush but obviously had not had time to use it.

"Father Thomas, Rux Come in," she said. "I wasn't expecting...." Her cheerful demeanor changed abruptly. "Where's Joe?" she demanded. "Has something happened?"

"Auren," the Padre said, stepping forward to take her hands. "There's been an accident. Joe is...well, he didn't make it. I'm so sorry."

Before he could finish his sentence, Auren screamed "No! No! No!" Her screams faded as she crumpled toward the floor in a dead faint. Rux helped Rector Richter lay her on the couch, then checked to be sure the clergyman was in control of his faculties.

Satisfied that the Padre could function well enough to perform his priestly duties, whatever they were, Rux went outside to check on the cows. He took several bales of hay and spread them in rows across the lot, then broke the ice off the water troughs with Joe's shovel.

In spite of the cold, he spent the morning examining the cows, the barn, the fences, anything that might need his attention.

Rux didn't object to commiserating, he just did it better with animals than with people. Cows and horses allowed you to pour your guts out without worrying about your choice of words.

"As far as I know," Rux said to the cows, "all animals live in mortal fear of danger or injury, but simply ignore death. Except for elephants. I read once that elephants cry over the death of a herd mate. Me and the elephants that knew Joe will miss him, but I guess you guys don't care as long as someone throws out the hay."

By midmorning, the word had spread and friends and relatives were coming by to help. Rux watched from the barn as a gray-haired old rancher scuffled over from the back porch. A brown, wrinkled hand offered Rux a mug of coffee, then shook hands.

"I'm Farley Smitherman, Joe's uncle," he said. "You had anything to eat?"

The elderly gentleman looked Indian, Rux thought. Farley Smitherman must be English for Red Feather, or something.

"Rux Tuttle, nice to meet you. Naw, I didn't get a chance to eat before I left the house. I'll get something directly."

"Too bad about Joe. Wife and I drove over from Peyson as soon as we heard."

"Yeah, real sad. How's Auren doing?"

"She's still pretty upset. Hanging on to that priest like a possum on its momma's tail. I was the one who married her and Joe, you know."

"You a minister?"

"Naw, I mean, I didn't really marry them like that. They eventually got married in the church, but when Joe first brought her out here they were all into this native American heritage stuff. Wanted to have a traditional Indian ceremony."

"Like what?"

"Well, first they tried to find a Comanche marriage ritual, but there weren't no such thing. All the Comanches did was just mate up, with no public fanfare. So we fixed them up an Apache ceremony."

The uncle paused, took out a sack of Bull Durham and paper, and rolled a cigarette. His dark eyes twinkled behind the puff of smoke as he lit up. He obviously enjoyed telling this story.

"I got to be the father of the bride, see, cause Auren had no folks out here. Joe brought her to stay with us. Then he was obliged to stake his horse outside. This is his proposal of marriage. Now the girl has four days to accept. She does this by feeding and watering the horse. Auren accepted the first day."

"That was fortunate for the horse."

"And for me and Joe. Once she accepted, he had to give me a sufficient number of horses in payment for his bride. I only demanded one, since that's all Joe had, and I didn't want one half-starved."

Rector Richter waved from the porch and Rux started for the house. Uncle Farley followed, obviously intent on finishing his story.

"Then we had the marriage feast. People danced all day and into the night. Course, none of them knew the old Apache dances, so we hired a country and western band. The idea was for Joe and Auren to slip off to a place away from the village for their honeymoon, but we had several old ladies chaperoning them all day. The old ladies finally pretended to fall asleep, and Joe and Auren took off for the Holiday Inn."

Uncle Farley shook Rux's hand again and Rux left with the Padre.

Rux asked, "Did you discuss the funeral arrangements with Auren?"

"No, she's in no condition to do that now. I'll talk with her again tomorrow."

"She may want to have an old Apache burial ceremony."

"What makes you think that?"

"Just a wild guess."

* * *

The following Monday, cold, gray skies greeted the mourners filing into St. Anne's. Auren had opted for a traditional Catholic funeral.

Rux followed Missy, Juanita and Emilio into the dim sanctuary. He settled beside them on a wooden pew near the front and studied the elaborately carved altar and furnishings. A stoical bronze casket rested in front of the altar, closed for obvious reasons.

Auren had insisted on placing Joe's medicine bag, peace pipe and bird bone whistle in the coffin with him.

Rux understood little of the service, most of which was in Latin. What did impress him were the boys in white smocks walking down the aisles swinging smoking pots. The dimness and smoke gave the church the appearance of Moose Ball's.

Eventually, the great Apache warrior was wheeled out, followed by the priest and then Joe's grieving widow. Auren clung to Rector Richter for support.

The rest of the mourners silently trudged out and waited, shivering in the cold as the casket was placed in the hearse. Then they piled into trucks and cars and began the long trek to Whiteriver. There was no snow in which the white buffalo could leave tracks.

The hearse and funeral home limo led them to a little cemetery on a bluff above the river. Hawk was home, finally.

Rux and the other bereaved huddled against the wind as the priest said his words of comfort. Rux noticed Joe's grave site was situated so that his eyes were facing east, assuming someone put them back in his head.

Unable to hear the priest well, Rux comforted himself with the thought that at least Auren didn't mutilate herself and slaughter Joe's cows.

* * *

Two days after Joe's funeral another norther ripped through the mountains, seducing the skiers with more snow and adding to Rux's irritation. Chester, cross-tied in the wash rack, suffered the brunt of his owner's exasperation with his usual "I'm bored" expression. Rux picked furiously at the mud and manure in one rear hoof.

"Sammi hasn't called in a week," he said to the horse. "I'm ready to head for California. Or better still, maybe you and me should just pack it in and get on to Texas."

"Not just yet," a voice said behind him.

"What?" Rux said, turning as far as he could and still hold on to the hoof. "Oh, hello, Padre. Didn't hear you drive up. I thought Chester answered me."

Rux set Chester's leg down and stepped around the horse, noticing that Rector Richter wore a nylon jacket over a heavy wool shirt, open at the collar. "You on sabbatical?"

"How did you...Rux, I need to talk to you."

Auren eased up behind him and popped into the half-light of the forty-watt bulb.

"Hi, Rux. How are you?" she said. Her face glowed. Rector Richter had the sad eyes of a puppy who had just missed his potty training newspaper.

"Hey, Auren," Rux said. "I'm fine, but you look great. Hope you're feeling better."

The Padre took Auren's hand and asked in a low voice if she would mind waiting in the truck while he talked to Rux. The two men fiddled with Chester until she left the barn.

"Rux, Auren's afraid to go back to her house. I was wondering if she could stay here for a few days until she sort of gets back to normal."

"Sure, it's okay by me. There's an extra room in the house. I need to check with Deke, but I'm sure he won't mind. You and Auren go on up and talk to Emilio and Juanita. I'll get Chester in his pajamas and be up in a minute."

"Thanks, Rux. I knew you'd understand. There's one more favor I need to ask before we go to the house."

"Nothing I'd rather do than help out a man of the cloth. I need all the help I can get with the big fella upstairs."

Rector Richter stepped out of the wash rack and looked up and down the barn, apparently making sure no one else could hear him. This is all I need, Rux thought. More snow and now a clandestine priest.

The Padre edged back into the wash rack and walked around to Chester's rear. Rux shuffled a couple of steps closer. Whatever the Padre was up to must be very sensitive if he doesn't even want Chester to hear.

"Rux, I know you were kidding with me when you asked if I was on sabbatical, but I am. At least, I'm going in tomorrow to ask for one. I'm no longer worthy of my robes. Could I possibly bunk with you in the barn for a while?"

Rux noticed Chester had one ear cocked toward Rector Richter, or was it now just plain Tom Richter? "Well, I ain't gonna turn a friend out in the cold, although the foaling room ain't much warmer. You should feel right at home, though. It's kinda like a monastery."

"I've never been in a monastery."

"Good, you won't know the difference. Take Auren on up to the house before she freezes. I'll be along shortly."

Rux turned his attention back to the horse as Rector Richter left. The horse picked up a leg and waited for Rux to clean the hoof.

"Never mind that," Rux said. "Let's bed you down for the night so I can get to my confession booth. I have a feeling I'm going to be playing father confessor to a priest."

As if he were house broken, Chester relieved himself before going into his stall. "My sentiments exactly," Rux said. "Maybe we'll go to California next week."

By the time Rux reached the house, Juanita had already sanctified Auren and the two were busy comparing Juanita's herbal cures with Auren's ancient Indian medicinal practices. Rux called Deke, who found the whole situation very amusing and agreed everyone was welcome to stay as long as they liked.

Rux located a cot for Rector Richter and helped him get set up in the foaling room. The Padre laughed at his host's attempts to brighten his spirits with levity, but the sad expression in his eyes never changed.

"Ain't much entertainment out here," Rux said. "Would you like a book to read?"

Rector Richter sank heavily into the rocker and warmed his hands over the small heater for several minutes before responding. He finally said, "I need to tell you something, in strictest confidence."

Rux pulled up a straight back wooden chair and waited as his new roommate contemplated the orange glow of the heating element in the electric heater. I suppose this is kinda like hat studying, Rux thought.

Rector Richter leaned back and sighed heavily. "Rux," he said, then paused again. "You were right about Auren wanting an Apache burial ceremony. After Joe's funeral she asked me to go to the desert with her so she could grieve in the way of her people."

"Did you go?"

"I didn't want to. I told her it was against the teachings of the church. But she would have gone without me. I thought maybe I could help guide her along the path of truth."

"Well, at least the desert is warmer than up here in the snow. Then again, so is standing too close to hell."

The weakness of the Padre's smile betrayed his agony. He got up and walked to the window of the foaling stall, absently fingered the curtain for a few minutes, then returned and stood with his back to the heater.

"Undoubtedly," he said, "hell is warm in the winter. Desert nights are definitely not. I built a large fire, but no matter which way I faced, half of me froze while the other half roasted."

"What about Auren?"

Rector Richter winced and made another visit to the foaling stall window before answering. "Auren had no trouble keeping warm. She brought along a tape of drums beating and people chanting. In Apache, I suppose. For hours she gyrated and contorted around the fire, chanting in this haunting monotone that increased in volume with the pace of her dance. Rux, do you know why Joe drank at Moose Ball's every night rather than going home?"

Rux started to relate Joe's tale of being a great Apache warrior who came and went as he pleased, but held his tongue. He sensed this was not a question expecting an answer.

The Padre returned to his chair. "He was impotent."

"Joe? You're kidding. If that don't scald the hair off a javelina. Joe Hawkins, the great Apache warrior, couldn't get a—Oops. Sorry, Padre. Can you imagine, being married to a woman as gorgeous as Auren and not being able to perform your husbandly duties? Well, of course, you can't, being a priest and all."

"Perhaps I can."

Rux decided it was his turn to make a trip to the foaling stall window. He had to do something to quell his own rutting. After a lengthy review of an empty stall, his carnality subsided enough to let the Padre's last comment sink in. Rux wasn't sure what to make of it and let it pass.

"Padre," he said, addressing Rector Richter's reflection in the window, "didn't Joe ever try to get any help?"

"Not as far as Auren knows. Apparently he was just too proud to let anyone know. Auren said she did everything she could think of to help him, but nothing worked."

"Wouldn't that have been grounds for an annulment?"

"Sure, but I guess she just kept hoping."

"For a whole year? She must be starving for, uh, something. Did she tell you all this in the desert?"

"Afterward."

"After what?" Rux returned to his chair by the heater, his passion momentarily in check, he thought.

Rector Richter took his turn at the foaling stall window. "That's what I really need to tell you," he said. "After what seemed like hours of simultaneously roasting and freezing, and listening to that incessant chanting, I began to hallucinate. At first I saw rattlesnakes seeking the warmth of the fire, then Auren whirling in and out of the darkness...." His voice quivered and trailed off to a whisper. "The top part of her buckskin outfit had been removed."

Rux felt the sudden need for another visit to the foaling stall window, but the Padre already had it staked out. Rux eased over to the window by his bed, facing the yard. Across the yard stood the old ranch house where, he convinced himself, Auren tossed and turned in the darkness, craving his body. Rux picked up his pillow and twisted it in his hands.

Rector Richter, not seeming to notice, went on with his story in a now husky voice. "I turned away from the fire and tried to shake the illusion from my head. When I turned back, I saw nothing but heavy smoke."

Rux relaxed his grip on the pillow.

"Then she came swirling out of the smoke, as naked as Eve in the garden of Eden."

"Before or after the discovery of fig leaves?"

"Before. The next thing I knew, we were hopelessly entangled."

The pillow ripped, feathers wooshed into the air. Rux tried to herd them under the blanket.

Rector Richter still did not notice. He now stood slump shouldered, with his forehead resting against the glass and his hands stuffed into his pockets. "My friend," the Padre said, "I'm afraid I yielded to my passion."

Rux suddenly forgot about his own lust, struck by the fact that a man of God would consider him a friend to whom he could bare his soul. He watched Rector Richter slowly lift one hand and make a mark in the fog gathered on the cold window pane. Rux wondered if it was the sign of the cross. He wanted to go to the Padre but hesitated, fearful that he might intrude on holy ground.

Rector Richter edged back to the rocker, seated himself and buried his face in his hands. Rux tried without success to wave the remaining feathers off the bed, then joined the Padre.

"Couldn't you go to the bishop or someone and ask for forgiveness?" Rux asked.

"I could, but that's the problem. I'm not sure I want to. Auren says she wants to share me with God. Right now I'm trying to sort out a universe rushing madly toward a black hole, one created by a vortex of unordered events."

That's the kind of world most of us live in every day, Rux thought, but he did not say it. Not knowing what to say, he left the Padre to appreciate the silence, although he doubted he would find much comfort in it.

He imagined the Padre in the desert night, desperately needing to escape the darkness but fearful of the exposing light of day. Somewhere in the depths of hell a sinister voice would be cackling hideously, "Boys, we got us a big one."

Rux shook his head to clear his mind. This father confessor business is getting to me, he thought.

Rector Richter leaned back in his chair and, after a while, dozed off. Rux pulled the heater a safe distance away in case the Padre fell out of the chair, then stripped to his skivvies and climbed into his feather filled but pillowless bed. He rolled up his pants for a pillow, then tossed them back on the floor after he realized they smelled a lot like the muck he had been picking out of the horses' feet.

For a long while Rux thought on the vortex of unordered events, both Rector Richter's and his own.

"Chester," Rux mentally said to his absent horse, "as I recall, when we teamed up we were headed for Texas to check on my daddy. Somewhere along the way, we acquired a beautiful singer and her lovely daughter who's not really her daughter, lost the mother but inherited the daughter, and now we've adopted two Mexicans, an Indian beauty queen and a horny priest. Good thing we can both see in the dark. Otherwise, I'd say we might be headed over a tall cliff."

From a stall at the far end of the dark barn, Chester nickered his concurrence.

I sure need to find Sammi, Rux thought, particularly after the Padre's erotic tale. But Rector Richter is a good friend. I can't abandon him now.

Seventeen

Rux had often heard Juanita proudly proclaim herself the personification of profound profundity, although she had no idea what it meant. The honor had been bestowed upon her by her uncle, the oral surgeon, who invented the phrase as a test for his patients to see if they were candidates for tongue reconstructive surgery.

Regardless of what the phrase meant to anyone else, it bore ill tidings for Howard and Rux.

Juanita joined Rux, Emilio, Rector Richter and Auren in the center of the barn. All of them welcomed the chance to be outside provided by a relatively mild January Sunday afternoon.

"I have announcements," Juanita said, in a futile attempt to still her slowly turning audience as they watched Missy and Chester circling the natural show ring created by the massive expanse of the barn. "I have decided Howard must join the ranks of the Macadamians. The time for his neutering has arrived."

"Anyone else?" Rux asked.

"Not for the moment," Juanita said, waving her hand in front of her face to settle the dust being stirred up. "But you guys better watch your step. Rux, I've also decided we're all going to Scottsdale with you and Missy."

"I didn't know Missy and me was going to Scottsdale."

"Sure you are," Juanita said. "To the horse show, the one Missy asked you about. Remember?"

Rux stepped away from the revolving band of onlookers and faced Juanita. "Yeah," he said, "but I didn't promise her we would go. She would have to miss a week of school. Besides, that's three weeks away. Sammi will be back before then."

Juanita took Rux's arm and guided him outside. "Sammi's been gone almost two months now," she said. "Something's wrong out there. No mother would leave her child like this unless she was on drugs or something. I've known mothers to get hooked on that stuff so bad they would sell their own kids for a fix."

Rux took off his hat and wiped his forehead on his sleeve even though it was too cool to sweat. He momentarily dwelled in the hat. Obviously, Juanita didn't know Missy was not Sammi's real daughter. But they were mother and daughter in every other way. Sammi had raised her.

Juanita's usual tactful approach, closely akin to performing a lobotomy with a meat cleaver, exposed something he had carefully hidden, especially from himself—fear.

136

Rux quickly covered the wound with mental cosmetic surgery, then emerged from the hat. "I'm sure," he said. "But Sammi's not like that. She sounds fine when she calls. If she needs help she would tell us. They're just keeping her busy with the band and recording and all."

Commotion from the barn precluded Juanita's reply. They watched as Missy brought Chester to a sudden halt, causing Emilio, Rector Richter and Auren to stumble into each other.

Missy dismounted and led Chester toward Rux and Juanita. Her cortege followed dutifully.

"How did we look?" Missy asked.

"Great," Rux said. "You've really got him bridled up and moving."

"What do you think about Scottsdale?" Missy asked.

Rux looked at Juanita, then back to Missy. "I think you've been recruiting. Scottsdale is like the Nationals. Big show barns from all over the country come to that one. You'll have to go against the top riders in your age group. Think you're ready for that?"

Missy handed the reins to Rux and began to unsaddle her horse. "Probably not," she said. "But Chester is. Even if we don't win I'd like to see how good the other riders are. Maybe you could show Chester in the Cutting and Working Cow Horse classes."

"I don't think even Chester can do that. We've got him set up for English Pleasure. If we let him drop down and work cows it will just confuse him."

Emilio said, "I bet he can do it. Why don't we find us a calf or two and let him work them. Then we can see if he will bridle up again."

Rux frowned at Emilio and playfully swatted the reins at Missy's legs. "You really have been recruiting, little lady. I suppose the Padre and Auren are in on this, too."

Rector Richter said, "Hey, we're just innocent bystanders." He winked at Missy as he took the saddle from her and headed for the barn. A giggling Auren followed.

Rux slipped the halter and lead rope over Chester's head as Missy removed the bridle. "He worked up a pretty good sweat," Rux said to Missy. "Cool him out good before you put him in his stall." He watched as Missy ambled the large gray gelding through the barn and out toward the back pasture. The barn door unwittingly framed a striking portrait of a small girl and her horse profiled by a brilliant sun.

"How's that for a picture of life as God intended it," Rux said to Emilio and Juanita.

"Yeah," Juanita said, "Howard's pretty artistic."

"Howard?" Rux had failed to notice the big, yellow cat thumping along behind Missy, his tail extending straight up as though he were scanning for messages from outer space. "What's artistic about a cat?"

The three of them wandered toward the tack room, talking loudly so as not to surprise Rector Richter and Auren in some compromising embrace.

"When we ran over Howard," Emilio said, "seems like we messed up his plumbing as well as his leg. We fixed him up a litter box in the kitchen, but every time he relieved himself he soiled his cast as well as the wall."

"Juanita," Rux said, "finicky as you are about germs, I'm surprised you let Howard in the house."

"Me, too," Emilio said. "Half the time she won't let me in. I have to remind her I live there. She solved Howard's germ problem by bathing him six times a day. If cleanliness is next to Godliness, Howard is ready for sainthood."

"Oh pshaw," Juanita said, kicking a dried road apple at Emilio.

Rux asked, "Why didn't he use the sand box?"

"Emilio doesn't need a sand box," Juanita said. "He can use the toilet."

"Not Emilio," Rux said. "Howard."

Emilio retrieved an old rag from the tack room and began cleaning the green slime off the bridle. "Howard did use the sand box," he said. "But the poor fella had diarrhea. Before he could get his hole dug he would let fly. Juanita tacked poster board on the wall so we could throw it out after each session, but then she realized Howard's uncontrollable urges were creating intricate patterns."

"Sort of like spin art?" Rux asked.

"Exactly," Juanita said. "So we let them dry, sprayed them with lacquer and sold them at an art auction in Peyson. Howard would be rich by now if I hadn't cured his diarrhea with my alfalfa-goldenseal-ginger herb remedy."

Rux's side hurt from laughing so hard. "Howard Spinart, the famous artist," he said.

"Soon to be Howard Spinart Macadamia," Juanita said. "You boys take him in to the vet first thing in the morning and return him to me a new man. Or at least less of a man than he is now."

"Why do you want to neuter him?" Rux asked. "There's no other cats around here."

"True," Juanita said. "But no telling what he'll find to carouse with in Scottsdale."

"Howard's going to Scottsdale?" Rux asked. He looked at Emilio, who simply shrugged and handed him the bridle.

"Sure," Juanita said. "He can't stay here by himself. Besides, Chester would miss him."

* * *

After supper, Rux returned to the barn to discuss the Scottsdale conspiracy with Chester and Howard. He kindly omitted any mention of the impending demise of Howard's manhood.

"Might as well amuse them," Rux said. "But the only way we're going to Scottsdale is if we pass through there on our way to Los Angeles."

Rux wondered what to do about Rector Richter and Auren when he left. It seemed to be his year for adopting strays. "Dang, I sure could use that old hat," he said.

Chester and Howard both ignored him.

* * *

Three weeks later, Rux sat in his old truck behind a huge chromed and brightly painted tractor-trailer, waiting patiently to enter the exhibitor's gate for the Scottsdale show. Missy squirmed excitedly on the seat between Rux and Emilio. Chester and Howard kept each other company in the trailer while Rector Richter, Auren and Juanita followed in the Red "C".

"Ruxstone Arabians," Rux said to the steward as he took his turn at the gate. "We've got two stalls."

"Howdy, Rux," the steward said. "Nice to see you back. Got your own farm now, I see. How many horses you showing?"

"Just brought one. Harry Beauchamp showing?"

"Naw. Harry's off in Florida or some place. Got himself a year's suspension for peppering a horse. Hey, did you hear somebody doctored old Harry's butt with pepper at last year's show?"

"You don't say. That's terrible. How'd the auctions go this year?"

"Pretty bad. They had all the usual glitz, but the million-dollar buyers weren't here. Several of the well-heeled owners bid the prices up to keep the market from collapsing any more'n it already has."

Rux took his packet from the steward and waved. "Truck behind is with me," he said, and headed off to find his stalls.

"What happened to Harry Beauchamp?" Missy asked.

"Oh, nothing serious. Somebody was just funnin' with him, I suppose."

Emilio asked, "People paid a million dollars for a horse?"

"They did in years past," Rux said, "But not this year. Several of the ranches here have barns that look like palaces. The rich and famous used to show up at their auctions stoned out of their minds and try to outbid each other for the shiny objects being paraded in front of them. Imagine their surprise when they woke up the next morning and found out they paid a million dollars for a horse."

"Wow!" Missy said.

Rux wasn't sure if her "Wow" referred to his million-dollar horse story or the pompous surroundings of the show grounds. The hot dog concession stand at the local shows she attended had been magically transformed into a whole street of kitchen trailers with false store fronts.

Vendors hawked everything from funnel cakes to Greek pita pockets with roasted lamb. The tantalizing aroma of sausage grease dripping onto hot coals drifted all the way to the stalls before yielding to the pungent odor of manure.

A separate street featured tents and booths selling seven-hundred-dollar riding outfits and ten-thousand-dollar furs.

Rux set up one stall for Chester and Howard and curtained off the other one with canvas for his sleeping quarters and tack room.

Missy asked, "Can I stay out here with you, Rux?"

"This ain't no place for a lady," Rux said. "It gets powerful cold at night and you have to shower in the rest rooms. I think you'll be a lot more comfortable at the motel. You can bunk in with Juanita and Auren. Emilio and Rector Richter can have the other room."

Missy went skipping off with Juanita and Auren to see the sights while Emilio and the Padre helped Rux get set up.

"Missy's really wound up," Rector Richter said. "But I bet she will be asleep before we get to the motel. Couldn't you find one closer than Mesa?"

"Not one we could afford," Rux said. "Everything in Scottsdale is two hundred bucks a night. You'll enjoy the drive, though. Scottsdale Boulevard is right out of a travel brochure for the jet setters."

Rux's merry band of travelers were like kids at a circus. They reluctantly headed for Mesa only after he insisted.

* * *

"We got a break," Rux said to his excited conglomeration as they arrived Monday morning. "The Working Cow Horse class is tomorrow but the Equitation is not until the weekend. That should give Chester time to learn how to bridle up again for the Eq classes. If he can't, we'll scratch him and go home."

Missy stuck out her bottom lip in a pretend pout. "He can do it," she said. The rest agreed, although Rux suspected they were just glad to be out of the mountains and didn't want to go home early.

Rux worked Chester in the practice ring, maddened by the wardrobe changes required by the fickle February weather. One minute, the sun would warm you to your shirt sleeves. Then just as quickly it would dart behind a cloud and a cold wind would blast you with sand and send you scurrying for a jacket.

The horses were distracted by the constant commotion created by spectators along the fences putting on, then taking off their coats.

* * *

The next afternoon, Rux emerged from his tack stall in clean jeans and his white western shirt with silver buttons and matching tips on his shirt collar.

"My, don't you look spiffy," Juanita said. "Isn't that your performing shirt?"

"Sure," Rux said. "It works whether I'm performing on stage or in the show ring. Same for my boots and hat, just gotta clean 'em up a little."

Rux mounted Chester, and Missy wiped the dust off his newly polished boots. The little groom had the horse so shiny his gray coat looked iridescent in the bright afternoon sun.

"You must have used a lot of show sheen on him," Rux said.

Juanita said, "She used all of my hair conditioner. Now I have to find some more nettle and Ho-lien-hua to mix up a new batch."

Missy ducked under Chester's neck and looked up at Rux with an impish grin. "Pick your foot up so I can check the girth," she said. "If you get off you'll get your boots dusty."

"Yes, ma'am." They went through the exact routine in reverse roles when Missy showed.

"Good luck," his merry band shouted as he rode off toward the old barn and the adjoining wood-fenced arena. The main show ring, an enormous oval defined by a low adobe wall, did not have facilities for cow pens. Chester could be equally at home in either setting, but his rider preferred the old rodeo style facilities.

They waited at the entry gate for their go. Rux silently admired the performances of the horses going ahead of him, wishing luck to each rider as they entered and offering a "nice job" as they returned.

"Number Seven Fourteen," the loud speaker called. Rux nudged his horse toward the open gate.

Once in the arena, Chester focused totally on the small door where he knew the calf would enter. They drew a good one. The calf had no intention of remaining at one end of the vast pen but Chester headed him at every twist and turn until Rux backed the horse off.

They had two minutes to complete the required exercises of confining the calf in the area of the entry gate, herding him along one side rail and then back, then circling the calf in both directions.

Rux let the calf have the left rail but kept Chester right beside him. The calf ran flat out, then skidded to a stop and tried to turn into the arena. Chester stopped with equal deftness and kept him hemmed against the rail.

The calf ran again but Chester caught up and skidded to a halt in front of the calf, heading him into a U-turn before he reached the fence. The horse worked the calf with equal skill back down the same rail, then turned him into the center.

They circled the calf, first to the left. Rux's heart skipped a beat when Chester slipped in the loose sand, but he did not lose the calf. They were still circling to the right when the whistle sounded.

Good horses preceded them and good horses followed, but Chester stamped his name among the national contenders. The judge scored him five points higher than the second place horse. When the scores were announced, Missy threw herself into Rux's arms for her customary victory squeeze.

He held her while acknowledging the congratulations of his fellow riders, then remounted and rode in to receive Chester's blue ribbon and trophy.

Missy took charge of Chester, bathed him and cooled him out, then iced his front legs good before rubbing all of them with liniment.

"Maybe we shouldn't show him in the Eq class," Missy said. "I didn't realize how much stress cow work puts on his legs."

"Let's give him tomorrow off," Rux said. "If he looks okay we'll try bridling him up and see how he responds. Right now my guess is he'd be pretty sour."

Rux borrowed some deck chairs from one of the large show barns and sent Rector Richter for pizza. "Be sure and get onions and bell peppers on them," he said. "Otherwise Juanita will gripe us out for not eating our vegetables."

They huddled in the extra stall to escape the cold air and partied the night away.

"Emilio, you look like a street urchin with that sweater tied around your head," Juanita said.

"I am a street urchin," Emilio said. "At least I feel like one. This cold wind makes my ears ache."

Emilio grimaced and bit his fist, but it was too late.

"Aha," Juanita said. "We can take care of that." She dug through the oversized straw bag she carried for a purse, produced a long, hollow wafer-like tube, stuck it in his ear and lit it like a cigar. "Ear candle," she announced, holding a cup under the end of the tube to catch the oozing ear wax.

"Dang," Rux said. "Remind me never to complain about a stuffy nose."

"We can fix that, too," Juanita said.

"I have no doubt," Rux said. "I'm just worried the remedy might be worse that the ailment."

"Oh, stop bellyaching," Juanita said. "None of you has had so much as a cold all winter, have you? Look how healthy Missy is."

Auren patted Missy on the knee. Rux had to admit the concoctions Auren and Juanita had come up with appeared to be keeping them all healthy. And Missy's teachers were reporting improvement in her math skills.

"Missy's going to live to be a hundred and fifty," Juanita said. "Even after the rest of her quits, we'll have to beat her liver with a stick to make it lie down."

Rux leaned back into his improvised hay bale couch and surveyed his impromptu family—Juanita intently holding Emilio's head still to facilitate her sanitation of his auditory cavity, Emilio and Rector Richter joking with each other as though ear candling constituted a part of their daily routine, and Auren and Missy huddled together under a blanket, giggling at Howard's antics.

Amazing, Rux thought, how people thrown together by happenstance will adopt each other.

He pulled back the canvas curtain and looked out at the clear night sky. A strip of blue buffeted the desert from the inevitable blackness, interrupted only by a quarter moon and Venus. A wise man would follow that star, he thought, all the way to California.

Eighteen

Sammi tried to focus on the figures standing in the doorway of her small, scantily furnished apartment. The setting California sun bathed them in an aura, suggesting the presence of either Beelzebub's minions or escaped Disneyland characters.

Given a choice, Sammi would have opted for the former. She ignored the intrusion and returned to the window to watch her freshly bathed horse rolling in the dirt.

The crack pipe had done its job well.

Sammi enjoyed the pleasant exhaustion spawned by an afternoon riding the dark bay quarter horse stallion around the pastures of her grandparents' farm. The creaky ceiling fan in the dark parlor of the ancient Victorian farm house eased the stifling heat, and the open windows provided a portrait of horses grazing in undulating green fields interrupted occasionally by giant spreading oaks and loblolly pines.

For as long as she could remember, the farm had consumed her summers. Her grandfather disdained the use of a pickup to herd his cattle, preferring to tend them on horseback as he had done since his youth. Sammi had fond memories of sitting in the saddle in front of him until her fourth summer, when she was assigned her own horse and her own duties.

Grandpa had promised to give her the stallion when she graduated from high school next year. Actual ownership made little difference so far as riding him was concerned. Grandpa rode very little since he "retired" from ranching. The colt had been half wild when she returned to the farm each of the last two summers. But his substantial stud fees would be Sammi's to use for college expenses. The horse had won several cutting horse championships and produced excellent offspring.

Sammi leaned back in the old rocker and watched the fan's blades lazily churn through emptiness. After supper, she, Grandpa and Grandma would retire to the massive porch and enjoy the chorale of katydids and whippoorwills welcoming the evening. They would talk of college. Sam Houston State and North Texas both had good music programs. Julliard was not out of the realm of possibility.

Sammi closed her eyes and pressed her fingers into her temples, then shook her head violently. Somehow a concrete and steel freeway had replaced the pastoral scene. The constant vibrato of buzzing and whining from a varied assortment of vehicles created a dual-keyed sonata.

Their unwitting passengers traversed the endless ribbon of pavement, going from nowhere to somewhere and then back again.

The room revolved around Sammi until she again faced the eerie manifestation in her doorway. Even though still mellow from the crack, something inside Sammi told her she should sense fear.

The tiny Anaheim apartment suddenly seemed crowded as the minions merged into one. Peter stepped into the room.

Sammi struggled to relate time and events. It was spring when the sheriff ran Peter out of town, and it was snowing in the mountains when she left for L.A. But it was hard to distinguish the seasons in southern California.

She seemed to have a vague recollection of Peter being in Los Angeles earlier. Surely, she imagined that.

Sammi looked again for the green pastures of East Texas, but found only concrete and cars.

"Hello again, Sam. I've come to take you back to Houston."

The words echoed, sort of bouncing off the walls.

Peter picked up the well-worn black cowboy hat hanging on the back of the dining chair. He toyed with it, apparently trying to distinguish front from back, then placed it on his head. "Always wanted one of these," Peter said.

Sammi pretended not to notice. That's Rux's hat, she thought. He has no right to it. He has no right to take me back to Houston either, but obviously he's going to.

She stood, massaged the small of her back with both hands, and stretched. "I can't go to Houston just now," she said. "I have important business here in Los Angeles."

Peter stared at her. No one moved. Sammi thought, hey, maybe that worked. She turned, still trying to appear nonchalant, and walked into the bedroom. She felt movement behind her. Peter took her arms, gently twisted her to face him, and helped her sit on the edge of the bed.

"Sam, are you listening? Can you hear me?"

She nodded. The room and everything in it blurred, then became topsy-turvy. Finally, she realized Peter had eased her to a prone position.

The cold rag on her face startled her. Sammi grabbed Peter's hand and tried to pull it away.

"Easy now," he said. "I need you to wake up a little."

She offered only token resistance as Peter lifted her head and ran the cold rag around the back of her neck, then over her chest. Eventually, he came more into a focus of sorts.

"I'm okay," Sammi mumbled.

Peter sat beside her and stroked her matted hair. "Think you can get cleaned up? We have a plane to catch."

With considerable difficulty, Sammi propped herself on one elbow.

"Plane? Where are we going?"

"Houston, remember?"

"But...I thought...what about the band, my contract, my recording?"

Peter placed his hand behind her head and pulled her to his chest. "We've gone over all that. The studio could never get a decent demo tape. Evan Vaughn cut you loose. We're going to Houston to start over."

Sammi freed herself and flopped back on the pillow. "No. If I have to start over I can go back to...to...wherever I came here from...Pine Nuts. Pine Knot."

A rush of images jolted Sammi into consciousness. Rux, Missy, Deke, Moose Ball's, all flashed in her mind simultaneously but each was a distinct engram. She forced herself to sit up.

"I have to get home," she said.

"Home? To Pine Knot, you mean? That will have to wait. Going back there, singing the rest of your life in a smoky saloon is a dead end. Remember your dream, Sam. Our dream. We just need to find a way to transfer your charisma from the stage to the recording studio."

"How?"

"We'll figure it out. You'll have Missy and Rux back with you in no time. Now come on, let's get you cleaned up."

Peter started unbuttoning her blouse. The garment was on the bed and he was twisting the catch on her bra before she fully realized he intended to undress her.

"No, stop." She grabbed his hands. "I can do this. If I go with you, it will be strictly business."

"That was our arrangement. I don't expect you to move back in with me. The little garage apartment over on the north side that I use for rental is available. You'll stay there."

Good, Sammi thought. It's in my old neighborhood, and Tyrone's. The area's a bit shabby these days, but then, so am I.

She held the bra in place and stood. "You wait in the other room while I shower and change. I'll be out in a few minutes."

Peter extracted himself from the bed and eased toward the living room. With some reluctance, it seemed to Sammi.

"Okay, but don't be too long," he said. "Are you okay now? I have something to help you relax but you're almost floating as it is."

"I'm fine."

Sammi stepped into the tiny bathroom and closed and locked the door. She was floating, but her faculties seemed to be coming back. Richard had kept her supplied with uppers, downers, everything else they thought might work. Nothing did.

As good as she was before a crowd, she could not duplicate her live performance in the little glass cubicle. Even bringing Earle and the Red Neck Band to the studio did not help.

The cold water of the shower brought another chilling reality Sammi had refused to admit until now. She was addicted, big time.

I can't go back to Pine Knot like this, she thought. I might as well go on to Houston, give it one more try. But no more uppers, no more downers, no more crack. I'll kick this stuff. If we can find the key to studio recording, fine. But regardless, as soon as I'm clean I'm heading for Arizona.

Sammi toweled off, then dried her hair. She toyed with the idea of styling it and applying makeup but that required too long in front of a mirror. The drooping eyes with dark bags under them were hard to look at. The hair was slicked into a pony tail. Clean jeans and a fresh shirt completed her travel attire.

She exited to the bedroom and found Peter already had her clothes packed and waiting.

She also found a grinning Hector Romero.

Nineteen

Chester's day off had given new life to his sore legs, although for several days he resisted Rux's attempts to elevate him with the double bridle. Rux had been reluctant to push him too hard. But by the weekend the horse was responding well, and seemed to appreciate Missy's soft touch with the reins.

On Saturday morning Chester roared into the vast show ring with his usual flair, but it would be hard to get noticed. There were twenty-five riders in the thirteen and under Equitation class.

"See number six eighteen, the blond girl on the big chestnut," Rux told Missy before the class. "She's one of the top riders from California. The judge will watch her. Try to stay close to her and, if you can, cover her up as you go down the rail in front of the judge. You'll get noticed."

Rux watched in amazement as Missy did exactly that. Number six eighteen won, but Missy took fourth. "Not bad for a national caliber show," he told Missy.

More pizza and ear candles produced another party in the extra stall. Chester received his usual icing and liniment rub and another well-deserved rest. The only thing left was the long trailer ride home.

"Hey, Rux, you got a message on the bulletin board next to the show office," one of the grooms yelled.

Who the heck would be calling me? Rux thought. Sammi doesn't even know we're here. The message was from Sheriff Mohlmann.

"Hey, Sheriff. What's up?"

"Rux, we got a problem. When's Sammi gonna be back?"

"I'm not sure. Why?"

"Hold on to your hat. Some ladies up here claim they saw you fondling Missy. Said it happened at one of the shows here and they saw you doing the same thing down there."

Rux exploded into the phone. "Mo, you know I wouldn't do anything like that. This is ridiculous."

"I know, Rux. But I'm in an awkward position. They got some case worker from Child Protective Services snooping around. If you come back up here I may have to arrest you. Stay put until I can get a handle on things. Meantime, try to get Sammi back. The CPS lady is concerned Missy's not living with a parent."

Rux's mind spun with the whirling dust. It had to be the mothers of the girls Missy competed against. What they saw was a simple hug, the same kind of affection a man shows his horse. Or his daughter. Where the hell was Sammi?

He called her apartment and received the friendly recorded message announcing the number was no longer in service. Good grief, he thought, maybe she's back in Pine Knot. But Sheriff Mo would have known if that were the case.

"Could I speak to Mr. Vaughn?" he asked the polite secretary who answered Evan Vaughn's phone.

"I'm sorry, Mr. Vaughn is out of the city. May I take a message?"

"Maybe you can help me. I'm trying to locate Sammi Stone."

"Miss Stone no longer works for Mr. Vaughn. I don't know how you might reach her."

Rux had no idea if he could get through to Lee Wiley Willcox. The lawyer was constantly in trial or preparing for one. He might be handling my trial if I can afford him, Rux thought.

"Rux, you ornery old goat," Lee Wiley said. "Good to hear your voice. You in town for the show?"

"Hey, Lee Wiley. Yeah, we won the Working Cow Horse. Chester did great. Listen, I hate to bother you on Saturday but I need to find out how to locate someone."

"You're not bothering me. Who are we looking for?"

"You remember Sammi Stone, the singer up at Moose Ball's?"

"Do I. Really pretty girl, lots of class. And man could she sing. Something happened to her?"

"She signed with Evan Vaughn the weekend you were up there. Left for L.A. before Christmas. We haven't heard from her in over a month. Vaughn's office doesn't know how to reach her. Last we heard she was traveling with a band Vaughn placed her with. Since she's cut her ties with Vaughn I assume she's no longer with the band."

"Let me make some calls and I'll get back to you. May take a few days."

Rux gave Lee Wiley the number of the show office and walked back to the stalls, studying his hat. Missy had to be back in school Monday. How could he explain all this to her?

"Send Missy back with the merry band and go on to Texas," read the message in the hat. Rux didn't like the message and assigned the hat to its secondary duty, keeping his head warm.

Rux explained his dilemma to the adult contingent of the merry band. They collectively decided to say nothing to Missy other than the need to stay an extra day for Rux to attend to some business. Monday was D-Day. The show closed Sunday and the motel in Mesa did not board horses.

* * *

The "D" in D-Day turned out to stand for disaster. Rux envied his companions as they arrived at the show grounds with their usual merriment. His current predicament had no noticeable affect on them.

Rector Richter handed Rux a cup of coffee and the remainder of their donuts. "Any word?" he asked. "Are we ready to pack up and head home?"

Rux sent Missy out to walk Chester before responding. "No and no," he said. "I called Lee Wiley this morning. He's got some people checking on Sammi but they don't have anything yet. Why don't you guys drop me at the airport and drive on back to Pine Knot? I'll fly to Los Angeles and wait there for some word on Sammi."

"We can't do that," Rector Richter said. "The State may very well take custody of Missy and I'm not sure what they would do with her. She might even end up in some foster home."

"They wouldn't do that," Juanita said. "We're taking good care of her. She's in school. We're better than any foster family."

Rector Richter said, "Yes, but remember what Rux is being accused of. Since we were all together, they might look with suspicion on all of us."

Juanita said, "Even a priest?"

The Padre lowered his head and felt his throat, where his clerical collar would ordinarily be. Rux knew what he was thinking—a priest on sabbatical, having an affair with one of his parishioners. The state would be more likely to place Missy with a gypsy circus.

Rux tossed the extra hay bale in the back of his truck, then checked the field behind the practice arena to be sure Missy remained out of ear shot. "None of us is her legal guardian," he said. "What kind of trouble are we getting into if we don't get her back?"

Juanita said, "You're following the sheriff's instructions, aren't you? That should be legal enough. None of us has any pressing need to be back in Pine Knot. We'll all go to California."

"That's crazy," Rux said, handing the saddles to Emilio.

Old sawdust mixed with manure came flying out the back of the trailer. Auren stuck her head out and said, "It is crazy, but it sounds exciting. I'm ready."

"See," Juanita said. "Even Emilio agrees."

"No he didn't," Rux said. "All he did was grunt when he tossed the saddles in the truck."

"With Emilio, a grunt is as good as a yes," Juanita said. "Right, Paco?"

Emilio shrugged and ducked back into the stall.

"I think they're right," Rector Richter said from the back of the pickup. "We are all in this together, and our first responsibility is to Missy. Right now, finding her mother is the best thing we can do for her."

"Well, thank you for your support, Padre," Rux said. He shoved his hat on his head and stomped off toward the grass field to retrieve Missy and Chester.

"Maybe I'll just turn myself in to the local sheriff," he mumbled to himself. "Ash Chalmers will probably take Chester back if I explain my situation. The rest of this lost tribe of Israel can either go home or spend the next forty years wandering up and down Scottsdale Boulevard."

He stopped to wait for Missy, who had spotted him and was leading Chester back. A familiar yellow cat arched his back and rubbed his jaw against Rux's boot. "Oh, I forgot," Rux said. "We've added a jake leg cat to our wandering troupe."

He picked the cat up and scratched between his ears. "Don't worry, Howard. You can go to jail with me."

I sure could use that old hat, he thought, although the new one seemed to be developing a pretty good wisdom of its own. The message still read the same but with added emphasis. If Missy didn't return he might be accused of kidnapping. And if he took her across state lines, Lord knows what that would involve. He calculated again and figured he and Chester could be in No Water in twelve hours.

Twenty

Rux sat on the edge of his cot and listened intently. Howard and Chester both had their ears cocked forward and were eyeing the upper end of an arroyo separating a sizable hill from the plateau where he had set up camp. The roadside park had seemed like a good spot to crash the night before.

He could not make out anything in the canyon, still half hidden from the pink light that precedes the dawn. But he could definitely hear something rustling through the brush. "Cows?" he said.

Chester apparently satisfied himself there was no danger and resumed breakfasting on the sparse vegetation within the confines of his tether. Rux pulled on his boots, walked to the edge of the park and contributed to the water erosion that undoubtedly formed the divide. He watched for several minutes as wranglers yipped and yahooed their herd into the canyon, past a small lake at the bottom, through a large culvert under I-10.

"Nice of California to provide entertainment for us campers," he said to Chester and Howard. "We best get the Padre and Emilio up and go find the womenfolk."

Rector Richter still slept soundly on his canvas and hay bed in the back of the Red "C". Emilio, cramped inside the cab, was already up and stirring.

"Where in the heck are we?" Emilio asked.

"Couple or three hours east of Los Angeles, I would guess," Rux said. "You guys should have gotten a room at the motel."

Emilio grunted his agreement and wandered off to the rim. Rector Richter stretched, yawned, then curled up under his blanket.

"I could do with a shower," the Padre said.

"Me too," Rux said. "Let's go grab some breakfast, then we'll roust the girls out of the room and shower while they're eating."

By nine o'clock, Rux had his own herd gathered in the motel coffee shop, showered, fed and ready to move on.

"I'd better go call Lee Wiley before we leave," he said. Rux slid out of the booth and motioned the Padre to follow him.

"Padre," he said, "tell Auren to find some excuse to go back to the room with Missy. Whatever Lee Wiley comes up with, we need to talk about it. I don't want to get Missy upset, or create any false hopes for her."

When Rux returned to the table, Rector Richter, Emilio and Juanita were alone. "Good news," he said. "I just talked to Lee Wiley. We're on the right highway. Sammi has an apartment in Anaheim."

The merry band reacted with renewed merriment. "How far is Anaheim?" Juanita asked. "We'll just drive down there and pick her up."

"Great idea," Rector Richter said. "Let's roll this convoy."

Rux said, "Hold on a minute. Her phone has been disconnected. We don't know for sure that she's at the apartment. Remember, she's been traveling with her band."

Juanita waved her cup at the waitress for more coffee. "Disneyland is in Anaheim," she said. "Why don't we get a motel near the park. Rux, you and the Padre can go look for Sammi while the rest of us take Missy over to Disneyland."

"Good thinking," Rux said. "That will keep Missy occupied. We'll have to find a place for all the animals, though."

Emilio rescued a last bite of bacon as the waitress removed his plate. "We should be able to find a boarding stable along the way for Chester," he said. "Howard has his litter box, he can stay in the motel with us."

No point in arguing with this group, Rux decided. "Load up the animals first," he said. "I'd hate to get halfway there and find out part of this zoo was missing. Of course, who knows what else we might pick up along the way."

* * *

Chester welcomed the pasture of a boarding stable on the outskirts of San Bernardino. Rux and Rector Richter deposited the rest of their roving flock at a motel on Harbor Boulevard. Rux felt certain they would return with Sammi before nightfall, but he was purposely vague with Missy. Her excitement about the Disneyland venture indicated the distraction would work, at least for the afternoon.

"You sure this is the right place?" Rector Richter asked as Rux circled a tall, wooden fence topped with spirals of barbed wire.

"Twenty-Nine Palms Apartments, on the Santa Ana Freeway," Rux said. "Sammi's last known address in Los Angeles or more precisely, Anaheim, according to Lee Wiley's contact."

He found the entrance, pulled up to the access code box, and read the instructions. "Enter access code or push star for information." He punched star. The wrought iron security gate swung open.

They drove through a maze created by three-story, charcoal gray buildings. What a dump, Rux thought. If twenty-nine palms ever graced these grounds, they had long since succumbed to the neglect that threatened like extinction for the buildings.

The only thing resembling a palm tree was a forlorn creosote pole encased in trumpet vines sprouting green plumage from the top of the pole, a Farmer's Almanac version of the hanging gardens of Babylon.

Rector Richter said, "This place sure looks run down. Not anything like what she described to you and Missy."

"Well, let's hope she hasn't been here long. But more importantly, let's hope she's still here."

They parked by the laundry room and followed a narrow concrete path to apartment thirty-three fifteen. Rector Richter tried to smooth down the peeling paint as they waited patiently for Sammi to answer their knock.

"Looks vacant," the Padre said. "Why don't we try the manager's office?"

Rux's optimism dwindled steadily as they trudged around to the office.

"How do, Ma'am," Rux said to the small, brown-haired girl behind a metal desk. "I'm Rux Tuttle, this is Tom Richter. We're looking for Miss Sammi Stone, apartment thirty-three fifteen. We tried her apartment but no one answered."

This little lady is probably no more than twenty, Rux thought. Working her way through school with free rent in this glorified ghetto.

The girl eyed them over black-framed reading glasses perched on her thin nose. "And how are you related to Ms. Stone?" she asked.

Rux said, "We're friends of hers from Arizona. It's important that we find her."

The overseer of the ghetto removed her glasses for closer inspection. "I normally don't give out information about our tenants to strangers," she said. "But you two look harmless enough."

Nice judge of character, Rux thought, considering the elfish manager was staring up at two behemoths across her desk.

"Besides," the girl said, "Sammi's no longer our tenant, and I think she just may be in need of friends right now. Her rent is overdue. We changed the lock on her apartment a week ago, but as far as I know she hasn't been back."

Rector Richter asked, "Do you know where we might find her?"

"Not really. I know she was with Earle Steiner's band. When they're in town they play at the Elk Horn Saloon, a big country and western dance hall over on the Riverside Freeway. You might try over there."

Rux and Rector Richter got directions, thanked the girl and retraced the pathway to the truck.

"Wonder what made her think we were harmless?" Rux asked.

"Probably the dust on your hat and the manure on your boots. You look like you just came in off a long trail drive."

"Well, in a manner of speaking, we did. But I think it was you. Even in that plaid shirt and blue jeans you have the innocent face of a priest. Are you sure you want to come with me? This place might be a little seedy for a man of your calling. I can drop you by Disneyland and you can catch up with the rest of our outfit."

Rector Richter fingered his chest, obviously wishing for the cross that normally hung there. "I doubt if I will be too shocked," he said. "Remember, I've spent quite a bit of time on the other side of the confessional booth."

"Yeah, but you probably don't want to witness first hand what your parishioners have been confessing to."

The Padre laughed as Rux crossed himself and mumbled, "Forgive me, Father, for I have sinned. But you don't want to know the details."

"Blasphemy," Rector Richter said in mock scolding. "But you may be right. If it gets too vile, I'll wait in the truck."

"I'm not sure what you consider vile. You may spend a lot of time in the truck."

The Elk Horn Saloon was not hard to spot. A huge, yellow-on-black sign extended across the entire front of a half block long, windowless metal building. Inside, the dim cavern was choked with dust stirred up by three janitors sweeping the concrete floor.

"We ain't open yet," a voice yelled from behind the bar as Rux and the Padre made their way through the round tables stacked with chairs.

"We know," Rux called back. "Need to ask you something."

The large-bellied man shoveling ice in the beer cooler straightened as they approached the bar. "What?" he demanded. "This ain't the tourist information bureau."

Rux asked, "Earle Steiner's band play here?"

The bartender dried his hands on his apron, then used the garment to wipe sweat from his bald head. Must be something they learn in bartender school, Rux thought.

"Did," the man said. "Band broke up about a week ago."

Rector Richter asked, "Know where we can find Earle?"

"Heard he moved up to San Francisco."

"Actually," Rux said, "we're looking for the girl that sang with the band, Sammi Stone. Do you have any idea where she is?"

"Nope." The man took a beer from the cooler, twisted off the cap and took a long swallow. "Byaak, still warm."

Rux asked, "Anyone around here that might could give us a lead on Sammi?"

"No." The bartender returned his attention to his beer icing.

Rux stepped closer to the cooler. The man straightened again, looked up at Rux, and apparently decided something in the kitchen needed his immediate attention. He kept his eyes on Rux as he swung his belly off the cooler and edged down the bar, then stopped.

"Aw, what the hell," he said. "Sammi don't mean nuthin' to me. She hung out with Lila. Used to be one of our waitresses. Last I heard of Lila she was dancing at a nudie club over on Slauson. Called Fancy Panties, or something like that. Never been there myself, you understand. I mean, Lila weren't much to look at with her clothes on. Don't know that I'd pay to see her dancing naked."

"Thanks," Rector Richter said as he grabbed Rux by the arm and guided him back through the tables.

"We need to get some directions," Rux said.

"That's okay," Rector Richter said, tugging harder on Rux's arm. "We'll find it."

They stopped at the phone booth outside and looked for the Fancy Panties Club on Slauson. "No such place," Rux said.

"Here's one on Slauson," Rector Richter said. "Fantasies."

"Worth a try. Hey, you're pretty good at this, Padre."

"Phonetics," Rector Richter said as they climbed back in the truck.

The sign identifying their arrival at Fantasies got second billing to a much larger one proclaiming Totally Nude, outlined in white Christmas lights revolving in sequence. Similar lights traveled around pictures displayed on the front of the building, each portraying a girl *au naturel* except for strategically placed black strips.

Rux parked in front of the adult book store across the street. "This looks pretty vile," he said to Rector Richter. "Maybe you should wait here while I go in and check."

The Padre waved back at the girl on the corner who had motioned them over when they drove up. "This whole place reeks of hedonism," he said. "I think I'd feel safer with you."

They crossed the street to Fantasies, circling behind a bus that had stopped at the corner. A plain looking girl got off the bus and walked toward them, then turned into the alley separating Fantasies from the empty building on the corner.

"I wonder if that might be Lila?" Rux said.

"Could be," Rector Richter said. "We should have gotten her description from the bartender."

"At least more than someone you wouldn't want to see without her clothes on."

A thin gray man huddled in the alley entrance, apparently warming himself in the sparse sunlight filtering through the brown haze. Before Rux could approach the girl, she stepped over the man, hurried into the shadows of the alley and ducked in the back door of the club.

More pictures of nude women, minus the black strips, beckoned them as they entered Fantasies. A hefty matron, sporting enough powder, rouge and lipstick to disguise a car load of circus clowns, greeted them from behind a counter.

"Afternoon, boys," she said. "First time, huh?"

I guess we're pretty obvious, Rux thought. I wonder what a regular patron looks like. Rector Richter appeared to be in total shock.

"Yes, Ma'am," Rux said. "We're not here for the show, we just need to find someone."

The lady threw back her large collection of red hair and laughed. "Don't worry about it," she said. "A lot of our first timers are a little sheepish. Show starts in thirty minutes. Twenty bucks apiece.

"You each get a private booth where you can see all the girls performing. They can see you, but no one else can. There's glass between you and the stage, so you can't touch them, but you can talk to them. They'll come over and do anything you want, up close and personal."

From the corner of his eye, Rux saw Rector Richter shudder.

"Thanks," Rux said to the lady. "But we really don't want to see the show. We need to find a girl who may work here. Her name is Lila."

The smiling woman quickly soured. "Forty bucks or hit the pavement. You perverts think you can come in here and fall in love, then try to get next to one of my girls? No way. Get your jollies some place else."

"Please," Rector Richter interrupted in a squeaky voice. "I'm a priest. We desperately need to find a young lady that may be in trouble. Lila has information that could help us."

"Yeah," the lady said, "and I'm Mother Theresa. I don't care if you're the Pope. Go ask God."

They repeated their exit from the Elk Horn Saloon, the Padre tugging Rux with one hand while crossing himself with the other.

"Holy Mary, Mother of God," the Padre mumbled. "I've died and gone to hell."

As they left the club, another girl darted down the alley, dodging past the wino relieving himself on the wall.

"What kind of place is this?" Rector Richter asked. "These ladies look like ordinary housewives, or someone's secretary."

"Who knows," Rux said. "Maybe Lila can tell us if we ever find her. Let's wait in the truck for the next bus. If another girl gets off, we'll try to talk to her before she gets in the alley."

The girl on the corner who had waved to them earlier flashed a broad smile as they crossed back to the truck. The air was cool, but she wore only a halter top and very short hot pants. Her high platform shoes made her look taller than she really was.

Rector Richter waved again, triggering a provocative undulation of the girl's ample hips.

"Don't do that," Rux said, unlocking the passenger door for the Padre.

"Why not?"

"She's a hooker. Looks like she's got a customer."

They watched as a stocky, middle-aged man wearing a Dodgers cap approached her. The girl and the man talked for a moment, then she took his arm and they started to cross the street. When they turned, the man saw Rux and the Padre in the truck. He stared at them briefly, said something to the girl, then hurried away without her.

"Wonder what that was all about?" Rux said.

The girl eyed them carefully as she walked to the pay phone in front of Fantasies.

"Maybe he just wanted her to call him a cab," Rector Richter said.

Several minutes later, Rux saw a large red Cadillac appear in his rear view mirror. A slim, black man behind the wheel studied the pickup for a few seconds, then stepped out of his car, walked behind the truck and emerged at the passenger window.

"How you boys doing?" the man grinned, flashing a gold front tooth. He had hair similar to the girl on the corner, plastered to his head and shining with the same luster as his blue shark skin suit.

"Fine," Rector Richter said, leaning away from the window to avoid the man's face.

"You boys like a little action?" the man said. "I can get you a nice white girl, or Mexican. Even got a Chink if you like it slanted."

"No, thanks," Rux said. "We're waiting for someone."

The man's smile never changed. "Wait somewhere else," he said. "That girl over there. You're scaring off her customers. They think you're Vice."

"Sorry about that," Rux said. "We'll be gone shortly. Tell her to work another corner."

The gold toothed smile turned into a tortured sneer. "This is my street," he hissed as his hand slapped the top of the truck. "Move." The dapper little man took a deliberate step back, pivoted and swaggered back to his Cadillac.

Rux was halfway out of the truck when Rector Richter grabbed his shoulder. "I wouldn't do that," the Padre said. "We have more important things to deal with right now."

Rux agreed, but he got out anyway and glared over the top of the truck at the Cadillac screeching off down the street.

"You stay there," the pimp yelled, flipping them the bird.

The Cadillac raced around a corner, then reappeared going the opposite direction. The pimp pulled up to the curb in front of his hooker and motioned her over to the car. He grabbed the girl's head, pulled it down to the open window, and appeared to be whispering in her ear.

Another bus pulled up and honked at him to move out of the bus zone.

"What do you think he's up to?" Rector Richter asked.

Before Rux could answer, the girl screamed and attempted to pull back, but the pimp had her ear locked in his teeth. His door suddenly flew open and slammed hard into the girl's midsection, knocking her free of his bite.

Rux lunged around the truck and started across the street, dodging quickly to his left as the red Cadillac roared passed him. The hooker slumped to the sidewalk, gasping for breath. Rector Richter joined Rux and together they eased her into a comfortable position. The Padre applied his handkerchief to the girl's bleeding ear.

A tall, dark-haired girl got off the bus and headed for the alley.

"Stay with this one," Rux said. "I'll be right back."

Several exaggerated strides of his long legs caught Rux up with the tall girl just as she stepped over the now prone wino.

"Pardon me, Ma'am," he said. "Are you Lila by any chance?"

The girl quickened her own stride, glancing back over her shoulder at Rux only after she reached the back door of the club.

"No," she said, "go away."

Rux stood with his thumbs hooked in the front pockets of his jeans and stared at the door for a few seconds. "This ain't working," he said to the wino as he stepped back over the ragged legs.

Rector Richter still knelt beside the hooker when Rux returned. He could hear the Padre mumbling something that sounded like, "Holy Mother, Mary of Jesus," as he wrapped his jacket around her shoulders and pulled it tight over her sizable bosom.

"Can we take you some place?" Rux asked the girl.

"I live in the hotel, right over there," she said between gasps.

Rux looked up the street where she pointed but did not see a hotel. He and Rector Richter helped her make her way toward home, wherever that was. Short fingers extended by long black-painted fingernails clung to his and the Padre's arms as they walked.

"What was that all about?" Rux asked.

"My man hittin' me, you mean?" she asked. "'Spose he's entitled. I spent his share of my take on a fix. Gonna be lot worse I don't earn some serious bread, like today. Here we are."

She directed them into the doorway of a vacant building.

"This isn't a hotel," Rector Richter said.

"Upstairs," the girl said. "Several of us got rooms up there. Bathroom, kitchen and everything."

And a bedroom, Rux thought, as they helped her up old wooden stairs. "How does your man expect you to earn any money if you can't work?" he asked.

"I'll be okay. Besides, you scarin' off customers. They see two guys in an old truck and they be thinkin' cops on a stake out."

"We're not cops," Rux said. "We'll be gone soon. How much could you have made during the time we were here?"

"At least one trick. Fifty."

Rux took out his wallet. "How about forty?"

"Fair enough," the girl said as she took two twenties from him.

The hooker drew out her key and opened her door.

Rux said, "One more thing. Do you know any of the girls that work in Fantasies?"

"No, man. Different kicks, you know? Like, I earn my bread the hard way. Those girls in there dancing behind glass, nobody can touch them. My johns won't settle for that. They gotta waller in it."

Rux and Rector Richter made their way back down the stairs and to the street. "Please, haven't we had enough?" the Padre asked.

"I guess. The girls at Fantasies aren't going to talk to us. Let's go back to the Elk Horn. Maybe the bartender or someone else there can give us a better lead on Lila."

From the front of the hotel they could see a policeman inspecting the truck. "Oh no, now what?" Rux said.

"This your truck?" the officer asked when they approached.

"Yes," Rux said. "Is there a problem?"

"For openers, you're parked on the wrong side of the street. But that's not the problem. We have a complaint about two men harassing some of the girls at the club over there."

Rector Richter spoke up before Rux had a chance to think. "That would be us," he said. "But we weren't harassing anyone. We are trying to find a young lady...."

Rux and the officer listened while the Padre related the whole story, all the way back to Pine Knot. He remembered to include the part about him being a priest.

The officer said, "Let me see some I.D."

Rux produced his driver's license. Rector Richter handed the officer a card that apparently identified him as a clergyman.

Not your typical cop, Rux thought. Young, clean cut, looks Mexican. With any luck, maybe he's Catholic.

The officer seemed satisfied. "You have to understand, the girls working over there might be a little skittish of strange men," he said, "considering the work they're in."

"What seems strange," Rector Richter said, "is people calling the police about two men sitting in a truck. Didn't anyone complain about the wino exposing himself to the world while he urinated on the building? Or about the pimp beating up his girl? Or, for that matter, about the prostitute working on the corner all afternoon?"

"All that's normal in this neighborhood," the policeman said. "Two white guys in a pickup, that's different. What's the name of the person you're looking for?"

"Sammi Stone," Rux said. "A girl named Lila works at the club. We think she may have some idea where Sammi is."

"What is Ms. Stone's address here in Los Angeles?"

"Twenty-Nine Palms Apartments down in Anaheim," Rux said.

"That's Orange County. Hold on a second."

The policeman walked back to his black and white cruiser and spoke to his partner waiting in the car, then returned to the truck. "Did you check to see if she was on the missing persons report or anything like that?"

Rux assumed "anything like that" meant in jail. Even that would be better than dancing at Fantasies. "No, not yet," he said.

The officer asked, "What's Lila's last name?"

"We don't know," Rector Richter said. "Lila is all we have."

"Okay. Give me the address and phone number where you're staying. I'll see what I can do."

The policeman took the information, walked back and spoke to his partner again, then said to Rux and Rector Richter, "Wait in the truck. I'll be right back." He crossed the street and entered the club as Rux and the Padre climbed back into the pickup.

Dusk settled around them in the few minutes the police officer was gone. "What do you think he's doing in there?" Rector Richter asked.

"Beats the heck out of me. Probably getting us free passes to the show. Or maybe he's checking it out to see if it's worth our money."

"I don't think so." Rector Richter continued a steady drum beat on the side of the truck with his fingers. "He seems like a nice young man."

"He's not the ordinary cop, that's for sure. If he was, we'd probably be sitting in jail nursing lumps on our heads."

The officer emerged from the club and waited for a red Cadillac to pass before re-crossing the street. The car drove slowly. The pimp and several cohorts glared at Rux and Rector Richter.

"You know those people?" the officer asked as he reappeared at the passenger side window.

"We had a run-in with one of them earlier," Rux said. "That's the pimp that beat up his girl."

"Figures," the policeman said. "Listen, I know where to reach you if we turn up anything on Ms. Stone. I also left the information with the lady who runs the club. There is a Lila working there, but I can't promise you she'll call."

"Thank you, Officer," Rector Richter said. "You've been very helpful."

"I'm going to do you one more favor and follow you back to the freeway. Don't come back over here."

The old pickup needed little encouragement as they sped onto the Santa Ana Freeway towards Anaheim.

"Well," Rux said, "it took all day, but maybe we've made contact with Lila. I just hope she calls."

"And knows something when she does," Rector Richter said. "Let's find our troupe and get something to eat."

"Tell you what, I better hang around the room in case Lila calls. Do you mind bringing me something back?"

"Sure. But Missy is expecting some news about her mother. Before we go eat, you should take her to get something to drink and explain where we are. If Lila calls, I can find out what she knows."

"Yeah, I suppose you're right." He may be right, Rux thought, but what am I going to tell Missy? We have no clue where her mother is or if she is even still in Los Angeles. We can't go back to Pine Knot because the state may put Missy in a foster home. And I'll most likely be arrested.

On top of all that, her mom has my old hat with all the wisdom in it. The only good news is, Chester and Howard are not traveling, for the moment.

Rux opened the door to their motel room and immediately wished Howard were traveling, at least some place else to potty. The smell of the litter box would slay dragons. Rux walked to the middle of the boulevard, dumped the litter box in the esplanade and returned to be greeted by the Red "C".

The Pine Knot contingent of the Mouse parade appeared tired, hungry but as giddy as ever. Missy's giddiness faded considerably when she realized her mother was not there.

"Hi, Rux," she called from the old truck. "Where's Mom?"

"Don't know just yet." Rux opened the gray door with the faded red C and helped Missy, Auren and Juanita out of the pickup. "Missy," he said, "let's you and me get something to drink. I'll explain what we found out today."

Rux handed the litter box to Rector Richter and motioned for him to place it in the other room reserved for their female counterparts. The Padre directed Emilio, Juanita and Auren into the room while Rux steered Missy toward the restaurant.

"Coffee for me," Rux said to the waitress as they slid into a booth. "Root beer all right for you, Miss?"

Missy nodded. Rux sensed the apprehension in her silence. "We didn't find your mom today," he said. "But I think we just missed connections. I'm expecting a call tonight from a lady who should know where she is."

That's a stretch, he thought. Don't lead her into counting on something you can't deliver. Missy's lower lip quivered as she stared at the table. Rux ached inside. He wanted to slide in the booth beside her and hold her, but he was in enough trouble already. He took her hands instead.

"Rux, I know something's wrong. Mom is either hurt or in trouble. She wouldn't leave us like this without calling or something." Her voice trailed off and the tears began to flow. Missy freed one hand and shielded her eyes.

The waitress sat the coffee and root beer on the table and politely left without saying anything.

"I know it looks bad, Miss. But we really don't know anything at this point. We shouldn't imagine the worst until we find out more."

Missy glanced from behind her hand but remained silent except for her sniffling.

"Wherever your mom is, I'm sure she's thinking of you right now. Everything will be okay, I promise."

Auren, Juanita and Emilio entered the restaurant, then hesitated by the cash register when they saw Missy. Rux motioned them over. "Here comes our compadres," He said. "I'm going to go back to the room and wait for the phone call so Rector Richter can come eat. Hang tough a little while longer, Missy. We'll get through this."

Missy gave him a weak smile as Auren sat down beside her and gave her a big hug. Rux excused himself and hurried off to relieve the Padre. I need to hang a little tougher myself, he thought. I wish I had punched out that puke of a pimp this afternoon.

Rector Richter and Emilio had long since crashed when Rux caught himself nodding. He looked at the clock radio on the night stand between the two beds. Two o'clock. Maybe Lila works the night shift, he thought. I'll just wait her out.

At five o'clock, Emilio shook him awake. "Rux, I'm going to get a shower. Why don't you get in bed and sleep for a while. You'll hear the phone if it rings."

Two hours later, Rux jerked up from a dead sleep when someone knocked on the door.

"I'll get it," Emilio said. "Probably the girls wanting to go eat breakfast."

"Yes?" Emilio said, opening the door only a crack so as not to expose Rector Richter coming out of the bathroom in his underwear. Rux could barely make out a small figure in a blue jacket.

"Are you Mr. Tuttle?" a feminine voice asked.

"No," Emilio said. "Just a second, I'll get him."

Rux already had a mouth full of toothpaste and boots on his feet before Emilio turned around. Rector Richter stepped back in the bathroom as Rux opened the door.

"Hi, I'm Rux Tuttle...You must be Lila."

"Yes, You're looking for Sammi?"

"Right. Would you like to get some coffee?"

Rux tried to hide the excitement in his voice as he stepped into the cool morning air and led Lila to the restaurant. From his vantage point across the table, Rux concluded the bartender was right. There seemed to be little to recommend Lila for exotic dancing other than her pretty green eyes, which were hard to notice behind her large, sequined glasses.

"Do you know how to get in touch with Sammi?" he asked.

Lila unzipped her jacket, displaying a T-shirt from a Fleetwood Mac concert. The caricature on the shirt lay relatively flat. "Why do you need to find her?"

Her voice had more than a little hostility. Not good, Rux thought. "I, we, are friends of hers from Arizona. Her daughter is with us."

"You're telling me she left her ten-year-old daughter with two men?"

Better, Rux thought. At least she knows Sammi well enough to know Missy's age. "No, she left her with a Mexican couple that lives on the ranch where she was staying. They're here also. Sammi got a deal with an agent here in L.A., had to leave in a hurry. She intended to get settled and come back for her daughter in a week or so."

Lila sat quietly for a moment, stirring her coffee and occasionally glancing at Rux over her glasses. Finally, she lay the spoon down, picked up the cup with both hands and stared hard at Rux. "Maybe," she said.

"Maybe what?"

"Maybe I don't know what to think. You know where I work, right?"

Rux hesitated. "Yes, that's how we found you."

"I understand." Lila sat the cup down and lowered her eyes. "What I want you to understand is, it's not something I would ordinarily be doing. My husband left me with no money, two kids and a ton of bills."

Rux had a sudden sinking feeling he was about to add three more to his traveling side show. "Hey, look," he said, "I'm sorry."

Lila fixed him with another stern look. "It's not your concern," she said. "The point is, working in the club you have to be careful. The type of people that come in there I don't want to meet on the street."

Lila leaned back and sighed heavily. "You don't look familiar, though. Have you been in the club?"

"No, not to see the show." Rux realized he needed the Padre and his clergyman's identification card. "Me and another guy, a priest, came in yesterday looking for you. The lady out front wouldn't give us the time of day. A policeman took the number of our motel and left it with her."

Lila hunched over the table and alternated between studying Rux and studying her coffee. Finally, she smiled at him. "Okay," she said. "Everything fits. You're either honest or you have a smooth way of luring a girl out."

Rux's own grin relieved his anxiety. "Maybe both," he said.

"Unfortunately, I don't know where Sammi is. I was hoping you would know. After her band broke up, she went with me to the Fantasies Club. But that wasn't for her. Sammi is way out of that league."

"Where was she living then?"

"Over at the Twenty-Nine Palms. But I think she's left there. Another friend who lives in the apartment right below hers saw her leaving with two men about a week ago. She hasn't seen her since."

"Did your friend know the men?"

"I don't think so. She said one was tall, blond-headed. The other one looked like a Mexican hood."

Rux had a sudden flashback to Moose Ball's, several months earlier. "Peter and Hector," he said.

Lila dumped several creamers into her coffee. "Who's Peter and Hector?"

"Mutual acquaintances. That may be who Sammi left with. Did the Mexican have a pony tail? And did the blond guy have a crooked nose?"

"I don't know. Let me call my friend and ask." Lila checked her watch before sliding out of the booth. "I guess she's awake by now."

Rux debated about whether he was awake yet. He twisted his neck and back to loosen the kinks left by his long night in the plastic chair.

"Any luck?" He asked Lila as she returned from the phone.

"Sort of. She thinks she remembers the pony tail, but she wasn't close enough to tell about the nose."

"Lila, you're a sweetheart. You've told me exactly what I need to know."

The girl's smile appeared genuine. Apparently she wasn't used to being called a sweetheart without a glass window separating her from her admirer. "That's great," she said, patting his arm. "You can find Sammi now?"

"Not quite, but I know where to start looking. She's back in Houston."

"Well, good luck," Lila said. She stood to leave. "I need to get home. I hope you find her. Sammi is a sweet girl. I wouldn't want anything bad to happen to her."

Rux watched Lila as she walked out of the restaurant and across the parking lot. Her short-cropped, dishwater blond hair seemed to have a bounce it did not have earlier. And he was sure he could discern an ample figure beneath her heavy coat.

"That bartender doesn't know a real woman when he sees one," he said to himself. "I'd pay to see her dance without her clothes."

Rux quickly dropped money on the table for the coffee and tip, and rushed out to the parking lot. "Lila, wait," he called, catching her in the process of backing out of her parking space. "One more question. Why did you come out here today?"

Lila's green eyes looked puzzled. "To help Sammi," she said.

"I know, but you had no idea who we were. We could have been customers from the club. I left the phone number. All you had to do was call."

Lila laughed. "I guess I wanted to meet you," she said. "You came highly recommended."

"Recommended? By whom?"

"Well, the manager of the club for one. She said the cop spoke well of you and your friend. And you didn't want to see the show. But the person who really convinced me was the dancer on the bus."

Rux pushed his hat back and thought for a second. "What dancer?"

"The one who ran from you when you asked if she was me. She saw what happened between the pimp and his hooker, and you and your friend running over to help. Listen, if you...when you find Sammi, give her my love. Tell her to call and let me know she's okay."

Lila touched his cheek lightly with soft fingers. "I need to go," she said.

"Thank you," Rux said. He straightened and stepped aside, then watched as she scooted her little car into the freeway traffic. The bartender was right, but for the wrong reason, he thought. I'd like to have her for a friend, fully dressed.

Rux hurried to his room and called Lee Wiley Willcox. The lawyer assured him he had contacts in Houston and told Rux to stay in touch until they found something.

"Houston?" Rector Richter asked.

"Yes," Rux said. "I'm sure of it. I've got to get down there right away so I can move as soon as Lee Wiley has a lead."

"I agree," the Padre said. "But what about the girls and Emilio. We can't leave them here."

"Right," Rux said. "I'm not thinking clearly."

He thought, what is this "we" stuff, Padre. But regardless of who went to Houston, they all had to be shepherded somewhere. We'll pick up Chester and drive back as far as Phoenix. If things are okay in Pine Knot, they can drive on back home and I can fly to Houston. If not, well, we'll bridge that cross when we come to it.

* * *

By mid-afternoon, Camel Back Mountain loomed on the horizon. "Another pit stop?" Rux asked Missy.

"Sure. We need to get Chester out and let him stretch a while anyway."

Rux steered into the rest area amongst the eighteen wheelers and Volvos with U-Hauls. He waved Rector Richter up to the parking lot for passenger cars.

As Rux walked out of the rest room, another pickup pulled up and parked beside the Red "C". The truck appeared to be loaded with all of the driver's worldly possessions. A rooster in a small wire coop crowed in loud protest.

"Aw, shut up," the driver yelled as he disembarked and headed for the rest room. The roster quieted to a jerky rattle that sounded like he had swallowed his tongue.

Missy walked up and spoke to the chicken, starting his squawking again.

"Aw, shut up!" the man yelled from the rest room.

Missy and Rux hurried to their trailer. "I hope that guy's not going too far," Rux said. "Traveling with a horse and a cat is bad enough, but at least they're quiet."

"I think the guy with the rooster just solved his problem," Missy said.

Rux turned to see the truck speeding out of the rest area. The cage with the rooster sat on the pavement beside the Red "C". The patron saints of the animal world, Juanita and Auren, mothered over the bird.

"Oh, no," Rux said. "I hope they plan on cooking that chicken for dinner."

"I doubt it," Missy said.

Rux knew she was right. The bonding process had already begun.

"Juanita," Emilio pleaded, "if you have to take him with us, is there any way you can keep him quiet?"

"Let's load him in the trailer with Chester and Howard," Juanita said. "Maybe he just needs a little company."

Rux deposited the screaming beast in the front of the trailer underneath Chester's water bucket. Chester and Howard refused to go back in the trailer.

"Try putting him in the back of the pickup," Auren suggested. "We'll put a blanket over him. If he thinks it's dark maybe he'll go to sleep."

To everyone's amazement, it worked. The chicken reduced his volume to a low, guttural noise. Auren asked, "What's he doing now?"

"Clucking," Emilio said.

Juanita said, "That's not a cluck. Hens cluck. Roosters crow."

"We all know his crow," Emilio said. "This is not crowing."

Auren asked, "If he's not clucking and he's not crowing, what's he doing?"

Juanita leaned over the cage, cocked her ear and listened carefully for a few seconds. "He's chortling," she said.

The rooster obligingly remained in his clucking, chortling mode while Rux and Missy loaded Chester and Howard. Rector Richter, Juanita and Auren retreated to the Red "C".

Rux fired up his truck. The rooster immediately started crowing again. The convoy rolled down I-10 through Tucson and Benson with their arrival heralded by an agitated chicken.

Each time they stopped, the rooster quieted.

Auren said, "Maybe he's car sick."

Rux said, "Maybe he'd prefer to walk. The town of Willcox is just ahead. Let's get some dinner and find you ladies a motel. I'm sure we can find a decent place on the outskirts of town that will accept small pets."

"Fine," Juanita said. "Just don't tell them one of your small pets might crow all night."

"Never mind," Rux said. "We'll find another roadside park for me and the traveling grange. Emilio and Padre, you guys want to get a room tonight?"

Emilio shrugged. Rector Richter said, "The truck is fine with me. If the rooster stays quiet."

Willcox was not big enough to have outskirts but did have a motel and a decent chicken-fried steak restaurant. Rux studied his map while they waited on their food. He marveled at the merry band, laughing and picking at each other just as they did around the kitchen table at Deke's ranch.

Juanita distributed everyone's daily vitamin dose and Auren deposited the purification drops in each water glass.

Pine Knot sat more or less due north on the map, a winding four-hour journey up route 666. Houston appeared to be an eighteen-hour bus ride straight down I-10. Rux folded his map to make room for his plate.

The gap-toothed teenager delivering the food offered no resemblance to Sammi, but her uniform twanged a pleasant chord, reminding Rux of his mornings at the coffee shop where they first met.

I knew I should never have gotten involved with her, he thought. But I gotta admit, I went to Pine Knot as much to see Sammi again as to say good-bye to Deke.

Rux took advantage of Missy's trip to the restroom to again broach the subject of Pine Knot. "Listen," he said, "we are not that far from the ranch. I could catch the bus to Houston and you guys can take the trucks on back home."

Rector Richter asked, "What about Missy? I assume the CPS lady is still looking for her."

"I'll talk to Sheriff Mo," Rux said. "Maybe he can keep Missy clear of the CPS lady for a few days until I can get Sammi back."

Juanita busily stirred catsup among the cream gravy covering her steak, then stabbed two French fries and waved them in the air. "Too risky," she said. "Besides, Rux, you can't go back even with Sammi until this child molesting mess is cleared up. I vote we go on to Houston."

Everyone else agreed. Rux kept one eye on the bathroom door to be sure Missy was still detained. What kind of a mess will I be in, he thought, if I get pulled over by the highway patrol? How do you explain a squawking rooster, a jake leg cat, a horse, an Indian who lives in the past century, and a horny priest on sabbatical from his sabbatical? On top of all that, I'm probably traveling with two illegal Mexicans.

Rux said, "We may come across an immigrations check point, driving this close to the border."

"So what?" Juanita said.

"Well," Rux said, "aren't you and Emilio worried you might get caught?"

Juanita held up her hand for silence while she swallowed a large bite of her steak. "Rux," she said, "How do you come up with this stuff? Emilio and I were both born in Los Angeles. And I'm not even Mexican, I'm Greek."

"Greek?"

"Yes, Greek. From Greece. You know, like Plato and Aristotle. You have heard of Plato and Aristotle, haven't you?"

Rux could see Missy returning to the table. "Certainly," he said. "I know Aristotle. He's a big, liver chestnut stallion. Last I heard of him he was on a ranch down in San Antonio. At least think about what I said. We can decide in the morning."

* * *

The rooster seemed perfectly content as long as he was not moving. He slept right through the sunrise, although Rux did not.

Rux perched himself on the pipe fence separating the roadside park from the adjacent desert. He absently tossed twigs at a beetle hole, waiting for the sun to stir his traveling companions. He reached for his hat, realized it remained on the mirror of the truck, and pacified his studying needs with serious contemplation of reeds in a stock tank some distance out in the desert.

"I've got to be firm," he said to the reeds. "They will understand. Missy will, anyway. She needs to be back in school. It will be a lot easier getting her mother back if I don't have to worry with keeping tabs on my endlessly expanding family of friends and animals."

Rux shook his head and then looked back at the tank. The reeds appeared to be moving about the water although they maintained the same spatial relationship to each other. "Oh, ducks," he said, as one of the reeds skimmed across the water's surface and took flight. "I wonder if they would like to join the rest of the animal kingdom on our journey to Houston. All I need is an ark and a good rain."

Rux swung his legs back across the fence rail and lowered himself to the ground. Better get moving, he thought. I've got a long bus ride ahead of me.

Twenty-one

Rux assured himself he was on the right road, although there is little to distinguish one part of the high plains of West Texas from any other. The old house, still the yellow with brown trim he remembered from his youth, loomed closer and closer. But somehow it seemed strangely unfamiliar.

As he crossed the cattle guard it occurred to him. The cottonwood tree, the only thing taller than a grain silo for two hundred miles in any direction, no longer dominated the yard. The front of the green-shingled house stood naked to the world, its porch railing with several missing pickets grinning sardonically at the endless prairie.

Jeremiah Tuttle held the screen door open with one hand and used the other to shield his eyes against the morning sun. Rux bounded across the brown yard in long strides and bear-hugged him with his familiar, "Hi, Dad."

Jeremiah stood ramrod straight, with no hint of stooping from old age.

Rux asked, "What happened to the cottonwood tree? I almost didn't recognize the place. Nothing out here now higher'n a telephone pole all the way to El Paso."

The elder Tuttle struggled free from his son's embrace and fixed him with a stern glare. Rux pretended not to notice the tears moistening his father's eyes, and blinked his own as though dust had gotten in them.

The first words Rux heard from his father were, "Rux, I ain't goin' to no nursing home."

Before Rux could respond, Missy slunk up behind him and tried to make herself invisible. Emilio, Rector Richter, Juanita and Auren followed in short order. Rux made the introductions and each of his traveling companions assured Jeremiah they were happy to meet him.

Jeremiah mumbled the appropriate "hellos" and "how are yous," then regained his full voice. "I don't know if you're all so glad to meet me or just happy to be out of them trucks. Looks like you folks been on the road a while."

Rux asked his dad, "What's this about a nursing home?"

"Nuthin," Jeremiah said. "The cottonwood just shriveled up and died of old age, like most everything else around here. Couldn't find a nursing home for decrepit trees."

Jeremiah ushered Emilio, Juanita, Rector Richter and Auren into the house, then joined Rux and Missy to help unload the animals. He held Chester while Missy removed the horse's leg wraps, then turned him loose in the pasture behind the barn.

"Nice horse," Jeremiah said.

"Thanks," Missy said, obviously assuming the remark was addressed to her. "He belongs to Rux." She hung the halter and lead rope over the gate, then scooted for the house.

"Could you use a rooster?" Rux asked his dad.

"I suppose. The one I got's about spent. You sure don't believe in traveling light, do you? Where you headed with all these folks?"

Rux explained his plight as best he could. "Dad," he said, "I know it's a big imposition on you, me just showing up out of the blue with a small circus. But I need to run down to Houston and find the girl's mother. I should be back in a couple of days. Can they bunk here until then?"

Rux watched his father take off his hat and study the inside while running a gnarled hand through his thick gray hair. "Sure," he said. "Might be nice to have company. Been a spell since a female voice graced this old place."

As they walked toward the house, Rux noticed the deep tan of his father's face included his forehead, normally left more pale by his hat.

"You look good, Dad. You been working outside without your hat?"

"Some, I guess." Jeremiah stopped and turned to face his son. "Truth is, Rux, ever since the good Lord called your momma home I just been waiting to die myself." The old man lowered his head.

"Aw, Dad. No. I didn't realize...look, I never should have left after Mom's funeral. It just never occurred to me...."

Jeremiah glanced up to meet Rux's eyes, then lowered his own again and feebly gestured toward the prairie. "This," he said, turning to face the brown grass extending beyond the barn and all the way to the horizon. "I love this land, but seventy years in this sun and wind is enough. I'm ready to go, I just want to die on my own terms. Not like your momma, off in some nursing home with tubes stuck all in her."

Rux felt awkward talking to his father's back, but he sensed Jeremiah was tearing up again. "Dad," he said, "I'll take care of you, wherever you want to live."

"Oh, here's fine."

A sudden surge of guilt left Rux unsteady. The last thing a man waiting to die needs, he thought, is his prodigal son showing up to disrupt the process. "Fine with me, too," he said. "Soon as I get this other mess straightened out I'll move back here and we'll get this old ranch humming again."

Jeremiah walked back toward the barn. "See that fence yonder?" he said, pointing to a new barbed wire fence.

"Yeah."

"Well, Rux, that's another problem I really didn't want to tell you about. But I guess it's better you hear it from me than some lawyer. That fence is now our boundary. Bank took the rest of it."

Rux stared at the fence in stunned silence. Jeremiah and his brother had inherited equal portions of their father's two thousand acre ranch. That two thousand had originally been a part of ten thousand acres settled by Rux's great-grandfather, who arrived on the plains shortly after the windmill.

He had often heard his dad repeat his great-grandfather's tales of grass as high as a man's head, millions of buffalo, and wild Indians.

"They took the whole thousand acres?" Rux finally asked.

"All but twenty acres the house and barn sits on. Bank held a perpetual mortgage on everything else. I would have hocked that, too, but Carter Hamilton advised me not to, many years ago."

"You and Carter have been friends all your lives. How could he foreclose? The bank always saw the farmers through the crop failures and bad weather. And they always got repaid in the good years."

Jeremiah turned and smiled at his son. For as long as he could remember, that big, friendly smile had assured Rux everything would be okay. "Weren't his doings, I reckon. Carter was president of the bank, but he only had a minority interest. He and his brothers and sisters inherited the bank from their father just like we inherited the land.

"His brothers and sisters sold their interest to a national banking syndicate out of Dallas. They tolerated a couple of years of partial payments, then foreclosed. Happened to a bunch of us. Carter got fed up and moved to Lubbock."

Jeremiah took Rux by the arm and gently guided him to the house.

I should have been here, Rux thought. I'm not sure I could have done anything, but at least he wouldn't have had to go through this alone. "Sounds like the new bankers ain't much into understanding."

Jeremiah chuckled. "Kinda like mother nature, I suppose. You gotta deal with what they bring you."

"Neither of them has a sense of humor, that's for sure."

Inside they found the men standing in the middle of the kitchen with their hands in their pockets and their elbows tucked in. The womenfolk were touring each room, "ooohing" and "aaahing" over his mother's collection of collectibles the way people did at a fireworks display.

Jeremiah said, "My wife did all this," obviously wanting to make sure they understood the menagerie was not his.

Rux marveled in silence. Everything appeared to be in place and sparkling clean, just as if Mom had never left. They may have belonged to Mom, he thought, but I think Jeremiah has accepted them. His dad had railed for years about having to spend ten minutes every night unloading the fancy pillows and ceramic cats from the bed before he could get in it. But there they sat, every last pillow and sterile feline neatly in its place.

Juanita and Auren shortly took over the kitchen and exiled Missy and the men to the living room.

Juanita asked, "What would you like for dinner, Mister Tuttle?"

Jeremiah eased back in his rocker, scratched behind the ears of the jake leg yellow cat curled up in his lap, and said, "Anything but meatballs and spaghetti."

* * *

After dinner, Missy scraped a few bites of leftover steak in a pan for Howard and asked, "Rux, do you think it's too cold to ride Chester?"

"Shouldn't be if we get out there before the sun sets. I'd go easy on him, though. Remember, he's been in that trailer for several days."

Missy turned to Jeremiah. "Mister Tuttle, would you like to come with us?"

"Sure thing, Missy."

Rux, Jeremiah and Missy all donned their jackets and headed for the pasture. Chester, obviously in no mood for work, stood in the corner farthest from the gate and watched Missy approach with the halter and lead rope.

Jeremiah and Rux met them in the barn with the grooming tray and tack. They held the horse while Missy brushed him and checked his feet.

Missy said, "Mister Tuttle, do you ride?"

"Well yes I do, little lady. Least I did once. Sold my horse along with the cows some years back."

"Rux is going on to Houston to find my mom. Can you help me with Chester until he gets back?"

Jeremiah's chest swelled noticeably as he tried to stifle a grin. "That's a mighty frisky colt, Miss, but I reckon I been on worse. Used to rodeo in my younger days."

Missy asked, "Did you ever get bucked off?"

"Oh, I probably come off one a time or two. Been a while though. Wouldn't want to do that now."

Missy tossed the blanket and saddle on the tall horse like the professional she had become. "Chester's easy to ride," she said. "Let me warm him up a little, then you can try him. Do you ride English?"

"No, I'm afraid not. All these old range ponies out here knows is go, get there and stop."

Rux gave Missy a leg up into the saddle and she reined the horse back out to the pasture.

"Chester can do western or English," she said, "depending on whether you set him up in the bridle or let him drop over."

Rux shrugged in answer to his father's questioning look. Missy worked the horse in a slow walk and canter, then pushed him into an easy trot. Once he had worked up a sweat, she brought him to the back of the barn where Rux and Jeremiah stood watching.

"You ready to ride?" she asked Jeremiah.

"Sure," Jeremiah said. "But I don't think I can get him to do all that."

"You'll do fine, Mister Tuttle."

Rux watched with the glowing smile of a proud father as Missy and Chester spent the next half hour teaching Jeremiah the finer points of English riding. Rux was sure his dad had forgotten all about tubes and nursing homes, although Chester did his best to remind him.

Chester and Jeremiah gave a simultaneous sigh of relief when Missy finally called a halt to the lesson. Rux took the horse's reins as Jeremiah slid off and wobbled into the barn.

"These old legs ain't used to this," Jeremiah said, rubbing the insides of his thighs. "That was more fun than I've had in a while though, Missy. Thank you."

"You did great," Missy said. "But...."

Rux volunteered to remove the horse's tack and cool him out as Missy launched into a series of explanations about Chester's idiosyncrasies and how to deal with them. He led the horse around the pasture, marveling at his dad's attention to the instructions being given him by someone young enough to be his granddaughter.

Chester nudged forward and rubbed his muzzle against Rux's arm. "Thanks, buddy," Rux said. "Nothing I like better'n horse slobber all over my sleeve. I guess you're entitled though, seeing as how you and Missy done a world of good for Jeremiah."

Rux's grin sagged in consort with his shoulders as the new barbed wire fence appeared in the fading light. Missy and Chester could do wonders for Jeremiah's spirit but they couldn't bring back the nine hundred and eighty acres the bank took. And the gaiety of the riding lesson could only temporarily gloss over Rux's shame for having left his father so soon after his mom's death.

"Well, Chester," he said. "We set out to get Sammi back, and get this bunch home to Pine Knot. Now we've added Dad to the clan, and from the way he's taken a shine to you and Missy, looks like he may be coming along as well."

Rux removed the halter from Chester and allowed him to search the dead grass for something on which to graze. No way, he thought. Tuttles have been a part of these plains for four generations. Dad's roots here are too deep. If they ran a seismic test his feet might be mistaken for a new oil bearing stratum.

Rux ignored the fact that he was now conversing with the horse's rear end and continued to outline his plan. "I'll go get Sammi," he said to the swishing tail. "And we'll get them all back to Pine Knot. But then you and me's coming back here to take care of Dad."

Twenty-two

Sammi adopted Juanita's dieting theory as the preferred method for kicking her cocaine habit. She would go cold turkey, starting tomorrow. It would be tough, but her mind would be occupied with cleaning her little garage apartment.

Mostly, she had to get herself clean. Promises to herself were easily put off. But she had also promised Tyrone. She knew he would do everything he could to help.

In less than a week she had managed to turn the apartment into a pig sty, with dirty clothes, dirty dishes and half-eaten food all over the place. Her roaches had invited their friends from all over the city. "Tomorrow," she said as she rose to answer the knock at the door.

She stood on her tiptoes and peeked through the small triangle of a window high up on the door. All she could see was a bushy Afro, but she recognized it as belonging to Tyrone.

As she opened the door the full brightness of the midday sun almost knocked her backwards.

"Whoa," Sammi said. "Come on in, buddy. I'm not used to this much daylight."

"Hey, Sam. Man, you need to get outside more. Little sunshine ain't gonna hurt you."

Sammi knew he was being kind. She was pale and gaunt. Singing at Cactus George's at night and mellowing out on crack during the day were taking their toll.

"Tomorrow," she whispered.

Tyrone followed her through the maze of unwashed clothes and pizza boxes to the little bar that defined the kitchen area.

"Enough with the tomorrow bidness," Tyrone said. "Sam, you gotta kick this stuff. Be tough for a week or so, but you can do it. If you don't mind stayin' with black folks I can take you over to Mamma Henry's. She'll hang with you 'till you get through it."

"Thanks, Tyrone. Tomorrow, I promise, but I'm singing at George's tonight."

Tyrone deposited his grocery sack on the bar. "Tomorrow," he said. "For sure. No more puttin' off after that. I gots to head on."

"More philodendrons?"

"Azaleas. Spring comin', white folks be wantin' flowers."

"I assume your supplier has a good stock."

"Nice ones, already startin' to bloom. Snuck 'em out last night."

Sammi laughed. "And you still put back what you don't sell. You ever worry about getting caught?"

"Hey, bro gotta make a livin'. I'm gone."

Sammi returned to the window overlooking Patton street and watched Tyrone's grandmother's old Chevy back out of the driveway and head for I-45. She dropped a rock of coke into the plastic bottle, lit it, and took a long, slow pull on the straw inserted in the side of the bottle.

Her eyes focused on the neon blue cross in front of the small white church across the street. The blue neon spelled out "Jesus Saves." Tomorrow, she would kick her habit and go back to Pine Knot. Tyrone could come, too.

Thinking of Pine Knot was too painful. Sammi forced her mind elsewhere while she waited for the crack to take effect. California. The dream still enthralled her even though it had been a disaster. Traveling with Earle and the Red Neck band, performing before boisterous crowds, she could live that again.

If Evan had stuck with her they might have eventually found the right high for her to perform in the studio the way she did on stage. But the band fell apart and Earle split for San Francisco.

Earle had roused her early one morning in Oxnard. They had performed the night before and normally slept until around noon, but the phone rang at nine o'clock.

"Sorry to call so early," Earle said, "but we have to leave. Pack your stuff and meet me at the van right away."

"Don't we have another show tonight?"

"It's canceled. I'll explain on the way."

Sammi tossed her bag and guitar into the van and climbed in the passenger seat with only a casual glance at Earle through leaden eyes. Nothing unusual. She normally rode with Earle and the equipment and the others came in their own cars.

"Why are we leaving so early?" she yawned. "Or more precisely, why are we leaving at all? I thought we had a three-day gig."

"We did, but the band no longer exists. I think you know Kenny and I are an item, or were. We broke up last night."

Kenny was the band's drummer. Sammi knew he and Earle were lovers, they made no secret of it. The sight of them holding hands repulsed her at first. But what the heck, she reasoned, this is California. Nineteen-Eighty-Seven.

"Couldn't you two break up and still keep the band together?"

"Under different circumstances, maybe. Kenny moved out of our apartment in L.A. Said he wanted more time to himself. I didn't like it, but I could understand that. When we booked this gig he asked for a separate room, which I agreed to although it meant extra expense. Then he shows up last night with his new lover."

Sammi looked at Earle for real. Red whelps dotted his face. "What happened?"

"The three of us had it out after the show. They look worse than I do. Sam, I'm going up to San Francisco and start a new band. I want you to come with me."

"I can't, Earle. I'm under contract with Evan Vaughn. Why don't you call me after you get your new band together? Maybe we can work something out."

Sammi didn't know herself if she meant that or was just being polite. It made no difference anyway, once Peter came back. She took several long pulls on her pipe and flopped on the bed. "Tomorrow," she muttered in her half stupor. "Maybe."

* * *

Noises from the street below woke Sammi from a deep sleep. She sat up, trying to orient herself in the dark. "Mama? Daddy?" Her words were absorbed by unfamiliar walls without reply. Little slivers of light danced through what appeared to be slats in a Venetian blind. She wasn't at home. Their house had window shades with curtains. She stumbled to the window and pried apart two of the slats. The street below looked vaguely familiar.

"Oh," she said, focusing on the blue "Jesus Saves" sign across the street. "Oh, no. I'm supposed to be at Cactus George's."

Sammi found the lamp by the bed, flipped it on and located her watch. A little after seven, I'm okay, she mused.

The top drawer of a small dresser provided her last clean pair of underwear. "I've got to find a washing machine," she said as she opened the bottom drawer and extracted her last clean pair of jeans and next to last clean shirt.

She dressed, grabbed the guitar and zipped down the stairs to the little blue car, a loaner from Peter. After several tries, the tiny car started and, at Sammi's careful urging, chugged off toward Airline Drive.

Fifteen minutes and lots of tender, loving care later, the blue bug gasped to a halt in Cactus George's parking lot. Sammi climbed out, gingerly patted the hood, and trucked in the back door.

"Hey, you look great," the bartender said.

"Thanks," Sammi said. "What kind of crowd do we have tonight?"

"Aw, usual for a week night, I guess. Several tables of ladies catching up on the latest gossip. All the husbands keeping the guy who owns the video and pin ball machines happy. Nobody drinking much, though. Sing 'em a few tear jerkers, see if you can get 'em crying in their beer."

"I'll try." Sammi hung her coat on a nail by the door, uncased her guitar and made her way to the corner where she performed. There was no stage, just a mike and a stool. She tuned the guitar, warmed up a little, then nodded to the bartender.

He unplugged the juke box and she started her first number. None of the customers seem to notice.

Several hours later, the crowd had dwindled to one couple arguing in a drunken slur and two men locked in mortal combat at one of the pin ball machines. The bartender motioned Sammi to shut it down. Sammi packed up and walked to the bar.

"Thanks," the bartender said. "Good job. You coming back tomorrow?"

"Sure. By the way, when do I get paid?"

"Oh, I thought you knew. I'm paying your agent, Mister Del Ossio. I assumed he would take care of your end."

A shudder rippled through Sammi. She had not talked to Peter other than him telling her he had arranged the job for her at Cactus George's. Peter controlled her money, and Hector controlled her supply of crack.

"You're right," she said, "Peter handles everything for me. Sorry."

"No problem. Come on, I'll walk you to your car."

Sammi led the bartender out the back door to Peter's little blue loaner car, wished him good night, and climbed in.

The bartender waited until she had locked the doors and started the engine, then waved and walked back inside. He seems nice, Sammi thought. Maybe I should explain my situation to him. Or maybe not. He obviously knows Peter. He would already know I'm only here temporarily, until I get my recording contract.

A cab pulled up in front of Cactus George's and honked. The soused couple that had been arguing inside protested loudly as the bartender shoved them in the cab and slammed the door.

The cab sped off. The bartender glanced at Sammi's car, hesitated, then turned and walked back in the bar.

Sammi followed the cab onto Airline. "Tomorrow, I promise," she said, remembering the one remaining cocaine rock Hector had left with her. The little blue car coughed, sputtered, then lurched down the dimly lit street as if there were no tomorrows.

Twenty-three

Before dawn the next morning, Rux pondered his fate relative to catching a flight out of Lubbock or driving to Houston. Flying would be quicker, but given his experiences with fat women in airplanes, he seriously considered giving the old truck a running start off the edge of the cap rock and soaring at least as far as Fort Worth.

hile he debated the fastest way to get to Houston, find Sammi and return, the old truck, on its own volition, made a hard right turn onto U.S. Highway 82 at the Ralls by-pass and bee-lined it for Lubbock.

"So much for executive decision making," Rux said to the automatic parking ticket dispenser at Lubbock International Airport. He carefully noted down the location of his parking spot on his ticket, deposited the ticket in the ash tray of the truck and headed for the terminal.

Good decision, he thought. If Lubbock is international, it's bound to have a direct flight to Houston Intercontinental. After all, he reasoned, Houston is a major drug distribution center. Lubbock, home of the Texas Tech Red Raiders, should be a primary destination, although the last time he was in Lubbock the student population had not yet advanced beyond peyote and chewing tobacco.

The bean pole behind the Southwest Airlines counter obviously indulged in both.

"Morning, Ma'am," Rux said. "I need a round trip to Houston Intercontintal."

The gangly, suntanned woman fixed him with a tobacco stained smile and immediately began punching her computer keyboard.

"Certainly, sir," she said. "We've got a flight leaving in thirty minutes. When will you be returning?"

Rux hesitated. He planned to be back tonight, but that plan had a familiar, hollow ring to it. "Tomorrow," he said. "I'll need a window seat."

"I'm sorry, sir," the ticket agent said. "We don't assign seats on Southwest Airlines. Here's your boarding pass with your number. We board on a first come, first on basis."

Rux's boarding pass bore number one hundred fifteen. The one hundred and fourteen passengers in front of him would each be a fat lady with a weak bladder and a strong body odor. He thought again of driving off the cap rock. He would be dead by the time he reached Houston anyway.

"Thank you," he said to the calf roping queen of West Texas. He stuck boarding pass number one hundred fifteen in his shirt pocket where he had intended to store his parking ticket with the location of his truck, picked up his bag and trudged off to find gate three.

A survey of his fellow passengers lounging in the boarding area confirmed his fears. He would be flying with the Texas Tech female sumo wrestling team, all no doubt perfumed with Stock Yard Number Five. Weak bladders were a given for lady sumo wrestlers.

"I need a drink," Rux said to the team in general.

One of them looked up from her Wrestler's Weekly magazine and pointed to a pizza stand across from the rest rooms. Pizza will work, he thought, dragging himself twenty yards further down the concourse to Lubbock's version of a gourmet restaurant.

"Coffee," he said to the first runner-up for calf roping queen of West Texas tending the pizza bar. Too much inbreeding, he thought. Rux handed her his money and unraveled against the standup counter.

At the opposite end of the counter a thin Latino woman struggled to open a plastic orange juice container. An equally thin boy shifted his weight from one foot to the other, apparently impatient to receive the juice. Rux guessed the kid to be of preschool age based on his size and mannerisms, although his slim face and slicked down black hair made him appear older.

Rux tipped his hat to the lady and said, "May I help?"

"Thank you, sir," the woman said, handing him the container.

Rux deftly sliced the top off the container with his pocketknife, returned the juice to the tiny lady, then re-focused his attention of the wresting team. Could this little lady possibly be on my flight? he wondered.

"Naw." He sipped his coffee and let his mind wander to Houston.

If Lee Wiley's information proved correct, finding Sammi would be easy. Convincing her to come back might be something else. What had happened in L.A.? How could she have just faded out of contact with them? Juanita was right. No mother would leave her child like that.

"I hope Peter is involved in this," he said to his cup. "Last time we met I bent his nose. The least I can do is straighten it out for him."

West Texas slang over the speaker system welcomed him to Lubbock International. "We are now ready to board flight number ten-ninety-seven to Houston," the gate attendant announced into a microphone she did not need. "With intermediate stops in Austin, San Antonio, Corpus Christi and Victoria."

My word, Rux thought. Good thing I didn't book a flight back tonight. I won't be in Houston before tomorrow. He watched the herd of woolly mammoths lumber out the door, across the tarmac and up the stairs to the unsuspecting plane. He accepted his plight, picked up his bag and joined the circus parade.

"I could have been half-way to Fort Worth by now," he said, surrendering his boarding pass to the gate attendant.

"Good morning," an obviously surprised stewardess said as Rux ducked into the tan and orange aircraft.

"I'm the trail boss," Rux said, and began the long, futile walk down the aisle in search of a window seat.

Fat ladies sat in every window seat, except the very last one at the back of the plane. The thin Latino lady had seated herself on the aisle and was busily buckling the boy into the middle seat next to her. Rux rushed back and smugly settled into the window seat beside them. The young lad had the scent of fresh pine soap.

Rux grabbed a pillow, pulled his Sunday-go-to-meeting hat over his eyes, and laid back for the long haul to Houston.

The kid threw up twice before they left the runway.

* * *

Six hours later, Rux staggered from the plane and gulped the stale air of the loading ramp in a desperate attempt to cleanse the stench of vomit from his nostrils. He flagged down a porter and asked, "Where can I rent a car, cheap?"

"How cheap, boss?"

"Cheap cheap. All I want is something to keep me dry while I drive into Houston and back."

"Try Ron's Rent-a-Rambler over on Greens Road. Take the shuttle to the Park-and-Ride lot and go west two blocks. Can't miss it."

The walk through Houston Intercontinental behind the stump-legged wrestlers took almost as long as the flight. At least the erupting orange juice kid and his mom had gone ahead on the porter's courtesy cart.

Rux crammed into the shuttle bus with three of his fellow passengers. He got off at the Park-and-Ride lot, found Greens Road with no problem, but determining west proved more difficult. The sun had conveniently hidden itself behind a leaden canopy.

His best guess was that west would be to his right. With swift calculation of the day's event's so far, he turned left. It worked.

Two blocks up the street he found a white portable building with "Ron's Rent-a-Rambler" plastered on the side in bright red plastic letters. The clanging of a cow bell attached to the door produced a bushy-haired young man from the adjoining room.

"Welcome the Ron's Rent-a-Rambler. I'm Ron," Ron said. "Need a car?"

"Right. What do you have in a subcompact?"

Ron slapped a sheath of forms on the counter and flipped through them. "A Rambler," he said.

"Rambler? As in Jeep?"

"No, Nash."

"Nash," Rux said. "They ain't been around for thirty years. What do you have in a compact?"

Ron made a grand production out of paging back through the forms. "A Rambler."

"How big do I have to go to get something produced in the second half of this century?"

"Actually, you can't. All I have is Ramblers. Three of them. You can have your choice."

"I'll take the Rambler."

"Good choice. Comes with a gas can and a set of jumper cables. I'll give you the businessman's discount."

Rux declined the insurance, reasoning if he wrecked the Rambler he could replace it with his pocket change. Ron agreed.

"Ever heard of Cactus George's?" Rux asked.

"Sure. Over on Airline. Here, I'll draw you a map."

Much to their mutual surprise, everything in the car worked except the driver's side window, which did not roll down. At least the weather's cold, Rux thought. Even the windshield wipers managed to remove most of the collecting mist, although they squeaked loudly in protest.

The minuscule excuse for modern transportation lumbered onto Greens Road and headed in what Rux hoped was the general direction of Airline and Cactus George's.

Ron's handwritten rental agreement indicated Rux's time of rental as three fifteen p.m. With any luck, he would have Sammi back at the airport by six o'clock.

Thirty minutes later, Rux steered the Rent-a-Rambler Rambler through the pot holes in the shell parking lot shared by Cactus George's and the Stop-n-Shop next door.

The number of cars in the parking lot in the early afternoon surprised him. Probably housewives meeting their lovers, he thought.

Inside, the housewives and their lovers tucked themselves into their booths as far as they could, casting nervous glances at Rux to be sure he wasn't a misplaced husband. The few singles at the bar eyed him for what he assumed were more productive reasons.

"Howdy, Pardner," the bartender yelled over the nasal twangs of Willie Nelson blaring from the juke box. "What'll it be?"

"Miller. Draft if you got it. I'm looking for Sammi Stone. Understand she works here."

"Sometimes. She may be in later tonight."

A chubby blonde with a pretty face, seated two stools down the bar, tapped her cigarette on the ash tray and re-crossed her legs, revealing more of her ample thighs. The smile she directed at Rux showed small white teeth and an equal amount of gums.

Rux tipped his hat and returned his attention to the bartender. "Know where I might find her?"

"Naw. You might try the Dead Man. He hangs out at Mama Henry's over on Cavalcade."

Rux drank his beer, got directions to Cavalcade Street, and returned to the Rent-a-Rambler Rambler. As he drove out of the parking lot he noticed the chubby blonde with the pretty face and small teeth using the pay phone in front of the Stop-n-Shop.

A fruitless hour driving up and down Cavalcade produced a number of bars but none called Mama Henry's. Rux finally spotted "Henry's Bar-B-Q" hand printed on a faded Orange Crush sign attached to one of several small, unpainted houses.

As soon as he parked and opened the car door, Rux realized Henry's clientele obviously didn't need a sign to find the place. The "Q" smoking on the cement block pit in the driveway filled the cold, damp air with a fragrance that attracted every stray dog and cat within a five mile radius.

The small black man tending the meat hunched low to avoid the roof of a rusted carport. Four thin metal posts, each bent at about the height of a truck bumper, suspended the roof in midair.

Rux entered the house, careful to set the screen door back in place, then turned to face several sets of maroon eyes. One set belonged to a figure awkwardly bent over a pool table in the back. His cue stick remained poised for the shot while the shooter's eyes studied Rux.

Three diners sat at one of several chrome-legged tables crowding the small room. A large, muscular man paused with his sandwich half way to his mouth, dripping barbecue sauce on the red checkered oil cloth.

The man with the drippy sandwich said, "Looka heah dis white boy wanderin' in like he was at the Steak and Ale."

Rux's eyes watered from the stifling cigarette and "Q" smoke. The plank floor creaked under him although he had not moved. Two of the men sitting at the table started to stand. The sound of a large wooden spoon slapping the counter stopped them half way out of their chairs.

A gargantuan woman cooking at a heavy black stove ordered them to sit. They sat.

"You lost, mister?" the woman asked.

"Looking for the Dead Man," Rux said.

"You da Man?" The woman's voice was stern but the tufts of gray hair sprouting from underneath her chef's hat and her large, friendly eyes suggested a gentle presence.

"No, ma'am. I need to locate someone. Understand the Dead Man can help me find her."

"Who she be?" a voice from the pool table asked.

"Sammi. Sammi Stone."

"An' who be askin'?" The voice merged with a thin black man moving around the pool table.

"Rux. I'm a friend from Arizona."

"Yeah. She talked about you. I'm the Dead Man."

Rux's tension eased as the small man with a large Afro extended a friendly hand.

"Tyrone Dedman. Come on back. We got some conversationin' to do. How'd you find me?"

"Guy at Cactus George's sent me over. Said you would know where to find Sammi."

Tyrone wiped barbecue sauce from a torn red vinyl seat and directed Rux to sit. "I'm glad you showed, man. But this ain't good. If Cactus George's people sent you that means Peter and Hector knows you're here, too. We best be movin' our dumb asses. You got wheels?"

"More or less." Rux tipped his hat to the woman by the stove as they stood to leave.

She acknowledged his silent "thank you" with a gold-toothed smile.

The gray February afternoon succumbed to early darkness as Rux followed Tyrone's directions west on Cavalcade, then south on I-45. The lights of downtown Houston loomed almost on top of them.

Rux swallowed his apprehension of Tyrone and asked, "Have you had much contact with Sammi since she returned?"

"Yeah. Nuthin' I'm proud of, though. I be tryin' to get her off crack. She's hooked bad, was when she got here. We talked maybe she should kick it while she still got a chance at singin', but so far she ain't. Romero just waitin' for Peter to give up on her, then he'll put her on the streets."

"That's not going to happen. What can I can give her to ease her off the cocaine?"

"Nuthin' I know of. She gotta go cold turkey."

'We owe you, Tyrone."

"Y'all don't owe me nuthin', bro. Me and Sammi go way back. Not many comin' outta Jose Urrea High School 'mount to much. But she was so sweet, you know, and so good with them cowboy songs. Everybody loved her. We all wanted her to make it. Exit here at Patton and go right."

"She was doing just fine up in Pine Knot. Never should have left. Something happened when she got to Los Angeles. You mentioned Peter.

Would that be Peter Del Ossio, Sammi's former husband?"

"Yeah, he's an agent. Singers, musicians, stuff like that."

"He connected with Romero?"

"Appears to be. Makes sense. That home boy's so eat up with the dumb ass he need Peter to keep from gettin' lost in his own driveway."

Tyrone pointed out a small garage apartment across Patton from an old white church with a blue "Jesus Saves" sign. A small patch of grass separated the garage apartment from a run down frame house that faced the black-topped street intersecting Patton.

On the opposite corner, a high cedar fence protected a neat, white brick house from the encroaching weeds covering the vacant lot bordering Patton.

The street light transformed the darkness into cascading shades of gray across the front half on the vacant lot. The back half of the lot and the small yard between the dilapidated house and the garage apartment were left in a dark void. Only a hint of light shimmered from the edges of drawn Venetian blinds in the two windows of the garage apartment overlooking Patton.

"Turn the corner and park down there past the fence," Tyrone said. "Sammi's in the apartment. Here's a key. I'm gonna split now, but I gotta warn you so you don't puke. Rotten food's all over the place. You'll smell it walking up the stairs. When you open the door the stench will take your head off."

"You gonna need any help?"

"Don't you worry 'bout me, bro. Just get her out quick."

"Thanks, man. If you're ever in Pine Knot...."

"Yeah, I know. Mention your name in any crapper and I'll get a good seat. Hurry up."

Roaches scattered from the half-eaten food when Rux flipped on the light. He heard Sammi stir in the bedroom as he stepped over the mounds of trash and moldy clothes. Her face lit up when she saw him, then froze in horror. She dove to the bed and under a blanket.

"No, No, No, Rux," she cried. "You can't see me like this."

Rux held her, perceiving her thinness and feeling the warm tears on his neck. "It's okay, Sam. We've got to get out of here."

The slamming of a car door jolted him to quickly kill the lights. Around the edge of the blinds he could make out the shadow of a large car parked behind the Rent-a-Rambler Rambler.

The silhouette of a short, stocky man stood by the car. Two larger figures were walking past the vacant lot toward the apartment.

"Peter," Rux said, although it was too dark to recognize anyone.

Sammi stiffened.

"Where's the back door?" Rux asked.

"There isn't one."

"Call the police."

"I can't. There's no phone."

"Great planning," Rux mumbled. "Wait in here." He grabbed what felt like a brass lamp and crept to the door. Through the small glass in the door he watched the two stealths ease up the stairs.

Rux stood against the wall opposite the door's hinges and listened as the door creaked open. One lanky leg attempted to feel its way inside. Rux swung. The lamp rang with a dull clank as it smashed into flesh.

The possessor of the flesh delivered something between vocalization and a guttural grunt and crashed into his equally surprised accomplice. Both men tumbled down the stairs and sprawled on the damp ground.

Only after he slammed and locked the door did Rux focus on what he thought he just saw in the darkness. A hat flew off the man's head. "Damn, that's my hat!" Rux said.

Both figures lay still in the dead grass. Rux bolted down the stairs and found his hat. One of the prone characters rolled about, holding his nose. Rux thought he could make out a head of blond hair. Peter!

The other man Rux assumed to be Hector struggled to his hands and knees, snarling like the Abbot's dog.

Rux wheeled and kicked him hard in the midsection. Hector whooshed and rolled onto his side, holding his ribs. Rux unleashed a wicked punch to his face. Hector brought his hands up. Rux aimed another fist at the howling face.

Peter grabbed Rux's leg and bit hard into his calf, hissing like an alligator. Rux snatched a handful of blond curls and pulled his leg free. He jerked Peter's face into his knee, coming with equal force from the opposite direction.

Peter clutched his face and pulled away. Rux turned quickly, sensing another attacker coming at him from the street. Hector was on his hands and knees again, apparently poising to charge at Rux. A hard kick to Hector's groin dispatched him to the fetal position, motionless and sucking wind.

Rux quickly assessed the two on the ground as temporarily disabled. He spun to face the figure looming out of the dark.

"Rux, wait! It's me!" Tyrone said, barely avoiding the oncoming fist.

"Arrggh!" Rux yelled as his fist slammed into the wall, sending a tremor through the garage. Rux slung his hand, trying to restore the feeling, and wished he hadn't. "Tyrone?" he said. "Where did you...I thought you left."

Tyrone waved a large garbage bag filled with something. "Thought we might need this."

"What?"

"I'll splain later. Po-leece on the way. Go get Sammi. We gots to git. I'll see these two don't bother us."

Rux glanced at the cars but could not locate the third man he had seen from the bedroom window. He grabbed both hats, bounded up the stairs and slammed the door behind him.

"Sammi, where are you? We've got to move."

"Right here," Sammi said, dragging herself out of the bedroom. "Are you okay?"

"Who knows. Here, take my jacket and one of the hats. I'll carry you to the car."

Rux wrapped his jacket around Sammi's shoulders and picked her up.

"Who's down there?" Sammi asked.

Peter and Hector, but they ain't in too good a shape. Tyrone's watching them. Plus another guy I can't account for."

Rux eased Sammi back to her feet but clung to her hand. They crept to the bedroom window and pried a crack in the blinds just large enough to see the street below. The "Jesus Saves" sign glowered at them.

Faint thumping signaled someone coming up the stairs. Rux pulled Sammi behind him and felt the darkness for another lamp.

Tyrone burst through the front door. "Rux, Sammi, you in here? We gotta move, now! Drug bust 'bout to go down."

"We're coming," Rux said. He picked Sammi up again and followed Tyrone down the stairs.

Hell of a time for a drug raid, Rux thought. But Tyrone's right. We don't want to be here. No telling what Sammi has stashed in the apartment.

In the yard, two figures writhed in obvious pain. Rux hurried behind Tyrone across the vacant lot. Tyrone ran ahead of them to the car parked behind the Rambler.

As he got closer, Rux could make out another body lying in the ditch. He quickly rehashed the previous ten minutes of his life and concluded this must be the stocky guy he saw standing by the car when they first pulled up.

Tyrone bent over the body, then opened the door to the large car and shoved the garbage bag under the front seat.

Rux ran past with Sammi and plopped her in the front seat of the Rambler. "Come on, Tyrone," he said, circling around to the driver's side. "We got bodies everywhere. This place looks like a war zone."

Tyrone piled into the back seat of the Rambler.

"Where to?" Rux asked.

"We gotta get out of this neighborhood," Tyrone said. "Get back on the freeway."

Rux made a sharp U-turn and zipped onto Patton toward I-45. "What was that guy doing in the ditch?" he asked Tyrone.

"Restin'. I tapped him in the back of the head with a brick. He be survivin' okay. Sammi, how you doin'?"

Sammi groaned but managed to say, "I'll make it. How about you?"

Tyrone let out a long, exaggerated breath. "We all gonna make it now," he said. "Rux, drop me back at Mama Henry's. Then y'all get out of this area. You got a place to stay?"

"No," Rux said. "We'll go to the airport and see if we can get a flight out tonight."

"Good idea." Tyrone leaned over the seat and patted Sammi's shoulder. "Get rid of this car, too, as quick as you can. This one of Ron's Rent-a-Rambler's?"

Rux floored the Rambler and forced his way into the freeway traffic. "Yeah," he said. "How'd you know?"

Tyrone laughed. "Not a whole lot of Ramblers around anymore. Won't be hard for the cops to trace it back to you if any of the home boys seen it."

Rux flipped on the blinker, zoomed off the freeway and made a right on Cavalcade. "Tyrone," he said. "What happened back there? How'd you know there was going to be a drug bust?"

"Hey, man, I was walking past the church when Peter's car pulled up. Ran inside and called my po-leece contact, told him where to find Peter and Hector. And that they had enough coke and horse to mellow half the Fifth Ward."

"How'd you...that's what was in the garbage bag?"

"Yo, baby."

"Should I ask where you got it?"

"From the church, inside the little stand they use to baptize babies. That's their drop."

Rux twisted to look at Tyrone. "And we don't wanna know how you knew that, right?"

"Right."

"Right," Sammi repeated. "Tyrone, why don't you come with us?"

Rux wheeled the Rambler into the driveway in front of Mama Henry's barbecue pit. Two young blacks sitting under the bent carport jumped up, stared hard at them, then started toward the car.

Tyrone hustled out onto the driveway. "Hey, man, it's me," he said. "Everything's cool."

The two men stopped and returned to their concrete bench, but continued to watch the car.

Tyrone ducked his head back into the open car door. "Sammi, I can't," he said. "I got things need takin' care of. If it gets too hot here, I'll catch up to you in Pine Knot, wherever that be. Here, I brought you a change of clothes."

Tyrone tossed a shirt into Sammi's lap.

Rux stretched across Sammi and extended his hand. "Thank you, my friend," he said.

Tyrone slapped Rux's palm, then grasped his hand and shook it. "Hey, any time, bro. Don't stop 'til you get to Ron's."

Rux didn't.

Sammi sat quietly on the toilet in Ron's Rent-a-Rambler's restroom while Rux groomed her matted hair as best he could. Jeans, a gray sweat shirt and Rux's jacket hung on her hollow frame.

"A little of Chester's mane and tail conditioner would do wonders for your hair," Rux said.

She nodded, then met his gaze with half-closed eyes and smiled. She was never more beautiful, Rux thought.

"How did you know that was your old hat Peter had on?" Sammi asked.

"I don't rightly know. Just a feeling, I guess."

"Kind of like lovers sensing each other's presence in the dark, without seeing or touching."

"I'll buy that."

A knock on the bathroom door interrupted them. Ron said from the other side, "Hey guys, I'm closing. You two want a ride to the terminal? No extra charge."

"Sure," Rux said. "We'd really appreciate it." He pulled Sammi to her feet and helped her into the office.

Ron looked at Sammi and said, "Hope y'all don't have to fly too far."

"The end of the runway would be too far," Sammi mumbled.

Rux left Sammi in one of the soft chairs in the lobby of the terminal and approached the Southwest Airlines ticket counter. A gray-haired little man in a tan blazer represented Houston's version of Lubbock's calf roping queen.

"I'm booked on the flight to Lubbock tomorrow morning," Rux said. "And I need one more ticket. One way. Any luck on getting out tonight?"

The man took Rux's ticket, examined it and said, "Sorry, nothing tonight. First flight to Lubbock is at eight-fifteen tomorrow morning. I can get both of you on that one."

Rux thanked the attendant, accepted his tickets and returned to Sammi. "Bad news," he said. "No flights to Lubbock until tomorrow morning. Let's go find a motel."

Sammi, staring at the floor with her elbows on her knees and her hands supporting her head, answered without looking up. "I need a fix worse than I need a motel. Why are we going to Lubbock?"

"Oh, I haven't had a chance to tell you. Missy is in No Water with my dad. Along with Emilio, Juanita, Rector Richter, Auren, Chester, Howard and the rooster. Lubbock is the closest town with an airport."

Sammi lifted her head just enough to level arched eyebrows at Rux. "Rector Richter? Auren? What rooster?"

Rux laughed, sat in the chair next to her and massaged her neck. "We've got a lot of catching up to do, and I don't know any way to get you a fix. Besides, you've got to kick this stuff. Tyrone said the only way to do that is go cold turkey. Might as well start now."

Sammi leaned against him and pressed the back of her neck hard into his hands. "Oh, no," she said. "I wish we were in Pine Knot. I miss my baby."

She sat up straight and turned to face Rux. "No point in going to a motel. I'll be heaving my insides out all night, and there's a restroom right over there. Let's just stay here. It's not that long before the plane leaves anyway."

"Good thing Tyrone brought you that extra shirt. Please try not to heave on my jacket."

* * *

Sleeping in the chairs in the airport lobby did little for Rux's disposition. "How are you feeling?" he asked as Sammi returned from the restroom and accepted the coffee he had purchased from the restaurant.

"Don't cancel the funeral just yet."

"We'll be back in No Water this afternoon. Missy will make you forget your death wish."

"Just thinking of her does that, but it doesn't do anything for my nausea. I hope she doesn't hate me. I intended to come back. I really did. But not like this. I'll be throwing up all the way to Lufkin."

"Lubbock." He held her close and patted her like the small child she had become. Missy needs her mom, he thought, but right now her mom needs Missy.

"Don't worry about throwing up on the plane. I'm well versed on that subject. We've got the first two boarding passes so we can sit in the back near the restroom. You can have the aisle seat. Of course, that means a fat lady with a weak bladder and a bad body odor will sit in the window seat next to us."

"How do you know that?"

"It's required by the Warsaw Convention or whatever governs

airplanes."

"How many fat ladies with weak bladders and bad body odor would be flying to Luling...Lubbock on any given day?"

"I dunno. It depends on how many window seats the plane has."

* * *

Rux anxiously awaited the heavenly music made by the sound of the plane's door closing. Passengers had stopped trickling on, and they were two minutes past departure time. The window seat next to them remained unoccupied. At the last minute an orangutan that would dwarf Mama Henry slogged on board wearing a bright yellow dress and a Dallas Cowboys jacket. A huge straw bag hung over each flabby arm.

Rux thought about grabbing the man in the business suit across the aisle and forcing him into the window seat. Something in the Articles of the Warsaw Convention probably made that illegal. He put his new hat in the seat and propped the "seat occupied" sign on top of it. Nothing worked.

The orangutan climbed into the window seat beside him, dragged both straw bags across his crotch, and then pretended the two bags were going to fit under the seat with her rhinoceros legs.

Sammi nudged him and whispered, "See, you were wrong."

"Wrong about what?"

"She smells like lilac water."

Rux tossed the new hat into Sammi's lap and pulled his old one down over his eyes. He slumped to as much of a prone position as he could muster with his seat back in its upright position for takeoff.

"It's early yet."

Twenty minutes and one stewardess' demonstration of seat-belt-buckling later, the captain droned over the speaker, "Good morning, ladies and gentlemen. Welcome aboard Southwest Airlines' flight Seven-Sixty-One to Albuquerque, with intermediate stops in Austin and Lubbock. Right now we're flying over Brenham, home of the Blue Bell Creamery...."

From the corner of his eye Rux could see the orangutan grip the arm rest and tilt her bulk slightly to the right. He rolled his head to the left and buried his face on Sammi's shoulder.

"Don't buy any ice cream for a while," he said.

"Why?"

"The milk of the Blue Bell cows just got curdled."

Twenty-four

Sammi leaned her throbbing head against a pillar supporting the Lubbock terminal building and wished she were Samson. Eternity had passed twice since Rux left to find his truck. Samsonette the orangutan walked by and wished her a nice day, then waved to Rux as he pulled up in the passenger loading zone.

"Sorry I took so long," Rux said as he helped Sammi into the truck. "I couldn't remember where I parked. Even went to the trouble to write down my location on my parking ticket and still forgot."

Rux slammed the passenger door, then mouthed "Sorry" through the window as Sammi pressed the heels of her hands into her temples. He quickly circled the truck, slid in behind the wheel and eased the door closed.

"Thank you," Sammi said. "Why didn't you look on your ticket?"

"For what?"

"For the location of the truck in the parking lot."

"Oh. I couldn't. The ticket was in the truck." Rux raced the engine, patted Sammi's knee, and crept into the moving traffic.

The cab of the Ruxmobile welcomed Sammi like a long lost friend. The frayed seat, cracked windshield and dusty dashboard eased her chills and aches with the same comfort as hot soup and a favorite sweater. She relaxed against the seat, closed her eyes to dim the bright midday sun, and let the truck's vibrations massage her neck.

"I missed you, old friend," she mumbled in a half stupor.

"I missed you, too," Rux said.

Sammi smiled. She meant the truck, but was happy Rux took the remark for himself. Even though they often miscommunicated, a special, unspoken bond allowed them to connect with each other when it really mattered. Right now, she realized, it mattered more than ever before.

Little thought atoms, each a unique image of Rux at various stages in their brief relationship, ricocheted through her mind. A montage of a ruggedly handsome, soft-spoken cowboy emerged, a gentle giant who made everyone around him laugh but kept his own feelings carefully tucked away.

The kaleidoscope of events produced a twinge of guilt. She had used Rux. He had to know this. Still, he took care of Missy. And when Sammi needed him most, he was there.

I'm in love with this big galoot, she finally admitted to herself. I want...I need a permanent bond. Love is a word he uses only in his songs, or maybe when referring to his horse or truck. I know he's been hurt, years ago by his wife and now by me. It won't be easy, but I've got to find a way to seduce him one more time, forever.

Sammi remembered her current physical state and decided it would be easier to seduce Chester. She scooted across the seat and cuddled Rux's arm.

"Are you cold?" she asked. "I can let you have your jacket back."

"No, I'm okay. This flannel shirt is warm enough inside the truck."

Rux put his right arm around her and kissed the top of her head. "Man, that wind's strong," he said, removing his arm to keep both hands on the steering wheel.

Rux held the wheel hard left, adjusting occasionally as the wind gusted, then died down.

"Where are we?" Sammi asked.

"On the high plains of West Texas, 'bout half way between Lubbock and No Water. Fascinating country, isn't it?"

Sammi watched the ribbon of concrete stretch as far as it could across the brown prairie and then seemingly merge into the horizon. "Yes," she said, "but does it ever end?"

"Not today." Rux chuckled and patted her thigh.

Sammi reached for his hand but he again returned it to the wheel to continue his struggle with the relentless wind. She lay her head against his shoulder and allowed herself to drift away again. Her fingers traced the steering wheel, found the big, leathery hand and placed it back on her thigh.

She didn't remember dozing but somehow sensed the passage of time. Serious vibration interrupted the hum of the highway. Sammi sat up and surveyed the countryside. Nothing had changed, except a pockmarked asphalt road had replaced the concrete ribbon. Her nausea returned.

"How much further?" she asked.

"Another five minutes or so," Rux said. "We're almost there. You feel okay?"

"No, I'm getting queasy again. I think it's this road."

"Sorry. I'll slow down a little. Maybe it'll smooth out the bouncing. Try to focus on the horizon. It won't move as rapidly as the fence posts and telephone poles. Let me know if you need to stop."

Sammi gritted her teeth and focused on the distant landscape. They rounded a curve to the left and two specks appeared on the prairie, making the land appear to rise gently.

"That's home," Rux said. "At least for tonight. We'll be there directly. We can get you cleaned up and bedded down for a while. I'm sure Juanita and Auren will have all sorts of cures for whatever ails you, although you may prefer the ailment."

"I doubt it. Did Tyrone say how long it would take to get the crack out of my system?"

"About two weeks. You're gonna feel pretty awful until you do. Maybe some of Juanita's herb remedies will ease you a little."

"I hope so. I feel terrible putting all of you through this, particularly your dad. He's never even met me. What will he think?" She clasped her head with both hands. "Oh, no. My hair. He can't see me like this."

"He adores you already. Your being sick won't bother him. Many a cold morning he's got up and pulled a calf from it's momma. Had to nurse some of them when the mother didn't make it.

"Besides that, he lived through ten years of my mother's cancer surgeries and chemotherapies. The last two years she didn't even have hair. My guess is, he'll welcome two weeks of helping us nurse a pretty lady."

The specks on the horizon began to take the shape of a house and barn.

"That's sweet," Sammi said. "Are we going to stay here for two weeks?"

Rux used his left hand to steer between the pot holes while he retrieved his new hat from the dash and placed it on Sammi's head.

"There," he said. "Now you don't have to worry about how your hair looks. I haven't really thought about where to go from here, or when. We need to talk about that with the others as soon as you feel like it."

Rux turned onto the dirt path cutting through the grass to the small yellow house. Much to Sammi's relief, he stopped, shifted into low gear and let the truck creep across the cattle guard.

"Breathe," Rux said.

Sammi removed her hand from her mouth and took a deep breath. "Didn't you say you had been gone from Pine Knot for two weeks? I imagine the others are anxious to get home. And we need to get Missy back in school."

Missy and an elderly man Sammi assumed to be Rux's father were standing on the porch. The rest of the "merry Band", as Rux called them, were filing out of the screen door and watching like little prairie dogs as the truck approached.

"Emilio and Juanita seem to be enjoying themselves," Rux said. "But I guess Deke would like to know if they're ever coming back. Rector Richter and Auren don't appear to be in any hurry to get anywhere. I don't really know what their plans are."

Sammi rolled down her window and waved. The cold air felt good. "If they're as infatuated with each other as you say they are, I don't think he'll go back to the priesthood," she said, grabbing the hat to keep it from blowing out the window.

She purposely did not say they loved each other, hoping Rux would pick up on it. It would be nice to hear him use the word with reference to people, as opposed to horses and trucks.

"I think you're probably right," he said. "And I know Missy needs to be in school. I'll call Sheriff Mo and see what the situation is."

Missy bounded off the porch and grabbed the door handle before the truck came to a complete stop. She jerked the door open and scrambled into Sammi's arms.

"Mom, you're home, you're home. I missed you, I missed you."

Sammi choked on her tears as she tried to speak. Missy's wet kisses smothered her cheek, and the child's own tears fell freely on Sammi's bosom. She could hear herself saying over and over, "My baby. I'm so sorry. I love you."

"It's okay, Mom. It's okay."

Only after Missy pulled away a little, pushed back her mother's hat and kissed her again did Sammi realize Rux had left them alone in the truck and was standing on the porch with the others. Missy ran her hand through Sammi's hair, apparently realized the necessity for the hat, and pulled it back over Sammi's forehead.

The child freed herself, took Sammi's hand and slid out of the truck. "Come on, Mom. Everyone is anxious to see you."

Sammi lost her voice again when everyone on the porch embraced her in a good imitation of the gang hugs from the Red Neck band. She couldn't help but notice the surprised look on Rux's face when even his father joined in. Amongst all the "how are yous" and "welcome backs," she could hear Rux saying, "Dad, this is Sammi."

Inside, Sammi felt the same comforting sensations that had greeted her when she climbed into Rux's old truck at the airport. There's something about Tuttles and old places, she thought.

Juanita and Missy hurried off to draw a bath for their returned prodigal while the rest of the group gathered in the kitchen. Auren served Sammi hot ginger tea with peppermint to soothe her stomach, then dished up chicken soup.

"Any chance that squalling rooster contributed to the soup?" Rux asked.

"Naw," Jeremiah said. "He's still out back with the hens. This one came from H. E. Butt's. Didn't think Missy would take too kindly to me wringing a chicken's neck."

Sammi's spoon dropped into her soup with a noisy splash.

"Oops. Sorry little lady," Jeremiah said. "I shouldn't be making chicken killing jokes in front of someone with your delicate condition."

"That's okay," Sammi said. "It's so nice to hear people laughing again."

Juanita and Missy returned to escort their patient to her waiting bath. Sammi thanked Auren for the soup and tea, received another hug from her, and followed her two nursemaids through a small bedroom and into a relatively large bathroom.

Woven Navajo rugs in front of the free standing sink and beside the claw foot bath tub protected bare feet from the cold linoleum floor.

"I put Epsom salt in your bath," Juanita said. "Missy insisted on adding the bubble bath. Should make you feel better."

"We'll be right here if you need us," Missy said, as she and Juanita backed out of the bathroom and closed the door after them.

Sammi pulled off her sweat shirt and realized she did not have on a bra. "I didn't bring any clothes," she said. "No bra, no clean underwear. I don't even have anything to sleep in."

She pulled off her jeans, searched for a hook, and found a soft pink gown hanging on the closet door. A little wooden wash basin contained neatly folded panties and a bra. Auren's, she thought. I guess Rux told them we left in a hurry.

"You look horrible," she said to her reflection in the mirror above the sink. "It's this greasy hair." She knew washing her hair would help, but it couldn't do anything for the wasted figure staring back at her.

Sammi slipped off her underwear and stepped into the frothing steam and bubbles. The warm water caressed her as she slid beneath the foam. I'll stay here forever, she thought.

A little ceramic heater warmed the room. At first, Sammi refused to acknowledge the chill coming over her. But her shaking and the strange gurgling noises in her stomach would not be denied. She propelled herself to the commode as her body rejected the nourishment of the chicken soup, insisting that it first be calmed with the narcotic of crack.

Cool water on her face aided her relief, and she returned to the tub. I need a fix, she thought. But where would I get anything out here? She closed her eyes and tried to picture the vast brown landscape meeting the bright blue of the sky. Her mind overrode the attempt at self-deception, echoing instead a deep voice saying, "She's hooked bad."

Sammi sat up, then realized she could hear Rux through the thin wall separating the bathroom from the kitchen.

Rux continued the now familiar litany. "Only way to kick it is to go cold turkey."

"How long will that take?" Juanita asked.

"At least two weeks," Rux said. "And Tyrone says it will be a miserable two weeks for her."

"We've got to detox her," Juanita said. "Otherwise, the cocaine will stay in her tissues. She'll always be addicted."

Rux asked, "How do we do that?"

Auren said, "Fasting and sweat baths."

"Right," Juanita said. "And we'll get as much plantain, Virginia snake root and Oregon grape down her as she can tolerate. She'll be pretty sick, but if she's going to be sick anyway, the faster we can flush out her system the better."

Sammi held her nose and ducked under the water.

* * *

Auren prescribed more ginger tea, this time with chamomile, to help Sammi sleep. It didn't work.

Sammi pulled the blanket under her chin and tried to control her shaking. Missy, her little nurse, had fallen asleep on the bed beside her. Sammi reached to stroke the girl's head, then drew back, afraid her damp hand might wake her. She sat for several minutes, absorbed in the graceful elegance of the sleeping child swathed in the soft glow the night light.

"Poor baby," Sammi said. "You deserve a better mommy. You certainly deserve a daddy."

Some time after the house had gotten quiet, Juanita tiptoed in. "How's everybody doing?" she asked in a hushed voice.

"One of us is doing fine," Sammi said. "She's sound asleep."

"Bless her heart. Be right back. I'll get Rux to carry her to her bed."

Juanita closed the door, then mumbled something under her breath as she reopened it to retrieve the skirt of her robe. A few minutes later, Rux emerged, carefully dressed in blue jeans and a white T-shirt. Juanita had obviously warned him about robes in doors.

He leaned over Missy, kissed Sammi's freshly washed hair, and picked up the gangly bundle of slumbering child. Missy stirred, put her arms around his neck, and continued her state of total relaxation.

Sammi returned Rux's smile and watched as he carefully guided Missy's legs through the door. Juanita reentered just as Sammi's own legs almost jumped off the bed.

"Still shaking?" Juanita asked.

"Bad. How could I have gotten myself into this?" Sammi began to cry.

Juanita sat of the bed and drew Sammi into her arms. "Shhh," she said. "Everything is going to be okay."

Crying seemed to help, and Sammi eventually relaxed a little. Juanita eased her back on the pillows. Several times Sammi almost dozed off, but on the very edge of unconsciousness an internal alarm system would use her legs for a lightning rod.

Out of desperation, Sammi extended her toes as far as she could, hoping to stretch out the tension. She succeeded in causing a severe cramp in her left calf. "Ow, ow, ow," she cried under her breath, trying to massage the cramp without disturbing Juanita.

"Sammi, what's the matter?" Auren asked.

"Auren? I thought Juanita was here."

"We're taking turns so everyone can get some sleep. Looks like you're not, though."

"I must have slept a little. I didn't know you had come in. Please don't worry about me. I'll be okay. Why don't you go on back to bed?"

"It's all right. Here, let me massage your legs for you."

Sammi lay back as Auren kneaded her screaming leg muscles. Finally Sammi said, "Rux told me about Joe. I'm so sorry."

"Thank you." Auren started to continue but paused.

Sammi sensed she was crying, but Auren's face hid behind her dark hair. This must really be awkward for her, Sammi thought. Someone sympathizes with her about her dead husband while she is running off with her lover.

Auren finally continued. "I guess you also know about Joe's problem."

Sammi caught her breath. "Yes," she said, wishing she had not brought up anything about Joe.

"I loved him dearly. Joe is...was...a good man. But we couldn't live like that. It was driving us both crazy."

Auren pulled her knees under her and moved up to massage Sammi's neck. "Something would have happened sooner or later," she said. "We were both about ready to explode. I just wish he could have found some help."

You did, apparently, Sammi thought. Auren must have read her mind.

"I guess you're wondering about me and Tom."

"Tom? Oh, Rector Richter."

Auren chuckled as she reversed herself to work on Sammi's jerking legs again. "Where did 'Rector Richter' come from?"

"That's how Rux refers to him. I guess the rest of us just picked it up. When we talk about him, he's 'Rector Richter.' When we talk to him, he's 'Padre'."

"Well, he was always Father Thomas to me. I feel terrible about luring him away from the church. He was so dedicated."

"He must have had some feelings for you. Romantic, I mean."

"I'm sure he did. Even though they are priests, they're still men. I guess the commitment to the church allows them to control their natural instincts. Poor Tom. I seduced him. I left him no choice."

Sammi could feel Auren's massage fade into mostly a gentle rub. "Why don't you rest for a minute," Sammi said.

The two of them swung their legs off the bed and sat for awhile, silently staring at the shadows on the wall.

"Auren," Sammi said, "are you and Tom in love?"

"Totally."

"What are you going to do?"

"I don't know. I obviously want us to get married and spend the rest of our lives together. But Tom is still struggling. He may decide to go back into the priesthood."

Sammi leaned back on her elbows and stretched. "Well," she said, "try seducing him again."

"Oh, Sammi, don't tease about that. I was wrong."

"You were desperate. Right and wrong get sort of blurry sometimes. I may try it on Rux, although, come to think of it, I already have. Maybe the trick is to keep him celibate."

"I don't think Rux has the same constraints Tom does."

"That's for sure. He has his own constraints, but he keeps them to himself. Let me know if you come up with anything that works."

"You too. You're shaking again."

Sammi crawled back under the blanket and Auren tucked it tight under her chin. "Thank you, Auren," Sammi said. "I'll be okay. Get some sleep."

Deep in the night, Sammi longed for another massage. She wanted Rux to hold her as well, but Missy still did not know they had become lovers. Juanita's herbs and her own exhaustion finally took their toll.

* * *

For the first time since her teenage summers at her grandparents' farm, Sammi woke to the sound of a rooster crowing. She moaned, turned over, and saw Rux peeping out the window around the edge of the drawn window shade.

"Dang," he said. "I guess now that that old rooster's not traveling anymore he's figured out he's supposed to crow at sun up."

"Great timing," Sammi said. She covered her head with a pillow. Around the edge of the pillow she saw Missy ease into the room with a tray of three brown bottles and a glass of orange juice.

"Good morning, Mom, Good morning, Rux," she said, chirping like a little bird.

"Good morning, sweetheart," Sammi said through the pillow. She peered out and noticed Missy and Rux were both dressed and ready for the day. "My, aren't you two the early birds," she said.

"Big day ahead," Rux said. He rounded the bed and paused at the door. "I'll let you get dressed. Do you feel like coming to the kitchen?"

"I suppose," Sammi said. "What's up?"

Rux said, "We'll fill you in at breakfast." He closed the door behind him, leaving Sammi alone with Missy.

"How are you this morning?" Sammi asked. "I know you stayed up with me last night."

Missy sat the tray on the night stand and hugged Sammi. "I'm fine," she said. "Juanita, Auren and I took turns, so we all got some sleep. Did you sleep any?"

"A little, I think. You are so sweet." She felt tears well up again.

Sammi realized she and her daughter had reversed rolls as Missy patted her and said, "That's okay, Mom. Go ahead and cry. Our tears nourish our soul."

"That sounds like a Juanita-ism."

"Auren."

Missy sat on the bed next to Sammi, keeping her eyes fixed on the window. Sammi realized her appearance must have been a shock to the girl.

Sammi touched Missy's hair and said, "Did Rux tell you what's wrong with me?"

"He said...you had the flu."

"But you know better, right?"

"Yeah, I guess so."

"Speed, crack, you name it. But it's over, finished. I'm getting clean and I'll never touch the stuff again. Missy, you see what drugs do to a person. Promise me you'll never, ever get involved in anything like that."

"I won't." Missy studied her hands for a minute, then looked up at Sammi and smiled. "Mom, you're still the most beautiful person in the world."

More hugs from Juanita and Auren greeted Sammi as she made her way into the kitchen. "Sit here," Juanita said, pulling out a white wooden chair from the end of the table. "I'll get your tea. Do you feel like eating anything this morning?"

"Not really," Sammi said.

Auren said, "You need to keep your strength up. Let the ginger tea settle you a little and then we'll try some oat meal and dry toast."

Missy and the men folk filed in from the living room, each greeting Sammi with a hug. Rux also patted her head, no doubt appreciative of her freshly washed hair. "Nice outfit," he said.

"Thank you for noticing," Sammi said, tugging at the collar of Rux's shirt that hung on her like an oversized dress. The jeans borrowed from Auren were a bit short but otherwise fit loosely.

"You sit here, Mister Tuttle," Juanita said, directing Rux's father as though he could not find a chair at his own table. "Rux, you're over there."

"Yes, ma'am," Jeremiah said. Sammi caught the quick grin he exchanged with Rux as he pulled out his chair.

Rux said, "Me and Emilio can eat off the counter so the rest of you can have a place."

Auren placed Sammi's oatmeal and toast in front of her. Juanita deposited a platter of fried eggs on the table, followed by a large bowl of steaming grits, then another platter of biscuits and bacon.

"Sammi," Rux said as he leaned over her to fill his plate, "we'd like to head for Pine Knot today if you feel up to it. Emilio, jump on in here. Be careful you don't lose a hand with this bunch."

Rux stepped back to the counter to make room for Emilio.

Sammi said, "I guess I feel okay. What did Sheriff Mo say?"

Rux nodded toward Missy, sitting with her back to him.

"Oh," Sammi mouthed to Rux. She suddenly realized Missy was not aware of the child molestation charges or the CPS lady.

"Sheriff and Deke are fine," Rux said. "Wondering when we're coming back."

Forks clattered against plates for several minutes as everyone busied themselves with the meal. Sammi dipped her toast in the oatmeal and took several bites. Everything tasted good, even the ginger tea with peppermint. Maybe it won't take two weeks, she thought.

Juanita finished her eggs, retrieved a white bottle from the counter and passed out two little pills to everyone, including Sammi. "Digestive aids," she announced.

Jeremiah downed his pills with coffee and pushed back his chair. "Mighty fine grub, ladies," he said. "Missy, if you're done you want to go with me to feed that horse and them old chickens?"

"Sure," Missy said.

Jeremiah grabbed their hats and coats from the spool hangers beside the back door and followed Missy outside.

"We won't be long," Jeremiah said. He nodded to Rux as he closed the door behind him.

"Sorry," Sammi said. "I should have known you wouldn't tell Missy about all this."

Rux circled the table and assumed Jeremiah's chair. "That's okay," he said. "I suspect Missy knows more than she's letting on. She's got to be curious about not being in school for two weeks. I talked to Sheriff Mo last night. He thinks it's okay to bring Missy back as long as you're with her."

Sammi said, "If he sees the shape I'm in he might not feel that way. What will the CPS lady think?"

Juanita made her way around the table with the coffee pot. "Don't worry about the CPS," she said. "You look fine. We just need to get a little weight back on you. Finish your oatmeal. As far as the CPS lady knows, you've got the flu. Good excuse for her not to be snooping around."

Sammi spooned down the rest of her cereal and finished the toast. "What about the molesting charges?" she asked Rux.

"Sheriff Mo's got that under control," Rux said. "Pulled off a little shuttle diplomacy with the husbands of the ladies who complained. Apparently, they agreed I didn't do anything with Missy but hug her, just like they do their own daughters."

Sammi quickly covered her mouth with her cup as her heart skipped a beat. Their own daughters? she thought. Was Rux now claiming Missy as his own? Don't get too excited, she cautioned herself. Still, this self-described old cowboy chose his words very carefully if there was any possibility they could betray his feelings. "What about your dad?" she asked.

The Padre said, "I think he plans on coming with us."

Rux asked, "He does?"

"That's what he said yesterday," Emilio said.

Sammi guessed what was coming next. Rux stood and plucked his hat from the spindle. He glanced out the back window, apparently making sure Jeremiah and Missy were still busy with the horse and the chickens, then leaned against the door and glared into the hat.

Rux finally asked, "Did he say anything else?"

Emilio started to answer but Juanita interrupted. "He's lonely, Rux," she said. "Maybe he doesn't realize it, but he really misses being around people."

Rux put on his hat and returned to the table. "He has his church friends," he said. "And his buddies in town. He goes in every day or so to pick up the mail. They all sit around the feed store and jaw for a bit."

"Not in a while," Rector Richter said. "Not since your mother passed away. Your dad told us he wants to follow her, but he wants to die naturally, without medicines, surgeries or tubes to prolong the process. He doesn't go to church anymore, and he only goes to town once a month now. Figures if he times it right, no one will miss him until he's gone."

Sammi watched the color drain from Rux's face. He stared hard at Rector Richter, then shifted his gaze to her. His eyes were those of a child pleading for help, but he remained silent for a few seconds. From the corner of her eye, Sammi saw Juanita start to say something, but Emilio placed his hand on her arm.

"Suicide?" Rux asked, turning back to the Padre.

"No, his religion doesn't permit that," Rector Richter said. "But he did tell us he drinks three gallons of water every day. Said he didn't think that was an unpardonable sin. I'm not sure why he thought it would hasten his demise."

"It might," Rux said. "Expectant mothers aren't allowed to drink it. Water out here is full of heavy chemicals from all the fertilizing. We always suspected our well was the source of Mom's cancer. What else has he been doing?"

"Nothing that works," Emilio said. "Jeremiah says he's healthy as pen raised rabbits. He tried working out in the sun without his hat. Appears the water and the sun agree with him."

Emilio's laugh relaxed everyone a bit, forcing a smile out of Rux.

Sammi stood and began to clear the dishes from the table. Juanita scowled at her, then apparently realized movement would be a good idea. She scooted out of her chair and started stacking dishes.

Emilio continued, "Even his old tractor wouldn't cooperate. Jeremiah said he was adjusting the carburetor one day when old John Deere jumped into gear and took off. But instead of running over him it went backwards and destroyed the chicken coop."

Rux leaned his chair back and roared with laughter. Sammi laughed with everyone else, then turned to the sink to hide her moistening eyes.

Her queasiness was back. She couldn't be sure if it came from her withdrawal symptoms or her inability to be alone with Rux. She wanted to tell him that he should stay here with his father, assure him she would be okay. She startled when Juanita clattered a stack of plates in the sink.

"I think he should come with us," Juanita said. "He needs us. Besides, Howard has adopted him."

"What would he do with his chickens?" Rux asked.

"Isn't there a neighbor who could use them?" Juanita asked. "We'll throw in the rooster. He's sort of gotten attached to the hens anyway."

"Roosters have a way of doing that," Rux said.

Sammi turned in time to catch his mischievous grin directed at her.

"Oh, good grief," Juanita said. "Don't you horny old goats ever think about anything else? It's all settled then. We'll find a neighbor to take the chickens and look in on the place while we're gone."

Rux asked, "Where's he gonna ride? We were three to a truck when we got here, and now we've added Sammi. Course, she ain't much bigger'n Missy now, but my dad is pretty good size."

Sammi noticed Auren look at Rector Richter, then lower her eyes.

The Padre said, "He can have my place. I need you to drop me at the airport in Lubbock."

Rux looked at Auren, then back to Rector Richter. "Why?"

The Padre stood, walked behind Auren and placed his hands on her shoulders. "I have to go to Chicago," he said, "to visit with my parents." Auren's hands grasped Rector Richter's but her eyes remained fixed on the table. "And," the Padre said, "I need to talk with the Bishop while I'm there."

"The Bishop?" Sammi asked.

"Yes," Rector Richter said. "He was my Parish's priest. He convinced me I belonged in the priesthood."

"Oh, I see," Sammi said. Her desire to comfort someone widened to include Auren along with Rux. Obviously, the Padre needed the advice of his family and his mentor before deciding on his future. And he had not volunteered Auren's place in the truck, just his.

Rux leaned over and placed his own big paw on top of the two hands already resting on Auren's shoulder. "I understand," he said. "Guess we can trade the Padre and one rooster for Jeremiah, but only for the ride back to Pine Knot. Right, Auren?"

Sammi watched Auren wipe her tears and try to return Rux's wink.

Juanita said, "Only if Jeremiah doesn't crow when he's riding."

"Or cluck when he's sleeping," Emilio said.

Juanita corrected him. "Chortles."

Twenty-five

Once back at the Ball Ranch the detoxification of Sammi Stone began in earnest. Rux sat in the kitchen with the rest of the merry band, more or less. His dad was the "more" and the Padre, off to Chicago, was the "less."

Juanita and Auren explained the wonderful world of cleansing to Sammi.

"When you fast," Auren said, "your body must nourish itself with nutrients. It will release stored toxins first to ease its task. In olden times my people would fast to cleanse both the body and the mind."

Juanita said, "Your people fasted because they couldn't find anything to eat."

"True," Auren said, "but the results are the same. My people also utilized the sweat lodge. Sweating will draw toxins from your skin. You will have to drink plenty of water to flush out your system. Otherwise, your body will just reabsorb the toxins."

Sammi opined she could deal with the sweating. Her queasy stomach pretty much took care of the fasting.

Juanita reassured her. "Just think of it as a religious experience."

"I'd rather not think of it at all," Sammi said.

She looked to Rux, her eyes pleading for his for support. He volunteered to soothe her during the process if that would help. "I've done that with mares while the vet palpated them for pregnancy," he said.

Juanita said, "You're so weak we will have to go slow. We can build you up gradually with lots of minerals, vitamins and herbs, and apple juice for nourishment."

Rux asked, "Where are we going to find a sweat lodge?"

Juanita said, "There's a sauna at the Holiday Inn. We can just walk in like we're guests. No one will know the difference."

Rux said, "My guess is you'll need a room key to get in the locker room. Three women wrapped in towels walking in off the street might look a little suspicious."

"Not a problem," said Auren. "Indians were using sweat lodges long before anyone invented Holiday Inns. You boys gather enough willow branches for a small wickiup and get some rocks, preferably lava if you can find them. I'll go over to Whiteriver and see if anyone remembers the ceremony. Oh, and be sure to leave some tobacco for Mother Earth where you pick up the rocks."

"We don't smoke," Emilio said.

* * *

With considerable reluctance, Rux relinquished his support duties in the wickiup long enough to retrieve Rector Richter from the Phoenix airport. When he spotted him at the passenger pickup, Rux immediately realized the Padre had also brought a replacement for his spot in the foaling room.

Tom Richter and Tyrone Dedman stood shoulder to shoulder, both grinning like mischievous possums.

"Found him at the airport in Dallas, asking for information on a flight to Pine Knot," Tom said. "I knew he had to be our Tyrone."

"This here's the Pine Knot shuttle," Rux said. "Climb aboard, Tyrone."

"Any black folks up there?" Tyrone asked.

"Don't worry about it," Rux said. "We'll get you a big, black hat and a rosary with a medicine bag on it. Nobody'll know the difference."

The Padre laughed. "That's sacrilegious."

"Speaking of which," Rux said, "How'd it go in Chicago?"

"Okay, I guess," Rector Richter said. "I confessed my sins to the Bishop, and didn't get condemned to everlasting hell."

Tyrone's head swiveled from the Padre to Rux as they relayed the questions and answers back and forth.

Rux asked, "You didn't tell him about your romp in the desert?"

"Sure I did," the Padre said. "He seemed very interested. Even pressed for more details. Said he often dreamed of becoming a missionary to the Indians himself."

The three men laughed, although Tyrone had a puzzled look on his face.

"It's a long story," Rector Richter said to Tyrone. "I'm a priest, or was."

"Was?" Rux asked.

The Padre reached in his jacket pocket and produced a small ring box. He opened it and displayed a sparkling set of wedding rings.

"Hey, congratulations," Rux said. "What did the Bishop think?"

"I told him my passion for Auren equals my love for the Church, and that I could not in good conscience return to my robes."

Rux asked, "He gave you his blessing, then?"

Rector Richter sighed as he returned the rings to his pocket. "Not right away. He was silent for several minutes, leaving me mortified with unholy fear. I fully expected centurions to appear with a cross and nails. If God had blinded me with light and called to me at that moment, I would not have recognized my own name."

Tyrone said, "Hey, I been there."

Rux asked Tyrone, "You were a priest?"

208

Tyrone laughed. "Naw, man. I mean I been that scared."

Rux wheeled the truck onto the highway to Payson as Rector Richter continued his confession of his confession.

"After several agonizing minutes, the Bishop addressed me as though he were housebreaking his pet dachshund. He told me I'm not the first man to leave the priesthood for the love of a woman. And he doubted if I would be the last. But he appreciated the fact that I had the decency to give up my robes. Apparently, many don't. He finally told me to go and sin no more, or at least be a little more discreet about it."

They drove in silence for a while. Darkness approached as the pine forest gradually replaced the sparsely vegetated sand hills. Rux, being a practicing pagan himself, wondered what a former priest did for a church.

He asked Rector Richter, "Are you going to go back to your church, as a lay person, I mean?"

The Padre said, "That would be a little awkward. I told the Bishop I might join the Baptist church. That's where Emilio and Juanita and Sammi and Missy go, isn't it?"

"Right," Rux said. "What did he think of that?"

"He said we've sent missionaries to every other heathen tribe in the world, we might as well send one to the Baptists."

"Sounds like my kind of church," Rux said. "Tyrone, what brings you to the fair city of Pine Knot?"

"Needed a vacation from my nursery bidness. Peter and Hector got busted okay, but they out on bail the next day. Didn't take long for Peter to figure out what went down. He saw me at the apartment with the garbage bag. And he know I know where his stash was in the church."

"Well," Rux said, "we're glad you made it."

* * *

Three days later, Sheriff Mohlmann called Rux and informed him he would be bringing by the lady from Child Protective Services. "Be sure everyone's on their best behavior," the sheriff said. "I wouldn't want to have to arrest anyone in front of a CPS agent."

"No more problems with the child molesting charges?" Rux asked.

"Oh, I doubt if you will get an apology from the ladies, but nothing else will come of it. None of them want to get their husband arrested for molesting their daughter."

"Yeah, but Missy's not my daughter."

"I know. You might want to get busy working on that. Otherwise, I may have to reconsider the charges."

"Is this like a shotgun wedding?"

"Take that up with the CPS lady. She's a lot more likely to shoot you than I would be."

After two hours around the dinner table with Missy's "family," the CPS lady pronounced the state of Arizona fully satisfied with the child's familial status. The agent seemed so relaxed they were afraid she would move in with them, even though Sammi had difficulty keeping her head from falling into her lemon meringue pie.

The CPS lady said, "The school tells me Missy is showing marked improvement in her math skills. What has she been doing?"

Everyone quieted in anticipation of Professor Juanita's dissertation, which was not long in coming.

"Vitamins and minerals," Juanita said. "Our brains need proper nutrition to stimulate neuron growth. The trick is to get the right balance of antioxidants, mainly Vitamins C and E, with zinc and a good herbal digestive aid so the body will assimilate the nutrients."

The CPS lady's eyes crossed. "Sounds good to me," she said. "Keep it up."

The sheriff and the CPS lady graciously agreed it was time to call it an evening when Sammi's face finally hit her pie.

Twenty-six

Of all his chores, Rux found his newest one the most pleasant. Each morning after breakfast, he would fire up the Indian sweat lodge, sit in it until he began to sweat, then install Sammi for her first of two daily saunas.

He also considered it his personal duty to stay and make sure she perspired sufficiently. Sammi wrapped in a wet sheet made it hard to leave.

"Not now, Juanita," Rux said through gritted teeth.

Sammi lay back on her cot and adjusted her sheet. "I didn't hear Juanita call you," she said.

"She didn't," Rux said. "But I can hear her beating her broom against the back porch. She said earlier she needed to talk to me. Broom beating is her form of saber rattling. Guess I'd better go see what she wants."

"Poor baby." Sammi teased him with a seductive smile, lifted a corner of the sheet and wiped the perspiration from her brow.

Rux waited a few minutes, then crawled out of the wickiup and made his way to the house.

"You rang, madam?" Rux said as he entered the kitchen.

"Yes, Cheeves. Sit down, I need to ask you something." Juanita poured two cups of coffee, handed one to Rux and plopped into the chair across the table from him. "Have you proposed to Sammi yet?"

Rux spit his mouth full of coffee back in his cup. "Proposed?"

"Yes, proposed. As in 'will you marry me.' You've heard of marriage, haven't you?"

"Well, yes...I just never thought...."

"Never thought what? That she'd have you? Couldn't blame her if she wouldn't, but she loves you. That covers a lot of sins. And you love her, too."

Rux never ceased to marvel at Juanita's propensity for stating things in the absolute. Her absolutes generally proved true. Against his better judgment, he chose to take issue with her pronouncement of his emotional state.

"Can't speak for Sammi," he said. "But I think in my case it's more like in fatchoused."

Juanita studied him for a minute, silently forming words with her lips. "You either mean 'fatuous' or 'infatuated.' In your case, both of them fit. We'll give you the benefit of the doubt. Look, love is nothing more than mature infatuation."

"Can't deny that. But Sammi and me, we're headed in different directions. She has all the potential to become a great singer. Only place

I'm going is to the barn and points beyond, like the manure pile. Broken down old cowboy like me would only...."

"Oh, poppycock. Don't give me any of your cowboy nonsense. Real cowboys went out with the nineteenth century. Nowadays we raise cows in feed lots. Herd them in with a pickup or a helicopter if they need rounding up. You modern day cowboys get caught up in a romance that never existed, still wanting to play cowboys and Indians. You're just a bunch of kids who never grew up."

"Wow." Rux found it necessary to focus on the whirlpool being created in his coffee by his violent stirring. He wondered if he could create one sufficient to pull him inside the cup.

Juanita stood and walked over to the sink, then turned to face him. "Rux, you need Sammi. And she and Missy need you. Give your love wings, boy. Put it into action."

The break up of Juanita's voice forced Rux to meet her eyes. They were moist with tears. "Yes, Ma'am," was all he could say.

Juanita stepped around the table and hugged him. "Now get out of my kitchen. I hate to see a grown man cry."

Rux placed his cup on the drain board and walked to the barn. Howard greeted him with his usual demand for jaw rubs. Rux picked up the cat and accommodated him.

"Howard," he said, "now I know how you felt after your neutering. Nothing worse than a scornful woman."

The cat's motor rattled his obvious concurrence.

Rux said, "How does this sound? 'Sammi, will you marry me'?"

Howard hopped out of his arms and jiggled his head.

"Pretty lame, huh? I guess everything about me is pretty lame. Well, not everything. How about this? 'Sammi, you've got to get better. We have a daughter to raise'."

Howard sat, hiked his jake leg and licked his posterior.

"Man, for someone who can't talk you sure have a way of making your opinions known. Never mind, I'll think of something." Rux hurried back to the sauna.

"Knock, knock," he said.

"Who's there?"

"The old sweat lodge shaman. I'm here to light your fire."

"Are you alone?"

"Yes."

"Come in."

Rux ducked through the flap and let it fall in place behind him. Just as his eyes were adjusting to the faint light, Sammi re-wrapped the sheet around her with tantalizing slowness. He stared, started to reach for her,

212

then checked the flap.

Finally, he sat cross-legged in the dirt facing the cot. "I...wanted to...."

"Wanted to what?"

The wet sheet revealed more than in concealed. "I forgot."

Sammi giggled. "Well, while you're trying to remember, I've been thinking. Let's put our act back together, then tape one of our shows at Moose Ball's. I'll get the recording studio to pipe in the tape and record over it. My energy level will be sky high. I'm sure the engineers at the studio in Hollywood can edit out a good demo tape and...."

Ten minutes later, Rux again found himself scuffling along the makeshift road leading to the barn. He kicked at a loose rock, driving the toe of his boot into the hard ground a fraction behind his intended target. He laughed at his return to his boyhood method of releasing anger and frustration, a welcome diversion from Sammi's new plan.

Actually, he thought, it's not new at all. Even with Peter out of the picture, Los Angeles and a recording contract still offered the possibility of fulfilling her dream. And what would Sammi do with her daughter this time? Did she expect Rux to look out after Missy again?

He thought back to her proposition when she left the first time. She would get settled and come back for them. They would load up the horses and all go to Los Angeles together. Had that been a ruse to get him to take care of Missy? Sure it was, he could see that now.

"Damn," he muttered. "You're stupid." He kicked at the rock again and sent it sailing into the side of his truck with a loud "thunk."

Jeremiah, Tyrone and Emilio looked up from the gate they were repairing, reminding Rux he was supposed to run into town and pick up some galvanized three-quarter inch bolts. He waved to them, climbed in the truck and spun out toward the main road.

The kaleidoscope twirling in his head suddenly merged into focus. He needed to talk to Deke.

Moose Ball's latest band was practicing when Rux arrived, as everyone within a three block radius knew. They needed the practice. Deke greeted Rux in the parking lot.

"Hey, Rux," Deke said. "What's going on?"

"Not much. Are you sweeping the parking lot or just trying to get away from the noise?"

"A little of both, and enjoying the sunshine. Let's walk over to the coffee shop. I'll buy you a cup."

Deke halted an eighteen wheeler in the middle of the street to allow them to cross. The driver, one of the Thursday night regulars at the bar, blasted his air horn just as they walked in front of the truck. "Take your time, ladies," the driver yelled as they made their way into the diner.

"Two coffees," Deke said to the waitress behind the counter as the two men each straddled a stool. "Man, that bass is rattling the windows all the way over here. Rux, when you and Sammi planning on coming back?"

Rux thought for a moment, waiting for the waitress to serve their coffee and leave. "I need to talk to you about that," he said. "We have no right to ask you to let us come back. The two of us pretty much abandoned you."

"Nonsense." Deke emptied enough sugar packets into his cup to make syrup. "Pass me the cream. You got yourselves in a little bind, that's all. I can always find a band to fill in. But these guys aren't getting any better, just louder. How's Sammi?"

"She's getting stronger every day, and she was just talking about practicing a little. I think in another week or so she may be ready."

Rux stared into his cup. From the corner of his eye he could see Deke turn his head to look at him, obviously picking up on the word "she" rather that "we."

"What about you?" Deke asked. "Lord knows, Sammi would make a vast improvement in this band. But that would hardly be fair to her. Look, we're getting into the shoulder season between the winter skiers and the summer weekenders. I need something to pick up the crowds. You and Sammi would sure do that."

"You've been a good friend," Rux said. It was Deke's turn to stare into his cup when Rux turned toward him, as though their heads were yoked. "We owe you more than that. Fact is, though, Sammi's talking about going back to Los Angeles. I think she got the taste of the good life and she ain't gonna rest easy until she tries again."

Deke gulped down his coffee syrup and called for more. "Can't say as I blame her," he said. "Anybody that good, and that pretty, she's gotta try. She'll make it. You go along with her this time to keep her out of trouble."

"Can't. I have to get my dad back to Texas. We still got a house and a few acres down there to look after. I'd be obliged if you'd let Sammi perform here for a while until she's ready."

Their heads reversed again, but this time Deke glared at Rux in silence, forcing him to meet his eyes. "I always knew you didn't use your head for much more than keeping your spinal cord from unraveling," Deke said. "But even you can't be that blind. You and Sammi are asses over eyebrows in love. How come everyone can see that but you?"

The waitress refilling their cups said, "I think the phrase is 'head over heels', Deke. But you got the idea. Yeah, Rux, why can't you see that?"

Rux looked from Deke to the waitress, then down at his cup. When he attempted to stir his coffee, the waitress placed her hand over his cup, obviously demanding an answer.

"I guess I can see that," he said, keeping his eyes tucked well under the brim of his hat. "In fact, I had my marriage proposal all thought out when I went to see her in the sauna this morning."

"Sounds sexy enough," Deke said.

"You guys are about as romantic as a bouquet of nose hairs," the waitress said. "What did she say?"

"Nothing," Rux said. "Least wise, not about the proposal. I never got to ask her. She was all excited about going back to L.A. That's no place for me. And Sammi can do a lot better than a broken down old...kid who never grew up."

"Oh, you're impossible," the waitress said. "Did you tell her you were going back to Texas?"

Rux glanced up at the waitress. Apparently she had been eavesdropping on their entire conversation. "No," he said, "I didn't decide that until the rock hit my truck."

The waitress said, "What does a rock hitting your truck have to do...oh, never mind. Don't you dare leave without telling her." She stomped from behind the counter and began refilling cups at several tables.

"Yes, Ma'am," Rux said. He turned on his stool and located the waitress at a booth by the window. Everyone in the restaurant looked at him in anticipation. "Why not?" he asked.

All the heads swiveled back to the waitress for her reply. "Because," she said, "she'll figure out a way to keep you here."

The women patrons nodded. The men all looked quizzical. Rux turned back to Deke, who simply shrugged his shoulders and added more sugar to his syrup.

* * *

Missy was home from school by the time Rux returned with the bolts. He didn't want to face Sammi, and he sure didn't want to have to tell Missy he planned to leave. He headed for the barn to find Jeremiah and Tyrone.

Rux shuffled through the soft dirt of the barn floor toward the wash rack. He could hear Missy explaining to Tyrone the fine points of picking muck out of Chester's feet. Rux stopped by the stalls and listened for several minutes. Missy rattled off instructions and answered Tyrone's questions as if she had been around horses all her life.

She'll be fine without me, Rux concluded. Her mother is another matter. Sammi has all the talent in the world, but she lets her passion for a singing career cloud her judgment. She needs someone.

Rux looked deep into his soul. Was he that someone? He tried to picture himself with Sammi and Missy in Los Angeles, or Nashville, or New York. His dad, Chester and the house in Texas came into clear focus.

With a discipline peculiar to lonely cowboys, Rux dismissed the sensation of Sammi's soft skin next to his, ignored the ache in his guts, and left to finish the gate.

* * *

Well after dark, Jeremiah and Tyrone filed into the foaling room. "Hey, Rux," Jeremiah said. "We missed you at dinner. Where you been?"

Rux kicked his boots under his bed. "I ate in town," he said. "Been checking the fence up on the ridge. Everybody okay?"

Tyrone said, "Seem to be. You missed a good meal. Folks eat good up here, 'cept for barbecue. I sure could use one of Mama Henry's 'Q' sandwiches."

Rux said, "I kinda need to talk to you two about that."

Jeremiah flopped in the rocker. "Not on a full stomach," he said.

"I don't mean the barbecue," Rux said. "About going back to Texas. Tyrone, I don't know what your plans are. Far as I know, you're welcome to stay here. I'm sure you can find a job in town. Work out something with Deke if you want to stay here at the ranch. But Dad and me need to be getting back home."

"We do?" Jeremiah asked.

"Yeah. You still got twenty acres with a house and a barn. And all your equipment. We can't just abandon the place."

"Reckon that's true," Jeremiah said. "What are you gonna do with Sammi and Missy?"

"Sammi's okay now. She's planning on going back to Los Angeles." The words came out with an edge Rux did not intend.

"Gettin' chilly in here," Tyrone said. He walked to the electric heater and flipped the "on" switch.

"We know about Sammi's plans," Jeremiah said. "She told us at dinner. Kinda thought you might want to talk her out of that."

Rux propped his pillow against the wall, leaned back and pulled his hat down over his eyes. "Not my place," he said. "Besides, it wouldn't be right. Sammi's a tremendous performer. You know that, don't you, Tyrone? She can make the big time."

Rux sensed both men were staring at him, waiting him out. After several minutes of listening to the ping of the heater warming up, Rux pushed his hat back. Jeremiah leaned his head back against the rocker. Tyrone turned to face the heater.

"When you figuring on heading back?" Jeremiah asked.

"Tomorrow morning, early. Another snow storm is due in. We don't want to be driving in these mountains when it hits. How about you, Tyrone? You want to come along?"

216

"Guess I'll stay," Tyrone said, still facing the heater. "You told Sammi and Missy y'all leavin' in the morning?"

"No," Rux said. "And I'd appreciate it if neither of you said anything either. Tyrone, if you're staying, you can tell them tomorrow at breakfast."

Tyrone and Jeremiah looked at each other but said nothing.

* * *

Route 666 winding through the mountains of eastern Arizona had to be a practical joke played by road construction engineers on an unsuspecting public. Some of the hair pin curves were so tight Rux knew he was going to connect up with the back end of Chester's trailer.

Rux welcomed his dad's snoring. Jeremiah had spent the first hour chiding him about leaving Pine Knot and Sammi, and the second hour dozing in the dark cab illuminated only by the dim lights of the dash board.

Dad's right, Rux thought, at least about me being a shiftless bum, a drifter afraid of being tied down. But a shiftless bum would have abandoned Sammi and Missy when they first started making demands on him.

Instead, he had stayed with Missy when Sammi left. And he brought Sammi back after she got herself in trouble. Not many men would have hung in the way he did.

Rux's head churned with a familiar litany. Cowboys aren't made to be tied down. They belong with their horses and trucks. If there's a problem, cowboys mosey into town and fix it, and then ride off into the sunset.

The truck finally trundled out of the mountains and eased onto I-10 along the desert floor. The pre-dawn gray suggested daylight would soon follow. Rux's audible sigh of relief caused Jeremiah to stir.

"Need a pit stop?" Rux asked.

"Naw, not yet. How much longer to No Water?"

"Nine or ten hours, maybe. We just hit the interstate."

Jeremiah stretched, yawned and picked up Rux's old hat from the seat. "Son, maybe you don't want to be out of Arizona at all."

"Aw Dad, don't start in on me again. I done right by those folks. Sammi and Missy are back together again, and Tom and Auren are married and starting a new life. Juanita will keep them all on the straight and narrow. I guess maybe I should have left Chester with Missy. Emilio could help her with him."

"Maybe you want to take him back. Have you read the note inside your hat?"

"You been talking to Missy. She's the one convinced me hats have messages in them."

"You're right, but there really is a message in here. You better read it."

Jeremiah pulled a crumpled slip of paper from the hat band and handed it to Rux. It read, "Dear Rux, I hope you will come back and be my daddy some day. Love, Missy."

Rux could hear Chester bracing himself as the old truck made a sharp U-turn through the "Emergency Vehicle Only" crossover. The fringe of the sun winked at the desert, inviting warmth and light for a new day.

* * *

Deke's marketing acumen outdid itself. For two weeks Rux had been skirting around questions from Moose Ball's customers asking if he and Sammi were coming back. Deke himself fueled the rumors, and scripted Rux's evasive answers.

"Tantalize them," Deke said. "Keep them guessing. Something big is going to happen, but they don't know what."

Madison Avenue couldn't have done it better. Moose Ball's had been packed every Thursday, Friday and Saturday night since Deke started his devious campaign.

On Saturday night of the last skiing weekend, Deke pegged across the stage and grabbed the mike to announce his new band, as was his custom.

"Ladies and Gentlemen, Moose Ball's proudly announces the return of the hottest act ever to grace our stage. Please welcome back Sammi Stone and Rux, now Mister and Miz Rux Tuttle."

The crowd went wild as Rux bounded across the stage to his keyboard.

Deke's final stroke of genius stunned everyone except Deke, Rux and Chester, Rux being a coconspirator and Chester no doubt considering himself above such frivolity. With the Rux Philharmonic blaring out a rousing rendition of the "William Tell Overture," Deke unveiled a banner above the stage.

The standard was so large the audience took turns walking from one side of the room to the other to read its entire contents.

In bold white letters across the top of the scarlet red banner were the words "Deke's Arabian Horse Farm." Centered underneath the title was a logo of a stallion and a mare lounging in the grass, smoking a cigarette; and underneath the logo the banner read "Home of Chester, Champion Working Cow Horse."

Along each side in smaller but still prominent letters were the titles of Deke's entourage: "Rux Tuttle, Head Trainer; Jeremiah Tuttle, Assistant Trainer; Juanita, Business Manager; Emilio, Barn Manager; Tyrone Dedman, Assistant Barn Manager; Missy Tuttle, Champion Equitation Rider."

Sammi came on stage with the final crescendo, dressed in her powder blue cowgirl dress and white boots and hat. The frenzy of the packed bar rose to a new level.

She stood for several minutes with her head bowed, turning once to cut her dark eyes to meet Rux's. The spotlight glistened the tears in her eyes in perfect harmony with the rhinestones on her dress. Finally, she lifted her hand to ask for quiet.

"Most of you know I've been away for awhile," Sammi said. "I left to pursue my dreams...but then I realized... everything I needed to fulfill those dreams is right here in Pine Knot."

She again glanced back at Rux, biting her lip and forcing back tears. "I missed you all, terribly. But one thing kept me going, the words from the song we always close with, 'Somewhere Out There'."

Sammi paused to recover her voice. Again she had to wait for quiet as the crowd took this as their cue to send up more cheers.

"And with your permission, we would like to open with that song tonight."

The room applauded in anticipation of Rux's keyboard introduction of the opening bars, then grew quiet as nothing happened.

Rux squinted into the spotlight, trying to focus on Joe Hawkins' table. Several seconds passed before he realized his old friend would not be there. He feared the lump in his throat would not dissolve in time for him to sing.

Sammi half turned and gestured with her palms for some explanation. Only the tinkling of ice in glasses interrupted the silence. Deke finally yelled from behind the bar, "Play the song Henry, you old fart."

The roisterous laughter shook Rux from his stupor, freeing his hands and his voice. He need not have worried. Sammi put her heart and soul into the song, carrying him through the duet parts.

The exuberance of the crowd shook water from toilets in the court house, three blocks distant. Five minutes after the last note, the clapping and stomping were still going strong. Sammi and Rux held hands and bowed for what must have been the thirtieth time.

Rux finally put his hand over the microphone and whispered loudly in Sammi's ear, "How would you like to honeymoon in Lubbock?"

"Lubbock? Why would anyone want to spend their honeymoon in Lubbock?"

"We've got to go back and get that clucking, chortling chicken."

"Rux, that's absurd."

219